Elizabeth Murphy was born in Liverpool and has lived in Merseyside all her life. When she was twelve, her father gave her a sixpenny book from a second-hand bookstall, *Liverpool Table Talk One Hundred Years Ago*, which led to her lifelong interest in Liverpool's history.

Throughout her girlhood, she says, there was an endless serial story unfolding in her mind with a constantly changing cast of characters; but it was only in the 1970s that she started to commit the stories to paper. Her first novel *The Land is Bright* was shortlisted for the Boots Romantic Novel of the Year Award in 1989 and the continuation of the story of the Ward family, *To Give and to Take* (also available from Headline), won even more readers and gathered critical acclaim:

'Hard to beat for good old-fashioned Northern common sense ... real "muck and brass" stuff tracing the fortunes of two sisters' *Manchester Evening News*

'A good long story (with) a good authentic feel' *Northern Echo*

Also by Elizabeth Murphy

The Land is Bright
To Give and To Take

There is
a Season

Elizabeth Murphy

HEADLINE

First published in 1991
by HEADLINE BOOK PUBLISHING PLC

First published in paperback in 1991
by HEADLINE BOOK PUBLISHING PLC

10 9 8 7 6 5 4 3 2 1

ISBN 0 7472 3672 0

Typeset by Colset Pte. Ltd.

Printed and bound by
HarperCollins Manufacturing, Glasgow

HEADLINE BOOK PUBLISHING PLC
Headline House
79 Great Titchfield Street
London W1P 7FN

For Ted with love

ACKNOWLEDGEMENTS

I would like to thank Mr Roger Hull, Reference Librarian, and the staff of Crosby Central Library, the staff of the Local History Department, Picton Library, Liverpool, and of the Museum of Labour History, Liverpool, my brother George Savage (ex. R.A.F.), my sisters Agnes Morgan and Theresa Kelly for memories they shared with me, members of Crosby Writers' Club and other friends and relations, and last but not least my husband Ted and all our family for all their help and encouragement for which I am deeply grateful.

To everything there is a season, and a time for every purpose under the heaven;
A time to be born and a time to die.

ECCLESIASTES iii.1.

Chapter One

Chapter One

The sun still blazed down although it was four o'clock in the afternoon. In Norris Street the air was stifling, and filled with dust scuffed up by schoolchildren returning home.

The front doorways of the tiny houses were flush with the street, and at most of them women in flowered pinafores stood by their open doors. Cathy Redmond stepped from the door of number twenty, next to which stood a baby carriage, and looked anxiously down the narrow street.

Her neighbours wore their long hair in a bun or braided around their head, like most women in Liverpool in 1926, but Cathy's dark hair had been bobbed. It clustered in short curls around her face, held back by a celluloid slide.

Opposite her, Mrs Parker, the matriarch of Norris Street, was sitting on a kitchen chair outside her house. She glared balefully at Cathy.

'You look peaky, girl,' she called to her, 'I told you it'd take your strength if you got your hair cut. Remember Samson in the Bible.'

Cathy made no reply but bent over the sleeping baby to hide the fact that she was blushing, as much with anger as with embarrassment. Nosy old faggot, she thought furiously. Greg had encouraged her to get her hair cut, and so had her mam and dad, and if her own husband and parents liked it, what business was it of Mrs Parker's?

Her silence annoyed the matriarch who said loudly, 'That baby carriage an'all – I carried me babies in me shawl, like me mam and me nin done before me.' She glared round at her daughters who stood or sat around her. 'What was good enough for them had better be good enough for youse, too.'

Cathy drew in her breath and stood up, but fortunately before she could speak her young daughter Sarah arrived, tugging her four-year-old brother, one hand clamped about

1

his wrist and the other gripping his fair curls.

'Sarah, you'll scalp him,' Cathy exclaimed, hustling the children before her into the house.

'I had to, Mam,' Sarah gasped. 'He was bursting tar bubbles.'

'Oh, Mick, and you know I didn't change your clothes after we'd been to Grandma's,' said Cathy. She took off his shirt and trousers, and replaced them with old and patched garments. 'Now don't go out of the street,' she said. 'And don't climb.'

Mick grinned cheerfully and ran off to play with his friends. Cathy turned to Sarah.

'Did you see anything of our John, love?'

'No, Mam, I didn't see any big boys,' said Sarah. 'They must have been kept in.'

They went through to the back kitchen and Cathy lifted a basket of dry washing from the top of the mangle.

'Help me to fold these, love,' she said, but as she lifted out the first sheet the door of the backyard burst open and her elder son raced up to them, waving a long manilla envelope.

'I've passed, Mam, I've passed!' he shouted. 'I've got the scholarship.' He held out the envelope. Before taking it, Cathy flung her arms around him and kissed him. Sarah could only reach his waist, but she hugged him, and he lifted her and swung her round, laughing with joy as his mother read the letter.

'I'm proud of you, son,' Cathy said, her brown eyes bright with loving pride as she looked at him. 'You deserve it too, John. You've worked hard for this.'

'You must be the cleverest lad in Everton – Liverpool, even,' Sarah exclaimed.

Cathy bundled the washing into the basket and put it back on the mangle. 'I can't be bothered with that now.'

There was a shout from the backyard and the next moment their neighbour's head appeared above the wall.

'Our Georgie's just told me about John getting the scholarship,' said Grace Woods. 'I'm made up for you, lad. Fancy a College boy in Norris Street. Aren't we getting posh?'

They all laughed and Cathy ruffled John's dark hair.

'He's done well,' she said proudly, 'but he's worked hard for it.'

'He has that,' Grace agreed. 'Staying in doing homework when other lads were out playing.' Cathy asked her to come in for a cup of tea but she refused.

'Billy'll be in before I can turn round,' she said. 'I just thought I'd give you a shout when our Georgie told me about your John standing out in front of the class and getting cheered. It'll cost tuppence to speak to you soon.'

They went back into the house and Cathy said to John, 'Is that right? Did you get cheered? How many passed?'

'Four of us. The partitions were pushed back and Mr Meade read out our names and we had to stand up. Me and George Mulholland and Joe Furlong and Sammy Roche – but Sammy doesn't think his dad will let him go. He was at sea when we got the forms and Sammy's mam signed them,' John explained.

'Maybe the teachers will talk him round?' Cathy said. John looked doubtful.

They went back into the living room and he said eagerly, 'Can I take the letter to show Grandad, Mam?' But Cathy shook her head and put the letter on the mantelpiece.

'No. Wait until you've shown Dad, John, he'll be home soon.'

The boy scowled. 'Why?' he muttered. 'Grandad'll be more interested.'

Sarah looked anxiously at her mother, but Cathy ignored John's remark and calmly took a tablecloth from the dresser drawer. 'Lay the table, Sarah,' she said, 'while I have a look at Kate.' She went out to the carriage and found the baby still sleeping.

As Cathy returned to the kitchen there was a clatter in the backyard and Greg Redmond came in the back door.

'John's got some news for you, Greg,' Cathy said eagerly. She thrust the envelope into John's hand. 'Tell your Dad.'

'I've passed the scholarship,' John said, grinning as his father shook his hand and clapped him on the shoulder. Greg read quickly through the letter then put his hand on John's shoulder again, and said quietly, 'I'm sorry, son. I always hoped that things would be better for us by this stage and I'd be able to send you to my old school, but I'm afraid there's no hope of that. You must just do as well as you can at the College.'

John pulled angrily away from his father. 'I don't *want* to go to Sheldrake,' he said. 'I want to go to the College. It's much better than Sheldrake.'

Cathy gave her son a quick consoling hug. Why did Greg have to mention Sheldrake now? she thought with exasperation. No wonder they're always at odds with each other, for all they seem so alike.

John looked like a smaller replica of his father with the same unruly dark hair and grey eyes and even the same cleft in his chin, but there was more of obstinacy and determination in his jaw, especially now as he stood glaring at his father.

'I wouldn't want John to go away from home,' she said quickly. 'He'll have a good education at the College, and I'm sure he'll do well there.'

'I don't doubt it,' Greg said shortly. He was a quiet man with a gentle manner but now Cathy saw anger in his face at John's rudeness.

'Scouse doesn't seem right for tonight, does it?' she said with determined cheerfulness. 'I feel we should have a goose or a leg of pork to celebrate.'

'The fire isn't lit. We wouldn't be able to cook it, Mam,' said Sarah practically.

Cathy laughed. 'Yes, that's the best thing about scouse. It can be cooked on the gas ring. Go and get Mick for his tea, love.'

Sarah went into the street but her brother was already running towards the house, bawling and holding his hand over his ear. His friends shouted to her above his cries and Sarah took him into the house. 'He climbed to the top of the lamp post and the lamplighter gave him a clout on his ear, Mam.'

'A smack, Sarah, not a clout,' Greg said as he drew Mick against his knee, but Cathy flashed angrily.

'Some of those fellows are a sight too free with their hands. You should go and tell him off, Greg. Look at the child's ear. It's all red.'

Mick's yells became even louder. Greg said quietly, 'He's been pressing his hand to it. That's the main reason why

4

it's red. I'll just wipe his hands and face.'

He picked up his younger son and took him into the back kitchen where Mick's cries soon died away. He was grinning when they returned to the kitchen and sat down at the table while Cathy served the meal. John picked up his spoon but laid it down again.

'I can't eat anything, Mam.'

'Never mind then, love, leave it. I'll warm it up for you later on. Do you want to run down to Grandma's now and tell them? We'll follow later on when we've finished our tea.'

John jumped to his feet and snatched up his cap. 'Thanks, Mam,' he said, his eyes shining.

'Don't they know yet?' Greg asked in surprise as John darted out of the door.

'No, I thought he should tell you first,' Cathy said with a shade of reproof in her voice.

Greg sighed. 'I'm sorry I mentioned Sheldrake. It was just – the years go too fast, Cath.'

'It wasn't the right time,' she said. 'I didn't realize you even thought of Sheldrake for John.'

'It's just been a vague idea. A pipe dream, I suppose,' he said, ruefully. 'I was glad to get this job, Cath, but I've always had the idea that some time I'd be able to provide the advantages for our sons that my father provided for me – with no very clear idea how I'd do it, I'm afraid.'

'I think we're very lucky. I saw Sam Benson's widow in Shaw Street, and honestly, Greg, she looks like an old woman. She had a job in a sweet factory but she was sick and had to give it up, she told me, and she's been trying to bring up those twins on a War pension. They all looked half starved.'

'I know. I agree we're lucky, but when I think what my father provided for me, and the advantages he gave me, I should have done better for my family.'

'Don't worry about it,' Cathy said. 'John doesn't want to go to Sheldrake and I'm sure I don't want him to go away to a boarding school. He'd be a fish out of water everywhere.'

'I *do* worry, Cath,' he persisted. 'I think I should have done more to try to trace that so-and-so who robbed me of the shop while I was in the Army, or else I should have tried to set up in business with what I had left.'

'The police couldn't find him so how could you?' she demanded. 'Anyway, we were too glad to have you back in one piece to worry about a thieving manager.' She noticed that Sarah was watching them anxiously and smiled at the child, knowing that her quiet and sensitive daughter worried unduly about any conflict in the family.

'Eat your scouse, love,' she said. 'And, Mick, stop gobbling, and close your mouth while you're eating.'

She glanced at Greg who seemed deep in thought, oblivious to her chivvying of the children.

'Cheer up. Don't brood any more about Sheldrake. John's perfectly happy about going to the College. In fact, he's made up that he's got the scholarship, and so am I.'

'And so am I, Cath. Don't misunderstand me – I know he'll have a good education there, but I feel that Sheldrake could have done so much more for him.'

Cathy shook her head. 'No. Sheldrake suited you because you had that sort of background, but it wouldn't suit John – or me either to have him away from home. All I want is for our children to be happy.'

'So do I, but I feel I've failed the boys,' he persisted.

'What about the girls? Haven't you been listening to me all these years when I've talked about girls having the same chances as boys?'

'Of course I have,' he said, smiling at her, 'and of course now you've got the vote, you can change the world.'

'It's not a joke,' she protested. 'Just wait and see. Soon girls will have equal chances, and maybe one of ours will be the doctor you wanted to be.'

'Perhaps,' Greg said. 'I wonder what's in store for Mick the menace?'

They looked at their younger son who had just finished eating. He smiled at them, showing the gap where his front teeth had been knocked out by a fall from a window cleaner's ladder. A half-healed scar ran down his cheek from a wound received when he toppled into a damaged beer cask, and there was a pale earlier scar beside his eye.

'He'll be able to appear in a circus if he doesn't alter,' Cathy said with a sigh. 'He's got scars all over him but he doesn't care if it snows.'

'His ear's all right anyway,' Greg said, looking quizzically at her.

'It looks all right,' she said. 'But I'll make sure that lamplighter doesn't hit him again, I can tell you!'

The baby had wakened and Cathy made bread and milk for her, then changed and fed her while Sarah and Greg washed the dishes. Mick's attempts to run out and play were frustrated and his clothes changed again, then Cathy put the baby in the carriage and they all walked the short distance from Norris Street to the home of Cathy's parents in Egremont Street.

Greg walked silently beside Cathy as she wheeled the baby carriage. She glanced at his serious expression and exclaimed impatiently, 'Cheer up, for heaven's sake! No one would think we'd just had such good news. I think we've a lot to be thankful for. Four healthy kids and our own house, *and* we can manage to keep John at school until he's sixteen. He'll have his fees paid and a grant for his uniform. When you think of the fellows we knew who were killed or maimed, and their families struggling to live now, I don't know how you can be so miserable.'

'I'm sorry I don't suit,' he said angrily, and they walked on in silence. Sarah looked anxiously from one to the other, but when they reached her grandparents' house they stepped immediately into an atmosphere of festivity and delight.

'What a day, what a day,' Lawrie Ward exclaimed, his arm around his grandson's shoulders. 'This is the lad who's going to realize all our dreams, aren't you, John?'

'I hope so, Grandad,' he replied, smiling with deep affection.

'A scholar in the family,' Lawrie went on. 'We've been waiting for you to come so's we can celebrate.' He picked up a stone bottle. 'Ginger beer for John and Mick and Sarah, port wine for you and your mam, Cathy, and a drop of rum for us, eh, Greg? How's that?'

'Just the ticket,' Greg said as he helped Lawrie to pour the drinks. John carried a glass of port wine to his grandmother and she drew his head down to her and kissed him. Sally Ward was less demonstrative than her husband but her delight showed in her shining eyes as she said, 'We'll all drink to John's success.'

He grinned and blushed as they all solemnly clinked glasses and drank to him. Sarah watched him proudly and gave a happy sigh. Her grandmother smiled at her. 'You'll be able to tell all the girls in your class about your clever brother on Monday, won't you, love?'

Sarah smiled and nodded, and Cathy said quickly, 'She'll be the next to take the scholarship, and she'll have a good chance of it if she works hard like John.'

'It's not so important for a girl,' Sally Ward said placidly as she unwrapped the baby's shawl.

Cathy immediately protested. 'It *is*, Mam. It's just as important. What was the use of fighting for the vote if girls don't get their chance now?'

'But girls only get married, and then even if they've managed to be teachers or nurses, they still have to leave.'

'But that's not right. Things must change, Mam,' Cathy said. 'There are plenty of single women now because so many lads were killed in the war, but it'll be different by the time Sarah grows up.'

The girl said nothing. She had already decided that she would leave school at fourteen so there would be no point in taking the scholarship.

One of her grandmother's neighbours, Elsie Hammond, had a florist's shop nearby and Sarah spent many happy hours there learning to make frames and to wire flowers for wreaths. Elsie had told her that she had a gift for floristry and that she would be taken on as an apprentice when she was fourteen. Sarah was looking forward to working full-time in the shop.

The men became aware of the exchange between Cathy and her mother, and Lawrie called jovially, 'No politics tonight. You should know by now, Sal, that if you scratch our Cathy you find a Suffragette.'

'Suffrag*ist*, Dad,' she said, and the adults laughed.

'The Suffragists fought for votes for women by peaceful means, love,' Cathy explained to Sarah, 'but the Suffragettes were willing to do violent things and get sent to prison, and I must say they really suffered for their beliefs.'

'And any time we said your mam was a Suffragette, she used to say indignantly, "No, I'm a Suffrag*ist*." We used to do it to tease her,' Lawrie said.

8

'And our Mary didn't give a button for either of them,' Sally said. 'She was more interested in the price of hats.'

'We'll have to write to America tomorrow, John,' Lawrie said, 'and tell your Auntie Mary and Uncle Sam about your scholarship. They'll be made up to hear about it.'

Sally sighed and said quietly to Cathy, 'This is the sort of thing that our Mary'll miss if she doesn't have children. I wish I could hear that she'd started with a baby.'

'Give her time, Mam. She's been married such a short time, and she'll want to be sure before she tells you.'

'Maybe,' Sally said. 'I just think Sam would make such a good father, it'd be a shame if they had no children. Anyway, never mind, love. Put the kettle on, will you? Your dad will have to get ready for work in a minute and he'll need a cup of tea before he goes.'

'Aye, *tempus fugit*, John,' Lawrie said. 'D'you know what that means, lad?'

'Time flies,' he said promptly, and his grandfather clapped him on the shoulder.

'There you are, lad. You're a Latin scholar before you've even started at the College.'

'Mr Meade told us that. How did you know it, Grandad?'

'I saw it in a book and I sort of guessed what it meant, but I asked the fellow at the Carnegie Library to make sure.'

'Remember that, John. If anything puzzles you there's always someone who can help you,' Greg said quietly.

John scowled, seeming to think that his grandfather was being patronized. 'Grandad knows nearly everything anyway,' he said, 'and yet you went to sea when you were twelve, didn't you, Grandad?'

Greg looked angry but Lawrie said with an easy laugh, 'Yes, but I wouldn't recommend it, lad.' He took a small book from the shelf. 'I'd like you to have this, John, to mark the occasion.'

'But, Dad, you love that book,' Cathy protested. 'I remember you reading out poems from it to me and our Mary when we were little.'

Lawrie smiled at her. 'That's why I want John to have it. I know most of the poems by heart anyway.' He took a pen and a bottle of ink from the dresser and wrote on the flyleaf of the book. "July 1926. To John Redmond on passing the scholarship. From his loving grandfather." He blotted the page and handed the book to John.

'There you are, lad. I hope you get as much pleasure from it as I've had.'

John's eyes filled with tears and he flung his arms round his grandfather and burrowed his head against him.

'Thanks, Grandad,' he said huskily, 'I'll always look after it.'

The kettle began to sing and Cathy brewed tea in a huge brown teapot. To distract attention from John she said brightly, 'You still use this pot, Mam, even though there's only two of you now.'

'What will hold a lot will hold a little,' Sally said. 'Anyway, Josh is usually here, or Peggy Burns, or one of the other neighbours.'

As though he had heard his name Josh Adamson, who lodged in Sally's parlour, tapped on the door and put his white head round it.

'I just wanted to say I'm glad to hear the lad's news,' he said diffidently, but Lawrie opened the door wide.

'Come in, come in, Josh,' he exclaimed. 'Come and have a drop of rum to drink to his success.'

The stout old man came into the kitchen smiling self-consciously, but he was soon at home as the children welcomed him eagerly. John pushed a chair forward and Mick climbed on his knee while Greg poured a glass of rum for him.

Meanwhile Lawrie was quickly drinking a cup of tea and pushing a teacan and a packet of sandwiches into his jacket pockets.

'It's all right for you clerks,' he joked with Greg and Josh. 'No turning out for night shift like us poor checkers.'

'And no lying in bed in the mornings for us either, eh, Josh?' Greg said, laughing. 'I wouldn't mind some shift work for a while.'

'Aye, summer mornings down on the allotment like Lawrie,' Josh said with a wheezy laugh.

'I think you're all very lucky to have jobs on the railway, whatever they are,' Sally said. 'I'm just thankful that Lawrie's not still out on the wagons in all weathers.'

John was standing close to his grandfather, reading

some of the lines of poetry aloud.

'Don't delay Grandad now, John, or he'll be late,' his father admonished him.

'I'm all right for time —' Lawrie began, but his wife interrupted him.

'You don't want to be rushing now, Lol, and losing your breath,' she said firmly. 'John can come and talk to you tomorrow.'

'Aye, come to the allotment if it's fine, lad, or if it's wet come here and we'll have a good talk,' Lawrie said, smiling. He bent over the rocking chair to kiss Sally, then Sarah and the baby on her knee.

'Don't forget, love, tell all your friends about your clever brother. I'll do some bragging myself tonight.' He punched John playfully then said goodnight to Greg, Mick and Josh before walking down the lobby, followed by Cathy.

'I'm made up about this scholarship, Cath,' he said as they stood for a moment on the step. 'This is just the start for John, you'll see. He'll go far because he's got a good headpiece on him, like his dad.'

'And his grandad,' she said. 'But you didn't have the chances that they've got today, Dad.'

'John'll make good use of his anyhow,' Lawrie said, kissing her and walking away, whistling cheerfully.

When Cathy went back to the kitchen Josh Adamson was leaving to prepare for his nightly visit to a nearby public house, but before he did he shyly slipped a coin into John's hand. 'For all your hard work,' he murmured.

John looked at the coin with delight. 'Two shillings!' he exclaimed. '*Thanks*, Josh.'

' "Mr Adamson", John,' Greg said sternly.

'Mr Adamson,' John muttered but Josh was already going through the door into the lobby and into his own room.

'We'll have to be going, too, to get this crowd into bed,' said Cathy.

'Will you need Sarah in the morning, or can she stay with me?' Sally asked. Sarah looked hopefully at her parents and Cathy said quickly, 'No, I won't need her, Mam.'

'And she doesn't have to go to school tomorrow,' added Greg. He smiled at Sarah, and she flung her arms round his

11

neck and kissed him. Sally and Cathy were wrapping the baby in her shawl and putting her into the carriage, while John put Mick's coat on him. Soon the family was ready to leave.

Cathy kissed Sarah. 'Be a good girl now for Grandma, love.'

Greg lifted Sarah in his arms and she clung to him when he kissed her. 'Take care of Grandma. I'll see you tomorrow, sweetheart,' he murmured, and kissed her again before putting her down. He saw John glance at him ironically as he turned away, but neither spoke. John tweaked his sister's straight brown hair.

'Goodnight, Fishface,' he said.

Sarah immediately retorted, 'Goodnight, Bunjaws.'

'Very nice, I must say,' Cathy said in a scandalized voice, but she smiled at the children before bidding her mother goodnight.

The streets were still thronged with people enjoying the cool air after the heat of the day. Cathy wheeled the baby carriage and Greg walked beside her, carrying Mick on his back, while John ran ahead, taking the front door key.

'Sarah'll be company for Mam while Dad's on night shift,' Cathy said. 'And she likes staying there.'

'Yes, she enjoys your mother's company and vice versa,' Greg said. 'They're certainly birds of a feather, aren't they?'

'Mam and Dad are made up about the scholarship. I know they've been as anxious about it as we have.'

Greg said nothing and they walked in silence for a few moments. Then he said in a low voice, 'I wish I had your father's knack with people, Cath.'

She looked at him in surprise. 'What do you mean?'

'Just the way he knew immediately how to make Josh feel at home, and giving that book to John.'

'But he's always been like that. He's just impulsive.'

'It's more than that, Cath. He seems to know instinctively how to deal with people.' Greg smiled ruefully. 'Your dad wouldn't have brought up the subject of Sheldrake during the excitement about John's scholarship, like I did.'

Cathy laughed. 'I was dropped on,' she admitted. 'I'd no idea you were thinking of it.'

'Only in a very general way. I was glad to get this job,

12

Cath, but I thought it would give me a breathing space to try to make a better life for us. I had vague dreams of getting back to the way things were before the war, but I realize now that that's all they were – dreams.' He smiled rather grimly. 'It was only when John's future was decided that I realized how long I'd been just dreaming.'

'Oh, Greg, you're never going to go back to the life you had when you were little, but it wasn't all good, was it? I'm happy now, and I thought you were too.'

'I am, Cath,' he assured her, giving her a quick hug and a kiss. 'Far happier than I'd believed possible, and far more than I deserve. I just wish I was a better provider.'

'You do all right,' she said staunchly. 'Don't run yourself down, Greg. I do wish we could get out of Norris Street but we will someday, and for now at least we've got a roof over our heads.'

'And Mrs Parker might decide to move,' he said mischievously.

'And pigs might fly,' Cathy laughed. 'She was giving out about my hair again today.'

'She's only jealous, love. The short hair really suits you,' he said. 'But that's something I *am* determined we'll do – move from Norris Street as soon as possible.'

'Yes, and it's one ambition of yours I *do* agree with,' she said. She looked up at him, her brown eyes bright, and dimples appeared in her cheeks as she laughed. Impulsively, Greg bent and kissed her.

'You're beautiful, Cath. I'm a lucky man.'

'I'm lucky too,' she said softly, and they walked on through the warm night, completely in harmony again.

Chapter Two

Sarah and her grandmother were up early the following morning, preparing breakfast and tidying the kitchen together. When Lawrie returned from work they all had breakfast, then he went to bed to sleep for a few hours, while Sarah scrubbed the front step and Sally cooked breakfast for Josh before he left for work.

When Sarah was on the step, the door of the adjoining house opened and Peggy Burns and her granddaughter Meg appeared.

'Hello, Sarah,' Meg said excitedly. 'Is your John with you?' At ten years of age Meg was taller than her dumpy little grandmother, a pretty girl with long fair hair and pale blue eyes, but there was something uncontrolled in her jerky movements and a wild look in her eyes.

'Your gran told me about his scholarship,' Peggy Burns said before Sarah could speak. 'I was made up. Did you stay with your grandma last night?' She had put a restraining hand on Meg's arm, and Sarah ignored the girl's question and answered Mrs Burns'.

'Yes, Mam said I could because there's no school today,' she said shyly.

'Well, you're a good help to her, I know,' Mrs Burns said. 'Like our Meg is to me. Come on now, love.'

She drew Meg away from the dividing railings between the two houses. 'She'll play with you later, Sarah.'

Sarah finished scrubbing the step and went indoors.

Her grandmother was troubled with arthritis in her right arm which had been broken many years before so Sarah helped with household tasks that Sally found difficult, then they went shopping together with Sarah carrying the basket.

It was a bright sunny day. When they returned Lawrie was downstairs with John who had just arrived.

'I only need a few hours' sleep this weather,' Lawrie said. 'We've had a bit of bread and cheese so we'll get off now, Sal. Make the most of the weather.'

They set off with John pushing the wooden cart that Greg had made for tools and produce. Sarah and her grandmother had their own simple lunch, then got out the rag rug that they were making.

The fine sewing which had been Sally's pride was impossible for her now but she and Sarah enjoyed sitting with a hessian sack stretched between them, making a rag rug to Sally's design.

Sarah felt very close to her grandmother at times like these, confident that she could ask about anything that puzzled her. On this Saturday they worked on the rug for a while then Sarah said suddenly, 'What's Sheldrake, Grandma?'

'Sheldrake, love? It's the school your dad went to.'

'Where is it?'

'A long way away, somewhere down London way,' Sally said. 'Why do you ask, pet?'

'Dad said he wanted John to go to Sheldrake, and Mam said she didn't want John to go away. Why did Dad want him to, Grandma?'

Sarah's voice trembled. Sally glanced at her troubled face and said gently, 'I think you've got hold of the wrong end of the stick, love. What did they say exactly?'

'Dad said he wanted to send John away to Sheldrake but it wasn't possible, and John said he didn't want to go. Mam said she didn't want John to go away, and I don't want him to go, Grandma, so why does Dad want to send him?'

'No, love, you've got it wrong. Your dad doesn't want just to send John away – he must think that it would be the best thing for him. You see, your dad wasn't brought up in houses like this. His father owned three jeweller's shops, and they lived in a big house over the water and had lots of money. Your dad was sent to a boarding school when he was only seven because his mother and father travelled a lot. Your dad wanted to be a doctor but his father died when he was sixteen and he had to work in the shop instead.'

'I saw that shop in London Road. Mam said it used to be Dad's.'

'Yes. When his father died the other shops and the big house had to be sold, and your dad and his mother lived over the shop in London Road. So you see, love, there's a lot you don't know about why people say things. Don't you be jumping to conclusions and worrying unnecessarily.'

'Anyway, John's not going away,' Sarah said. 'It was just – I wondered what Sheldrake was.'

They worked in companionable silence for a while, then Sarah said, 'Dad's mother died of the Spanish flu, didn't she, Grandma? Like Mr Anderson's family.'

'Yes, just after the war,' Sally replied. 'Your dad had a hard time then, love. All those years in the trenches, then when he came home in 1919 he found the man he'd left in charge of the shop had robbed him of everything, the dirty rat.' She stabbed the needle viciously in and out of the hessian, then went on, 'Your mam and John lived with us while your dad was in France, then when he came home they lived here until they got that house in Norris Street. He turned to and got a job, and never complains although his life is very different to what he was brought up to.'

'I wish –' Sarah said, then hesitated.

'What do you wish, love?'

'I wish our John knew that. John and Dad, they say things to each other and Mam gets ratty, but if John knew –'

'Don't worry about it, love, I'll sort them out,' Sally said, and Sarah sighed with relief and worked with enthusiasm on the rug until there was a knock on the door.

'We've done enough anyway,' Sally said, rolling up the rug as Meg pushed open the door and came down the lobby. 'You should be out playing on such a nice day.'

'Can we go to Shaw Street and play in the quarry?' Meg said eagerly. 'Gran says I can if I go with you, Sarah.' Although she was several years older and much taller than Sarah, it seemed natural for the younger girl to take charge.

'Yes, all right,' she said. 'But you mustn't climb too high, Meg, and you've got to come home when I say.'

'I will, I will,' Meg cried. She was bounding ahead down the lobby until Sally stopped her.

'Wait a minute, Meg. Sarah, I'm going over to see Josie Mellor's baby.'

'Josie Mellor?' Sarah said, puzzled.

'Mrs Meadows opposite, I mean,' Sally said. 'She used to be Josie Mellor. Her baby's sick, so if I'm not back you'll know where I am. Josh might be home anyway. He only works half day on Saturdays but he's started going for a pie and a pint on his way home, the last few weeks.'

'He'll probably keep on then,' Sarah said. 'We won't be long anyway.'

Sally took biscuits from a tin and gave a few to each girl and they ran off together.

The following Monday, when Cathy came to do her mother's ironing, Sally took the opportunity to probe gently about Sarah's worries. 'I believe Greg wanted John to go to Sheldrake, Cath?'

'It was just a pipe dream, Mam. It's out of the question even if we wanted it, and I certainly don't. Even Greg says he doesn't know why he came out with it then, just when we were all excited about the scholarship. It made it look as though the College was second best. I nearly said I wasn't an unnatural mother like his was, sending him away at seven years old so she could jaunt off with his father.'

'I suppose all that class of people do it, Cath.'

'But that's just it, Mam. Greg doesn't seem able to see that that sort of life is over forever as far as he's concerned. He worries because he can't provide that life for our children, but they don't want it. We're happy as we are.'

'He's adapted very well, love. I told Sarah how hard it must have been for him to get used to such a different life, and he never complains.'

'I don't see why he should,' Cathy retorted. 'He's happier now than when he was young, and he didn't have an easy life when they lived over the shop. God knows he's *far* happier now than when he was there with that horrible old mother of his.'

'Yes, but he's had to adapt himself and I think he's done it very well,' Sally persisted. 'If things had been different, *you* would have had to be the one to change and you wouldn't have liked that, would you?'

'I certainly wouldn't,' Cathy said with a grin. 'Our Mary would have taken it in her stride but I'd have hated it.'

'That's what I mean. Greg's had to change and you should

make allowances for that. Josh says he's very well liked at work although as soon as he opens his mouth they can tell he's different. You should see that John appreciates his father and treats him with respect, Cathy.'

'They're very fond of each other,' she said defensively. 'Eldest sons always clash a bit with their fathers.'

'Yes, but sometimes it only needs a word to keep the peace,' said her mother. 'I don't want to interfere, love, but you know I worry so much about all of you.'

'I know you do, Mam, but honestly there's no need to worry about John and Greg. You should just see the pair of them with that crystal set they're building.'

'That's all right then.'

And Sally spoke of other matters, but later, as they sat together having tea, Cathy suddenly said, 'Has Sarah been making out there was a row about Sheldrake or something?'

'No, she didn't,' Sally assured her. 'She didn't even know what Sheldrake was. She asked me, and I put two and two together and made five, as usual.'

'I know what a worrier she is though,' Cathy said. She looked quizzically at her mother. 'I don't know *who* she inherits it from.'

They both laughed, then Sally said seriously, 'The trouble is, she sits there so quietly and you don't know how much she's taking in. D'you know, I said Josh had started going for a pint and something to eat at Saturday dinner times, and she said, quite the thing, "He'll probably keep on then." You could have knocked me down with a feather.'

'She was right though,' Cathy said. 'Once Josh starts anything, he keeps right on. He's not a man for change, is he?'

'That's what I mean. Nobody's said that to Sarah but she's just weighed him up in her own quiet way.'

'I can see we'll have to watch what we say in front of her, especially if she's going to repeat it.'

'Now that's not fair, Cath. The child wasn't carrying tales, only asking me about something that worried her,' Sally said, but Cathy still looked vexed.

Within a few days the schools closed for the summer holidays and with no homework to worry about, John was able to spend more time with his grandfather. Greg and

Lawrie rented an allotment and while Greg was at work, John spent hours of the long sunny days there helping his grandfather.

Sometimes he went with Lawrie to meetings of the unemployed, held during the day because the men had long empty hours to fill. There he heard harrowing tales of the treatment of men and their families by the hated Board of Guardians.

With his heart swelling with indignation John listened as gaunt, ragged speakers told of having the pittance they received reduced on one pretext or another by well-fed men revelling in their power over the destitute men and women humbly petitioning them.

Lawrie was not a councillor but for many years had worked to try to help the destitute, and knew many influential people who also tried to ameliorate their conditions. Often he promised to write a letter or see someone to try to have a case reviewed, but he always warned that there was little hope. There were so many in the same situation.

Often John saw his grandfather furtively slip some money into a man's hand with the face-saving words, 'Just till things get better. You can do the same for me someday.' To John, the most heartrending aspect of all this was the way the desperate men tried to cling to their self-respect in spite of the humiliation they suffered at the hands of arrogant officials. He longed to have the power to help them.

After one such meeting Lawrie raged to John about the injustice of these terrible lives lived only a stone's throw from wealth and luxury, and his lifelong ambition to change matters.

'I remember when I first came ashore, lad,' he said, 'I was scandalized when I saw the crowds of barefoot hungry children in Liverpool. I thought that surely if rich and powerful people knew about them, they would do something. That's what I tried to bring about at first, but they just didn't care, John, even when they knew.'

'But what about the other rich men you know, Grandad, who took the soup out at night?'

'Aye, I've met plenty of rich men who do care, lad, and people like the Rathbones have worked for generations for the Liverpool poor, but it's the system that's wrong. That's what'll have to change. Never forget what you've seen here, John. Get a good education and speak up for them that can't speak for themselves.'

'I will, Grandad, I will,' John promised as though he was taking an oath.

Lawrie and Greg worked hard on the allotment, helped by the women and children of the family, and large crops of vegetables were produced there. A local greengrocer bought enough to cover their allotment expenses then after both families were supplied and some given to neighbours, there was still a surplus.

John and his grandfather often piled this into the wooden cart which John pulled down to the dilapidated houses near the docks.

On the way Lawrie would tell the boy to wait outside a butcher's shop while he went in, returning with several newspaper-wrapped parcels which he thrust into the cart.

Whenever possible they went through the back entries so that the vegetables could be delivered unobtrusively. The parcels of meat handed over with them often brought tears from the recipients.

'Just a few ribs or a bit of meat to flavour the veg,' Lawrie would say quietly as they were handed over. The emaciated children clinging to their mother's skirts watched eagerly. Years later, under a foreign sun, one of them spoke to John of his grandfather with deep respect and affection.

'He was solid gold,' he said. 'It wasn't just what he gave us but the way he did it. Me poor mam had to beg and be made little of by the fellers on the Board of Guardians for the bit they allowed her that cost them nothing, but she used to say, "God bless Lawrie Ward. They knock me down but he picks me up and puts me on me feet again. He's one of us, and he leaves himself short to help us, but he always makes you think you're doing him a favour taking it. There's decent people left in the world, Thank God." '

The man's words were no surprise to John. Even as a young boy he recognized his grandfather's goodness and sensitive concern for the despairing people he tried to help. Always he insisted that John should raise his cap to these ragged men and use the prefix 'Mr' when speaking to them.

'It's important, John,' he explained. 'It's the contempt some people treat him with that destroys a man, far more rapidly than hunger or poverty. I've been with them to the Board of Guardians and seen it, and I lived through it myself years ago, lad, so I know.'

Sometimes John spoke of these matters to his mother, knowing that she agreed with his grandfather and that she had tried to fight for justice by joining the Suffragists when she was young.

'Your grandad's always been like this,' she told him. 'No matter how little he had, he would always find someone worse off to help. Grandma used to go mad because he'd give away his carry out, and his penny for the tram, and walk home from the south end docks in pouring rain.'

'Grandma said the other day we should just do what we can to help people by doing what's next to our hands. Grandad was talking about Parliament when she said that.'

'I know. She's got no time for politics, but she practises what she preaches. Everyone goes to her for help if they've got someone sick or they're in trouble, but help from the likes of her isn't enough, John. The very poor are as badly off now as they were before the war.'

'Do you think things will ever change, Mam?'

'Of course they will,' Cathy said cheerfully. 'Now that women have got the vote. Women understand more about being short of money for food and coal and clothes, and if Miss Rathbone can make Parliament pass the Family Allowance Bill, that will make all the difference to mothers.'

During these holiday weeks when John was free of the restrictions of school and homework he felt that he saw unemployed men everywhere he went, even when he was not with his grandfather. Lawrie's own fervour blinded him to the dangers of speaking so freely to an impressionable young boy like John, and no one else was aware of the problem.

It seemed that the closer John drew to Lawrie, the greater the gulf became between his father and himself. After John had been to a meeting with his grandfather, he spoke at home about the shame the unemployed men felt when they ran out of Benefit and had to apply for relief tickets.

Greg said sharply, 'There's no reason for them to feel ashamed.'

He had been interrupted before he could finish what he intended to say: that men who tried hard to find work should feel no shame because there was no work for them, but John misunderstood and brooded sullenly on his father's words. He thought his father harsh and unsympathetic and avoided mentioning the unemployed before him again.

This meant that Greg was quite unaware of the depth of John's feelings on the subject, feeling only vaguely uneasy about the boy.

'John seems to spend an awful lot of time with your dad, Cath,' he said. 'They're doing wonders on the allotment but I think John should spend more time with his own friends.'

'That's the trouble,' she said. 'You know John's not like Mick. He has dozens of friends but John just has a few close ones, and they all seem to be missing just now. Jimmie Brady's gone to Ireland to stay with his grandmother for the holidays, and Joey Sutcliffe has gone to work on a farm with his uncle. Poor Sammy Roche is dodging the other lads, I think, until this scholarship business is settled.'

'There must be other lads he can play with, surely?'

'Who?' she demanded. 'There's no one of his age in this street, and the boys from his class are all in their own gangs. It doesn't worry John.' And Greg said no more on the subject.

Chapter Three

Most of the houses in Norris Street were occupied by relatives of Mrs Parker because for many years, whenever a house became vacant, she 'spoke to' the landlord to ask for the tenancy to be given to one of her daughters or other relatives.

Cathy had innocently applied for the tenancy of number twenty while Mrs Parker was busy with a daughter who had given birth to triplets, and had always felt that she was treated as an outsider, resented by Mrs Parker and her clan.

Whenever possible she escaped from the house in Norris Street, either to take the children to play in the park or to her mother's house in Egremont Street. She encouraged Sarah to make her friends among her classmates or the children in Sally's street. Friendship with children who lived in Norris Street could mean becoming involved in family feuds, some of them stretching back many years.

Mrs Parker disapproved of the Redmonds' baby carriage which was the only one in the street, but Doreen Bates who lived a few doors away from them braved the matriarch's wrath to ask if she could wheel Kate in the carriage.

At twelve years old, Doreen was a quiet, sensible girl, who loved to sit on the step nursing Kate and watching over other young children who played near her. Cathy felt that Kate was safe with her, and several times during the school holidays Doreen set off for Newsham Park, wheeling Kate in the carriage and surrounded by a crowd of children of various ages, including Sarah and Mick. Parcels of jam sandwiches were tucked in the bottom of Kate's carriage, and bottles of water to which pennyworths of lemonade powder would be added later. The children spent happy hours playing games supervised by Doreen or rolling down a grassy hill.

On one red letter day, they met Lawrie as they trooped down Boaler Street, and he bought penny ice cream cornets for the nine children with Doreen, and a tuppeny ice cream sandwich for her 'because she's the boss'.

'Eh, she's a born mother,' neighbours would say sentimentally when Doreen set off with the children, but Cathy listened to them with cynicism. More and more she hated living in Norris Street, and the gossiping and backbiting that went on there.

She had been pleased when Grace Woods had congratulated John on passing the scholarship until she heard later that Grace had said that it would make John even more bigheaded. Cathy had been bitterly hurt and avoided her neighbour as much as possible after that.

She did her housework quickly and went to her mother's house in Egremont Street, only returning in time to prepare the evening meal before Greg returned from work.

Egremont Street was wider and the houses larger than in Norris Street, and Cathy felt that there was not the same feeling of living in each other's pockets or the same sense of being always under close and hostile scrutiny.

Many of the people of Egremont Street had known Cathy all her life and took a genuine interest in her and in her children. She always had a sense of coming home when she turned into the street.

One day towards the end of the holidays she went there as soon as she had hung out the washing she had risen early to do. John's friends had returned and he had gone to play cricket with them but Sarah and Mick walked beside the baby carriage. Cathy wheeled it round to the backyard and Sarah and Mick ran in to see their grandmother then went off to play with their friends.

Sally welcomed Cathy with a smile and immediately stood up to take a letter from behind the clock.

'A letter from our Mary,' she said, 'and there's two snapshots in it too.'

Cathy took the letter eagerly. Letters from her sister, who had lived in America since her marriage to Sam Glover, were infrequent, but Sam sent a money order regularly every month with a short note.

He had always been made welcome by Mary's parents and

by Cathy when, as a gawky young man, he had faithfully but hopelessly courted Mary. He was a rich and confident businessman and Mary a widow when they met again after the war on a ship returning to Liverpool from New York, but he never forgot the early kindnesses he had been shown by Mary's family.

'Quite a long letter this time,' Cathy said, but she looked at the snapshots before reading it.

They showed Mary wearing a cloche hat, her face framed in her coat's huge fur collar, leaning against an opulent-looking car, with a big house in the background. She looked strikingly beautiful even in the black and white photograph, and Cathy glanced to where a painting of her, sent by Sam, hung on the wall.

It showed Mary's head and shoulders, her beautiful clear blue eyes fringed with dark lashes, thick red-gold hair clustering round perfect features and creamy skin. The proud tilt of her head was just Mary as they remembered her, but did anyone else, Cathy wondered, see the hardness in those lovely eyes and in the set of her full red lips?

Perhaps Greg did. He had said quietly, 'That's a clever artist. He's got the essence of Mary as well as just her appearance.' Cathy had made no reply and he said no more. There was always a slight constraint between them when they spoke of her sister.

Now Cathy came back to the present to hear her mother saying, 'Sam must be doing well. They've got another automobile, as she calls it, as well as that one.'

Cathy read through the letter quickly and put it back on the mantelpiece.

'Not really much news,' she said. 'Although the letter is a bit longer, but at least we know she's well and happy – and she keeps writing.'

'Aye, not like the war years when we never heard a word from her.'

'She's different now she's married to Sam,' Cathy said. 'He's a good fellow.'

'He is,' her mother agreed. 'He never fails to send that money although your dad won't touch it. He puts it straight into the Penny Bank.'

'But they must be able to afford it, and I'm sure they want

you to spend it,' Cathy said. Her mother shook her head.

'No. You know how independent your dad is, Cath. He doesn't think we should be kept by anyone else while he's able to work, but he doesn't want to hurt Sam's feelings by sending it back. That's why he puts it in the bank. He says it will be a little nest egg for them, or it might pay their fare if they want to come home.'

Cathy sighed. 'It's the other way round with us, Mam. You're always helping us instead of us helping you.'

'Don't be foolish, girl,' her mother said. 'We'd be lost without you. All the cleaning and ironing you do for me, and sending the children to help. All the things Greg does for us too. Those are more important than sending dollars – although it's good of Mary and Sam to think of us,' she added hastily.

'I miss her,' Cathy said. 'And I know you and Dad do too, don't you?'

'Yes, we do,' Sally said with a sigh. 'I wish she wasn't so far away. She might as well be on the moon for all the hope we have of seeing her.'

'Never mind, Mam,' Cathy consoled her. 'Who knows? Sam's a Liverpool lad after all, and he might decide to come back here. He'd do anything to please Mary.'

'Aye, that's the rub,' Sally said dryly. 'Would Mary want to come back here when they've got that beautiful house there, and the two automobiles, and no doubt a lot of posh friends there too. No, I don't see much hope of it, Cath.'

Sarah came in for a drink of water and Sally asked who she was playing with.

'Edie Meadows, and Meg and Jane Daly, Grandma.' Sally rose and took some biscuits from a tin.

'Share with the girls, love,' she said. 'D'you know where Mick is?'

'He's playing with Georgie and Tommy but I don't know where.'

'Never mind. His stomach will bring him home soon, especially if he sees you with the biscuits.'

Sarah looked back and smiled and Cathy felt a sudden shock of recognition. She turned to her mother as the child sped away. 'I got the shock of my life then, Mam. Sarah smiled at me and it was just as if she was Greg. Oh, I know she's not a bit like him in looks – she's the model of you – it was just the smile. I don't know why I've never seen it before.'

'Aye, you can't mistake Greg's smile,' Sally said, thinking that it was that smile which had charmed both Cathy and Mary and nearly caused a rift in her family. Aloud she said, 'I used to think John smiled like that but he's grown less like his father lately, in expression anyway.'

'*I* think he's still the image of Greg,' Cathy said quietly.

'Everything all right there, love?' Sally asked gently.

'Oh, yes, they're the best of friends.' Even to her mother she was reluctant to say how often John spoke impudently to his father, and how often Greg criticized his elder son. It will all sort itself out when John grows older, she told herself, and meanwhile ignored the frequent clashes between them.

Later, when they returned to Norris Street, the usual crowd of women was surrounding Mrs Parker. One of them called to Cathy, 'I seen yer washing out before the birds were up this morning. Yer bed can't be very comfortable.' They all sniggered and Cathy was annoyed to feel her eyes filling with tears. She made no reply and went quickly into the house. She sat down and Sarah came and stood beside her.

'Don't cry, Mam,' she said. 'Our John said they're only jealous.'

'I don't care about them,' Cathy said. 'I'm just tired. Get me a drink of water, please, love.'

Cathy waited until the children were in bed before telling Greg about the neighbour's remark. She was sorry she had mentioned it when she saw a worried look appear on his face.

'We'll have to get away from here, Cath,' he said. 'But I've asked everywhere and I can't find another house – not one that we can afford, anyway. We need something bigger than this, with three bedrooms, but the rents are too high.'

'I wouldn't mind even another two up and two down,' Cathy said. 'Not all these little streets are like this. That girl I walk to the school with sometimes from the next street – her mother lives there, and her sisters and cousins. They all go to their mam but she's different altogether from Mrs Parker. Freda told me she was really desperate one week. She hadn't a penny left until payday and her little boy lost one of his shoes on the way home from school. The baby was screaming with earache, so she went to her mam.

She put warm oil in the child's ear and nursed him off to sleep, then when she was on her own with Freda she gave her some money for shoes for Joey.

'Freda say she's always doing something like that for them if they're short – and she always says, "Just to tide you over, girl. Give it me back when you've got it." Catch Mrs Parker doing that!'

'I wonder whether we should apply for a Corporation house, Cath? It would mean moving to the outskirts of Liverpool but there'd be space, and a bathroom, and a garden.'

'But it would be more rent, and then fares for you to go to work and the children to school,' Cathy objected.

'I could get a bike, and there are new schools on those estates.'

'But John – the College – and I wouldn't want to go so far away from Mam. Anyway, those houses are only for people living in a couple of rooms or a slum house.'

'True,' Greg said. 'It was just an idea.' He slipped his arm around her waist. 'Try to ignore the comments, Cath. As Sarah says – they're only jealous of you.'

'It was John who said it. Sarah just repeated it,' she said. 'But I *will* ignore them. I've been a fool to let it bother me.'

When John started at the College and walked down the street in his new uniform, Cathy knew that there would be sly comments made, but her concern about this was soon forgotten in her shock at the amount of homework that he was expected to do. Often he had to work from immediately after his evening meal until eleven o'clock at night, and even at weekends he had little spare time to spend with his grandfather.

Cathy worried about his health but Greg assured her that things would be better when John became used to the work. This proved to be true, but as he settled into the College he soon became involved in the various sporting activities.

Though Greg admired Lawrie and respected him, he was secretly relieved to see John spending less time with his grandfather, and coming under other influences. Greg was not aware that the fires of anger against injustice lit by Lawrie were only temporarily damped down in John's mind, and still smouldered below the surface.

Now that John was so occupied, he and Greg came in contact only briefly, usually at meal times when the boy's conversation was chiefly about his school activities, so the tension between them was eased, much to Cathy's relief.

Greg's suggestion of moving out of Everton had alarmed her, and she determined to make the best of living in Norris Street and to ignore the pinpricks.

'What can't be cured must be endured' was a favourite maxim of her mother's, and Cathy determined to act on it. She would say no more about moving, but she would keep herself to herself and also make sure that her children were not suffering by living there.

John's time was fully occupied now, and Kate was still only a baby, but Cathy made plans for Sarah. Doreen Bates had told her that some of the bigger girls in the street 'talked dirty' so Cathy ensured that Sarah was kept away from them. Often on Friday nights Sarah stayed with her grandmother, and on Saturday played with her friends in Egremont Street.

She spent more time too in Elsie Hammond's florist's, and Sunday was always a family day. The family would go together to nine o'clock Mass, then after a hearty breakfast they would go to the grandparents' home in Egremont Street.

Greg and Lawrie, and John if he was free, would then go to the allotment. Josh would have had his breakfast and left to visit an old friend, returning after lunch, and in fine weather Cathy and Sally would take a basket containing meat and cheese sandwiches and some of Sally's homemade cakes for a picnic tea at the allotment. There was a spirit stove there and all that was necessary for tea. At first Josh accompanied them, but then he decided that he preferred to have a rest on Sunday afternoons, so Sally left him a substantial cold tea.

As winter approached the cold wet days meant that picnics at the allotment were finished but the family still spent most of Sunday together. Whenever possible the men worked on the allotment but they were always glad to return to Sally's warm kitchen and the plentiful spread she provided.

One day in November the meal was the cause of a resumption in the friction between John and his father, which Cathy had hoped was now finished. Lawrie and Greg came in, closely followed by John who had been playing for the College Rugby team, all cold and hungry.

Sally had a pan of soup to supplement the usual cold meat and pickles, and John had three helpings of this, followed by a generous serving of cold meat and several slices of bread and butter.

Rhubarb tarts and apple tarts followed, and Sally cut a generous slice of his favourite apple for John. She had already served Lawrie and Greg and the younger children, and Cathy brought a jug of custard to the table. John immediately seized it and poured a lavish amount into his dish.

Greg began angrily, '*John*—'

But Sally said quickly, 'It's all right, Greg. There's plenty more out there.' She smiled fondly at John. 'I suppose the football gives you an appetite, lad.'

'It does, Grandma,' he agreed. Greg was still frowning but John seemed unaware of his father's censure. As soon as he had eaten his apple pie, he asked immediately for some more.

This was too much for Greg who grew red with anger.

'Have some thought for others, John,' he snapped. 'Your grandma and your mam haven't had any at all yet.'

John blushed and muttered, 'Sorry, Grandma,' but he shot an angry look at his father.

Sally said placatingly, 'I'm glad to see them eaten, Greg. I made three rhubarb tarts as well as a couple of apple.'

'Aye, the rhubarb did well this year,' Lawrie said. 'We'll have to remember to force some next year, Greg. That chap on the end allotment had some in March just by putting a bucket over it in the winter.'

The uncomfortable moment passed but Sally noticed that John sat as far as possible from his father after the meal, and when the Redmond family had gone home she spoke to Lawrie about it.

'Do you think Greg feels we spoil John, Lol? I wouldn't like him to think we made any distinction between the children.'

'Greg couldn't think that, love. Look how close you and Sarah are, and we all spoil the baby.' He laughed. 'We couldn't spoil young Mick – he never stands still long enough.'

'But that business with the pie – I seemed to be taking John's part against his father, but there *was* plenty and I like to see a lad eat well.'

'Don't worry about it, Sal. Greg was just worried in case he left us short, that's all.'

'Maybe,' Sally said, but she still looked thoughtful.

Cathy had said nothing about the incident until they left her mother's house, then she gave John the key and told him to run ahead with Sarah and Mick. As soon as they had gone, she turned to Greg.

'I hope you're satisfied! Making a scene like that and leaving everyone feeling uncomfortable.'

'Something had to be said,' Greg snapped. 'He showed no concern at all for other people. Your mother was just about to sit down for her own meal when he demanded more pie.'

'He didn't *demand*,' Cathy said, 'he asked for another helping and Mam was pleased to give it to him. She knows he's a growing lad and always hungry.'

'Hungry!' Greg exclaimed. 'He was eating as though for a wager. It was an abuse of your mother's hospitality, and you know it, Cathy.'

They had reached home and nothing more was said while she hurriedly prepared the children for bed. The fire had gone out and the house was cold but John had boiled water on the gas ring and was filling a hot water bottle when they arrived. He had put the kettle on again for cocoa and Cathy said gratefully, 'That's a good lad, John. Put the bottle in Kate's cot for a minute then it can go in Sarah's bed, you and Mick will warm each other.'

John smiled at her and ran upstairs with the stone hot water bottle. Cathy glanced at Greg to see if he had noticed his son's helpfulness, but he had taken off his coat and seemed absorbed in cleaning out the grate and laying the fire for the morning.

Later, when the children were safely in bed and asleep, Cathy returned to the argument.

'It was ridiculous to say John "abused Mam's hospitality". She made those pies for tea and was delighted to see him enjoying them.'

'That's not the point,' he said. 'John was greedy and selfish, and I'm surprised that you defend him – although I know, of course, that he can do no wrong in your eyes.'

'And no right in yours!' she retorted.

They were interrupted by a loud cry from the baby. Cathy

dashed upstairs to attend to her. You can't even have a row in peace in this house, she thought, then the absurdity of the thought struck her, and she smiled.

By the time that Kate had been comforted and Cathy had returned downstairs, both she and Greg had had time to draw back from an argument in which things might be said that would be hard to forget. By tacit consent the disagreement was dropped.

Cathy spent a wakeful night. Kate was teething and when Cathy was disturbed by the baby's cries she lay awake worrying about matters which she could manage to push to the back of her mind during the day.

Chief of these was money. When she had only two children Cathy could manage to make ends meet on Greg's small wage, with the help of food from the allotment and assistance from her mother, but as her family grew it became increasingly hard. She could manage to provide sufficient food, with Sally's unobtrusive help, but clothes and other extras, particularly shoes, were an ever present worry.

John and Sarah rapidly outgrew their shoes and Mick's only seemed to last a couple of weeks before the sole was hanging off or the toecaps scuffed away.

When Sally bought a rabbit she always made a small pie for Lawrie and Josh and herself, and a larger one for Cathy's family, and part of her bread and cake baking was always passed to her daughter.

'I can't get used to cooking for a small family,' was always her excuse as Sally put bread and cakes into Cathy's basket.

The clothes she provided were a great help too. Sally's arthritis meant that she could no longer do fine sewing but she had kept her sewing machine and on it made dresses for Sarah and trousers for John and Mick from the material in second-hand clothes, bought for a few pence in the market or from a wardrobe dealer. A cutdown pair of men's Harris tweed trousers had provided a pair for Mick which had defied even his talent for destruction.

Shoes were another matter and providing them, and other items such as coal and pennies for the gas, became increasingly hard for Cathy. She had shopped at the Co-operative Stores when she began life in Norris Street, but gradually she had slipped into the habit of frequenting the corner shop which gave credit.

At first she told herself that it was just for a week or two until she could catch up, but instead she found that she was falling further behind. She paid her bill weekly and at first left only a shilling or two to be carried forward, but before she realized what was happening the debt had grown until she owed as much as Greg's weekly wage.

Every week there seemed to be some reason why she was unable to pay anything off the debt. Her only hope was a Christmas Tontine to which she paid two shillings a week. She had decided that her Tontine payment of two pounds must go to pay off the debt, and that there could be no extras for Christmas, but the woman who ran the Tontine had supposedly gone to nurse a sick friend in Wales and rumours that she had in fact absconded were growing.

What on earth can I do if she has? Cathy thought despairingly. Her worries were compounded by the fact that she had concealed her debt from Greg and her mother – from Sally because she was ashamed to tell her when she had given so much help and because her mother was such a good manager, and from Greg because she knew he would feel mortified that his wage was insufficient.

The rumours proved to be true, and although the woman was arrested the money was gone, and there was nothing for the members of the Tontine.

It was the main topic of conversation in the district. When Cathy went into the corner shop the woman there asked if she had been a member.

'Yes, I was,' Cathy admitted. She hesitated, blushed, then said nervously, 'I was hoping to pay my bill with it. I'm sorry – I don't know what I'll do now.'

Mrs Cain leaned over the counter. 'Well, don't go to no moneylender, Mrs Redmond. You know what I mean.'

It was something that had not occurred to Cathy, but the woman spoke so earnestly that she agreed.

'There's been some suicides when women have run Tontines and spent the money, but there's been more people done away with themselves because of moneylenders. Don't worry about what you owe me. I know you'll clear it when you can.'

'I will,' Cathy promised. 'Thanks for giving me time. I've been very worried about it.'

They talked for a while about the people whose Christmas would be ruined by the loss of the Tontine money and of similar cases which had occurred in other years.

'I suppose it would be more sensible to put the money in the Post Office every week,' Cathy said.

'Yes but would you do it?' Mrs Cain said shrewdly. 'It's because she came round every week on pay night that people put it away.'

'Yes, you're right,' Cathy said.

She turned to leave the shop and Mrs Cain said suddenly. 'It's a wonder you can leave your lad at school until he's sixteen, Mrs Redmond. I know the railway don't pay much. Grace Woods' lad is earning twelve shillings a week in the foundry and he's only fifteen.'

Cathy's face burned but fortunately a customer came into the shop and she was able to leave without replying.

In the small hours of the night she lay awake thinking of Mrs Cain's words. Was she mad to have such ambitions for her children? John's school fees were paid and a grant given towards the cost of his uniform, but there were many small extras for which money had to be found, and this was one of the reasons for her debt at the shop. She resented Mrs Cain's comments but she told herself that the woman was entitled to make them while money was owed to her.

The thought of the twelve shillings a week earned by Harry Woods, and the difference that such a sum would make for all of them, was tempting. But then Cathy thought of young Harry, pale and hollow-cheeked, too exhausted after work to do more than eat and sleep, and knew that that was not the life she wanted for her sons, no matter what sacrifice was needed from her.

Chapter Four

Cathy felt a sense of reprieve after talking to Mrs Cain and having her credit extended, but she resolved to watch every penny that she spent and to reduce her debt if it was only by sixpence a week. She felt that she was a poor manager. True, Greg's wage as a railway clerk was meagre but he only kept enough from it for a frugal five cigarettes a day, and walked to work to save fares. He got off-cuts of wood from someone he knew to save coal, and borrowed a last from her father with which to repair the children's shoes.

With help from her mother and food from the allotment, Cathy felt that she had no excuse for debt.

She remembered Greg's words about envying Lawrie's knack with people and thought that she envied her mother's knack with money. Then she remembered her old friend Mrs Malloy, and her cheerful saying, "Never mind, girl, we never died a winter yet", and felt comforted.

That Christmas was a happy one in spite of her worries. John brought home his first school report and they were all delighted by it. He was third in his class and described as "intelligent and industrious". His behaviour was described as "excellent". Cathy looked on happily as Greg shook John's hand and told him that he was proud of him.

'It's better than I expected,' John said modestly, but Greg told him that he had been sure that the report would be good. Lawrie commented on the word "industrious".

'That means that you're working hard, doesn't it? Don't forget what you're working for, lad.'

'I won't, Grandad,' John promised. In spite of all his other interests, John still occasionally attended meetings of the unemployed with his grandfather, and read accounts of Council meetings in Lawrie's newspaper. He also discussed them with Joe Furlong who had passed the scholarship examination at the same time and was now in his form at College.

Now he told Lawrie of a discussion he had had with Joe. 'He said I was a Communist like Bessie Braddock. Are the Communists any good, Grandad?'

'No. I've got no time for them,' Lawrie said. 'They don't stand up for the working man. Where were they when the General Strike was on? I admire John and Bessie Braddock though, lad, and they're not Communists.'

'Joe said they belong to the International Social Club in Byrom Street,' John said.

'Aye, they did,' Lawrie said. 'But they were out of it by 1924. You've got to remember, lad, people were desperate to get something done after the war. We were just beating our heads against a brick wall, and I suppose the Braddocks thought Communism might mean a just society. They found out their mistake though. The Communists just wanted to carve the country up, *and* they tried to tell Bessie what to do.'

'She wouldn't like that,' John said with a grin.

'What! She told them what they could do with themselves and I don't think they've recovered yet,' Lawrie laughed. 'By the way, do you ever see Sammy Roche these days?'

'No. I think he dodges me,' John said. 'He was so disappointed because his dad wouldn't let him take the scholarship.'

'That's a shame,' Lawrie said. 'But he can still do well, even without the scholarship.'

'Yes. He was the cleverest of all of us,' John admitted. 'And I like him the best. I think Joe's sly.'

'Give him a wide berth, then,' Lawrie advised. 'There's nothing worse than a false friend.'

'It's all right, Grandad. He doesn't want to be friends with me,' John said. 'His dad told him he should be making friends with people who could help him when he left school.'

'Well, by the hokey!' Lawrie exclaimed. 'That's ripe. Does he know he's aping his betters, as the saying goes? That's the main reason rich men send their sons to posh public schools – so that they can make contacts.' He laughed heartily, and John laughed with him.

All the adults in the family forgot their various worries in their efforts to make Christmas happy for the children.

Greg used scraps of wood to make presents for them: a doll's cradle for Sarah, a toy farm for Mick – with green-painted sawdust for grass, a broken mirror as a pond, and a tiny farm cart filled with hay – and an elaborate pencil case for John.

Cathy bought a celluloid doll for twopence, and dressed it to go in the cradle, and made a rag doll for the baby, and felt that they were well prepared for Christmas.

Sally had sewed new clothes for all the children: a coat and bonnet for Kate, a warm dress for Sarah, and jerseys and trousers for the two boys.

'What would I do without you, Mam?' Cathy exclaimed when Sally showed her the clothes. She had been cleaning and blackleading the grate in Egremont Street, and there was a smear of black on her cheeks, but her eyes sparkled with excitement, and Sally thought that she still looked like a young girl.

'Everybody's been so good to us,' Cathy said. 'Dad buying all that fruit and the sweets, and a man at work brought a pile of little farm animals in for Greg that his own son used to play with.' She thought but did not say that Mrs Cain had done her the greatest kindness of all in relieving her worry about her debt at the shop.

Sarah had been spending a lot of time at Elsie Hammond's shop, helping to prepare frames for the many wreaths which had been ordered. Although so young she was quick and deft, and on Christmas Eve spent several hours making bunches of flowers in the back room while Elsie and Celia were busy in the shop.

The flowers would be bought by people who visited the graves of relatives on Christmas Day, and Elsie was delighted when she saw them.

'You've mixed them colours lovely,' she said. 'You've got a real gift with flowers, love, there's no doubt.'

Sarah blushed with pleasure. 'I'll have to go home now,' she said shyly. 'Mam said I had to be back by twelve o'clock.'

'All right, love, but tell your mam you've been a real help to me,' Elsie said. She took half a crown from her pocket and gave it to Sarah. 'That's for helping me.'

Sarah flew home and showed her mother the money and

gave her Elsie's message. 'Can I keep the half a crown, Mam?' she said eagerly.

'Yes, but don't waste it,' Cathy said. 'Buy some new hair ribbons for yourself and a pair of stockings – you'll still have plenty left.'

Sarah raced to Brunswick Road, and bought the gifts she had been planning since she received the money. Tiny bottles of 4711 eau de cologne for her mother and grandmother, a rattle for Kate, a monkey on a stick for Mick, and a flat tin of De Reske Minor cigarettes for her father. Then she dived into a second-hand book shop. It was easy to find a copy of *Treasure Island* for John, but she found it hard to decide between a copy of *The Diary of Samuel Pepys* and a leatherbound copy of a book of sermons for Lawrie. Both were priced at fourpence but she dithered between them for so long that the old man who kept the shop came to her aid.

'Is your grandfather a religious man?'

'No, but he likes books with nice covers,' Sarah said. 'He often comes in here.'

The man asked his name, then put the book of sermons back on the shelf. 'Take the Samuel Pepys, love,' he said. 'You can have it for threepence and he'll be made up with it.'

Sarah was so pleased that she was half-way home before she remembered her hair ribbons and stockings and had to go back for them. She also remembered Josh and bought a box of dates for him.

As usual the family gathered at Sally's house for the Christmas dinner and soon after Cathy and Greg and the children arrived, a hamper from Fortnum and Mason, ordered by Mary, was delivered. There was much hilarity when it was unpacked.

'Quails in aspic,' Lawrie read out. 'Peaches in brandy. Pâté de foie gras. This must have cost a fortune, Sal, and all fancy stuff. Mary must have forgotten scouse is my favourite food.' He chuckled but Sally looked worried.

'You're right, Lol. This must have cost the earth. I know their intentions are good but I don't like them throwing their money away like this.'

'They must be able to afford it,' Cathy said. 'Gentlemen's Relish . . . that should be all right on toast, and you can eat the smoked salmon and crab and peaches, and things like that.'

'But those quails – ugh!' Sally said. 'And some of that other stuff – I couldn't face that.'

'Give it to Peggy,' Lawrie advised. 'Jimmie Burns would eat a horse between blankets. He'll soon polish it off.'

'Aye, that's a good idea,' Sally agreed. 'As long as they don't think our Mary's showing off, sending this stuff.' There were also carefully packed bottles of brandy, whisky and gin which Lawrie ranged on the dresser.

'We'll drink their health when we've had our dinner,' he said cheerfully. The gift seemed to bring Mary and Sam, though so far away, close to them in spirit, and Sarah always remembered that Christmas as a particularly happy one. It was the first time she had been able to buy gifts for the family and everyone had been delighted with her choice. Josh had been particularly pleased at being included, but Sarah felt that all the family seemed content that Christmas.

January was a miserable month with wet cold days and foggy nights, and in spite of Sally's precautions Lawrie caught a chill which rapidly became bronchitis. Greg and John carried the kitchen sofa upstairs and brought down instead the single bed from the third bedroom. The fire was kept going day and night.

'He's better in the kitchen than stuck upstairs,' Sally told Greg. 'The company does him as much good as the warmth.' She applied her well-tried remedies to such good effect that Lawrie was up within a few days and talking of going back to work by the end of the week.

Sally objected, and Peggy Burns who had called in told him he would be a fool to go back on Monday.

'The first three days aren't counted for sick pay,' she said. 'So if you go in on Monday you'll only get two days. If you wait till Tuesday to go in, Saturday and Sunday'll be counted for sick pay.'

Peggy was held to be an authority about such things but it was the weakness in his legs rather than the prospect of extra sick pay which made Lawrie stay off the extra day.

Sally made him wear a flannel vest soaked in camphorated oil, and so many layers of clothing that he protested.

'Good God, Sally, I won't be able to move never mind work if I wear any more.' But she was adamant.

'You're not taking any chances, not in this weather, not

while I'm here to stop you,' she said firmly.

He had returned from the morning shift and was sitting by the fire when Greg and John came to take the bed upstairs and replace the sofa while Lawrie declared that he was "as right as ninepence". Greg was surprised to see John, who usually evaded shows of affection, put his arms round his grandfather and kiss him.

'I'm glad you're better, Grandad,' he said.

Lawrie said with a laugh, 'Aye, there's life in the old dog yet, lad.'

Greg watched them sadly, wondering at the difference in John when he was with his grandfather. The boy had been the cause of another quarrel between his parents only a few days earlier.

He took his books upstairs directly after the evening meal every night, and Cathy had been furious when he came home with red and swollen hands after being given six strokes of the strap for scamped homework.

'It's not fair,' she raged to Greg. 'He was working from tea time till ten o'clock last night. You'll have to complain to the headmaster.'

'I can't do that, Cath,' Greg protested. 'Were other boys punished?'

'No. Only our John.'

'Then their work must have been satisfactory, and they must all have the same amount.'

'I don't care about them. I only know how long our John was upstairs with his books, and so do you,' she declared.

'I know how much time he spent in his bedroom but he can't have been working all the time. He must have been reading or day dreaming,' Greg said mildly. 'I can't complain about his punishment if he deserved it.'

'He *didn't* deserve it, and it was too much anyway. The palms of his hands were all red and swollen. If you won't complain I've a good mind to go myself, but I know they'd take more notice of a man.'

'It would be the wrong thing to do, Cath. It'd only make life difficult for John with the masters *and* with the other boys. He'll have to learn to stand on his own feet.'

'He'll get no help from you, that's for sure,' she snapped.

Greg made no reply although his expression was grim. He

42

took a packet of cigarettes from the mantelpiece and lit one. Cathy pushed past him to bang the flatiron against the glowing coals.

'You'd go quick enough if it was one of the others,' she fumed. 'But John—' She was near to tears. Greg glanced at her face and checked an angry retort, then he went out to the shed. Cathy could hear him hammering something as she angrily pushed the iron over the clothes. It was some time before the hammering ceased and he came back into the kitchen.

They had both had time to cool down and Greg said quietly, 'If I thought it was the right thing to do I'd complain, Cathy, but I know it isn't, and John wouldn't want me to.'

'But the state of his hands, Greg. It was cruel.'

'I know, but at Sheldrake we had far more than that to take and no one ever complained. The prefects had more or less a free hand to punish the younger boys, and it wasn't a few strokes on the hand either, but bending over with trousers down and being beaten. There was one prefect – boys couldn't sit down for days after he'd beaten them.'

Cathy was horrified. 'Did nobody stop it?' she demanded.

'One of the masters had a word with him, I think, because he was easier later. He was a big boy who didn't realise his own strength.'

'But that's disgraceful – and you wanted to send John there!'

'It happens in all schools. Men approve because it's a way of toughening boys up for later life. It's a hard world for men and John will be grateful later on for this discipline.'

'It's not such an easy world for women,' she retorted. 'I'm hoping both our girls will have a good education, but there won't be any nonsense like that in a girls' college. Women have got more sense.'

She said no more about complaining to the headmaster, however, and Greg hoped that the punishment had taught John a lesson. He felt that the good report had given his son false confidence in his abilities and hoped that he would now work harder. It seemed that he did as there were no more punishments.

Mick came home from school one day with a swelling in his neck and as soon as Sally saw him she said that it was mumps.

'John had them when he was two, didn't he? The other two will probably get it now.'

She was right and both Sarah and Kate became ill, but fortunately the attacks were slight. Nevertheless, it was an exhausting time for Cathy, kept awake by the fretful baby and by Sarah and Mick needing attention, and confined to the house with the bored and quarrelsome children.

She began to look pale and hollow-eyed, and on the first fine Sunday after the children recovered Sally announced that she would take charge of them and Cathy and Greg were to go for a tramride.

'A tramride. Where, Mam?' Cathy said.

'Anywhere. Woolton Woods or Calderstones Park,' Sally said. 'Anywhere you fancy so long as you're out in the fresh air. Take some sandwiches with you and get a cup of tea somewhere.'

Within half an hour the sandwiches were made, and their clothes changed, and they were hustled out by Sally. They set off with a feeling of adventure and decided to board the first tram that came along.

It proved to be one for Sefton Park and they went on the top deck, determined to make the most of the sunny day. Once inside the park they walked around the lake, watching the ducks being fed at its verge, and the rowing boats setting off, to be inexpertly rowed by young men in their shirt sleeves and straw hats, with a giggling or admiring girl in each boat.

Cathy and Greg rested on a grassy bank by the lake, listening to the shouts of a man with a loud hailer calling in the rowers whose time was up, and watching the fishermen sitting round the lake, patiently waiting for a movement of their lines.

After a while they wandered on to see the aviary and the Palm House, strolling round in the damp warmth to see the exotic flowers and strange large-leaved plants, all with identifying name plates. Cathy craned to read one and a burly man beside her said, 'I'd read it out to ya, girl, but I can't speak Dutch.'

A youth with slicked back hair said superciliously, 'It's Latin, actually.'

'Ho, is it?' the burly man said. 'We've got a smart one

here. You read it out then, lad.' The youth beat a hasty retreat and Cathy and Greg moved away, smiling, to join the crowd round the banana tree.

Later they found a quiet spot near the café, and unpacked the sandwiches and cake they had brought, and Greg brought cups of tea.

'Isn't it lovely and peaceful?' Cathy sighed. 'You'd never think we were so near the city, would you?'

'No. We must do this more often, Cath. Bring the children next time.' She agreed but looked up at him, smiling mischievously. 'I'm glad they're not with us now, though. I've seen enough of them lately.'

Her eyes sparkled and her dimples showed as she laughed, and Greg exclaimed, 'You look better already, Cath.' He put his arm round her and pulled her close to kiss her. A passing couple smiled at them.

'I wonder what they'd think if they knew we were an old married couple with four children,' Cathy said.

'They'd never believe it,' Greg said stoutly, 'not when they looked at you anyway.'

They sat in silence for a while enjoying the sunshine, then Greg returned the cups and Cathy scattered crumbs for small birds which hopped and pecked around her. They walked on to see the Peter Pan statue and the Wendy House, and then to see *The Jolly Roger* moored in a small lake.

'I don't know why we haven't brought the children here,' Greg said. 'We must bring them often this summer.'

'We always went out on Sundays with Mam and Dad when we were children,' Cathy said. 'Mam always kept Sunday as a day of rest. She said her father insisted on it although he wasn't a religious man because he said women should have a day off, too.'

'He sounds a progressive sort.'

'It's strange,' Cathy mused. 'I only remember him as a bad-tempered, bedridden old man, but he must have been different once. Our old neighbour Mrs Malloy thought the world of him and she was a good judge. Dad admired him too. They used to talk about politics and world affairs, Mam said once.'

'I think I fail your dad there, Cath,' he said. 'Perhaps that's why he talks so freely to John.'

'No. He's always been close to John from when we lived there.'

They suddenly realised that they were touching on a controversial subject, and Cathy exclaimed, 'Look, we're at the park gates already!'

Greg said, 'Look at the queues for the trams!'

They had been walking with Greg's arm around Cathy's waist. Now she drew away and straightened her hat, then walked along demurely with her arm through his.

'Oh, I have enjoyed today,' she exclaimed as they stood in the queue. 'I feel tons better.'

'You look better too,' he said. 'Your mam will be pleased.'

The children returned to school and life returned to normal for Cathy, but at the beginning of May Greg slipped and fell as he alighted from a tram, spraining his right wrist. He was unable to hold a pen in his right hand and although he practised writing with his left, the office manager refused to accept his handwriting and he was obliged to stay off work.

One of his colleagues brought the wages that were due to him a few days later. Cathy heard him say, 'Anyone but old Greenwood would have found you a filing job or something until your hand was right, but I'm afraid he's got it in for you, old chap.'

'Why has the manager got his knife into you, Greg?' she asked when the man had gone, but he was unable to tell her.

'I've never done anything to offend him as far as I know,' he said, 'but he's a queer man.'

Greg took out medical books from the Library and studied them, then worked on his wrist to such good effect that he was able to return to work after a week, much to Cathy's relief.

She felt sometimes that Fate was against her in her efforts to reduce the debt which seemed to grow larger instead of smaller. Mrs Cain was still accommodating about it, and partly for that very reason Cathy was determined somehow to pay it off.

She kept her worries hidden and was outwardly as cheerful as ever, singing as she went about her housework and greeting Greg with a happy smile when he returned from work.

On the twenty-eighth of June the children were all out when he came in from work and drew some transparent coloured eye shields from his pocket.

'These were given away in the newspaper, Cath. For the eclipse tomorrow. Apparently it's dangerous to look at it with the naked eye.'

'Sarah said they were told about it at school,' Cathy said. 'The teacher drew diagrams on the blackboard.'

'Yes, it's very important. I thought I might take John to see it, because there's no school tomorrow – a Holy Day of Obligation. The sun rises at twenty to five and the eclipse should be about twenty past six. They're allowing people on the flat roof of the school. What do you think, Cath?'

'You'd have to be up very early,' she said, 'I know John's off but you'd still have to go to work, wouldn't you?'

'I'm not worried about that,' he said. 'I wouldn't like John to miss it. It will be so many years before it happens again.'

Before he could say any more the door burst open and John rushed in. 'Hello, Dad,' he said breathlessly. 'Mam, Dad, can I go to Crosby with Grandad to see the eclipse? The world will go dark, Grandad says, and it won't happen again until I'm old. Can I go?'

'But—' Cathy began, looking at Greg in dismay.

He slipped the shades in his pocket and said quickly, 'Crosby? That should be a good vantage point. Yes, of course you can go, John.'

'Thanks, Dad,' he said, darting away to tell his grandfather.

'Oh, Greg! But you wanted—'

'It doesn't matter Cath, really. Don't let your father know I'd suggested it. He just hasn't thought of John going with me.'

'I know,' Cathy said, but she still looked troubled. Then her face brightened.

'I've just thought, Greg, why don't you take Sarah? She'd love it, and it's just as important for her to see these things.'

'But is she old enough to understand?' he asked doubtfully.

'Of course she is. I told you – her teacher told them all about it.'

Sarah was delighted when she was told, and the eclipse was something she remembered all her life: walking through streets even at that hour thronged with people, then waiting

47

in the crowd on the flat roof of the school, then the awe-inspiring seconds of utter darkness and silence and an eerie feeling. Then the relief when normality returned, and most of all the feeling of closeness to her father as she walked beside him, clutching his arm.

For John too the morning was memorable, but less for the exciting moments of the eclipse itself than for a conversation with his grandfather which channelled all his vague plans for the future.

They arrived early at Crosby and as they strolled from the railway station to the shore, Lawrie talked about an item in the newspapers about a Bill which had come before Parliament for its third reading.

'The Trades Union and Trades Disputes Bill, but the papers are calling it the Freedom Bill. *Freedom*! Freedom to starve, that's what it is.'

'What's it about, Grandad?'

'About making a General Strike illegal – they say no man is to be intimidated into striking or forced to contribute to any political party, but they know fine well no intimidation is needed. The last time men rushed to come out was because it was the only way they could protest about what was being done to them. It's all eyewash, this Bill.'

'What do you mean – eyewash?'

'I mean they're pretending it's for the benefit of the working man, and really it's to make sure that working men don't stand together to get justice.'

'Like last year when everyone came out to support the miners?'

'Aye, God help them. Their pay was so low that their families were going hungry even while the men worked long hours. When the masters wanted to cut it even lower, the men had to do something. More shame to us that we weakened and left them to stand alone,' Lawrie said with a sigh.

They walked in silence for a while then John said, 'What about the other bit, Grandad? About contributing to a political party.'

Lawrie gave a short bitter laugh. 'By "political party" they mean the Labour Party, lad. It doesn't matter to the other two parties with money being poured into them by newspaper barons and businessmen who know they'll benefit by having laws passed that'll line their pockets. That's why Clines and Lansbury and Thomas have tried to fight this Bill, but they've got big guns against them.'

They had been walking slowly but suddenly Lawrie had a fit of coughing so severe that he had to sit on a low wall nearby. John stood beside him, watching anxiously, unable to help.

'Sit further along and lean on this, Grandad,' he said when the bout of coughing was over. 'Do you think you've talked too much?'

Lawrie wiped his face and took a deep breath. 'I always do, lad,' he said with a grin. 'But it'd take more than the ould tickle to stop me. I'll just sit here for a minute and get me breath back.'

They sat together for a few minutes with John darting anxious glances at his grandfather.

'It's a good thing you *didn't* go on the Council, Grandad,' he said presently. 'Although it's a shame in a way because you'd be better than any of them.'

Lawrie smiled. 'Aye, I always said I didn't want to get mixed up with their squabbles about religion, but the truth is, lad, your grandma put her foot down good and proper on the idea because of me cough.' His face grew serious.

'The old cough stopped me, John, but I hope you'll carry on the fight. The Council for experience, then get into Parliament. That's the only way. Get into Parliament and help to change the whole rotten system from inside.'

'It'll take a long time that way,' John said doubtfully.

'You've got time on your side, lad,' Lawrie said. He gripped John's arm. 'I don't know what I'd do without you. It's not just your company, John. You're my hope for the future. It crucifies me to see poor kids hungry and barefoot, and women worn out and old before they're thirty, and not be able to fight for them. But you'll do it, won't you?'

'I will, Grandad,' said John, feeling as though he was taking a solemn oath.

'Men too,' Lawrie went on, 'standing for hours at the dock gates, soaked to the skin and hungry, then fighting like animals for the chance of half a day's work. Turned away too, as often as not. I know what it's like. I did it myself when your mam and Auntie Mary were children.'

'I know,' John said. 'I heard Grandma saying to Mam that was how you got your bad chest.'

'Aye, but it was only a bad patch for me and we came out of it. Some fellers never know anything else all their lives – except when they're wanted to fight for their country.'

People were beginning to hurry past them towards the shore and Lawrie stood up. With a sudden change of mood, he said cheerfully, 'Never mind that now, lad. We've come out to enjoy ourselves, haven't we? This has been good for trade anyway, with the pictures open all night, and the pubs having extensions for music and dancing until the early hours. It's a bit of excitement for us too, isn't it?'

They had reached the shore and found a comfortable seat among the sandhills, where Lawrie produced a can of tea and sandwiches. They settled down to enjoy a picnic but even during the exciting moments before the eclipse John was thinking of his grandfather's words and storing them away in his mind.

Cathy and Sally had hot cocoa ready when they all returned, and Cathy insisted that they all went to bed for a few hours' sleep and saved all talk of the eclipse for later. She knew that Greg would be up and out to work before John came downstairs to talk about his outing with his grandfather, and hoped that the subject would be exhausted before he came home. Although Greg had said nothing, she had an uneasy feeling that he had been hurt because John had gone with Lawrie.

Chapter Five

Greg had not forgotten his plan to take the children out on Sundays, but he needed to spend a great deal of time on the allotment and Sunday was his only free day. Cathy told him not to worry about it as they all enjoyed spending sunny days at the allotment and having picnic meals there, but he still felt that he would like to show the children the Park's sights.

He was pleased, however, that John was spending less time with his grandfather. Even when Lawrie and Sally were at the allotment with Cathy and Greg and the younger children, John was often elsewhere playing cricket.

He had been chosen for the school team and as with his other enthusiasms, for the moment it was all he could think of. He had formed a team to play in the park and they were now challenging boys from other areas and travelling round to various parks to play.

Greg had a stroke of luck at this time. A man who had one of the other allotments had admired the hut which he had built on theirs and asked him to make one for him.

Greg had access to a cheap supply of wood through a timber firm owned by a man who had once been a shop boy in his father's jeweller's shop. He built a sturdy shed and fitted it with shelving. The allotment holder was delighted with it.

'You got the wood cheap because of your contacts,' he said. 'You should have the benefit of that. I'll pay you full price for the wood, and for your labour. How about a quid?'

Greg said he would only take what he had paid for the wood.

'No, lad, I said you got it cheap through your contact but I'll pay the full price. I reckon I'm still doing well. I'm made up with that shed,' the man said.

Greg hastened home and put a one pound and a ten shilling note on the table by Cathy.

'How about that?' he said triumphantly. 'For building that shed.' Cathy gazed at the money in disbelief then flung her arms round his neck.

'Oh Greg! Oh, what a relief,' she exclaimed.

'He paid me a pound for my work and the ten bob is the difference between what I paid Stan Johnson for the wood and its retail value. He insisted on paying the full price,' Greg said, smiling broadly. 'Should pay for new shoes for the menace and a few extras, shouldn't it?'

Mick had arrived home from school with the sole of one shoe torn away from the upper and Cathy had kept him indoors as a punishment. Now he grinned unrepentantly at his father.

'You'd better look after your next pair of shoes,' Cathy warned him. 'Dad's worked hard for this money.' But she was too happy to scold him further. Her mind was filled with plans for the pound note, including paying something off at the corner shop, but she pushed the ten shilling note to Greg.

'You should keep this. It will be a chance for you to get new shoes yourself. That split's beginning to show.'

He glanced down at the heavy boots he wore for the allotment. 'Pity I can't wear these for the office,' he said ruefully. 'I must admit I was getting worried about my shoes.'

'Well, this is a golden opportunity for you to get new ones,' she said cheerfully.

The money gave a lift to their spirits as well as helping them in a constant battle to make ends meet. Cathy was able to pay a few shillings to Mrs Cain, and buy various small neccessities she had been unable to afford from Greg's small wage.

Greg took Mick with him and bought his shoes as well as his own from the ten shillings, and Cathy was able to buy shoes for Sarah and replace a worn-out pan and towels. She also bought a leather cricket ball for John to use instead of the tennis ball he usually played with, and Greg insisted that she bought something for herself.

She chose a prettily flowered wraparound pinafore. As Grace Woods had once said to Cathy: "These pinnies cover a multitude", and though the clothes beneath them might be worn and shabby, and their shoes patched and stockings darned, the women of the neighbourhood felt that they looked respectable if they had a clean pinafore to wear.

Cathy wore a sacking apron in the morning for the heaviest and dirtiest housework in her own house and her mother's, but always washed thoroughly and changed into her floral pinafore in the early afternoon. Although Cathy had worried about Sarah hearing "dirty talk" from the girls in the street, she never worried about Mick. He had always been his own man, having hosts of friends but always set on doing whatever his inventive mind suggested at the moment. He seemed as oblivious to quarrels between the other boys, and their conversation, as he was to scolding for damaging his clothes.

It was a shock to her when he came in one day while she was putting clothes through the mangle and said bluntly, 'Mam, where do babies come from?'

'Just a minute,' she said folding a pillowcase to give herself time to think.

Sarah was there, helping to put the clothes through the mangle, and before her mother could speak replied calmly, 'Eileen Reddy said they grow inside their mam. We were doing the altar flowers one day and there were some irises, and you know how the little bud grows on the stem?'

'No, I don't know what irises are like,' Mick said.

But Sarah went on, 'Eileen said that's how babies grow inside their mam. I thought Mrs Carter brought them.'

Cathy had been about to tell Mick that Mrs Carter the midwife brought the babies so she felt that she had had a narrow escape.

'But how do they get out?' he asked Sarah.

'Through their mam's belly button,' she said in her quiet way.

'Mams must have big belly buttons,' Mick said doubtfully.

'It's like balloons,' Sarah explained. 'Eileen said the babies come squashed flat then they blow up properly.'

Cathy had gone into the living room and was rummaging in the dresser, her lips twitching as she listened to Sarah's confident explanation. Suddenly her expression grew thoughtful. She went back into the kitchen.

'Who've you been playing with, Mick?'

'Bertie Woods and Bob Bailey and some other fellows,' he said.

'But they're older than you,' Cathy exclaimed.

'Yes, but they've got a go cart. Bertie got the wheels but I got the box for it so they have to let me play with them.'

'Never mind the go cart,' Cathy said. 'Those lads are too old for you. Play with boys your own age.'

Bertie Woods, she thought. I don't like that lad. Bertie was the second son of Grace Woods next door and very like his father, a big bullying man who frequently beat his wife and children. Grace was expecting her eighth child and Cathy wondered whether Bertie had overheard conversations about the birth.

She told Greg about the incident later. 'You could have knocked me down with a feather. Not just Mick springing that on me, but the way Sarah talked to him about it.'

'Eileen Reddy seems a nice girl,' Greg said.

'She does,' Cathy agreed. 'She lives in Field Street though, so she goes the other way home from school to Sarah. Still, I'm glad they play together in school. There's a few nice girls in that class, not like the girls in this street, except for Doreen.'

'I'd better have a talk with Mick,' Greg said. 'I've had a word with John on the subject.'

'Have you? I didn't know.'

'I thought it might be wise,' was all he said, but Cathy was pleased. I'll have to stop looking for trouble between them, she thought. They get on all right now.

She made up her mind that she would take the children out to the park during the school holidays, or for days out further afield. The children could have four rides for a penny on the tram and the baby would go free, so it would cost very little and would keep them away from other influences.

John had other plans, but as soon as the holidays started Cathy put hers into effect. She packed a bottle of cold tea and packets of bread and jam into the bottom of the baby carriage, and set off for Newsham Park with Sarah and Mick walking beside her.

They also took a bat that Greg had made, and a ball, and played rounders and catch. Cathy enjoyed the games as much as Mick and Sarah, and Kate toddled about picking blades of grass and playing with a knitted ball that her grandmother had made for her.

Sometimes Cathy joined forces to go to the park with her friend Freda who lived in the next street. She was a plump jolly girl with a carefree attitude to housework.

'It'll be there when I'm gone,' she would say airily. 'Come on, kids.' Her baby would be dumped in with Kate, and Freda would fill a bag with jam butties and broken biscuits, and a bottle of tea.

They all enjoyed these excursions. Usually they went first to Sheil Park and played on the swings, then walked on into Newsham Park. There they had their lunch and played on the grassy hill, then watched the tennis players or the boats on the lake, before going to the pond.

Mick and Freda's son took jamjars and fishing lines, made from bamboo canes and black cotton, to catch "jacksharps" in the pond. Mick was always successful and usually collected a crowd of onlookers as he quickly filled his jamjar, but Cathy was always glad to leave the pond.

She hated to see the unemployed young men who stood or crouched around the pond with makeshift fishing rods. Gaunt and shabby, without work or money, they tried in this way to fill in their long, empty days, and it grieved Cathy to see the waste of young lives.

Mrs Parker disapproved of her jaunts with Freda. 'Her own street isn't good enough for her,' she said loud enough for Cathy to hear, but otherwise resolutely ignored her. Cathy never stopped to talk to her neighbours except to comment on the weather, but one day as she returned from the park, she was hailed by a group of women standing at the end house.

'Have y'heard about Grace Woods?' one said. 'Got took to hospiddle.' They all began to talk at once, but the first woman had the loudest voice and soon shouted the others down.

'In Lipton's, she was getting syrup when she was took bad. Miscarriage. She lost the baby and the manager got the ambulance and she got taken off to the hospiddle. I seen where they had to put fresh sawdust down on the floor.'

'And how is she? How's Grace?' Cathy asked, but the woman shrugged her shoulders and looked mournful.

'Not many come out of them places once they go in.'

Another woman said, 'I believe she was real bad, screaming and crying when she got took away.'

Cathy was conscious of several children listening, including two of Grace's, and said brightly, 'She was bound to be upset but I'm sure she'll soon be better.'

She looked at the woman who had spoken last and jerked her head at the children, and the women said hastily. 'Oh, aye, she will. I've took Lizzie and she's going to sleep with our Nellie, aren't you, love?'

Other women announced that they too had taken in one of the Woods children and Cathy left them and walked home, thinking that her neighbours had good points too. They were enjoying the drama of Grace's misfortune but they had immediately offered to look after her children who would be comforted and well treated.

Cathy said this to her mother when she went to Egremont Street the following morning, and Sally agreed.

'I don't like the children playing out there though,' she said. 'A lad of Mick's age asking a question like that! They're better playing round here if you can't take them out.'

'I'll have a job to get Mick away from here from now,' Cathy said with a grin. Lawrie had managed to acquire a set of pram wheels and Greg had built a wooden seat on them so Mick was now the proud owner of a go cart or "trolley" as boys called them.

The only stipulation was that the trolley must be kept at Egremont Street. Mick was out now with a group of boys, proudly steering the cart by a rope attached to the front wheels.

Grace Woods was in hospital for ten days. Shortly after her return, she came to the back door to thank Cathy for the cake and sweets she had sent. Cathy invited her in for a cup of tea, and Grace seemed glad to accept. She looked thin and pale and Cathy asked if she could do anything to help.

'No thanks. You can't help what ails me,' Grace said. Cathy thought that she was referring to the baby she had lost and tried to comfort her.

'You'll soon feel better now you're at home with your children,' she said, but Grace smiled bitterly.

'I was glad to get away from them. And even more to get away from Billy.'

Cathy sat in silence, not knowing how to reply. Grace went on, 'I've had time to think there. To realise what a mess I've made of my life. I didn't want to come back here, Mrs Redmond, and that's the God's truth.'

'You're bound to feel low spirited. Everyone does after a miscarriage,' Cathy comforted her, but Grace shook her head.

'No, it's not just the miss. I was glad of that, to be honest. I was thinking about my life. I bet I'm younger than you, although I don't look it. I had our Harry when I was sixteen.'

'You were only a kid yourself then,' Cathy said sympathetically.

'It was me Aunt Maud made me get married,' Grace said.

'Mrs Parker!' Cathy exclaimed. 'How are you related – I mean, is she related to your father or your mother?'

'Me father, he's like her too. Me mam died in childbed when I was fourteen and I was terrified when I found out I'd got caught at sixteen. I was sure I'd die over it, and went crying to Aunt Maud. I said to her, "I'm sure I'll die like me mam," and she said, "You'll die, all right, if your dad finds out." And she got hold of Billy and made him marry me. I'd only been with him four times and he throws that up to me when we have a row. Me aunt didn't do me no good turn marrying me to him. The beatings I've had!'

'Never mind, the boys are growing up and they'll stop him,' Cathy tried to console her, but Grace laughed bitterly.

'Don't you believe it! They'll all clear off as soon as they're earning and old enough. I've seen it with other women like me. A kid every year till you're too old for any more, then they all go off and you're left to be the only punchbag for him. Unless you've snuffed it, and then your feller gets married again in a couple of months. I know what's in store for me.' Cathy could only pour more tea for her in silent sympathy, then Grace said, 'I don't suppose your feller's ever lifted his hand to you, has he?'

'Er, no.' Cathy said. She was in a dilemma. She felt that if she praised Greg it would be tactless but if she criticized him it would be disloyal as well as dishonest, so she said no more. But Grace was intent on her own troubles.

'Me only chance is if he snuffs it first. There y'are now – I've said straight out and I mean it. I hate him. I'm terrified of him and so are the kids – and no wonder. There's fellers on the docks frightened of him too. The only one he's afraid of is me Aunt Maud.'

'Then why don't you get her to warn him?'

'She wouldn't. She thinks a feller's got a right to beat his wife if he wants to. She told me that once.'

'Did her husband ever hit her?' Cathy exclaimed.

'No, but she might have belted him once or twice,' Grace said. They giggled together, and finished their tea in a more cheerful mood but before she left her neighbour said to Cathy, 'Don't let on about me being in here, will you, or what we've talked about?'

Cathy promised. As she closed the back gate after Grace she reflected that Billy was not the only one afraid of the redoubtable Mrs Parker.

The children all enjoyed their holidays and returned to school very reluctantly. Soon Sarah had even more cause to be downcast. She was now in the Juniors and the system in her school was that at about eight years of age several promising pupils were selected to form an elite class which leapfrogged up the school, making up by homework for the classes that they missed. When they took the scholarship examination at eleven years old they were working with the fourteen year olds in the top class, Standard Seven, and the school was assured of a virtually one hundred per cent success rate for the examination.

Sarah was one of the girls sent for to receive a letter for her parents from the smiling headmistress. The other girls were pleased and excited, knowing what the envelope contained, but Sarah walked home slowly, wondering how she could persuade her mother to let her leave school at fourteen and become a florist.

Cathy was delighted when she read the letter. 'It says you're going into the scholarship class, love,' she said. 'You're almost sure to pass when you're picked for that class.'

'But I don't want to, Mam,' Sarah said. 'I want to leave

when I'm fourteen and be a florist with Elsie.'

'Oh, no, Sarah. I know you like playing about in Elsie's shop but this is such a chance, love. You could do anything – be a teacher in a posh school or go into politics like Margaret Beaven or Miss Rathbone. This is why we fought for the vote, and soon we'll have it for all women, not just those over thirty. There are women doctors now. You might even be one of them.'

Cathy's eyes were sparkling as the words tumbled from her lips, but Sarah looked down, her own mouth set stubbornly.

'I don't want to, Mam,' she repeated. 'I want to be a florist.'

'Don't be *stupid*!' Cathy cried. 'I'd have given my right arm for a chance like this. I know what's best for you and I don't want to hear another word about Elsie's shop.'

Cathy seemed to think that the last word had been said on the subject as she put the letter away and went back to her cooking, but Sarah sat twisting the belt of her gymslip, dry-eyed but determined that she would never give up her dream.

Cathy showed the letter to Greg while Sarah was out, and told him that she had said that she wanted to leave school at fourteen. Later, before Sarah went to bed, Greg put his arm round her and drew her to the side of his chair.

'Your mother tells me that you don't want to enter the scholarship class, Sass.' It was his pet name for her.

She slipped her arms round his neck and laid her head on his shoulder. Her mother was busy in the back kitchen. Sarah whispered, 'I want to be a florist, Dada. I'd have to start when I was fourteen, Elsie says.'

'Yes, but you see, pet, that's what you want now. Don't forget, Sass, you're only eight. You might change your mind.'

'But I won't, Dad. I've always wanted to be a florist and I always will. Elsie says I'll be a good one.'

'I'm sure you would but a lot can happen in six years. Although you think now that you won't change your mind, in a few years' time you might wish to enter for the scholarship and you'd have missed your chance with this peculiar system they have,' Greg said.

He seemed to have forgotten for the moment that he was speaking to a child, until Sarah raised her head and kissed his cheek. He smiled at her and said gently, 'On the other hand, love, you can resign from the scholarship class with no harm done if your ambition doesn't change. Your mother only wants what's best for you, pet.'

Sarah smiled her agreement and hugged her father, and a moment later Cathy came into the room.

'Come on now, Sarah, up to bed and don't make a noise,' she said. 'I hope I'm not going to hear any more whingeing about the scholarship class. You're lucky to have the chance, you know.'

'Yes, Mam,' Sarah said meekly, but she gave her father a conspiratorial smile as she kissed him goodnight.

The next day she accepted the congratulations of her teacher and the envious remarks of the other girls without mentioning her own doubts. As she was always quiet, her lack of enthusiasm went unnoticed.

Cathy believed that Sarah had accepted her decision and said no more on the subject, and Sarah meekly accepted being moved into another class and given homework, but decided that she was going to be a florist, no matter what.

Chapter Six

Cathy had worked hard for the Votes for Women campaign before the war, and as 1928 drew near she was excited by the prospect of women between the ages of twenty-one and thirty being able to vote, as well as those over thirty, and by the fact that Liverpool had a woman Lord Mayor.

Margaret Beaven was well respected and popular, known as the "little mother" of Liverpool because of her charitable work. With her as first citizen, Cathy felt optimistic about the future.

The early months of 1928 brought sadness to the city, however, with the death of Archbishop Keating in February and Bishop Chavasse in March.

It also brought more trouble between Greg and John. On the day that Bishop Chavasse died, Greg came in with the *Evening Express* in his hand.

'Cathy, Bishop Chavasse is dead,' he said in a loud excited voice as she came through from the back kitchen. 'God, this brings back memories.' His face was flushed and Sarah and John looked up in surprise at their father, usually so quiet and reserved.

'What sorrow that man endured,' he went on, 'but no man ever had braver sons.' He looked at their uncomprehending faces and exclaimed, 'Captain Noel Chavasse – what a man! He was awarded the MC and *two* VCs, the second one after he had died of wounds after saving other men. He was the kindest, bravest man – no medal was enough for all he did. He was a hero every day that we fought.'

Greg's voice was uneven as he went on, 'And now his father's dead. Poor man, he lost another son on the Somme too, but how proud he must have been of his family.'

Sarah looked up at him with shining eyes, but John muttered defiantly, 'I don't see why. Grandad doesn't believe in war. He says working men are only cannon fodder. They should all refuse to fight, then war would stop.'

Greg looked as though cold water had been thrown in his face. He started towards John, but Cathy grabbed the boy's arm and thrust him into the back kitchen.

'Get out,' she hissed at him, 'and just you wait, m'lad.'

She turned back to the kitchen and took Greg's arm. 'Sit down, love. You've had a shock. What else does the paper say?'

But Greg said through clenched teeth, 'That young fellow'll go too far one day. If I start on him, I'll kill him.'

Sarah had slipped away. Cathy put her arms round him. 'I know, love,' she soothed him. 'Take no notice. He's too young to realize, and too stupid.'

'Yes, Cathy, but your dad – he speaks too freely to John.' He sat down and picked up the poker to stir at the fire in agitation. 'I've never said this but I've thought for a long time – it's not wise. Your father talks to him man to man, but that fellow half digests the ideas and thinks he knows everything.'

Cathy stood beside him looking into the fire, her face troubled. Greg took her hand and said more calmly, 'I'm not blaming your dad for John's impudence. That's something I should have done something about long ago.'

'I've thought myself once or twice that Dad shouldn't say so much to him,' she said. 'I think he likes to talk over his ideas and you know how impulsive he is. He says himself that he speaks first and thinks later, and he doesn't realize how far ahead of him John's jumping.'

'I'm not criticizing your father, Cath – you know how much I respect him and I agree with many of his views – but I don't think he allows for John's undeveloped character and for how impressionable he is.'

'And how cheeky,' Cathy said grimly. 'Dad would go mad if he heard him giving lip to you like that.'

Greg sighed. 'It's difficult,' he said. 'I don't want to hurt your dad's feelings, Cath, but something must be done. Do you think you could give your mother a hint?'

'I'll have to, I suppose. If it was anyone else she'd see the danger but where it's something that makes Dad happy, she just doesn't see past that.'

Cathy fully intended to alert her mother to the situation

but there never seemed to be an opportunity. However, she spoke sternly to John about his behaviour.

'Don't you ever dare speak to your father like that again,' she said. 'Trying to be smart! Noel Chavasse was a doctor and his brother was a padre so you'd got hold of the wrong end of the stick, as usual.'

'It doesn't make any difference,' John said sullenly. 'I was only repeating what Grandad said, and I agree with him. It's stupid to talk as if there's anything good about war.'

Cathy's hand shot out and boxed his ear. 'You damned little upstart!' she said furiously. 'Making out your dad's stupid.'

John stood speechless with shock and she went on, 'D'you think your grandad would speak like that? He respects your dad too much, and by God *you'll* show him respect or I'll know why. Most fathers would have given you a good hiding long ago for your cheek, but you'll try your dad too far one of these days and then you'll get the shock of your life.'

She clattered dishes together angrily and John took his cap and slipped out. He walked for miles, shocked and humiliated by the blow from his mother, and thinking of her words, not with shame or repentance, but with growing resentment towards his father. He felt that his father had turned his mother against him, and was angry that they had criticized his grandfather who was the cleverest man he knew.

When he returned home he seemed quiet and subdued and Cathy, always optimistic, congratulated herself on having solved the problem without upsetting anyone. She regretted striking John but believed that he had been thinking over her words and gave him a loving hug when he returned. With his mother John had always been a good son, quick to see if she needed help with heavy jobs in the house, and to notice if she was tired and urge her to rest. The close relationship between them was soon restored.

Greg and John managed to avoid each other for a few days until their tempers cooled, but Greg's anger was deep and he was determined to keep a tighter control on John in the future, while John was equally determined that he would take all his ideas from his grandfather, not his father.

Cathy still watched them anxiously. She felt that since the

63

quarrel on the day of the death of Bishop Chavasse, Greg had become sterner and more critical of John, and he had avoided his father as much as possible. She grieved about the situation, and loving them both felt torn between them.

She had always been on the defensive with Greg about John because she had brought the boy up alone while he was away during the war, and felt that any criticism of John was a criticism of his upbringing by her. But she had begun to see clearly how headstrong and self-willed the boy had become, and how impudent to his father.

She loved Greg deeply, but thought that he failed to realize how over-ready he was to find fault with John, and that he was less loving towards him than his other children. Cathy could see too that John's closeness to his grandfather widened the gulf between his father and himself and how he was constantly comparing the two men to Greg's disadvantage. Still, she consoled herself, it was only a phase. As John grew older, the situation would change.

All these worries were forgotten when the three younger children became ill with measles. Sarah and Mick had only a slight attack and they recovered quickly, but Kate was very ill.

The other children went to stay with their grandparents and Cathy nursed Kate in the small back bedroom of Norris Street. The doctor recommended a carbolic-soaked sheet hung over the door and Cathy stayed with the sick child night and day, until the doctor at last announced that she was out of danger.

Kate had been a very pretty baby, with her Aunt Mary's delicate features but with brown eyes and dark curls like Cathy. She was totally unlike shy Sarah, fond of attention and always ready to sing or dance for any audience, but after her illness she was thin and pale, and most of her hair had fallen out. There was a slight squint in one eye too but this eventually righted itself, and her hair grew thick and curly and much lighter than before her illness.

While she slowly recovered Kate was happy to lie in her father's arms as he read to her or told her stories. There was no trace of a Liverpudlian accent in his deep, pleasant voice and as Sarah sat listening to him reading to Kate one night, she remembered a conversation she had overheard between her grandfather and Josh Adamson. Josh worked in the same railway office as Greg and he told Lawrie that there was no hope of promotion for Greg.

'Too much of a gentleman to suit them, y'see, Lawrie,' the old man said. 'The way he speaks an'all.'

'I don't see why that should hold him back,' Lawrie protested.

'Aye, well, some of the bosses don't speak as good as him and they don't like it. A general clerk showing them up.'

'But he's not putting it on. It's the way he's always talked. He's not one for showing anyone up or throwing his weight about, not Greg,' said Lawrie.

'Yes, he's well liked by the lads and he's always very quiet – but that's another thing holds him back. There's some pushy fellows would tread on anyone to get on, but Greg's not like that, see.'

Now Sarah felt indignant, as she recalled the conversation, to think that people might be jealous of her father for the very things she loved about him: his voice and his gentle manner.

Sarah was in difficulties at school at this time because she had not been doing her homework and was falling behind in class. She had been away from school while she had measles. When she returned she was staying with her grandparents while her mother nursed Kate, and they were unaware that she should be studying at home.

With so much else on her mind Cathy had not thought of Sarah's homework. It was a shock to her when she received a note asking her to call on the headmistress.

'Why does she want to see me?' Cathy demanded, and Sarah was forced to admit that she had not been doing her homework.

'I don't know how to do the sums, Mam,' she said. 'Mary Cullen is supposed to show me what we'd have learned in Standard Two, but she doesn't know herself. She copies the answer off the girl in front, then when I have to do sums for homework I don't know how to do them.'

'That's no excuse. Why didn't you ask your dad or John to help you?'

'I didn't want to tell them I couldn't do the sums.'

Cathy made a gesture of impatience. 'The truth is, you're

not even trying because you've still got this idea in your head about Elsie's shop,' she said. 'What did your teacher say?'

'She asked me why I didn't do the homework. She said my work was a disgrace and I wouldn't pass the scholarship if I didn't do better,' Sarah muttered.

She lifted her head and looked defiantly at her mother. 'I told her I didn't want to pass it.'

'You stupid girl!' Cathy exclaimed. 'I'll never forgive you if you waste a chance like this.' She seized Sarah and shook her. 'I'll go to the school, all right, and I'll tell them you'll do what *I* tell you to do, so don't think you'll get your own way like this. Now go to bed.'

Sarah fled upstairs to cry herself to sleep, but when Greg came home and read the letter he was against the idea of forcing her to take the scholarship.

'If the child is good at floristry and wants to do it, she'll be far happier working in Elsie's shop. I believe in a square peg in a square hole. Sarah's happiness is what counts, not our ambition for her.'

'*My* ambition, you mean,' Cathy retorted, but she felt guilty when she saw how pale and miserable her daughter looked the following morning.

On the way to the school in the afternoon Cathy called in at her mother's house to leave Kate with her, and confide in her the reason for the visit to the headmistress.

'It's about the scholarship class, Mam. Sarah admitted she hadn't been doing her homework, and she turned round and told her teacher that she didn't want to pass.'

'I don't see the sense in forcing her, Cathy,' her mother said. 'She's got a real gift for flowers. Elsie Hammond says she's as good as any apprentice she's had, even at *her* age, and if she'd be happy there—'

'That's what Greg says, but I don't want her to throw away a chance like this for a child's whim,' Cathy protested.

Lawrie was sitting by the table reading a newspaper. He looked up. 'A chance for what, love? What sort of job d'you think she'd get in the end?'

'She could do anything, Dad. Be a teacher or even a doctor if she worked hard, or a politician like Miss Rathbone.'

'Cathy, girl, come down to earth. I thought I was the one who built castles in the air,' he said with a sigh. 'The truth is, love, the girls who do that sort of thing have monied families behind them. How far do you think Eleanor Rathbone would have got if her father had worked for the railway and they'd lived in Norris Street?'

'But times are changing,' she argued.

'For the worse, as far as I can see,' her mother said. 'Jobs are getting harder to come by all the time.'

'Aye, and when it comes to it a girl hasn't much hope of an office job, even if she's been to College,' Lawrie said. 'You've seen it yourself, Cath – the queues of girls outside any office where there's a job going – but it's not what you know but who you know that counts.'

'That's true,' Sally said. 'There was a job going in that office where Peggy cleans, and she said it was a shame to see the long line of girls waiting to apply when the job had already gone to the niece of a friend of the boss.'

'Well, I don't know what the headmistress will say,' Cathy said. 'It's such an honour to be picked out for that class – I don't know how I'm going to tell her that Sarah doesn't want it. She'll blame us, I suppose, for not making her do as she's told.'

'Tell her you can take a horse to water but you can't make it drink,' Lawrie said with a grin.

And Sally added, 'Yes. The trouble is that Sarah's as stubborn as you are, Cathy.'

'Me! I'm not stubborn,' she said in amazement.

'Of course you are,' her mother said placidly. 'But you might have met your match in Sarah.'

'Aye, what do they say?' Lawrie said laughing. 'The irresistible force meeting the immovable object. That's you and Sarah, Cath.'

She was only half convinced by her parents' arguments, and as she walked to the school decided that she would apologize for Sarah's behaviour and ask for her to remain in the scholarship class. So much might change in a few years, she felt.

At the school she was kept waiting outside the headmistress's room for ten minutes, and when she was finally admitted the nun greeted her coldly. She was a small woman, standing with her hands inside the wide sleeves of her habit, wearing a deceptive air of humility belied by the set of her thin lips and the cold glare she directed at Cathy.

Before she could speak the nun said cuttingly, 'I hope you're ashamed of yourself, Mrs Redmond. To deny the child this opportunity simply to send her out to work at fourteen is most unfair.'

Cathy's temper rose. 'That's not the reason, Sister,' she said. 'Sarah doesn't want to stay on at school. She's been promised a place as an apprentice in a florist's when she's fourteen, and that's what she wants to do.'

'So, you allow a girl of eight years of age to dictate to you?' the headmistress said. 'We teach our girls obedience, but if the parents don't continue the training our efforts are wasted. She will be moved to Standard Two and her place given to a girl who will appreciate it. Good afternoon.' She swept forward and opened the door and Cathy found herself in the corridor again, before she could say any of the things she had meant to.

She waited for Mick and Sarah to leave school. When Sarah came out her face was pale and tear-stained, but Cathy waited until they were away from the crowds of children before she took out her handkerchief and wiped her daughter's face.

'Did Sister say anything to you, love?' she asked gently.

'Yes. She said I was a wicked, ungrateful girl and teacher had wasted six months on me. She said another girl would have been glad to go in the class, and I was being moved to Standard Two because I was too stupid for the scholarship,' Sarah said. Her voice trembled and Cathy drew in her breath in anger.

'That's not true, love. I told Sister you had a job promised with Elsie because you'd be such a good florist. Don't worry about what she said – she was just annoyed with me.'

Sarah looked happier. When they reached Miss Tulley's sweet shop, Cathy gave the children a halfpenny each.

'I'm going to call in to see Elsie. When you've got your sweets, go straight to Grandma's. I won't be long'

Elsie Hammond welcomed her with a smile. 'Hello, Cath. On your own?'

'Yes, I sent the kids on because I wanted to talk to you, Elsie,' she said. 'I've just been to the school to see the headmistress about Sarah.'

'Why? What's wrong?' Elsie said anxiously.

'Nothing really, only Sarah hasn't been doing her homework so she's being moved out of the scholarship class.'

'Is she? Does that mean she'll leave at fourteen?' Elsie said eagerly.

'Yes. She'll go in Standard Two now,' Cathy said.

'So she'll be able to come to me. Well, I can't say I'm sorry she's left that class. It would have been a waste, Cathy.'

'That's what I wanted to see you about, Else,' Cathy said, looking embarrassed. 'I don't want you to feel – well, that you're sort of obliged to take her just because she's left the class. I don't want to take things for granted.'

'Cathy, I can't wait to start her here!' Elsie exclaimed. 'I wish she was fourteen this minute.' She looked down the shop to where a thin pale girl was slowly pressing a handful of moss against a wreath frame and binding it with thin wire. Elsie lowered her voice. 'Sarah'd have that frame done in half the time that Celia takes. It's always the same – they're either careful but slow, or quick and slapdash. Sarah's one in a thousand.'

'Celia looks delicate,' Cathy whispered.

'She is. The whole family are. She's lost two sisters already with galloping consumption and her mam's not well. That's why I have to keep her on,' Elsie said.

A customer came into the shop and Cathy left. When she reached her mother's house Mick and Sarah had gone out to play. Sally poured tea for her.

'How did it go?' she asked.

Cathy shrugged. 'That headmistress is a faggot, Mam, nun or not,' she exclaimed. 'She tried to make out that we just wanted Sarah to leave at fourteen so she could go to work. I stood up to her though and told her about Elsie. You should have seen her face when I answered her back.'

Sally smiled. 'You've changed, love,' she said. 'You wouldn't say boo to a goose when you were little. Our Mary was the one who enjoyed a row. You were as different as chalk and cheese – not a bit like sisters. I never thought you'd stand up to anyone.'

'Someone's got to stand up for the kids. Greg won't – he just lets people walk on him,' Cathy said.

'Including you,' her mother said dryly. 'Greg's gentle and well mannered, Cathy, but he's no weakling.'

'I didn't say he was,' she flashed, more sharply than she intended. She added quietly, 'I didn't say half I wanted to. All the way home I kept thinking of things I should have said.'

'I usually do that in bed at night,' Sally said. 'I think of great things I could have said if only I'd thought of them.'

They laughed, then Cathy said seriously, 'She told Sarah she was wicked and disobedient and too stupid for the scholarship. I told her it wasn't true and I'd told Sister about the shop. I went in to see Elsie too, and said she mustn't feel obliged to take Sarah, but she said she can't wait for her to start.'

'Sarah'll be happy there with her too. Elsie's a nice girl and she'll be kind to Sarah. She's been a good daughter, looking after her mother all these years and working hard in that shop to keep them.'

'It's a wonder she never married,' Cathy said. 'She's such a nice-looking girl.'

'It's the old story,' Sally said with a sigh. 'The lad she was engaged to was killed in Mesopotamia and she's never looked at anyone else. It's a good thing she's got the shop.'

Cathy called Sarah and Mick and they set off for home. Cathy said nothing about the school and only asked how they had spent their halfpennies. Sarah had bought a sherbet dab and Mick had bought a gobstopper. He told her happily that a boy had given him a go with his boomerang for a suck of the sweet.

'You dirty thing,' Sarah said. 'You could catch something out of his mouth.' They were passing the corner of a street where a group of ragged young men sat on the pavement, passing a Woodbine from hand to hand, each taking a puff of it. Mick stopped beside them.

'You don't catch anything off that, do you?' he said. He pointed at Sarah. 'She said I'd catch something because a feller had a suck of my gobstopper.'

Cathy was horrified and tried to pull Mick away quickly but the men laughed. They seemed to know him and one of them said to Cathy, 'He's a case, isn't he, Missis?'

'He certainly is,' she said emphatically, pulling Mick's arm. He only shouted cheerfully to the men, 'Ta ra, fellers,' and left them smiling.

When Greg came home Cathy delayed him in the back kitchen to whisper a brief account of her visit to the school and its outcome. Later, when the children were in bed, she spoke again about her visit to the school and also told him of the conversation with her parents about jobs.

'I'm afraid they're right, Cath,' he said. 'But I suppose I shouldn't complain since Josh recommended me for my job.'

'I never thought of that,' she confessed. 'I was really mad about Sister telling Sarah that she was stupid. I didn't think a nun would be so nasty and spiteful.'

'They're only human beings,' he said tolerantly. 'I suppose she's become autocratic because she's a headmistress, or else she was chosen for the job because she's naturally autocratic. Either way she doesn't like being thwarted. Anyway, Sarah will be happy with the result.'

Cathy agreed, rather grimly, but it was true that Sarah was much happier. She liked the teacher in her new class who was younger than most of her colleagues with a fashionable hairstyle much admired by her pupils. The large class of forty-six girls gave her little time to offer individual attention, but the teacher was enthusiastic and did what she could to encourage any talent.

Sarah found that she enjoyed writing essays and often her work was read aloud to the class by Miss Holden. The teacher had a great love of poetry which she tried to instil into her pupils, and was delighted to find that Sarah knew many of the poems that she read to them.

'They're in my grandad's books, Miss,' Sarah said shyly, and Miss Holden encouraged her to talk about her grandfather and the many books he bought from second-hand shops or barrows.

'That explains why you have such a good vocabulary, Sarah,' she said kindly. 'Develop the habit of reading, dear. It will be a pleasure to you all your life.'

Sarah was not sure of the meaning of the word "vocabulary" but she knew that she was being praised, and the teacher's kindness and encouragement did much to restore her self-confidence.

Chapter Seven

Although Sarah was such a quiet little girl her happiness seemed to imbue the whole family, and Cathy felt that she had much to be thankful for at this time.

She still spent wakeful hours worrying about money, but she was happy to see Kate fully recovered and a bonny child again, and John and Greg on better terms.

Kate's hair had grown fairer since her illness and the contrast between her light-coloured curls and brown eyes was very attractive. She was a pretty child and a favourite with Josh Adamson, who declared her the image of Shirley Temple. As a result she pestered her mother until she was taken to see a Shirley Temple film. After that she was always ready to sing "The Good Ship Lollipop" or to dance holding out the skirt of her dress as Shirley Temple did. She was encouraged by Josh who unearthed a mouth organ to play the music for her.

Sally watched her grimly. 'She's very like our Mary was as a child,' she said to Cathy. 'Don't make the mistake I made with her. I often think if I'd been firmer when she was little, it would have been better for her in the end.'

'Kate's not as moody as our Mary was,' Cathy said defensively.

'She can throw a tantrum just like Mary if she doesn't get all her own way, I've seen her,' her mother said. 'You've got a better chance of stopping yours than I had with Mary. I was living with your grandfather when she was little, and between him and your dad she was well spoiled. I couldn't prevent it.'

Cathy could see that Kate was growing very wilful but she found it hard to scold her. She was too pleased to see the child well and happy.

John was still enthusiastic about cricket and Greg, who

had been a useful bowler at school, had begun to coach some of the boys in the team John had formed. They had also decided to replace the crystal cat's whisker wireless set that they had built together with a set with a loudspeaker so that all the family could listen, instead of just the one who had the headphones. Cathy was pleased to see Greg and John with their heads together poring over blueprints and fiddling with valves and other parts.

Greg put up a shelf for the loudspeaker and bought a Bakelite panel for the front of the set. Soon dance music began to sound from the loudspeaker. Greg and John were delighted although to Cathy it sounded as distorted as the sound from the crystal set, and there were as many whooping sounds and howls coming from it.

'Only oscillation,' they assured her. She was too pleased to see such harmony between them to complain further.

Cathy's only remaining worry was about money and particularly her debt at the corner shop. She fancied that Mrs Cain had become cool with her and worried in case she was about to ask for the debt to be repaid. Sometimes she felt that she would have to share the worry with Greg, but always she drew back before the words were said.

She knew that Greg would blame himself because his wages were so poor, and she was ashamed that she had allowed the debt to mount up. Her mother had never owed a penny, even when she was desperate for food, and Cathy had been trained to think that it was better to go without than get into debt.

I'd die of shame if Mam knew, she thought, but she could see no hope of paying off the debt. She knew that she never wasted a penny yet the battle to feed and clothe six of them on Greg's wages was becoming impossible.

There was no chance that she could get a job herself. Married women were not employed in shops or offices, nor in factories or workshops, and cleaning jobs were rare and jealously guarded. A woman who lived in Norris Street had gone to clean an office even while she had shingles rather than risk losing the job to someone else while she was ill.

It was galling, while she was so worried, to go to her mother's house and see another parcel from Fortnum and Mason's and to read another letter from Mary. Again there was a snapshot in it, this time of Mary and Sam standing outside a log cabin. "How do you like our holiday cabin?" Mary had written. "One of Sam's business friends and his wife have a cabin too and we have splendid times there, although Sam is so busy it's hard for him to get away."

'They seem to be doing well,' Cathy said, handing back the letter. I don't envy Mary, she told herself, not while I've got Greg and the kids – but I wouldn't mind some of her money!

Aloud she said to her mother, 'More quails, eh, Mam?'

'I haven't unpacked it yet,' Sally said. 'I was hoping you'd give me a hand, but I suppose it'll be the same as last time.' They began to unpack the hamper of luxury foods, and Sally looked worried.

'I don't care how well they're doing, I don't like them wasting their money like this. I know it's lovely food but it's not what suits us, is it?'

'I meant to ask you, Mam – did you ever give that stuff to Peggy Burns?'

'Yes. She said Ritchie wouldn't touch it – he's more faddy than his dad – but Jimmie enjoyed it, and so did Meg.'

'Meg did?' Cathy said in surprise.

'Yes, well, poor child, she doesn't know what she's doing half the time,' Sally said with a sigh. 'I was glad it wasn't wasted but I felt a bit uncomfortable about it, you know, Cath.'

'Why, Mam?'

'Well, Peggy didn't say anything, but you know she didn't think much of our Mary and I could sense her thinking it was showing off, sending this posh food. You see, I've never told her about the money Sam sends because she wouldn't understand why your dad won't use it, and so she might think Mary's not thinking what would be best for us.'

She was standing turning a small jar round and round in her hand as she spoke. Cathy said gently, 'I think you're worrying about nothing, Mam. I'm sure Peggy doesn't think all that. You think she thinks that Mary should have sent you money instead, but I'll bet Peggy was just glad to get the food and thought no more about it.'

'I suppose you're right,' Sally said with a smile. 'I know I worry over nothing.'

'I don't really know why Dad won't use that money, you know, Mam.'

'I do though. I know Dad always seems lighthearted, but he feels things very much, Cath. We had a bad time when you and Mary were young and it's still there, deep down within him. He said once that it does something to a man to see his family going short and not to be able to do anything about it, no matter how hard he tries.'

'But what's that got to do with the money?'

'It's his pride. He was so thankful when he got a job and could provide for us, and he wants to go on doing it, so he won't take anything from anyone while he's able to work. Do you understand, love?'

'I do, Mam,' Cathy said, giving her mother a quick kiss. 'But I don't know why these hampers worry you.'

'I don't like waste,' Sally said. 'And I'm ashamed when I look round the way people are these days and think the price of this could keep a family for a week.'

Cathy said nothing but still looked puzzled. Her mother said suddenly, 'To tell you the truth, love, it's all to do with what I was just saying – about how your dad feels. He doesn't like the idea of food parcels, as though we're hungry. Neither do I, for that matter.'

'Oh, Mam, Mary doesn't think you're hungry, I'm sure!' Cathy exclaimed. 'You know her. She probably likes the idea of ordering from Fortnum and Mason, or else one of her friends has done it so she thinks she'll do the same.'

'You've probably hit the nail on the head,' Sally agreed. 'But I think I'll write to our Mary and tell her not to send any more. Say the food's too rich for us.'

Sarah and Mick had arrived home from school and Sally gave each of them a slice of bread and jam. Mick rushed out immediately with his trolley but Sarah sat down by her grandmother to eat the bread, then took a ball from the cupboard and went into the backyard.

'The kids have more toys here than they've got at home,' Cathy said. 'Mind you, I'm glad, because I don't like them playing out in our street.'

Sarah suddenly reappeared. 'Mam, Grandma, come quick,' she whispered. They followed her but she paused by the door into the yard. 'Look.'

Flagstones had been lifted in the yard to make a tiny garden. Mint and parsley, mignonette and snapdragons grew there. A butterfly hovered over the tiny plot. It was larger than the cabbage white butterflies which sometimes came to the little garden, and its velvety wings carried russet and cream markings.

They all watched entranced as the butterfly settled on a flower and folded its wings then opened them to their fullest extent. It rose in the air and fluttered above the flowers for a moment, then flew up and away over the backyard wall.

'Wasn't it lovely?' Sarah said, looking at her mother with shining eyes. 'It was like Auntie Mary.'

Cathy looked surprised then she laughed. 'The colours, you mean, love. Like her red hair – or Titian as she liked it called – and her brown clothes.'

Sarah said nothing. Even to her mother she found it hard to explain what she meant. The butterfly, exotic and beautiful, fluttering into their lives, alighting briefly then leaving, had reminded her of the time her beautiful and wealthy aunt had suddenly arrived a few years earlier. After charming them and showering them with gifts, she had departed for life in America with her new husband.

A little later Cathy and the children left. Kate sang to herself but Sarah was silent. Cathy too was thoughtful. At first she thought briefly of her sister in America, then she remembered her mother's words about her father's pride and the reason for it. Who would have thought he was influenced still by such bitter memories when he always seemed so carefree? And Greg's pride, which she was afraid to wound by telling him about her shop debt, and his reluctance to assert himself . . . That's because of the life he had with that damned old mother, always criticizing him, she thought angrily. I suppose we're all like icebergs with only the tips showing.

She herself was determined that her children would have only happy memories of their childhood, so she concealed her money worries from them and somehow managed to find coppers for anything that was required at school, meanwhile devising as many small treats as possible.

In the school holidays she took them out, sometimes with her friend Freda and her family from the next street, and sometimes with her childhood friend, Josie Mellor, now Mrs Meadows, who had five children but still lived with her mother in the house in Egremont Street opposite Sally's.

Sometimes the three mothers combined families to go to the park, and the children all played noisily and happily together. On one such occasion Cathy and Josie, with their children, went to Freda's house to call for her. Her mother was sitting on a chair at her front door. She laughed heartily at the sight of them.

'I always say I'm like an ould hen with me chickens around me, but youse look like a Sunday School treat with all the kids.' She took her shabby purse from beneath her apron. It opened out like a concertina and she took sixpence from it and gave it to Freda.

'Ee are, girl. I can't go round all this lot but you three girls get a cup of tea for yourselves. The big girls can look after the little ones while you have a rest.'

They thanked her and the convoy moved off, but Josie said to Freda, 'You're lucky having a mam like that. And I know your mam's good to you, Cathy, but mine! She never stops finding fault and trying to stir up trouble, and the older she gets the worse it is. Remember my old gran, Cathy?'

'I do,' she said, laughing. 'I remember a clout she gave me one day for going near her foot. I thought I'd been sent for.'

'I got plenty of those clouts too,' Josie said. 'And now me mam is going just like her.'

'But you've got good neighbours, though, Josie,' Cathy said. 'That Mrs Parker in our street is a horror. Greg said, when he was off that time, she was like a spider sitting at the centre of a web. Women are going in and out of her house all day but I'm sure it's not because they're fond of her. In fact, they seem afraid of her.'

'That's because she's a moneylender,' Freda said.

'A moneylender!' Cathy exclaimed. 'I must be thick, living opposite her and I never knew.' She suddenly remembered Mrs Cain's words about getting in the clutches of a moneylender and almost blurted them out, but Josie was speaking again and Cathy was able to keep her debt secret.

These were happy days. The children rarely quarrelled and Cathy was happy to see how much Sarah and Mick and Kate enjoyed themselves. Quiet Sarah screamed as loudly and raced about as much as the others and Mick was in his element playing leapfrog and tumbling about on the grass in mock battles with the other boys. Kate joined in the games but she always looked as neat when they finished as when they started, unlike Sarah and the other girls.

John considered himself too old to go with his mother, but Cathy never worried about him as he had a wide circle of friends now because of the cricket, and seemed to enjoy his days. He still spent some time with his grandfather, who was often off during the day because of shift work, but Cathy went to her mother's house at some time most days and it seemed to her that John and Lawrie talked more about ships than about politics. They had travelled to Seaforth on the Overhead Railway and Lawrie had told John about the ships in each of the docks they passed, so another of her son's sudden enthusiasms had been born and he could talk of nothing but ships.

Greg was now writing to various firms asking to be considered if a vacancy arose but the replies were discouraging.

The children had been back at school for several weeks and the weather was warm and humid when two such replies arrived one morning before he left for work.

'Never mind, love. At least you've got a job, and a secure one,' Cathy consoled him when he silently handed the letters to her, but Greg looked downcast when he left, and she worried about him during the day.

It was only one of several anxieties, the chief of which was as usual money. It was a Friday and payday. She had been without a penny in her purse since the previous day. The insurance man was due but she would tell him she would pay double next week, she thought. She had potatoes and dripping but no money for gas and no fire to cook on.

She could do as many people did and buy chips and fish when Greg arrived with his money but that would put her further back the next week. Sarah and Mick rushed in from school and announced that they were starving. Cathy cut thin slices from the heel of the loaf and spread them sparingly with jam.

'Can I have a butty?' Kate said, and Cathy had to pare another slice from the loaf. Why are they always most hungry when I'm short? she thought. She was determined not to get another loaf on "tick" from the corner shop, but her head ached with all the planning and she longed for a cup of tea.

John arrived next, wearing a beaming smile. He had been returning from school when he saw a stout old lady trying to carry a Gladstone bag up Eastbourne Street.

'I'm blowing for tugs, lad,' she gasped when he offered to carry the bag.

John put the bag on his shoulder and with the old lady clinging to his arm they soon reached the top of the steep street. Then he took her to the corner of the street where she lived.

She was still puffing, but said, 'That's far enough, lad. I'll take it to the door meself.'

'Will you be all right?' he asked. She winked.

'Me son should'a met me. I'll tell him I carried it up the broo meself.' She laughed wheezily and gave John a threepenny piece, and he went running back to the sweet shop and bought a pennyworth of stickjaw toffee for himself and a penny bar of Fry's chocolate for his mother.

He gave the chocolate bar to her. 'I carried a bag for an old lady and she gave me threepence,' he said, smiling broadly and handing her the remaining penny.

Cathy flung her arms round him and kissed him.

'Oh, John, that's a godsend,' she exclaimed. 'The gas has run out and I was waiting for Dad's wages to have a cup of tea. My head's splitting.'

John looked at her in dismay and her face grew red. She had always concealed her money worries from her children but relief at receiving the penny had made her incautious. Now she felt ashamed, but John, always sensitive to her feelings, turned away tactfully, saying, 'I'll put it in the meter then, Mam.'

He stayed in the back kitchen and made the tea and when he brought it in, told Cathy about the old lady and the trick she intended to play on her son. They were laughing together when Greg walked in, carrying an evening paper.

John glared at him. Spending money on a newspaper, he thought, and Mam not able to have a cup of tea for want of a penny. Greg could see no reason for John's hostility but it was unmistakable. Greg's temper rose all the more when Cathy said innocently, 'John got money for carrying a bag and he bought me this chocolate.' John's face was turned from her, so she was unable to see his expression and was surprised at the result of her words.

They had been meant to show Greg that John was a good son, but her husband said furiously, 'That sort of thing is easily done. It would be more to the point if he worked hard at school and justified the expense of leaving him there.'

Cathy stood amazed at the suddenness of the attack, but before she could speak, John said loudly and impudently, 'My fees are paid by the scholarship, and I *do* work hard – for Grandad's sake.'

'Then why am I informed that you've been punished for slovenly homework? Not by you, of course. You're too sly for that.' Greg raised a finger and shook it in John's face, 'If you can't be trusted, from now on you'll do your homework there, on that table, where I can watch you. I'll put a stop to all your gadding about, too.'

Cathy stood looking from one to the other, bewildered by the storm her innocent words had provoked, but she saw by the way John stood with his head thrust forward that he was about to answer back, and said quickly, 'John, go and call Sarah.' She gripped his arm and drew him to the door.

He was scowling but she said, 'Hurry, son,' and smiled at him so warmly that his scowl faded before he ran down the street.

Cathy turned back into the kitchen. Greg had put his wage packet on the dresser. She picked it up and walked through to the back kitchen, too angry to speak to him. John can do nothing right as far as he's concerned, she thought. He doesn't deserve such a good son.

Sarah came running in but John stayed in the street. 'Our John said you wanted me, Mam.'

'Yes, I want some messages,' Cathy said, taking money from the wage packet. 'Get a loaf from Cain's then go to the chippy.'

'Why couldn't our John go?'

'Because I'm telling *you* to go.'

Greg had sunk down wearily into the chair, regretting his angry words and overwhelmed by depression. It had been a disastrous day for him. He had been unable to sleep the previous night in the stifling heat of the tiny bedroom, feeling suffocated by the nearness of so many people and by the small houses crowded close together, and worrying about his failure to provide a better home for his family.

He had lain sleepless for hours while his thoughts turned this way and that, desperately seeking some way of improving their lives. All his efforts to find another job or a better house seemed hopeless. Finally he had decided that his only chance was to ask about his prospects for promotion or for a rise in pay, but exhausted by his sleepless night he had been tempted to postpone the ordeal.

It had needed great fortitude for Greg to overcome his natural diffidence and make his request and he had been humiliated by the attitude of the office manager.

The man had kept Greg standing before him while he lounged in his chair and told him contemptuously that there was no reason why he should have either a rise or promotion.

'I don't see why you need it anyway,' he sneered. 'You can afford to keep your lad at College instead of out at work like other lads.'

'His fees and expenses are paid for by his scholarship,' Greg said quietly, but the other man laughed.

'I don't see the point of it meself. He'll only grow up thinking he's better than other people, and you know y'self, that'll be no benefit to him.'

A hot tide of anger rose in Greg and he longed to punch the man, but he only said firmly, 'That's beside the point.' He laid a neatly written paper on the desk. 'These are my reasons for asking to be upgraded.'

He had listed several items: the fact that he had been carrying out the duties of a senior clerk who had died and not been replaced, extra responsibility and hours worked without pay, but the manager had scarcely glanced at the paper before pushing it aside.

'Are you complaining?' he said roughly.

'No, just making a request.'

The manager snapped, 'Refused. You make up this wasted time by working late.'

Greg returned to his desk, angry with the manager and furious with himself for not being more aggressive.

For the rest of the day he was conscious of sidelong glances from the other men, but only one spoke of his visit to the manager's office.

'Got nowhere with old Greenwood then, old chap?' he said. 'You won't, you know. He's still afraid to use the telephone. He never got over that time you spoke on it, and that London fellow thought you were the manager.'

'He couldn't be so petty,' Greg exclaimed.

'He could, y'know,' the other man said. 'You're not going to get any further while he's in charge, I'm afraid, so you might as well resign yourself to it.'

Greg still felt angry and humiliated as he walked home. James Furlong joined him. He was a small shopkeeper whose son Joe was a fellow pupil of John's, and seemed to delight in telling Greg that John had been in trouble at school.

'Got the strap, my lad said,' he announced with satisfaction, 'for slovenly homework. That's one thing our Joe will never be punished for, I see to that.'

Greg made no reply and left Furlong as soon as possible, making the excuse of buying an evening paper. He rarely bought a newspaper but was determined to redouble his efforts to change his job and move house, and wanted to search the paper for situations vacant and houses to rent.

One of the bitterest aspects of poverty, he found, was never having any money to spare for even the smallest treat for his wife and children, so it was galling to be shown the gift from his son to Cathy, then to be confronted with an impudent and hostile look from John, just when his spirits were at their lowest ebb.

When Sarah had left Cathy went back into the kitchen, intending to challenge Greg, but a glance at him as he sat slumped in his chair, his feeling of misery and failure clearly showing in his face, made her change her mind.

She recalled her mother saying once, 'You've got to give and take, love. Keep back the angry word when Greg's feeling low, and I know he'll do the same with you. Dad says we're like the couple in the weather house, taking turns to come out on the sunny side.'

Cathy had laughed at the time but now she remembered her mother's words and spoke gently and cheerfully to Greg.

Sarah returned with the loaf and the fish and chips,

followed by Mick and John. While Cathy served out the meal, Sarah stood with her arm round her father's neck, telling him about an order she had helped Elsie to make.

'It was a little chair all made of flowers for a lady from Scotland Road who had died. Her family all put together for it. Elsie put a little purple banner across it, saying "The Vacant Chair". It was very sad, Dad.'

'I'm sure it was, pet,' he said, hugging her. Mick and Kate chattered to him so that his spirits lifted and he was able to smile at Cathy before going to wash his hands.

Later he sat and read through the newspaper, but the only jobs advertised seemed to be for highly trained men or domestic servants. Among the news in the paper was a report from America describing New York as "Boom Town" with thousands of dollars changing hands in wild speculation. Perhaps I should have copied Sam and gone there, he thought, but he knew that Cathy would have been miserable away from her parents.

Chapter Eight

Greg told her nothing about his day until they were in bed, then he said in a muffled voice, 'I went in to ask for a rise today, Cath, but it was refused.'

She put her arms round him. 'You tried anyway, love.'

'Not very forcefully,' he said with a sigh. 'But Jack Almond told me I'd never get on while Greenwood's the manager. He's got his knife into me for some reason.'

'He can't sack you anyway,' she comforted him, 'And we're lucky that you've got a job. Plenty of people in Liverpool would give their right arm for one.'

'But it's so poorly paid, Cath, and I can't see any hope of getting anything better – or getting away from this house. I'm sorry I shouted at John like that but I was so fed up, and meeting that fellow Furlong was the last straw.'

'So that's who it was,' she said. 'I might have known!'

But Greg went on, 'It all seems so hopeless. Our lives are passing while I'm stuck in this job, not earning enough to keep us. I'm ashamed, Cath, that you have to scrimp and go short of so much.'

A street lamp shone into the room. Cathy could see the lines of worry on Greg's thin, sensitive face, and with a sudden rush of tenderness she drew his face down to hers and kissed him.

'Don't worry, love,' she whispered. 'We get by. We've got enough food and respectable clothes. Don't worry about another job either. You know you're safe in the railway job. Greenwood can't sack you.'

'No, but he can report me for misconduct and then I'd be sacked. I think that's why he's trying to provoke me, and he damn nearly succeeded today.'

'What do you mean?' she asked, trying to hide her alarm.

'I don't know how I stopped myself from punching him

this morning and telling him what I thought of him,' Greg said, 'but that would have been playing into his hands. I despise myself for keeping quiet while he pushes this extra work on to me, all the time finding niggling faults with it, but what can I do, Cath? You must despise me too,' he added bitterly.

'Indeed I don't,' she said. 'It was more manly to stop yourself hitting him, and a lot harder. I *respect* you for it.'

'You're so loyal,' he said, but the lines of worry remained on his face.

Cathy kissed him again, tenderly. 'Don't think about it any more, love,' she said. 'We've got each other so nothing else matters, does it?'

'Oh, Cathy, Cathy,' he murmured, holding her close and kissing her passionately. He kissed her throat and breasts and she responded with equal passion. Their worries were forgotten as their bodies merged in love.

Later, as she lay in his arms, he smoothed her hair back from her forehead and kissed her gently.

'I'm the richest man alive while I've got you, Cathy,' he said. 'I'm sorry I worried you with my troubles.'

'Don't be, Greg. "A trouble shared is a trouble halved," Mam says, and anyway I'm not worried. I'm happy, aren't you?'

Kate still slept in the corner of their room. Now she stirred and suddenly said loudly, 'No.'

'*Yes*,' Greg whispered, as Cathy buried her head against his chest to stifle her giggles. She could feel his body shaking with suppressed laughter, but Kate had settled again, and soon Greg too slipped off to sleep.

Cathy lay awake for a while thinking of the worry she was unable to share, her debt at the corner shop, but she pushed the thought away. Instead she thought of the day she had met Greg when she had been injured in the Bloody Sunday riots and he had carried her to lie on his mother's sofa in their flat in London Road.

She had opened her eyes and seen his face above her, his expression of concern and sudden sweet smile. For both of us it was love at first sight, she thought, looking at his dear face on the pillow beside her. He seemed relaxed and happy now, and Cathy smiled to see it. Our Mary wouldn't have made him happy, she thought. She only wanted him because he was the only man who didn't fall for her, and because he owned the jeweller's shop. I wonder how she'd have liked living in Norris Street . . . The next moment Cathy too had drifted off to sleep.

A few weeks later Jack Almond, who worked with Greg, asked him if he could get some wood for him at cost price. Jack's son, now eighteen months old, was able to climb the stairs and several times had tumbled down them.

'I'll have to make a gate for the stairs,' he said, 'but I don't want to use orange boxes because of the splinters, and new wood's so dear.'

Greg went to the woodyard on his way home but the owner, who had once worked for Greg's father, was busy. While Greg waited for him he wandered round the woodyard, talking to the workmen. He savoured the smell of new wood, and listened fascinated as one of the men filled an order from different stacks of wood and told him what they were best used for.

He was standing beside a stack of redwood, running his hand over it, when the owner, Stan Johnson, came looking for him.

'Hello, Mr Greg,' he said. 'What can I do for you?' He looked hot and flustered and when Greg asked diffidently if he could have the wood for Jack at cost, Johnson said in an abstracted voice: 'Yes, yes.' They walked together to the hut that Stan used as an office. Suddenly he said furiously, 'That bloody shark! Trying to say I haven't paid my bill. I know damn' well that I have, and he knows it too.'

'Didn't he mark it paid or give you a receipt?' Greg asked. They had reached the "office". Stan waved his hand.

'It's here somewhere, I'm sure, but how the hell am I going to find it by Tuesday?'

Greg looked at the confusion in amazement. Papers on the desk looked as though they had been stirred up by a stick, probably in more disorder than usual because of Stan's search, but they were also heaped on a chair in the corner and in boxes on the floor.

'Y'see what I mean?' Stan said. 'That's what the bugger's counting on – that I won't find it in time.'

Papers began to slide from the desk. Greg seized some as

they fell and pushed the others back. The bundle in his hand consisted of delivery notes, invoices, bills and orders, all mixed together. Greg found a clear space on the top of a small cupboard and sorted them on to it.

Stan Johnson watched him and gave a gusty sigh. 'That's what I should do, I suppose, but I wouldn't know where to start with all this.' He took a pencil from behind his ear. 'Did your mate give you the measurements?' he asked. Greg gave him a slip of paper with these and Johnson made a quick calculation, but they were interrupted by a workman who poked his head into the office.

'Will you have a look at this two by four before we load it, Mr Johnson?'

'Aye, all right,' Stan Johnson said. He turned to Greg. 'Hang on a minute, will you? I might be able to find a bit of offcut would do this.'

He bustled out and Greg began to tidy the papers on the desk and add them to the appropriate pile on the cupboard. He found a box of rubber bands and secured the piles on the cupboard with these. By this time he had cleared enough space on the desk to start fresh orderly piles. Stan paused in amazement when he came back.

'Bloody hell, it looks better already,' he said. 'I could do with someone to see to this for me, I suppose, but I don't want anybody knowing me business.'

Greg's face grew red. 'Sorry,' he said. 'I wasn't trying to butt in. I only glanced at the papers to see what they were.'

'I don't mean you, Mr Greg,' Stan said hastily. 'Bloody hell, you're no stranger; but I'll have to do *something*, I suppose. This is only the half of it. I've got boxes full at home as well.' He looked again at the papers Greg had sorted. 'I wish —'

'Yes, I'll sort them,' Greg said. 'I'll be glad to.' He smiled. 'You've done me plenty of good turns. If I get all the receipted bills together, you might be able to find the one you've been looking for.'

Stan was called away again and Greg settled down to sort out the rest of the papers on the desk. He enjoyed bringing order out of the chaos and worked quickly, careful though only to glance at headings to identify the type of transaction.

When Stan returned he went through the bundles of paid bills Greg handed to him, and soon gave a shout.

'Got it! Now I'll spike that bugger's guns.' He was like an excited child, slapping his thigh and chuckling as he waved the paper and said over and over again, 'I've got him. I've got him now.'

In his excitement he knocked the pile of bills to the floor and looked at Greg in comical dismay, but he laughed as he gathered up the papers and secured them again with the elastic band.

'That's saved me eighty pounds nearly,' Stan said when he had calmed down. 'As well as wiping that bugger's eye. We'll have to have a drink on this.' He groped in a cupboard and brought out a bottle of rum and two glasses then poured a generous amount for each of them.

'I'm bloody made up,' he said. 'You've done me a bloody good turn there, Mr Greg.' He took a gulp of his rum. 'You know, before you said you'd do this, I wasn't throwing a hint when I said "I wish". I was going to say I wished you could do the job for me permanently. But you've already got a bloody good job, haven't you?'

Greg's heart leapt but he only said quietly, 'I wouldn't call it that, Stan, but it's safe and there's a pension at the end of it.'

Greg felt that it was only the euphoria of the moment and possibly the rum also which had prompted Stan's offer of a job, but he said earnestly, 'I couldn't offer you no pension but the job'd be safe here for as long as you wanted it, Mr Greg. I need someone I can trust. Your father was as straight as a die, and I know you are too.'

'But could you afford another wage just for having paper-work done?'

'I'm beginning to think I can't afford *not* to have it looked after properly,' Stan said. 'It's not just this chancer today. I've mislaid orders and lost them, and I'm in a right bloody muddle all round. I hate this side of the business, and I'm losing money stuck in here while I'm needed in the yard. They're mostly good lads but there's a few skivers among them who take advantage, as well as things going wrong because I'm not on the spot.'

'But perhaps you only need someone for a couple of days

a week?' Greg said. 'I don't know what you've got at home but the paperwork here could soon be straightened out.'

'A few days?' Stan exclaimed. 'Bugger that for a tale. You know I've bought the land behind this yard? I'm growing all the time and this is only the start. Tell me straight now, Mr Greg, will you come here? I can only pay three pounds a week for a start, but as I make more so will you. The lads'll tell you I've always treated them fair.'

Greg stood up and held out his hand. 'I'll take the job, and glad to have it,' he said. 'I'll do my best to do a good job for you, Stan.'

'It's not a big wage,' he began but Greg interrupted him.

'It's a damn sight more than I'm getting now, and I hate the job I'm in. Rules and regulations galore, and a bully for a boss – I've been trying for months to find something else. Believe me, I'm very grateful for this job.'

'Right then, we're both suited because you're just the fellow I need,' Stan said. 'We'll have another drop of rum on that and then I'd better get home or me missus'll have me life. How about yours?'

'I often have to work late,' Greg said. 'Unpaid,' he added with a smile.

'What notice will you have to give?'

'A week. I could start here a week on Monday.'

'Good. Half-past eight till six, and twelve o'clock Saturdays,' Stan said. 'That wood you want, is the lad coming for it? Tell him there's no charge. Goodnight, Mr Greg.'

'Goodnight,' said Greg. He hesitated a moment then said quietly, 'We must change that. I'll have to start calling you Mr Johnson from now on. You'll have to stop saying Mr Greg too.'

'Bloody hell,' Stan said with a laugh. 'All right, Mr Redmond.'

Greg rushed home so quickly that he was breathless when he arrived. Cathy looked up in alarm. He lifted her off her feet and swung her round. 'I've got a job, a new job! Three pounds a week, Cathy, and maybe more later.'

She had just opened the oven when he arrived but he slammed the door shut and pulled her down to sit on the sofa with him. He poured out the tale of Jack Almond's wood and the missing bill and all Stan had said, but Cathy could only say dazedly: 'Three pounds a week. Oh, Greg!'

They were both too excited to eat but the children gladly accepted larger helpings of hotpot, and Cathy gave them recklessly large handfuls from a bag of broken biscuits Peggy Burns had given her.

Greg repeated the story of all that had happened at the woodyard several times, exulting in the prospect of giving his notice to Mr Greenwood, while Cathy planned all that she would do with the extra money, starting with paying off her debt to Mrs Cain.

After a while she said, 'I must tell Mam and Dad. I'll run down now, Greg – or do you want to tell them yourself?'

'No, it's all right,' he said, but Cathy felt it was mean to leave him alone on such an occasion.

'Why don't we both go?' she exclaimed. 'We'll take Kate. The others are old enough to leave.' She called Sarah and told her where they were going, and they went together to tell Sally and Lawrie the good news.

Kate ran into the parlour to Josh while Greg again told the tale of the wood for Jack Almond and all that had happened at the woodyard. 'I can't wait to see Greenwood's face when I say I'm leaving,' he said. 'I don't think I could have stood another day in that office.'

Greenwood did all he could to make life unpleasant during Greg's last week in the office, but he was too happy to care. When he arrived at the woodyard on Monday morning he was amazed to see a large sturdily built shed beside the old office hut, and Stan Johnson walking towards him with a beaming smile.

'Well, what do you think of that then?' he said. 'Plenty of room here for the papers, eh?' He flung open the door and Greg saw a long desk under the window and rows of shelves, at present filled with boxes of jumbled papers. Sacks containing more papers lay on the floor. A black stove had been fitted in the wall at right angles to the desk. Stan crossed to it and slapped a hand like a ham on it.

'You don't want this now but you'll be bloody glad of it in the winter,' he said. 'And what about that?' He pointed at an electric light bulb hanging from the roof of the shed like a giant acid drop, and then at the coconut matting on the floor. 'All the comforts of home,' he laughed.

'I can't believe it,' Greg exclaimed. 'How have you done it in a week – done it at all, for that matter?'

Stan pushed his cap back on his curly hair and laughed, obviously pleased at Greg's amazement.

'Not much I can't get done if I put my mind to it,' he said. 'And there wasn't enough room in the other place – specially when we grow. Think you'll be comfortable here then?'

'I will indeed. Thank you, Mr Johnson.'

'So you meant that about the names? You're probably right,' said Stan.

Greg was happy in the new job from the first day. Stan Johnson was a good employer and well liked by the men who worked for him. Unlike most employers he had always used his men's Christian names and treated them with respect, which Greg found a welcome change from Greenwood's bullying, contemptuous manner.

Typical of Stan's behaviour was the fact that the old hut was not demolished when all the papers had been moved, but was kept for the men to use for their dinner break. He provided a primus stove, and wood for them to knock up stools for seats.

The workmen's hours were seven-thirty until six-thirty, and while he was striving to sort out the backlog of paperwork Greg worked these hours also. He found it no hardship, sitting in his comfortable office sorting the jumbled mass of papers into orderly files. Stan insisted that Greg was always called Mr Redmond, and described him to customers as his Office Manager, but the men liked his quiet, unassuming manner and the fact that he was fascinated by the different types of wood. He was amused to find that they had nicknamed him the "Bisto Kid" because of his habit of savouring the smell of the wood.

For Cathy the relief of the extra money was immense. To be able to pay a regular amount each week to reduce her debt instead of helplessly watching it creep even higher was like having a weight lifted from her, and there was the joy of replacing the children's shoes or buying coal without the anxious juggling with pennies.

Best of all was seeing the change in Greg. He became again the quietly happy man he had been until a few years earlier, always ready to make a joke or to see the humour in any situation.

'I didn't realize how miserable I was in the railway office until I left it,' he told her. 'The difference now is unbelievable. Stan swears like a trooper but he's a fine man and straight as a die. He treats everybody fairly and all the men are friendly and helpful.'

Cathy smiled at him, delighted to see him full of enthusiasm for the job. He went on, 'The days fly past. We all get a lot done, yet there's always time to talk.'

'Couldn't you talk in the other place?' she asked.

'Not a hope. We daren't lift our heads with Greenwood sitting there, glowering at us. It's degrading to a man to be as afraid as we were, but he had such power over us.'

'Well, it's all behind you now,' she said. 'But I'm made up that you're so happy there, as well as having the extra money. Remember that day when you were so fed up? It's like Mrs Mal always said – it's always darkest before the dawn.'

By the time that Greg had been at the woodyard for two months he had succeeded in sorting out the accumulated papers and found among them several unanswered order queries.

'I could answer these if you could offer a price,' he said to Stan.

'No, they've been there too bloody long. They'll have got the wood somewhere else.'

But Greg persisted. 'It's worth trying. Only the cost of a stamp.'

Greg's carefully worded letters written in his copperplate handwriting brought several new orders and Stan was delighted. Greg was pleased to make some return for Stan's kindness and to justify his wages, but was astounded to find an extra pound note in his pay packet at the end of the week.

He thought at first that two notes had stuck together and tried to return one to Stan, who waved it away.

'No, fair's fair. The lads'll tell you I pay them a bonus if we get a specially big order,' he said.

The Jazz Singer was showing at a nearby cinema and when Greg suggested that they should go there to celebrate, Cathy agreed eagerly. She had even more cause to celebrate than Greg knew, as she had been paying for her groceries as she bought them, and gradually paying off her debt. On this Friday the extra money meant that she was able to clear the debt completely. And I'll never again get in a mess like that and have to deceive Greg, she promised herself.

Now that John was nearly fourteen they felt that he was old enough to leave in charge, and their Friday night outing to the cinema became a regular treat for them. The house was always peaceful when they returned with the three younger children asleep and John doing his homework, and they brought back a pennyworth of chips for him as a reward.

For months everything went smoothly, then one night Cathy and Greg returned to find all the neighbours in groups in the street, chattering excitedly. In one heart stopping moment images flashed through Cathy's mind: the house burned down with the children trapped inside it, Mick falling to his death from a bedroom window or a maniac running amok with a hatchet, but the women hurried to enlighten them.

'Billy Woods has got took to jail,' one said.

Another cried, 'And Grace Woods has got took to hospital. You should'a seen her. Covered in blood she was – he might swing for it.'

'You mean she's dead!' Cathy exclaimed.

'Well, she looks very bad,' the woman conceded. The same thought struck Greg and Cathy simultaneously.

'The children!' they exclaimed, and dashed down to their own house. The front door was open. Inside John sat in his father's chair with Kate on his knee and his arm round Sarah, who sat on a stool beside him. 'Where's Mick?' Greg demanded as Cathy ran to fling her arms round the other children.

'Still asleep,' John said briefly. He looked at his mother. 'Don't cry, Mam,' he said. 'They were all all right.'

Greg put his arm round Cathy. 'Sit down, love,' he said gently. 'You've had a shock, but everything's all right, as John says. I'll make you a cup of tea.'

'See if Mick's asleep first,' she said. She found she was trembling and Kate moved closer to her. 'What happened? Were you all very frightened?'

'They were screaming, Mam,' Sarah said. 'Mrs Woods and all the kids, and Mr Woods was shouting.'

Greg returned downstairs and nodded to Cathy. 'Fast asleep,' he said, then to the children, 'It's all over now. Can they share your chips, John?' He agreed, and Greg busied himself making tea. Cathy felt better after that, and she and Greg talked about the Laurel and Hardy film they had just seen until the children were smiling and had forgotten their fright.

Cathy took the girls up to bed but Greg detained John to say, 'You did well tonight. Kept a cool head and looked after the others.'

'Mam won't stop going, will she?' John said gruffly. 'She needs a treat, and the kids are safe with me.'

'We know they are,' Greg said. 'I'll see that Mam still goes out. Goodnight, son.'

'I wonder what happened?' Cathy said when she returned downstairs, but she soon heard all the details from the neighbours.

She told her mother about it when she went as usual to help with the housework, and Sally was shocked.

'What about that houseful of children?' she asked.

'The neighbours have taken them. They're all related, you know, Mam, but poor Grace. I'm glad the police came this time.'

'I'm surprised they did,' Sally said. 'They don't usually interfere when it's a husband beating his wife.'

'I believe one of the kids ran into Everton Road screaming that his dad had murdered his mam so the two policemen came back with him,' Cathy said. 'Mrs Mills said Billy was like a wild animal. The police blew their whistles and more coppers came and they had to frog march him to the Bridewell.'

'And our children having to listen to all that,' Sally said.

'I know, Mam, and us out.'

'I hope you're not going to start blaming yourselves for that,' Sally said firmly. 'It was a chance in a thousand, and the young ones were safe with John.'

'Yes, he was the gear. Kate woke up and cried, and Sarah was frightened, but he brought them down and looked after them. Mick slept through it all.'

'He'd sleep through the Last Trump,' Sally said with a laugh. 'He's making up for all the nights he kept you awake when he was a baby.'

Cathy finished cleaning the windows and Sally made a pot of tea. She knocked on the back of the firegrate and soon Peggy Burns from next door came in. The friendship that had begun when Peggy moved in next door to Sally when their children were small, had lasted unbroken ever since. Cathy looked at them both with affection as they sipped their tea and ate bread and butter with keen enjoyment.

They never change, she thought. Both of them had endured many sorrows and even now had worries but it was hard to believe as they sat together placidly. Sally worried about Lawrie's bouts of bronchitis and Peggy about the orphaned granddaughter she was bringing up, who the neighbours said euphemistically was "a bit backward".

They told Peggy about the row and Cathy said she hoped Billy would be sent to jail for a long time.

'But who'll keep the children?' Peggy said practically. 'She'll have to go on the Parish, and he'll be worse than ever when he comes out.'

'I wish you could get away from that street, Cathy,' Sally said. 'And that nosy old woman opposite to you.'

'Grace told me that Mrs Parker thought a man had a right to beat his wife. She's Grace's aunt. I wonder what she thinks now?'

'I don't suppose she's changed her mind,' Peggy said. 'That sort don't. Did you know she's a moneylender?'

'Freda told me,' Cathy said. 'I must be thick. All the time I've lived there and never suspected it.'

'Well, thank God you've never got into her clutches, girl,' Sally said. 'You can afford to ignore her, but I wish you were well away from that street.'

Later, as Cathy walked home, she thought of her mother's words about the house and her neighbours. Since her money worries had been solved, Cathy had thought sometimes that if only they could find a new house life would be perfect, but then she told herself that she was being greedy to want more when God had been so good to them.

Nevertheless, she decided that as she had prayed for a solution to her money worries and her prayers had been answered, now she would start to pray for a new house.

Chapter Nine

Billy Woods was sentenced to six months' hard labour as he had also struck one of the policemen. Cathy went to see Grace and found her in great pain from her injuries, but glad to be in hospital.

She had a broken jaw, three broken ribs and numerous cuts and bruises on her body, but it was the deep cut on her head which had bled so freely that the children thought she must be dead.

'Can I do anything?' Cathy asked. 'Your cousins in the street have taken the children, but if there's anything you're worried about or anything I can do—'

'No, thanks,' Grace said wearily. 'Our Janey came in and told me which ones have got the kids, and that they've all been in to clean the house. I suppose they had a fine old time rooting round and finding out all my business.'

'Don't worry about it,' Cathy said sympathetically. 'Just get yourself well, that's the main thing. Everything will seem different when you feel better.' Neither of them mentioned Billy.

Cathy was truly sorry for her neighbour but nothing could mar her own happiness at this time. It was a happy time for all the family, and although Greg and John clashed occasionally when the boy aired his views, on the whole they were on much better terms.

Sarah was happy both at school and at home. She was a class monitor, was devoted to her teacher and consistently near the top of the class.

She still went often to Elsie's florist's shop, and sometimes stayed with her grandmother for the weekend. Sally was a thrifty housewife and bought her meat and fish in Great Homer Street where it was always cheaper than elsewhere, waiting until meat was auctioned off on Saturday nights to buy the Sunday joint. Sarah loved these expeditions, and also their trips to St John's Market. She loved the crowds, the noise and good humour as they strolled through the market, Sarah clinging to her grandmother's arm. Sometimes Sally would talk of the days when, as a young girl, she had worked in the market.

'I was very unhappy before I came here,' she told Sarah. 'My two brothers had just died and my little sister Emily had been adopted, but the market cheered me up. There were some characters here then, Sarah, and they were very kind to me.'

Sarah thought that there were still many characters in the market. The only thing that worried her was seeing ragged, barefoot children trying to snatch scraps of food – cabbage leaves or bruised fruit or a potato which had fallen to the floor – and being chased away by the stallholders.

One night she was standing beside her grandmother at a stall when she saw a barefoot boy crouching beneath it. The next moment a small dirty hand reached up and snatched a steaming pig's trotter from a dish on the stall. There was a shout from the stallholder and the boy darted out, nearly overturning Sarah, and raced away between the shoppers. The stallholder pursued him, waving a large knife he had been using, and Sarah gripped Sally's arm.

'Oh, Grandma, will he kill him?'

'No, love. He won't catch him. Those boys are like eels, and anyway the crowd has closed up behind him,' Sally said. 'Poor little beggar, I hope he enjoys the trotter.'

Usually, though, these weekends were peaceful and happy. Sally seemed to have unlimited time to listen to Sarah's tales about school, and she was always willing to tell the stories Sarah loved to hear, about the days when her mother and her Aunt Mary had been young in this house.

But the incident in the market troubled Sarah. She was puzzled that her grandmother, always so law abiding and conscientious, had seemed to approve of the theft of the trotter, and asked her father about it.

She told him what had happened and what her grandmother had said. 'I hope he enjoyed it too, Dad, but it was stealing, wasn't it? That's a sin, isn't it, Dad?'

Greg considered carefully before answering, then said gently, 'That's a question which has troubled cleverer people than us, love, but I don't believe that a child stealing something to eat because he's hungry is committing a sin. The sin belongs to those who allow him to go hungry in the midst of plenty.'

'But he stole it from the stall and that's a sin, isn't it?'

'In black and white terms, but circumstances alter cases, Sass. You have to have the intention to commit sin, and the boy probably didn't even know it was dishonest. To him it was a way to cure his hunger. It's a bit complicated for you now so don't worry about it, love.'

'So that's why Grandma said it.'

'Yes. But, remember, *you* must never take anything that doesn't belong to you,' Greg said.

Cathy came into the kitchen. 'You two look very serious,' she exclaimed.

'A small point of theology,' Greg said, smiling at Sarah. She ran out to play, happy with her father's explanation. She felt that she could always rely on him to explain anything that puzzled her.

Another parcel had arrived from Fortnum and Mason and Sally had finally written to Mary to ask her not to send any more hampers. She chose her words carefully but no more letters came from Mary.

'I think our Mary's taken the huff,' her mother said to Cathy. 'I tried to explain in my letter – said the parcels were such an expense to them that it worried me, and the food was too rich for us, but she must have taken it the wrong way.'

'I don't think so, Mam,' Cathy said. 'You know Mary. She's probably having a good time and hasn't realized how the the time's passing.'

When the usual monthly remittance from Sam failed to arrive, Lawrie said nothing to Sally but spoke to Greg about it.

'I wonder if they're in trouble,' he said. 'The newspapers are full of this Stock Market crash on Wall Street, and all the suicides and bank failures. Sam's got his fingers in a lot of pies there.'

'I wouldn't worry yet,' Greg said. 'All the better if Sam's got several business interests. If one fails, he can use another to bail it out.'

'He might just have been too busy to remember to send it,' said Lawrie, always ready to look on the bright side.

The weather was atrocious and in Arrowe Park in Birkenhead where the Scout Jamboree was held, the camping site rapidly became a sea of mud. Although the weather did nothing to dampen the spirits of the Scouts from many nations who were meeting there, it had a serious effect on older people.

Lawrie had a severe bout of bronchitis in early November and it was several weeks before he was fit to return to work. As soon as he was well enough he searched the newspapers for details of the aftermath of the Wall Street crash and the "knock on" effect of the spectacular failures.

When the next remittance failed to arrive he was convinced that Sam must be in trouble and his first outing was to the bank. He asked the manager for advice on the best way to send the savings to Sam.

'I don't want to send it in a way that'll see it gobbled up, with no benefit to Sam and Mary,' he explained.

'Of course you must do what is best for your daughter and her husband,' the bank manager agreed. 'Matters are rather complicated at present but I'll consider the options and inform you of them.'

Lawrie was too worried and too anxious to put Sam's mind at rest about money to wait for the bank manager's advice, and while Sally was out he wrote to his son-in-law.

Sally and me do very well with only the two of us to keep and a lodger into the bargain. I didn't want to hurt your feelings, lad, by sending the money back because we didn't need it so I put it in the bank, thinking it might come in useful for fares or something you'd need. By what I see in the paper this might be the time to send it to you, but thanks for thinking of us and I hope you won't think that me and Sally aren't grateful.

I asked the bank manager and he said he'll think of some way to send it so no one else gets their hands on it. The amount is 1,426 dollars. Keep your pecker up, lad. Love to Mary.

Yours faithfully,
Lawrence Ward

Sam's reply came promptly. He wrote that he had been very touched by Lawrie's letter and was sorry that he had been worried.

It has been a bad time here and everything is very disorganized. I could see that the bubble must burst and I planned accordingly, but many of our friends have not been so lucky. I was not over-extended so I was able to salvage enough for a fresh start. It has upset Mary to have so many friends scattered and houses sold, and she would like to make a start somewhere else. She fancies California because of the sunshine and I can see openings in supplying the film business so will give it a try. Rest assured, Mr Ward, that I will never let Mary experience hardship.

I hope you were not offended by my sending the money. It was the only way I could show my gratitude to you. I hope you will keep it in England and use it there as it might complicate things for me if it came here, although I appreciate your kind offer.

I can never be thankful enough not only to have Mary as my wife but also to have you and Mrs Ward as parents and Cathy as a sister.

Yours very affectionately,
Sam

Now that he knew that Mary and Sam were not in trouble, Lawrie showed Sam's letter to Sally who shed a few tears.

'I hope our Mary's been a comfort to him while he's had these troubles, poor lad,' she said. 'And I hope she realizes how lucky she is to have a husband like Sam to look after her. He'd pull the moon out of the sky for her.'

'I'm sure she does,' Lawrie said. 'She saw enough of the other kind to make her appreciate him.'

Sally dried her eyes. 'Aye, well, this explains why she hasn't been writing. It looks as if there's been a fair old upheaval there, and she wouldn't write while she couldn't boast.'

They were interrupted by the sound of Cathy opening the front door, but she paused on the step to speak to Peggy Burns who had come out of the house next door.

Sally looked down the lobby. 'There's another one who's got a good husband,' she said, 'Greg's one in a thousand, but at least our Cathy values him. Both our girls have been lucky.'

'And we've been lucky too, girl,' Lawrie said. 'Two lovely daughters, and sons-in-law like Greg and Sam.'

They could hear Cathy's voice rising excitedly, and then they heard her say, 'Oh, come in and tell Mam, Mrs Burns,' and the next moment the two women came into the kitchen.

Cathy's cheeks were pink with excitement. 'Mam, Dad,' she exclaimed, 'Peggy's heard about a house here in the street!'

'An exchange,' Peggy said. 'Miss Andrews' house over the road.'

'Miss Andrews,' Sally echoed, 'but —'

'I only heard this morning,' Peggy said. 'I got talking to her and she said her house was too big for her and her brother. I said why didn't she exchange into a smaller one, and told her Cathy was looking for a family house.'

'Oh, Mam, wouldn't it be lovely?' Cathy said.

'What are we all standing up for?' Lawrie interrupted. 'Sit down and tell us, Peg. Do you think she's serious?'

'You know her, Lawrie, she's not one for jokes.'

'I've seen her in the street,' he said, 'but I wouldn't say I know her. Tall, thin woman, very reserved?'

'Yes, with a patch of red on her cheeks. That shows she's got a bad heart. That's why she wants to move, I think,' Peggy said. 'The house is too much for her.'

'What should I do? Should I go and see her?' Cathy asked, but her mother advised caution.

'Don't rush the woman,' she said. 'Let Peggy have another talk to her.'

Cathy waited impatiently for Greg to return home, and as soon as he stepped inside the door she poured out her news. 'It wouldn't be much difference in rent either,' she said. 'This place is seven and threepence a week, and Mr Jones never puts his rent up so Egremont Street is only nine and sixpence. We could easily afford that, Greg.'

Her eyes were bright with excitement and she seemed unable to keep still. Greg felt compelled to warn her not to build her hopes too much.

'Miss Andrews may not want to live here, or one or other

of the landlords might object,' he said.

'But you'd like it, wouldn't you?' Cathy said eagerly.

'Of course I would. I've always liked Egremont Street. They're good sound houses and it's a much wider road than this.'

'Three good bedrooms, and a parlour, and all the rooms are bigger than these!'

'Which house is it?'

'Number twenty-three. Across the road from Mam's and a bit further up. Next to where the Bennets used to live. You must have seen Miss Andrews. "The Grenadier", we used to call her. She was so tall and thin, and her brother was little and fat. Oh, Greg, if only we could!'

He was walking about in excitement although he tried to appear calm. 'It would be splendid for the children. Even the youngsters there are different. Properly brought up.'

'Mam said we mightn't like being so close to them,' Cathy said.

'Oh, no. That might be the case with some people but not with your parents, Cathy,' he exclaimed.

"Like your mother," trembled on Cathy's tongue but she bit back the words. That bitter old woman was long dead and now her malice should be forgotten.

It all seemed an impossible dream but suddenly all their problems seemed to be solved. Miss Andrews visited the house in Norris Street and declared that it would be perfect for her and her brother. The front door opened into the living kitchen but Greg had put up bookshelves at an angle to the door which screened the room from the street.

He had also made bookshelves for John's books and added a lean-to shed in the backyard which gave extra storage space. The little house was spotlessly clean and perfumed by flowers from the allotment, and Miss Andrews announced that she and her brother would be very comfortable there.

Cathy felt compelled to warn Miss Andrews about the inquisitive neighbours, but the spinster gazed at her in mild surprise.

'I shall keep them at a distance, dear,' she said firmly. 'My dear mother always advised against familiarity, and Herbert will know how to deal with any impertinence.'

Cathy hid a smile. The Andrews family had certainly followed that policy in Egremont Street, she thought, but she wondered what the effect of their reserve would be on the people of Norris Street, particularly Mrs Parker.

They had finished their tour of the tiny house and Miss Andrews declined Cathy's offer of tea.

'I am perfectly satisfied with this house, Mrs Redmond,' she said, 'but you must inspect my house.' Cathy assured her that it would not be neccessary as she knew the layout of the houses in Egremont Street but Miss Andrews said with dignity, 'Nevertheless, I should prefer you to do so.'

It was arranged that Cathy would call later that day and if she was satisfied they would go to see both landlords and get the matter settled.

Later Cathy went to her mother's house before going to number twenty-three, and told her of Miss Andrews' visit. 'I asked her if she needed to consult her brother but she just said, "That will not be neccessary." It's funny, Mam. He's such a peppery little man, and she's so stiff and quiet.'

'I think she rules the roost there all right,' Sally said. 'I'd like to see those nosy neighbours of yours trying anything with *her*.'

'So would I,' Cathy laughed. 'It didn't take her long to decide that Herbert would have the back bedroom. You know, when I was little I thought they were married and I used to think how funny they must have looked at the altar, with Miss Andrews so tall and thin and her brother little and fat.'

'There was a big family there when we came to this house,' Sally said. 'But they were always very superior and kept themselves to themselves. I think they were interested in amateur theatricals, and they used to go to the theatre and the choir together.' She sighed. 'There used to be lots of families like that before the war, but not any more.'

'Weren't some of the sons killed?'

'Three joined up right away and two were killed early in the war, on the Somme, I think. One was killed in the last week, I remember now. Some of them married and the house seemed to empty out suddenly. The mother died a few years ago but she'd been bedridden for years.'

Cathy went to see Miss Andrews and was solemnly

conducted round the house. It was totally different to her mother's although the rooms were the same size. The parlour was in semi-darkness, with an aspidistra on a bamboo plant stand and heavy chenille curtains and Nottingham lace shrouding the window. There was a rosewood piano with candle sconces and a massive picture above it of a St Bernard dog rescuing a small boy from a pond.

The rest of the room was filled with a round mahogany table and massive dining chairs, and a sideboard with a curved marble top and a heavy ornate mirror above it. Every inch of wood was elaborately carved and Cathy was just thinking how hideous it all was when Miss Andrews remarked, 'Most of the furniture will be too large but we must take the sideboard and that dear picture. It was Mother's favourite.'

They went into the kitchen, the heart of the house in Sally's house but here as dark and overcrowded as the parlour. The bedrooms were the same but although tidy they smelt fusty and airless. Dust lay thickly in the folds of the heavy curtains.

Cathy was not deterred. She was sure that with the dark hangings and heavy furniture removed, she would soon make a clean and comfortable home for her family here.

They went next to see the landlords who both agreed to the exchange which was arranged for the end of the month.

Excitement had carried Cathy forward as though on the crest of a wave, but that night in bed she was suddenly filled with panic. How on earth would they pay for the move, and for furniture for the new home? Since her debt had been paid, she had enjoyed having the extra money to spend but somehow now it was only just enough to last the week and she was never able to save from it.

She tossed and turned, unable to sleep, and looked pale and tired when she went to her mother's house the next day.

'You don't look well, love,' Sally said. 'Didn't you sleep?'

'I'm just excited,' Cathy said. She had not intended to tell her mother that she was worried but suddenly found herself blurting out her fears over the move.

'I don't know what you're worried about,' Sally said calmly. 'Peggy knows someone who'd move you for five shillings, and your dad and I have already decided that we'll pay that and for any new oilcloth you need for the floors.'

'I can't let you do that, Mam,' Cathy protested.

'Don't argue,' Sally said. She stood up and took down the handleless teapot that stood on the mantelpiece. She took three pound notes folded together from it. 'I drew my Co-op divi and it was good this time. Josh got his new suit and shoes and he gave my number because he's not in the Co-op himself, so I did well.'

'I'm sorry I said anything,' Cathy exclaimed. 'I wasn't trying to scrounge.'

'I'm going to get annoyed in a minute,' her mother exclaimed. 'If your own mam and dad can't help you out, who can?'

Cathy looked down. 'I feel ashamed,' she said in a low voice. 'I should have been able to save out of the big jump in Greg's wages, but honestly, Mam, it just goes.'

'I'm not surprised,' Sally said, 'with six mouths to feed and four growing children to clothe. I don't know how on earth you managed before, but don't worry yourself any more about this move. Me and your dad can't wait to have you all just across the road.'

She seemed to assume that the question of the money had been settled and Cathy could only accept with thankfulness. During the following weeks she gradually packed up what she could and scoured every corner of the house so that it would be clean and fresh for the new tenants.

A niece had appeared to help Miss Andrews sort out what she could take and what must be sold. Cathy went to the house again and arranged that she would buy the Nottingham lace curtains which were too large for the Norris Street windows, and some other small items.

'We won't be able to furnish the parlour yet,' she said to Greg, 'but if the lace curtains are up it'll look all right from outside.'

'The main thing is having the house,' he said. 'We can take our time and furnish it gradually.'

'Oh, Greg, it's all like a dream come true, isn't it?' she said, putting her arms round him and leaning her head on his chest.

He kissed her gently. 'Our lucky star's shining now all right, Cath,' he said.

The day of the move was bright and pleasant and all went smoothly. The family were up early. Sarah helped Cathy to strip the beds and pack the bedding and the last few pots and pans into a tea chest, while Greg and John dismantled the beds ready for the removal men.

Kate had stayed with her grandmother, and the rest of the family went off to school or work. When the removal van arrived Mrs Parker was sitting outside her house opposite, surrounded by relatives, all shamelessly scrutinizing every item as it was carried out. Cathy swept out each room as it was cleared and then took out the brush and shovel to the van. As it drove away the rent collector came down the street. He raised his bowler hat and shook hands with Cathy.

'I know your rent has been paid at the office, Mrs Redmond,' he said, 'but I wanted to say how sorry I am to lose such a good tenant, and to wish you every happiness in your new home.'

Aware of the watchers across the road, Cathy blushed but said warmly, 'Thank you, Mr Carnegie. I'm sure Miss Andrews will be a good tenant and her brother is a bookworm, you know.'

'I'm glad to hear it, but I'll miss you. Thank you for all your kindness.' He raised his hat again and moved away. Cathy went back into the house and through to the back kitchen away from the prying eyes, her own filling with tears.

In her early days in Norris Street she had invited the rent collector into the house on a bitterly cold day and had offered him a hot drink which he had gratefully accepted. Cathy had been amazed and hurt by the sly comments of her neighbours about her innocent action, but she was too proud to be intimidated by them and had since often repeated her action.

The old man had become a friend and had often borrowed books from the bookcase behind the door. Most of them were from second-hand shops and a few were school books of Greg's but Mr Carnegie always made brown paper covers for anything he borrowed and brought the books back promptly.

The house next door was still empty. Billy Woods was still in jail and Grace was making little progress back to health.

Cathy had been again to the hospital but had found her weak and dispirited.

'They think me rib damaged me lungs,' she told Cathy. 'I was going to go to the Tired Mothers Home for a holiday but now I might get sent to Fazakerley instead.' She showed little interest in her children, except to say that her cousins were not able to keep them any longer.

The eldest boy had taken lodgings near the foundry where he worked and one of the girls was in service. George, who was now fourteen, had obtained a living-in job as a boot boy in a hotel, and of the five remaining children, three had been sent to an orphanage in Seaforth, and the two youngest who suffered from rickets had been sent by Miss Beaven to the Open Air Hospital for Children in Leasowe.

Cathy went into the backyard for the last time and glanced up at the windows next door, feeling sad for Grace. But nothing could depress her for long on this day. She went in and toured the house to make sure all was in order, and put a penny in the gas meter. She had already put a large lump of coal on the fire, and satisfied that she had done all she could to leave the house warm and welcoming for Miss Andrews, she stepped out and shut the door behind her.

'Ta ra then,' one of the woman standing near Mrs Parker called. 'We'll have to watch our step with the new woman, won't we? She looks as if she could flatten us with one blow.'

The women sniggered and another one called, 'The rent man'll miss his comforts, won't he? His cups a' tea.'

Several retorts rose to Cathy's lips but she suppressed them and simply said goodbye, walking away with her head held high. Three of her children had been born in the little house but any pang she might have felt at leaving it was speedily cured by the malicious comments. She walked away with no regrets, only an added thankfulness that she would be living in Egremont Street, among friends.

Chapter Ten

Sarah thought that the day that they moved in to Egremont Street was the happiest of her life. To have a house like Grandma's with two steps up to the front door and a railing between their house and the one next door, a bedroom just for herself and Kate, and best of all Grandma and Grandad just across the road, was heaven.

She sang as she ran round exploring the house then helped her mother to hang curtains and make up the beds. John was helping his father to lay linoleum and her grandmother was unpacking dishes. Just as Sarah began to feel tired and hungry Sally called, 'Come on, Cathy. We all need a break, and dinner'll be ready.'

They went over to her grandmother's house where her grandfather welcomed them, singing, "Come to the Cookhouse Door". 'You didn't know I could cook did you?' he said to Sarah, as he served them with spareribs and cabbage. To her it was the food of the gods. She sat smiling to herself with pure happiness.

For all the family, but particularly for Cathy, there was a sense of homecoming as they settled in to the house in Egremont Street. She had never openly quarrelled with her neighbours in Norris Street but she had never made any friends there either. Her friends were still the friends of her youth who lived in and around Egremont Street and thankfully she settled back among them, while her ties with her mother and father grew stronger and deeper.

She knew that Greg too was happy in the new house. In Egremont Street he became friendly with a man named Tom Faulkner who walked with a limp as a result of a war wound, but who was an enthusiastic member of the St Johns Ambulance Brigade. Greg enrolled in the same unit.

For John the greatest advantage of the new house was

that he now lived just across the road from his grandfather. He was still studying hard, spurred on by the hope that he would fulfil his grandfather's ambitions, although he had no clear idea of exactly what he would do when he left school.

Cathy's greatest pleasure in returning to live in Egremont Street was being able to see her childhood friend Josie Mellor, or Meadows as she now was, every day. Josie still lived with her mother in the house opposite Sally's.

Cathy had been able to see Josie briefly on visits from Norris Street, but now there was time for a chat over a cup of tea or a joint expedition to town. Old Mrs Mellor had always been fond of Cathy, and although now very cantankerous she welcomed Cathy and told her she should never have left the street.

Josie had been a noisy scatterbrained girl when she was young, and not such a close friend of Cathy's as another girl, Norah Benson, but after the War, when Norah had married and moved away and many of their friends had died or been scattered, Cathy and Josie drew closer together.

Four of Josie's brothers had been killed during the war, and she had been constantly worried about Walter, now her husband, who was serving at sea. Grief and anxiety had made Josie quieter and more sensible, but like Cathy she had an irrepressible sense of fun.

Although the Redmond family were happy, elsewhere in Liverpool misery and hardship were on the increase as the shock waves from the Wall Street crash were felt around the world. The queues outside the Labour Exchanges and the Assistance Board grew longer, and the bitter weather when even the sea froze made the plight of the destitute even worse.

Some of the girls in Sarah's class were ragged and neglected, or wore the distinctive navy serge dress piped in red and clogs issued by the police charity, but most were poorly but neatly dressed.

Many of them were undernourished and it was not unusual for a girl to faint and fall to the floor. Sarah was class monitor and often would be told to sit with the girl who had fainted while the teacher took the class out for playtime.

When the teacher returned Sarah would be told to wait in the corridor while the teacher asked the girl what she was getting to eat. It was impossible for Sarah to avoid hearing some of the conversations.

'What did you have for your breakfast, dear? And your tea last night? And when you went home yesterday dinner time?'

Invariably the answer was, 'A jam butty, Miss.'

Then the teacher would come into the corridor and send Sarah for a ham barmcake and a gill of milk from the carters' cafe near the school, with a warning that nothing must be said to the other girls.

Most of the teachers were strict and hard with their large classes of forty or more girls, but Sarah saw the kinder side of many of them.

'If only I could give my girls a cup of milk every day,' Cathy heard one teacher say to another, 'it would make such a difference.'

'Save the lives of some of them,' the other teacher agreed.

'At least four of mine show all the signs of consumption, but what can you do?'

Sarah told her mother but Cathy could offer little comfort.

'We'll just have to hope that Miss Rathbone can get Parliament to give Family Allowance, pet,' she said. 'I'd be more hopeful if they weren't nearly all men there.'

Later Sarah was surprised to hear her mother and her grandfather disagreeing about Family Allowance.

'You've got to see it'd be a good thing, Dad,' her mother said. 'Remember the war? Women who had never known how much or how little they would have to feed their families each week – once they got a regular amount every week, paid directly to *them*, and God knows the Army allotment was little enough, you could see the difference in the kids.'

'I know, Cathy,' Lawrie said. 'But you've got to realize that it would take away a man's power to bargain for a pay rise or stop a cut in wages. And what about a chap on relief? He'd only lose the same amount and be no better off.'

'The truth is, Dad, men don't like the idea of women not having to depend on them for every ha'penny,' Cathy exclaimed.

'Now stop arguing, you two,' Sally intervened. 'I've said it before, Cathy – the best way of helping people is to do what's next to your hand. You don't have to go far to see someone you can help.'

Grandma's the most sensible, Sarah thought, and put her grandmother's ideas into action immediately. Jane Clark, who sat next to her in school, was a thin pale girl who always seemed tired. Sarah took a slice of bread and jam to eat at playtime and the next day gave it to Jane Clark, saying that she felt a bit sick and couldn't eat it.

The school was in a poor area half-way up the ground which rose steeply from the river. The greatest poverty and deprivation were in the narrow streets and overcrowded courts below the school and near to the River Mersey, but after school Sarah walked up the hill to Egremont Street and better living conditions. She was sorry for the girls who lived in the slums but while she was giving away her playtime jam butty she felt that she was doing all she could, and for the rest of the time simply enjoyed herself, listening scornfully to John as he talked about speakers he had heard at the Pier Head.

He rarely spoke of these meetings or of his own ideas while his father was present, but one day when he was arguing with Sarah about them, Greg walked in unnoticed.

'Keep away from those meetings, John,' he said sharply. 'Spend less time on politics that you don't understand, and more on your school work.'

'I *do* understand them,' John said hotly. 'I bet I could answer any questions *you* asked me.'

The unspoken inference was clear – that Greg knew nothing about the subject. He grew pale with anger. A small pile of books lay on the dresser. He picked them up.

'*Riches and Poverty* by Chiozza Money; *Life and Labour of the Poor of London* by Charles Booth; *Round about a Pound a Week*, by Maud Pember Reeves . . . So that's where you get your information. Well, you can take these back wherever you got them from.'

'I got them from Grandad,' John shouted, 'and I've got more too, by Engels and Rowntree.'

Greg's face grew even whiter. He put the books under his arm. 'Then *I'll* take them back, and tell him the use you're making of them,' he said as Cathy came in at the back door. She looked round at them, Greg as white with anger as John was red, and Sarah nervously twisting the belt of her gymslip.

'What's happened? What's going on?' she exclaimed.

Greg said shortly, 'Nothing for you to worry about. I'm taking these books back.'

He walked rapidly down the lobby. John started after him. 'If he makes a row – if he upsets Grandad – I'll kill him!'

'Don't speak like that about your father,' Cathy cried. 'What's happened anyway? Good God, I can't turn my back.'

'I'm going out,' John said, snatching up his cap and rushing out of the back door.

Cathy sat down, and Sarah said timidly, 'It was just those meetings, Mam. John was telling me about them when Dad came in, and John had some books there from Grandad.'

Cathy shut her eyes and sighed deeply. 'Dear God, I thought all that was over with them,' she said. 'I'd better go and see what's happening.'

She stood up, but the next moment Greg came down the lobby. He was still pale but said quietly, 'No need to be upset, Cathy. I've simply returned the books and told your mother that John was neglecting his school work to read them. Your father's out.' He looked round. 'Where's John?'

'He's gone out,' she said. 'I don't know why you can't agree.'

'Agree?' exclaimed Greg. 'I'm his father, and by God he's going to show me respect or I'll know why. I'm having no more of his impudence.'

Cathy had been annoyed with John but instantly her anger turned on Greg. 'He's got compassion for other people,' she snapped. 'What's wrong with that? I don't know why you have to make these scenes.'

Sarah was still standing where she had been when the row started and Cathy said sharply, 'Don't be standing there listening in, Sarah. Get out and play.'

'Everyone's at fault except your precious son,' Greg said furiously. 'Even Sarah who's done nothing.'

'Of course you can't see any fault in *her*,' Cathy said. It was a childish tit for tat retort, but Sarah heard it as she reached the door and was pleased to think that she was her father's favourite.

She ran down to call for Edie Meadows and told her that her parents were quarrelling about John.

'I think your John's awful hardfaced to your dad,' Edie said frankly. 'We wouldn't dare talk like that to my dad. He'd murder us.'

'I wish Dad and John didn't fall out all the time.'

'Fellows are soft,' Edie said. 'My Auntie Mary hates men.'

'All men?' Sarah asked.

'Yes. Mam told me it was because her husband was cruel and everybody was glad when he got killed in the war.' She giggled. 'She's buying new shoes for me and our Sophie but she won't buy any for the lads.'

'Good job you're a girl then,' Sarah said with a grin.

Sally had been uneasy about Greg's appearance when he returned the books, and spoke of it to Lawrie when he came home.

'White as a sheet, he was,' she said. 'All he said was that John was neglecting his schoolwork, but there was more to it than that. There'd been a row there, I could tell.'

'But John hasn't *just* borrowed these books,' Lawrie said. 'He's been taking them gradually for months.' He jumped to his feet. 'I'd better go over and explain.'

'No, leave it, Lol,' she said. 'Let it simmer down.' But she still looked worried.

They sat in silence for a few moments, Sally knitting and Lawrie scraping out the bowl of his pipe, then Sally put down her work. 'John's getting very cheeky to Greg, you know, Lol, and our Cathy doesn't back Greg up like she should when he checks the lad.'

'Don't worry, Sal. John's just finding his feet, that's all,' said Lawrie.

'But I'm wondering if we spoiled him,' she said. 'When he was a baby and Greg was away at the war, we all made much of John. You remember how he resented Greg when he came home?'

'Good God, love, how old was he then? Three or four years old. He's long got over that, Sal.'

'I hope so, but I don't like to see trouble in the family. Greg's been like a son to me and I don't want him hurt.'

'It's just a spell,' Lawrie comforted her. 'Most lads go through one like this. It's just like their voice breaking.'

'I suppose so, but if John grows up half as good a man as his father he'll do well, and I hope he realizes it,' Sally said.

There was a strained atmosphere in the Redmond household for a few days but the books were not mentioned again, and John said nothing of the reason for their having been on the dresser. He had been planning to put them in the parlour, ready to pick up on his way out to school the following day, to lend to a friend there.

The cricket season had started again and John had been chosen for the school team. Through this he had become friendly with a boy he would not otherwise have met, the son of a local doctor, and through him with the son of a solicitor, whose elder brother was at Cambridge.

Gerry, the doctor's son, had heard John talking about a meeting which had been broken up by the police, and had invited him to supper at his house.

Cathy and Sally were delighted that John was making such "nice" friends but they would have been horrified if they had heard the discussions which took place in Gerry's bedroom after supper. Gerry and Peter, the solicitor's son, were greatly influenced by Peter's brother who was a member of a Communist group at university. Their talk of social reform was wild and unrestrained.

John had been slightly overawed at first by these well-dressed, confident boys, but soon forgot his shyness when the discussions started.

'There'll be trouble in Germany,' Peter declared. 'My brother says the so-called Peace Treaty was a mistake and Jewish financiers have moved in to wreck the country.'

'My grandfather says one man in four is on Public Assistance in Germany,' John said. 'It's not only in England that the working man is suffering, it's in every country.'

'Money's useless in Germany. Men who are working are taking their wage home in a handcart yet it won't buy enough to eat,' said Peter. 'Financiers cause wars and profit by them.'

'My grandfather says if all working men refused to fight there would be no more wars,' said John.

He had looked forward to telling his grandfather about the talk but when he did Lawrie looked very dubious. 'And this brother is against the Jews, you say, lad? Are you sure he's a Communist? I don't like the sound of it, John.'

'The Jews are good people,' Sally said. 'Your mam worked for a Jew, Mr Finestone, and he was a real good old man.'

John felt exasperated. Old people don't understand, he thought, for the first time including his grandfather in that category.

He determined to say no more about the meeting but a few weeks later, Gerry's father overheard some of the wild talk and the meetings were promptly stopped. Homework had been increased as the time for the Matriculation Examination drew near, and John had little time anyway for any other reading.

Greg made a point of praising John for working hard. 'This final year is important if you're going to get a good result,' he said. 'I'm pleased to see you preparing so well.' He was careful not to repeat his mistake at the time of the scholarship by regretting that John must leave at sixteen years old, and John refrained from saying why he was working hard, so there was peace between them.

Cathy felt that she could stop worrying, but soon Mick was the cause of more anxiety. He often rescued animals or birds which had been injured, and one day climbed on to the roof of a warehouse to release a pigeon which had been trapped by a loose slate.

He managed to release the bird but it flew up in his face, causing him to lose his balance and fall from the roof. He was lucky to suffer nothing worse than a broken collar bone and arm, but was admitted to hospital where his temperature rose alarmingly.

Cathy and Greg rushed there when they heard the news. They were told that the collar bone and arm had been set, but there might be internal injuries causing the rise in temperature. They were allowed to see Mick for a few minutes. Cathy bent and kissed him.

'Is it very sore, love?' she asked.

Mick said in a die away voice, 'Very, Mam.' He closed his eyes and composed his features into a look of suffering.

'Do you have pain anywhere else, son?' Greg said. 'In your chest or your stomach?'

'Everywhere,' Mick said in the same die away voice, and closed his eyes again. They had to leave after kissing him and telling him he must be brave, and Cathy's tears flowed as they left the hospital. She felt that she had never loved Mick enough and regretted scolding him so often.

'You only told him off for his own good, to try to make him more careful,' Greg said.

'I know, but I wish I'd cuddled him more and made more of a fuss of him. Oh, Greg, what will we do if anything happens to him?'

'I'm sure he'll be all right,' he said, and looked thoughtful. 'D'you know, Cath, I've got a feeling that Mick's enjoying this, in spite of the pain.'

'Enjoying it? How could he enjoy being in pain?' she said indignantly.

'Just an impression I got. I think he's a born actor. Now he's playing the part of an injured hero, as he sees it.'

Cathy was annoyed. 'It's no effort for you to play the part of a heartless father,' she stormed, increasing the speed of her steps until Greg had to hurry to keep up with her.

'I don't mean he's not in pain, only that he's enjoying playing the part,' he said, but Cathy could only think of her child's suffering.

Visiting was only allowed twice a week, on Sunday and Wednesday afternoons. The following Wednesday Cathy and Sally hurried to be first in the queue outside the hospital. Anxious inquiries at the hospital lodge had met only with the formula "As well as can be expected", and Cathy longed to see for herself how he was.

The Ward Sister met them with a grim expression on her face. 'How is he, Sister? Is his temperature still high? Have you found out why?'

The nurse answered the last question first.

'We have,' she said sternly. 'He has chicken pox and has probably given it to the rest of my patients. The ward is closed to visitors.'

Her voice was loud and there were cries of dismay from the other relatives. Cathy felt that they all looked at her reproachfully as they went away without seeing their children.

'I'm sorry, Sister,' she said. 'I'd no idea he had it. Is he all right?'

'As well as can be expected,' Sister said austerely, then she caught sight of a nurse without her cap and set off after the luckless girl like a ship in full sail.

There was nothing that Cathy and Sally could do but turn away as the other visitors had done, but a cleaner who was wiping down paintwork slipped round the corner after them.

'Are youse belonging to the lad with the broken arm?' she hissed at them urgently.

'Yes, but we can't see him,' Cathy said tearfully. 'Have you seen him? Do you know how he is?'

'He's all right. She cudda let yer see him, the old cow. He's in a little room on his own, and he couldn't have give the others the chicken pox neither.'

'I couldn't even ask if he could have this cake and sweets. She went off so quickly after the nurse,' Cathy said.

'Bloody old mare,' said the cleaner, peeping round the corner. 'Here, give it to me and I'll slope it to him. He's a case, isn't he? Should'a been on the stage.' She put the parcels beneath her voluminous sacking apron, and with a parting wink slipped away.

'I feel sorry for the other children and their mothers,' Sally said later. 'It doesn't sound as though there was any need to close the ward.'

'Chicken pox!' said Cathy. 'Trust Mick to get it just at the wrong time. Still, I'm glad that was the reason for his temperature, so long as he isn't too ill with it. I wish we could have seen him, even for a minute.'

'You and Greg will have to try again on Sunday,' Sally said. 'And try to see that cleaner too, I'll make a cake for you to give her.'

Cathy walked home, thinking of the woman's words that Mick should have been on the stage. Could Greg have been right? It seemed unimportant though. If only they could have seen Mick! But at least he would know that they had been to the hospital, and the cleaner might be able to give him the cake and sweets.

Lawrie was indignant when they told him what had happened. 'It's a damn disgrace,' he said. 'Those Sisters have too much power. I suppose no one will bother to tell the kids

118

that their mothers came to see them and got turned away. Mothers should be allowed to see their children every day when they're sick – it's the time they need them most.'

'Every day?' echoed Sally. 'They'd never allow that, Lawrie. None of the hospitals would, unless the children were on an urgent note and we don't want that for Mick.'

'Aye, when a child's dying and doesn't even know his mam and dad, then they'll let them in to see him. It'd do the kids good, and help them to get better, if they could have visitors every day.'

'Sister doesn't even like twice a week visiting, one of the women in the queue told me,' Cathy said. 'She says it upsets the children and makes more work for the nurses, and it makes the ward untidy too.'

'It's a pity about her,' Lawrie said. 'I suppose a tidy ward is more important to her than the poor kids who must think their mothers have dumped them there.'

His face was flushed and he was gasping for breath. Sally went into the back kitchen and came back with a glass of water.

'Drink this. Why do you always work yourself up about everything, lad?' she scolded him. 'All these impossible dreams, trying to set the world to rights single-handed.'

He managed a smile but was too breathless to reply. She put her hand to his forehead. 'You're burning hot. Do you feel all right, Lawrie?'

'Yes, I'm fine,' he said, but leaned back in his chair as though weary. Cathy kissed him and went home, leaving him to recover quietly.

'I'm nearly as worried about Dad as I am about Mick,' she told Greg later. 'I've never seen him like that.' She went over again later but her mother told her that her father had insisted on going to work.

'He's worried about having so much time off sick in the winter,' she said. 'He says he can't stay off in the summer as well. He had a couple of hours' sleep and didn't seem so bad when he went.'

The next morning when Lawrie came home his body was covered in a rash. 'Shingles,' Sally told Cathy. 'I thought it was, and Peggy said the rash was the same as their Michael had.' Cathy went up to see her father who greeted her with a smile though he looked ill.

'How do you feel, Dad?'

'Glad to be home in bed, to tell the truth, love,' he said. 'Mind you, I was glad to see the rash in a way. I felt so bad and didn't know what was wrong. At least now I know why.'

'Have you got a lot of pain?' Cathy asked.

'No. I've had some of Mam's jollop,' he said with a grimace.

'Never mind, she's got some good remedies. She'll soon get you right, Dad.'

'Aye, I'll be getting back to work to get away from them,' Lawrie said, but he was plainly tired, and Cathy left him to sleep.

She inquired every day at the hospital lodge about Mick but the reply was always "Comfortable" or "As well as can be expected". Sally was unable to leave Lawrie so Cathy went alone on Wednesday afternoons and on Sundays with Greg, but several visiting days passed before they were allowed to see Mick.

He seemed quiet and subdued but the attack of chicken pox had fortunately been slight. He whispered to Cathy that the boy in the next cubicle had been badly burned and screamed every time he heard the nurse approaching with the dressings trolley.

'He's only four, Mam, but he screams awful loud,' Mick said. 'I can't stop thinking about him, 'specially when I can't sleep at night.'

'Can't you get to sleep, love?' she said, tenderly stroking back his hair.

'I get to sleep but I keep waking up,' he said. 'When can I come home, Mam?'

Greg went out and braved the Sister to ask about Mick's progress. She was unexpectedly gracious.

'Michael is a good patient and the bones seem to be knitting well, Mr Redmond. Of course, he is strong and well nourished.'

'When will he be discharged?' Greg asked. 'I know you need the beds, Sister. Could he be nursed at home?' Mention of the need for beds had softened the Sister, and she said that she would ask Doctor on his next visit and Michael might be discharged on Friday.

Greg thanked her and returned to tell Mick that he might be coming home "fairly soon".

'Sister said you'd been a good patient, son. Mam and I are proud of you.'

'I'm proud of myself,' said Mick, smiling at them. What a handsome little boy he is, thought Cathy. The chicken pox had not marked his skin permanently, and although he still bore scars from various accidents, his face was fresh and clear and his teeth had grown white and even, in spite of all the mishaps with his baby teeth. With his deep blue eyes and fair curls, he showed signs of the handsome man he would become and Cathy watched him with pride.

They had taken him a comic to read. Greg's head was close to Mick's as they laughed together at the pictures. Cathy felt a pang as she watched them. Why was it that Greg was so different with John? He's so close to the younger ones, she thought, and yet with John, I never know when the next row will break out over nothing. I suppose Greg would reply he treats them all alike, if I said anything, and blame John for the rows.

When they left the hospital, Greg told Cathy that Mick might be discharged on Friday. 'Friday? Why didn't you tell him? It would've cheered him up.'

'But excitement might have sent his temperature up, and then he'd have been kept in.'

'I wouldn't have thought of that. I'd just have blurted it out,' she said. 'Mind you, I don't suppose she'd have told me as much.'

'She said she'd ask the doctor tomorrow, but I think she has the last word really,' said Greg.

'I hope so. Oh, Greg, wasn't it awful having to leave him there? Did you see the tears in his eyes when we were leaving, real tears, not like when he's just yelling about something?'

'He cheered up when you gave him the jigsaw,' Greg comforted her. 'It was a good idea to keep that until we were leaving. We'll just have to hope he's only got two more days there.'

Mick was discharged on the Friday and seemed thoroughly to enjoy the fuss that was made of him on his return home. Cathy found him an unexpectedly good patient, docile and obedient. Before long she put a cushion on the step for him to sit on and watch the other children playing, after making him promise not to join in their games. Fear of returning to hospital made him keep the promise.

Cathy felt that she got to know Mick much better during the weeks he spent safely at home, instead of rushing out to play all day.

'I didn't realize how much he knows,' she told Greg. 'He's really clever.'

'Yes, there are unsuspected depths in Mick,' Greg said with a smile. And in you, thought Cathy. Since the day in the hospital she had seen more clearly how close and loving the relationship was between Greg and the younger children.

It annoys me that he doesn't behave like that with John, she told herself, refusing to acknowledge that the twinge she felt was jealousy. It gave her an excuse to devise small treats for John to make up for his father's imagined neglect, without feeling that she was being unfair to the other children.

But there was little margin now for any extras, Cathy found. Her feeling of affluence when Greg first earned higher wages had soon vanished and she was dismayed to find that she was again barely stretching the housekeeping money from Friday to Friday.

Cathy talked freely to Josie about her problems, knowing that she had the same worries.

'I thought I was on Easy Street when Greg got this job, and it is better, but honestly, Josie, I don't know where the money goes. The rent's not much more here than Norris Street but it seems to cost more for coal and gas and cleaning stuff.'

'I know,' said Josie. 'It's the clothes that get me down. I don't know what I'd do without our Mary helping me, but she never gives anything without a dig at Walter.'

'I suppose you can understand it,' Cathy said. 'I can remember that time when she had the stillborn baby and that awful husband.'

'Yes, but all fellows aren't the same,' Josie said indignantly. 'Walter wouldn't hurt a fly and she talks about him as though he's a monster.'

'Mam does a lot to help me,' Cathy said. 'She gets clothes from that wardrobe dealer and cuts them down for the kids.'

'But you're handy with a needle yourself, aren't you, Cath? Not like me,' Josie said. 'Have you ever thought of taking in sewing like your mam used to do?'

'I couldn't,' Cathy said. 'There's barely enough work for Queenie and she keeps her and her mother with her sewing.' Queenie was a tiny woman with a club foot and a hump and Josie agreed that she needed the work.

'I've got half a promise of a few weeks' cleaning,' Josie said. 'Bella's cousin cleans those offices at the corner of Dale Street. She's lost three babies and the midwife says she got to give up the cleaning for a month before she has this one, so she spoke for me. It'll only be for about two months but it'll be a godsend – if I get it.'

'I hope you do,' Cathy said. 'I'll look after the baby, if you like.'

'It's all right, thanks all the same,' her friend said. 'It's before the kids go to school and after they come home, and our Edie's very sensible.'

'See if anyone else has got a midwife like that,' Cathy said, laughing. 'Then you can speak for me.' Then, more seriously, she said, 'I'm ashamed, Josie, that I can't make ends meet, or at least that I've got to scheme for things. I wish I was like my mam.'

'You're more like your dad, and money always burned a hole in his pocket, didn't it? I had many a penny off him. He's a lovely man.'

'He's not picking up after the shingles. He's not himself, really quiet and miserable.'

'It takes time,' Josie consoled her. 'Your mam will soon get him right.'

Chapter Eleven

Josie obtained the cleaning job which lasted for eight weeks, but before it finished she heard of another job as a part-time waitress.

'Walter doesn't like the idea of me working,' she told Cathy. 'I think the other fellows say things, and of course my mam is always stirring it. Saying he should be ashamed he can't keep his family.'

'Take no notice. Your mam's gone very moody, hasn't she?'

'She's gone like me old grandma used to be. Remember her, Cathy? The first word was a blow with her. Mam's the same with my kids.'

Cathy told her mother about Josie's job and old Mrs Mellor's comments about it. 'That's ridiculous,' Sally said. 'Walter's a good husband, but he doesn't get much as a baker's roundsman. All credit to Josie for trying to make something to help out.'

'She says she'll keep her ears open for a job for me,' said Cathy. 'So you wouldn't say anything if I got it, Mam?'

'No. Growing children take a lot of keeping,' Sally said calmly.

Josie started the new job just before the summer holidays and was too busy to go for outings in the park with Cathy and the children. During the previous bitter winter Freda's husband, who worked on the roads, had caught a cold which developed into pneumonia from which he died.

Freda's family had closed ranks around her to comfort her and care for the children, but Leslie had been a loving husband and father and Freda grieved deeply for him. Cathy still saw her taking her children to school, but she was a sad, withdrawn figure with no heart for outings.

John was often studying, and when he was free went with

a group of friends to camp on Seaforth Sands. They had acquired a small tent, and John begged an old pan from Cathy in which they cooked weird concoctions on the fires they made from driftwood.

Sarah and her friends preferred going for tram rides now, although they were happy to go to the park when pennies for the tram fare were not available. When they were, the girls could buy a ticket which gave them four rides, although the tickets were known as penny returns.

Sarah, and Edie Meadows, and another friend Lucy Ashcroft, were all considered capable, responsible girls, and the mothers thankfully handed over younger children to be taken on these days out. They usually took Meg Burns too. Meg's real name was Smith as she was the child of Peggy Burns' dead daughter but she had been unable to understand why her surname was different and had been distressed about it, so her name had been changed to Burns. Peggy usually kept her close, but was happy to put the backward Meg into Sarah's care.

The children gathered by Cathy's step and it amused her to see Sarah, whom she had always considered timid, firmly organizing the noisy group, and gently restraining Meg as she danced about, wildly excited at the outing.

They always came back dirty and hungry, but happy and full of stories about their adventures. Only Kate was never untidy. Among the motley throng of children with dirty faces and tangled hair, with hems coming down on their dresses and socks round their ankles, she looked as neat and clean as when she had set off in the morning.

'Why can't you keep yourself tidy like Kate?' some of the mothers scolded, but the older residents of the street told each other that she was the model of her Aunt Mary. 'The same temper and all,' they said, because Kate was ever ready to throw a tantrum when thwarted. But these were quickly over, and she was a favourite with most of the neighbours.

Sally had made her a dress for Sundays of spotted material, with a full skirt and deep white collar, similar to one worn by Shirley Temple. Kate believed that she was very like the film star. She had a sweet singing voice and had learnt to tap dance a little from one of Sarah's friends, and was always ready to perform.

Cathy took her to show Josie her new dress when it was finished. Josie's mother was there, a shapeless mass filling the armchair from which she rarely moved. Her beady black eyes were bright with malice.

'You'll have to watch *her*, Cathy,' she said. 'She's the spitting image of your Mary, and your mam had her share of worries with that one.'

'Your dress is lovely, Kate,' Josie said hastily. 'Your grandma's very clever, isn't she?' But old Mrs Mellor ignored the interruption.

'Always chasing lads, your Mary, and didn't think none of them good enough for her. I always said she'd come to a bad end.'

'Then you were wrong,' Cathy said angrily. 'She's got a good husband and a lovely home in America, and two automobiles.'

She was not sure whether the automobiles had been replaced but was not going to admit that to Mrs Mellor.

'And it wasn't Mary chasing lads, Ma,' Josie said. 'It was the other way round, and no wonder. She was so beautiful. Put us in the shade, didn't she, Cathy? But, never mind, we done all right for ourselves. We've both got good husbands and good children.'

She walked down the lobby with Cathy and Kate, and took a penny from her pocket. 'There you are, love. I think your dress is beautiful – just like Shirley Temple's.'

To Cathy she said in a low voice, 'Take no notice to me mam. She found out that our Frank was head over heels for Mary and she wouldn't have him, and that's why she's saying all that.'

'Poor Frank,' said Cathy. 'I thought he was lovely when I was young. Remember those parties? Frank was the first one I knew who was killed in the war.'

'Plenty followed him,' Josie said with a sigh. 'Either drowned like Frank and our other lads, or killed in the trenches. Lovely lads, all of them.'

They stood in silence for a while, their faces sad as they thought of those who were gone, then Josie shrugged her shoulders. 'Ah, well, no use brooding, I suppose. Thank God these kids won't go through what we had to.'

'Yes, the lads didn't die for nothing,' Cathy said. Mick

was outside, walking down the street with a rolling gait, and Josie laughed. 'Look at him,' she said. 'D'you think he'll be a sailor? He's got the walk.'

'He's probably got a stone in his shoe and can't be bothered to take it out,' Cathy said.

A few weeks later Josie came in at the back door to Cathy's house before the girls and Mick had left for school. 'I couldn't wait to tell you, Cath, there's a job for you. I've got to take you to see Mr Ireland this afternoon. Waiting on at functions with me. You'll love it.'

Fortunately everything happened so fast that Cathy had no time to be nervous. They went to see Mr Ireland who was a thin, harassed-looking man who could only spare them a few minutes. Josie started to introduce Cathy but he interrupted her.

'Yes, yes. As long as you vouch for her, that's all right. There's a job tomorrow night. See Mrs Nuttall. Wear a black dress and a cap and apron, Mrs Er – er. All right?'

He dashed away and Josie laughed at Cathy's bewildered expression. 'Don't worry, he's always like that – meeting himself coming back.'

'Who's Mrs Nuttall?'

'She's the supervisor. She's the real boss. There was no need to go and see him, but he likes everything done properly.'

They went in next to see Mrs Nuttall and she gave them details of the job. It was a dinner at an imposing building in Mount Pleasant and Cathy felt extremely nervous when she arrived there with Josie the following night. She was wearing a black dress of her mother's, and in a paper bag carrying a cap and apron borrowed from Josie.

It was only when all the arrangements had been made about the job, that Josie admitted that she had told Mrs Nuttall that Cathy was a silver service waitress. 'Don't worry, I'll show you what to do,' she said airily. She had given Cathy a lesson in serving vegetables with a spoon and fork, using pieces of raw potato and some sprouts, but they had both collapsed in giggles at Cathy's efforts. As she tried to grip the vegetables between spoon and fork, the sprouts shot into the air and pieces of potato flew across the table.

'Don't worry, you'll soon pick it up,' Josie assured her, but Cathy was overcome with panic as she followed her friend into the building. Her hands trembled as she took off her coat and tied the strings of the small white apron. Josie arranged the cap on her hair.

'I'll look after you, and the other women are good sorts,' she whispered, but Cathy was not reassured.

They went into a side room where four women were sitting. Josie made the introductions. 'This is my mate Cathy,' she said. 'This is Cissie, Doris, Bella and Janey.'

'Your first time, girl?' Cissie said. She was a small woman with a thin face and protruding teeth. Her cap, a strip of starched cotton with fancy edges, threaded through with black velvet ribbon, was perched at a rakish angle on her untidy hair.

Cathy nodded, unable to speak, but Cissie said scornfully, 'Don't worry over this lot. They're only tuppence ha'penny toffs. They'll be too busy wondering what knife and fork to use to take any notice to you, girl.'

For a moment Cathy thought she meant the other women, then she realized she was referring to the diners. Mrs Nuttall bustled in. 'Put your cap straight, for God's sake, Cissie. You look as though you've been on the ale.' She noticed Cathy. 'All right, love? Josie'll show you the ropes, or ask me. Cup of tea now, girls, before we start.'

A van arrived, and boxes and baskets were carried in, and suddenly the small room seemed to buzz like a disturbed hive. In a flash, it seemed to Cathy, the dining tables were laid with linen and cutlery and glass, and Cissie had claimed her to help unpack baskets of crockery.

Before she had time to realize what was happening, the diners were seated and she was serving soup, with Josie and Cissie rapidly serving extra people to make up for her slowness. A serving dish of meat was thrust into her hands then snatched away by Josie. 'Take the spuds, Cath,' she said, and set off down a row of seats, followed by Cathy with the potatoes and Cissie with vegetables.

The potatoes were mashed which made them easier to serve but Cathy was uncertain how large the portions should be. Josie was too far ahead for her to ask but Cissie noticed her dilemma. 'Give him a bit more, girl, he's a growing lad,' she said. That solved one of Cathy's problems but she was worried that she was too slow and was keeping Cissie waiting behind her, but that lady was unperturbed.

Hot and flustered, Cathy whispered to her, 'I'm sorry, Cissie.'

'Don't worry, girl. Take yer time. These aren't going anywhere, are yer?' she said to a man who looked round in surprise.

'Er – no,' he said, turning away quickly. Laughter bubbled up in Cathy and suddenly she felt that she could manage quite well. Josie had also noticed her friend's dilemma and slowed down in serving the meat so that Cathy was not too far behind her.

The same frantic pace of activity continued in the kitchen. Very soon, it seemed to Cathy, the meal had been served, with Josie and Cissie like guardian angels beside her, showing her what to do and covering for her slowness or mistakes.

The diners moved to another room and the tables were cleared as swiftly as they had been laid. Cathy helped to pack the dishes into baskets then went to fold the tablecloths and collect cruets. Small silver dishes of sugared almonds had been placed at intervals down the tables and few of the nuts had been eaten, so Cathy was surprised when Cissie handed her several empty dishes to take back with the tablecloths.

The dessert had been a rich chocolate cake and Cathy watched in amazement as Cissie cut a tiny slice from a whole cake and crammed it into her mouth, especially as there were several cut cakes on the side table.

When a young man arrived to supervise the packing of the unused food she saw the reason for Cissie's action. Several whole cakes were packed away and the young man looked at the cake that Cissie had cut.

'Good God, look at the bit out of that,' he said.

'A man just asked for a taste, Mr Owen,' Cissie said glibly.

'Aye, and pigs might fly,' he said. 'All right, girls?'

He pulled a bag from his pocket and handed out the wages. Four shillings for each woman and something extra for Mrs Nuttall.

'The carrier'll be here in a minute,' he said. 'Good night,

girls.' He departed, and Cathy saw the reason for the small cases the other women used to carry their caps and aprons. The leftover rolls and fragments of cheese were shared out, and the chocolate cakes that had been cut into were divided between them.

Cathy had taken her cap and apron in a paper bag but Cissie found another bag and put Cathy's share of the spoils in it. 'You've got kids, haven't you?' she asked, and when Cathy nodded her hand went under her apron and then into the bag too quickly for Cathy to see what had happened.

When she reached home she found a pile of sugared almonds at the bottom of the bag, and Josie told her that Cissie had also given some to her.

'I didn't tell you about the loot, Cath,' she said, 'because it would've looked bad if you'd seemed to expect it – if you'd taken a case the first time – but it'll be all right now.'

The children enjoyed the cakes and sweets and Cathy took some to her parents. Her father laughed heartily when she told them about Cissie.

'The quickness of the hand deceives the eye,' he chuckled. 'She could've made a living as a conjuror.'

'She was awful good to me, and so was Josie,' Cathy said. 'I'd have been in a right mess if they hadn't helped me the way they did. All the women were nice. They all mucked in with one another and we had a good laugh. Cissie's a comedian.'

Later Lawrie said to Sally, 'I saw you give me an old-fashioned look when I laughed about that food, Sal, but I reckon those women are entitled to it. Four bob for working all those hours! I wouldn't say anything to Cathy about being exploited, though, because she's made up with the job.'

'It'll be a help for her and a change from the house too,' Sally said. 'I'm not worried about the food either. It'd be thrown away otherwise and the boss seemed to know about it.'

The four shillings Cathy received provided the meal for the following day, and extra fruit, and she looked forward eagerly to the next job.

Within a few days a postcard arrived for her, saying briefly, "Please be at Horton Lodge, Meadowsweet Lane, at 2 p.m. on Tuesday". Cathy hurried to see Josie and found that she also had received a card.

'It'll probably be a tennis party,' she explained. 'I haven't been there before but I think some of the others have.'

Cathy enjoyed that job too and found the serving less nerve-racking. They served strawberries and cream to players and guests, and a selection of tiny sandwiches and delicious fancy cakes. The sun shone and everyone seemed happy, and Cathy felt that she was seeing another side of life as she served tea in the marquee on the lawn of the mansion, and to older people who sat on the terrace. The women joked lightheartedly as they worked, and Cathy felt that she had been quickly accepted by them.

Cissie was the comedian of the group, but she was kind-hearted too and had evidently decided to take Cathy under her wing. Cathy had provided herself with a small case, and at the end of the day it contained not only her cap and apron but also a basket of strawberries and a large medicine bottle full of cream, and a selection of sandwiches and fancy cakes.

Cissie had provided the medicine bottle and packed Cathy's case, handing it to her with a wink and a stage whisper of, 'You'll soon get to know the ropes, girl.' The sandwiches and cakes were rather squashed when Cathy unpacked the case but they were thoroughly enjoyed by the family. They enjoyed the strawberries and cream too, and as Kate finished her portion she closed her eyes and sighed.

'When I grow up I'm going to *live* on strawberries and cream,' she announced.

A memory pricked Cathy and a cloud came over her happiness for a moment. She remembered her sister Mary announcing her plans for a future life of luxury when she was still a child, and thought of the unhappiness her ambitions had brought her. Was Kate going to follow the same path?

Not if I can help it, Cathy thought. We'll just have to be careful not to spoil her because she's the baby, and as soon as she's old enough I'll warn her about these ideas.

Cathy had again received four shillings for the job and it was a great help with her housekeeping. She told her friend how grateful she was to her for recommending her, but Josie said she had been glad to do it.

'I know what a help the money's been to me,' she said. 'It's only four bob, but you get it in your hand, no waiting, and very often it buys the dinner for me. Mind you, Cath, some weeks there might be nothing, and then another week you might get three jobs. There's usually a lot round Christmas, Cissie told me.'

'She's a case, isn't she?' Cathy laughed. 'But awfully kind.'

'She doesn't give a damn,' Josie said. 'No matter who the people are. She dropped a sprout on the Bishop of Liverpool once, and she just said, "Sorry, cock," and wiped his sleeve with her cloth before she went on serving. Mrs Nuttall was having a fit. She gets the jobs, though, because she's a gear worker, quick as a flash.'

'She's been very good to me, and so have you, Jose.'

'What does Greg think about you working?' Josie asked.

'He only said he didn't want me to get too tired. He knows I enjoy it, and the money's so handy. We have a good laugh when I tell him some of the things that go on.' She said nothing to Josie of how careful she was to stress that the money she earned only put jam on the bread he earned for his family, in case his pride was hurt.

She knew that her father had never felt diminished by the fact that her mother's sewing had provided part of the family income, but then her father never held the orthodox view. Cathy felt that her care for Greg's pride might be unnecessary, but she knew how easily he could be hurt and that most men were ashamed if their wives needed to work.

As Josie had warned Cathy, the postcards announcing a job came irregularly but they were always very welcome and the family learned to look eagerly for the "Please be at's", as they were christened.

Cathy was very happy at this time. The extra money made many small treats possible for all of them, and life seemed to be flowing smoothly.

Even the tension between Greg and John was less evident, although it still showed itself in small ways. After the first of Cathy's jobs she had been excited but tired and Greg had taken her coat and pushed the armchair forward for her. He had turned to get the stool for her feet, but John had been before him, lifting Cathy's feet on to the stool and easing off her shoes.

Not an important incident but made so by the challenging look John had given his father. Cathy had hastily made a joking remark about the fuss they were making of her.

Thankfully such incidents were rare nowadays, especially as John was either up in his room studying or out playing cricket and Greg was spending so much time on the allotment. Lawrie was often with him and Sarah liked to go there, but Greg insisted that Lawrie did only the very lightest tasks.

'Just tell us what to do, and Sarah and I can do it,' he said. 'You're the one with the green fingers.'

'Sarah's got a knack for gardening too,' Lawrie said. 'She'll soon be telling us both what to do, won't you, love?'

'Oh, no, Grandad. I like gardening but I don't know all about it like you,' Sarah said seriously. Greg and Lawrie exchanged a smile, careful not to let Sarah see.

'I think you've inherited a love of flowers from Grandad,' Greg said. 'Another few years, love, and you'll be working among them all day.'

'I can't wait,' Sarah said, but her father and grandfather both told her not to wish her life away.

Sarah had grown tall and her resemblance to her grandmother was even more marked, although her hair was darker than Sally's had been. Sarah's hair was obstinately straight and resisted Cathy's attempts to curl it, but it was a true chestnut colour – 'Like my conker,' Mick had said – and thick and shining with health.

She still went to the flower shop whenever she could but she had less free time now. Since living in Egremont Street she had made many friends and there were always games to play. All the girls were expected to help their mothers in the house, and Sarah was a great help to Cathy. She was quick and deft and seemed to enjoy housework, which was invaluable to Cathy now that she was so often out working for the caterers.

Sometimes Cathy's jobs involved travelling to the Wirrall or to Southport, which meant that she was often out all afternoon and early evening. She knew that some of the women she worked with would have to return to an untidy house and piles of unwashed dishes, and take up the burden of housework immediately, no matter how tired they felt, but she was more fortunate. When she returned, Greg and Sarah between them would have ensured that the house was orderly, the dishes washed and put away, and a welcoming cup of tea was ready for her.

Chapter Twelve

The last outdoor job of that summer was at a large house in Southport where a charity garden party was held. The film star Daisy Duval was invited to open the garden party and Sarah listened eagerly to her mother's account of the star's clothes and the speech she had made.

Cathy unpacked her case which held several small pots of jam as well as egg and cress sandwiches and cakes, and put some of the food to one side for her mother.

'Take this over to Grandma, Sarah,' she said. 'I'm too tired to go over there tonight, but I'll see her in the morning. You're a good girl to have everything so nice for me.'

As soon as Sarah left, Cathy turned to Greg, her eyes sparkling. 'Oh, Greg, we had such a good laugh but I couldn't tell you while Sarah was here. You know we got the train to Southport. Well, there were two journalists in the carriage with us, going to the garden party because of Daisy Duval.

'When we went through the tunnel at Moorfields it was all dark, of course, and Doris leaned over and ran her hand up Cissie's leg. Cissie thought it was one of the journalists, and you should have heard her!'

Cathy began to laugh helplessly at the memory and Greg laughed with her. She wiped her eyes. 'Oh, Greg, those poor young men. She ranted and raved and told them she was a respectable married woman and just because she came out to work they needn't think they could take liberties with her. The two men were looking at each other, each thinking that the other one had done something awful, and Cissie was threatening them with her husband.'

'With Bert?' Greg said, laughing.

'Yes. I forgot we'd met them that day in town. You know the size of him. I was laughing at the idea of him tackling

137

these hefty young men, but at the same time I was indignant. It was only when we got off the train and Cissie was still going on that Doris told her *she'd* done it. The men had dashed off as fast as their legs would carry them, and they kept out of our way all day.'

'A monstrous regiment of women,' he laughed. 'You're seeing another side of life with these jobs, Cath.'

'I'm seeing the lives some posh people have,' she said. 'But I suppose you mean I'm getting to know people like Cissie as well. They're good women, Greg. They might be a bit tough but they're really good-hearted and we always have a good laugh.'

'So do I when I hear the tales,' he said. 'When you've had a rest, why don't you go over and tell your dad that story? It'll cheer him up before he goes to bed.'

Cathy's smile faded. 'Yes, I think I will. I never thought I'd have to cheer Dad up, but he can't seem to throw this off, can he?'

'He will,' Greg comforted her. 'The effects of shingles can last for a hell of a long time, you know.'

As Greg had predicted Lawrie laughed heartily at Cathy's tale, and Sally smiled too, but more because she was pleased to see Lawrie laughing, Cathy suspected, than because she appreciated the joke. They were all worried about Lawrie. Some of his strength had come back after his illness but all the fire seemed to have gone from him.

After work he rarely went out, seeming content to sit in his chair, silent and subdued, glancing listlessly through his newspaper. But as he laughed at Cathy's story, he seemed briefly to resemble the cheerful man they had always known.

Sarah had gone home to bed before Cathy went over. Sally came to the door after her daughter. 'Why don't you come to us for tea on Sunday?' Cathy said. 'We always come here, and the change might brighten Dad up.'

'No thanks, love. I'd rather you came here,' Sally said. 'We both look forward to it.'

On Sunday, when the family gathered round the table for tea, they all did justice to the lavish spread provided by Sally, and Mick and John especially enjoyed the good food.

'They've got good appetites,' Josh Adamson said wistfully.

'I don't know where they put it,' said Cathy. 'If you'd seen the size of the dinners they ate only a few hours ago! They must have hollow legs.'

'They're growing lads,' Sally said tolerantly. 'And they're both strong and healthy, thank God.'

Josh sighed. 'They might as well enjoy it while they can,' he said, and Cathy remembered that he had been told by his doctor to cut down on his food.

'Do you feel any better?' she asked him. 'Mam said your breathing was bad.'

'Aye, it takes me all me time to walk up the broo from Shaw Street,' he said. 'It's a good job I sit down to my work or I couldn't carry on. The doctor says I've got fatty degeneration of the heart, and I've got to give up meat and fried stuff.'

'That's hard,' Cathy said sympathetically. 'But, still, if it means you'll get better, it'll be worth it, won't it?'

'Maybe,' he sighed. 'But it's torture, Cathy, torture. I'm a man that likes his food, as you know.'

Cathy felt deeply sorry for the gentle old man and later said so to her mother.

'It's awful, Cath,' Sally said. 'It was a pleasure to cook for him because he enjoyed his food so much, but now I don't know what to do. With Dad working shifts, I can try to give them their meals separately but I'm trying to build Dad up, yet I'm afraid to cook anything that'll leave a savoury smell in the air to make it harder for Josh.'

'Do you think it's worth it for him?' Cathy said.

'Dad doesn't think so. He thinks it's too late to make any difference and Josh shouldn't deprive himself when it upsets him so much, but I'm afraid to give him meat. I'd never forgive myself if it killed him.'

'How old is he?' Cathy asked.

'I don't know. He seemed quite old when he first came here, but that might have been because he was so settled in his ways. It's hard to say.'

Josh seemed to forget his troubles when Kate sat on his knee or when she danced and sang for him. There was a deep affection between the old man and the lively little girl.

'They're well matched,' Sally said dryly to Cathy. 'He never gets fed up watching her and she never gets tired of performing.' And Cathy had to agree.

Nobody was sure whether the diet prescribed by the doctor was the cause or whether worry made Josh lose weight, but he soon became much thinner and his breathing improved. Kate spent more time at her grandmother's house now that Cathy was often at work, and most of that with Josh.

One day he shyly asked Cathy if she would allow him to pay for dancing lessons for Kate. 'I think she's got real talent,' he said earnestly. 'I'd be very pleased if you would allow it, Cathy.'

She found it impossible to refuse with Josh and Kate both looking at her expectantly, but later she was careful to warn Kate that Josh might be overrating her talent.

'He's fond of you, you see, love. And when people are fond of you, they often think that you can do things better than you really can.'

'But I *can* dance well,' Kate said. 'Everyone says so.'

'We'll have to wait and see what the dancing teacher says,' Cathy said, but when she spoke to her mother about it, Sally shrugged.

'The teacher's not going to quarrel with her bread and butter, is she? She'll say she's good whether she is or not. You'll have to watch that child, Cathy. She's getting too big for her boots.'

Kate's friend Rosie was already attending a dancing class in Breck Road, and Cathy took Kate to the same class every Saturday afternoon. On the rare occasions when a job for Cathy occurred on a Saturday afternoon, Greg took her. After one such occasion, he came home full of a new idea.

'Do you know there's a dancing class for grown ups?' he said to Cathy when she came home. 'Ballroom dancing. It's only half a crown for six sessions. What do you think?'

'For us, you mean? We're a bit old, Greg, and with four children.'

'Doesn't matter. Do you know Rosie's parents go to the Grafton every Thursday night? I'm sure she's older than you.'

Cathy was doubtful, but the following week Rosie's mother came to speak to Cathy as she waited for Kate. Cathy had always been too shy to speak to her because she sat with another group of mothers to wait for the little girls. Now the woman introduced herself as Nancy Dutton.

'I saw your husband here last week, Mrs Redmond, and he seemed interested in the dancing class upstairs. Why don't you join?'

Cathy blushed. 'I don't know. We're a bit old,' she murmured.

'Old? Good heavens, no. I'm sure you're no older than me, and some of the people who go are much older. Barty and I go to the Grafton every Thursday and we have a really good time. You'll be missing a lot of fun if you don't learn.'

'Greg's very keen,' Cathy said, but still looked doubtful. Nancy seized her arm. 'Come upstairs and peep in,' she said. 'The dancing teacher won't mind.'

Cathy looked in at the dancers, fascinated to see the couples plodding round to the music of a gramophone and the teacher's voice shouting, 'One two three, one two three.'

'I think I'll try,' she said, smiling at Nancy. 'I don't know why we never learned to dance.'

'You'll make a good dancer,' Nancy said. 'You've got a light step. Your mother has too, hasn't she? I saw her walking down our street, and she still has that quick, light walk that I used to notice years ago.'

'Mam used to go to dances when she was young,' Cathy said. 'Irish dancing. She enjoyed it.'

The following week Cathy and Greg left Kate at the tap dancing studio and went upstairs to learn ballroom dancing. They found the steps easy to learn and they could move to the rhythm of the music quite effortlessly. At their last session the dancing teacher asked them to demonstrate a waltz for some prospective pupils and they felt that they were ready for a visit to the Grafton.

Nancy invited them to accompany her and Barty, her husband, on their first visit, so that they could "show them the ropes" as she put it. They were glad to agree. It seemed, though, that Nancy and Barty went to the dances with two other couples who were waiting for them in the ballroom.

Cathy thought that the other couples looked momentarily dismayed to see the newcomers, and was relieved when after they were introduced, Greg said firmly, 'I think we'll just watch at first. We'll see you later.' He took Cathy's arm and they smiled at the group and went up to the balcony.

'I'm glad you did that,' she said. 'I think they change partners and they wouldn't want beginners with them. Look.' They stared down at the floor below which had filled with couples as soon as the music for a Veleta began.

Nancy and Barty and the other couples were among the dancers, but Barty was dancing with one of the other women and Nancy with another man. A tango followed the Veleta so Cathy and Greg remained on the balcony, watching the dancers, but when a waltz was announced Cathy looked at Greg, her brown eyes shining and the dimples appearing in her flushed cheeks as she smiled. He stood up and held out his hand.

'May I have the pleasure?' he said, laughing. 'Cathy, how could you ever think you were too old for this? You look about sixteen.'

They had a happy night, and when Cathy told Josie about it she looked wistful. 'I'd love to learn,' she said. 'But I don't think I could get Walter to go.'

'Come up to our house and we'll teach you,' Cathy said. 'Walter would come that far, surely?'

'He'll come if I have to frog march him!' Josie said.

The sessions in the Redmonds' parlour were hilarious. Cathy and Greg had bought a Fullotone cabinet gramophone by hire purchase so that they could play records for Kate to practise her tap dancing, but now they bought dance records and nearly every night the four adults danced to the music of Jack Jason and his Orpheans for the dreamy waltz music and Harry Roy for the foxtrot, with his opening announcement: 'This is your hotcha ma chotcha, Harry Roy.'

Walter picked up the dances very quickly. He had been a seaman for many years and thought that had made him light on his feet.

Josie was less adept but eventually managed to learn the steps of the dances, although for a while she chanted 'One two three, one two three' as she was guided round by Greg.

The parlour was ideal for the dancing classes. Cathy and Greg had put curtains up at the windows and linoleum on the floor but they had not yet managed to furnish the room, except for the cabinet gramophone which stood in solitary state. There was plenty of room for the dancers as they blundered about, Greg with Josie and Cathy with Walter, sometimes too helpless with laughter to move.

Soon the Grafton dances became a regular event for the four of them, the high spot of their week. The catering firm's cards came once or twice a week, more frequently as Christmas approached, and the extra money made a difference to the Christmas festivities for both families.

In the spring of 1931 John sat for the School Certificate Examination set by the Joint Matriculation Board and passed in seven subjects. He was awarded credits in French, Mathematics, English and Geography, and the family were sure that he would be able to secure a good job. But John soon found that his good school record and examination results made little difference to his prospects.

At this stage in the Depression jobs were hard to find. The magic key was to have a friend or relative who worked for the firm and could "speak" for an applicant, or to know someone who was friendly with an employer and willing to use his influence.

Lawrie raged about the injustice of the system. 'Here's a lad who's worked hard at school and done well in his exams, yet he's got no chance the way things are,' he said to Sally. 'Mind you, girl, for all I think it's wrong, I'd put my pride in my pocket and ask for him if I knew anyone who could help.'

'What about the councillors you know?'

'Not them,' Lawrie said grimly. 'It's a case of you scratch my back and I'll scratch yours with those fellers, and there's nothing I could do for them in return, you see.'

Cathy grieved to see John rushing off every time he heard of a job, his face shining with soap and water and his hopes high, only to see him return a few hours later, disappointed and dejected. At long length, though, his persistence was rewarded and he obtained the job of office boy in a fruit importer's at a salary of seven shillings a week.

Most of the office staff seemed to be what his grandmother called "tuppence ha'penny toffs". They tried desperately to give the impression that they belonged to a higher social class than they did, and talked grandly about

143

their superior friends and cultured lifestyle outside the office.

The opposite side of the coin was their contempt for those they saw as their inferiors, and John could find no kindred spirit among them. Before long he was in trouble for his outspoken comments.

A group of the clerks spoke slightingly of the Liverpool councillors John and Bessie Braddock, and John, stamping envelopes at a table nearby, immediately joined in.

'They're good people,' he said angrily. 'They've left the Communist Party now, and they only joined because they were banging their heads against a brick wall trying to get something done for the poor under the present system.'

'If people are poor it's their own fault,' one man said. 'They don't want to work.'

'That's ridiculous,' John flared. 'Listen, there are sixty thousand men out of work in Liverpool. Are you saying they're all shirkers? A shop owner said that in the Council and someone put a hoax notice in the paper that there were two vacancies in his shop. The police had to be called to clear the queues of people applying for the jobs. The street was full and customers couldn't get into his shop so he published a retraction.'

'That's enough,' the senior clerk said angrily. 'We don't want that sort of talk in this office. Get on with your work and keep your mouth shut. You've got too much to say for an office boy.'

John had to comply and although his grandfather told him he should stand up for what he thought was right, his mother and grandmother both warned him that he could lose his job if he was not more careful.

John tried to be more restrained but his fiery temper often landed him in hot water with his superiors and made him some enemies among the snobbish clerks. He told himself that it was a job at least and he must stick it out, but the only compensation for him was when he handed his wage packet to his mother each week.

She always told him how much it helped her although John knew that when she had given him a shilling for his pocket money and money for his lunch there was little left. He said this to her one day but she told him that it paid for something extra every week.

'I bought shoes for Mick last week,' she said. 'You know what a problem his shoes are usually.'

It was true that Mick's shoes were a constant worry to her. 'You use up as many pairs as if you were a centipede,' she scolded him. 'If you don't try to be more careful, I'll make you go to school in clogs.'

But neither scolding nor coaxing could make Mick alter his ways. He sailed happily through his days, oblivious to warnings. He had shown a flair for arithmetic and as his English was also good he was usually top of his class although he never seemed to work hard. Most of his spare time now was spent playing football in the park, and on alternate Saturday afternoons he went to stand in the Boys' Pen and watch Everton Football Club.

'At least it's safer than climbing on roofs,' Greg said, but to Cathy Mick seemed as boisterous and adventurous as ever, and his clothes and shoes suffered accordingly.

Cathy seemed to have few worries as the summer of 1932 approached. Her father had at last thrown off the effects of the shingles and had suffered only one bout of bronchitis the previous winter. She was enjoying her nights at the Grafton and her job as a part-time waitress, and all her children seemed happy.

Josh Adamsom was still paying for Kate's tap dancing lessons, and she was making good progress. Sally went every week now to the cinema with Peggy Burns, and copied Shirley Temple's dresses for Kate.

'I think Kate's growing more like your Mary in features, although her eyes are brown,' Josie said to Cathy. 'And she keeps her clothes clean like your Mary used to, didn't she?'

'Yes. Mam says even when times were bad for us and Mary had to go to school in patched clothes, she always made sure her hair was just so,' Cathy said. 'Sarah's more like us. Remember how we used to get our knees black, Jose, kneeling on the flags playing cherry wobs or jacks and ollies?'

They laughed together at the memory, then Josie said with a sigh, 'Sometimes I wish those days were back, when we had nothing to worry us.'

'Yes, but we still had the war years to face,' Cathy said. 'I wouldn't want to go through that again, and we were lucky. Our fellows came back all right.'

'Yes, and we've both got healthy kids,' Josie said. 'We've got a lot to be thankful for. When you think of poor Mrs Moore . . . she lost three before they were five years old. And Mrs Riley – she says she'll never get over losing Frances just before her eighteenth birthday.'

'Don't,' Cathy said with a shudder. 'I can't bear the thought of losing any of mine.'

'Yes, we're getting morbid,' said Josie. 'But, listen, is it true the girl from Elsie Hammond's shop has gone in a sanitorium?'

'Yes, poor Celia, but it might give her a chance,' Cathy said. 'Sarah says Elsie's taken on another girl on trial, but Sarah doesn't like her. She doesn't think Elsie'll keep her on because she's slapdash.'

'Pity Sarah's not just a bit older. It won't be long though, Cath, will it, before she's ready for the shop?'

'Eighteen months,' Cathy said. 'She says she can't wait.'

'It's strange, you know,' Josie said, 'when you look round the kids and see family likenesses coming out. Kate's like your Mary, and Sarah's like your mam, and our Edie's like our Mary – like she used to be before she went so bitter.'

'And your little Alice is like you,' Cathy said. 'And our John is the image of Greg.'

'Like Greg? I don't think so!' Josie exclaimed. 'I think they're completely different.'

'But, Josie, his hair and his grey eyes are like Greg's and he's as tall, although John *has* got a heavier build now.'

'Yes, but in other ways, Cath – in character, for instance. Greg is so quiet and reserved, he'd never push himself forward, while John is so – so self-confident. Nothing shy or diffident about John! Walter says Greg is a gentleman in every sense of the word.'

'And John's not, you mean?' Cathy said.

'I didn't say that. They're just different,' Josie said hastily. 'As long as none of mine turns out like my mam, I'll be satisfied. They say a person's character shows in their face, don't they? And just look at my mam!'

Later, while Cathy was ironing, she pondered on Josie's words, especially about the difference between Greg and John and about character showing in the face.

Greg was sitting reading and John was writing something in a notebook. She compared their faces. It's John's that has changed, she thought. Greg's thin sensitive face was the same as when she had first met him, and his sudden, sweet smile still had the power to make her feel weak with love. But Josie was right, John's features were entirely different although he had the same unruly dark hair and grey eyes as Greg, and even the same cleft in the chin.

She'd never noticed it before, Cathy marvelled, yet John's headstrong, reckless nature showed in the thrust of his jaw and the stubborn set of his lips.

But then, she told herself quickly, he's just impulsive and it's natural for a young man. Maybe Greg's *too* quiet and diffident. It doesn't mean that there's anything wrong with either of them, she thought, and at least now there's peace between them.

But she soon found that it was a fragile peace. The fire that had burned between them was not out but only damped down, and speedily flared up again.

Chapter Thirteen

Sarah was the innocent cause of the row between Greg and John. She had a school friend whose family shared a house in Plumpton Street with another two families. Maisie Doyle's family lived in the basement kitchen and had two bedrooms in the basement. All the family were unhealthy. When Sarah went down the basement steps to call for Maisie she hated to be asked into the kitchen to wait for her, especially in the summer.

A thickly encrusted fly paper hung in the window, and more flies crawled on the American cloth covering the table and swarmed round the open tin of condensed milk which stood on it. The room was crowded with furniture, including a large dresser with a carved eagle above it. Maisie's sister's hat and various caps hung on its outspread wings.

One day when Sarah was there, Vera Doyle took down her hat then flung it away from her with a scream as a large cockroach scuttled from within it.

Mrs Doyle was a pale, exhausted-looking woman who seemed to be in constant pain, and one boy of the family was in Alder Hey Hospital with a suspected tubercular spine while another had been sent to Heswell Children's Hospital on Miss Margaret Beaven's recommendation.

One night when Sarah was at home with her mother and father and John, she remarked that Mr Doyle said that the reason the family got sick was because they lived in the cellar kitchen.

'He says germs fall out of the air, and with them living below ground all the germs go in their kitchen.'

'Rubbish!' John exclaimed roughly. 'The man's a fool.'

'Don't speak like that about your elders,' Greg said sharply.

John laughed scornfully. 'Germs falling from the air – did you ever hear anything so stupid?'

149

Before her father could speak, Sarah said quickly, 'Mrs Doyle went to Copperas Hill to ask the people there to speak for them for a corporation house, and she told them what Mr Doyle had said about the germs. He told her to, but she said they all laughed. Mr Doyle said, "They can laugh their B legs off as long as they get us a house!" And I think they might be getting one.'

'So, the man's not such a fool, is he?' Greg said tauntingly to John. 'He's a lot smarter than a know-all like you, evidently.'

'I don't call that smart – making yourself look a fool to get something you should have anyway. I'd be ashamed to degrade myself like that.'

'That's not degrading yourself. I admire a man who'll go to those lengths to get a better home for his wife and family, and so would anybody with any sense. But of course you're like the smart guys in Copperas Hill who laughed and felt superior and didn't see that he was outsmarting them,' Greg said with contempt.

'I'm talking about a man having to sacrifice his principles,' John said angrily. 'But I wouldn't expect *you* to know what I'm talking about.'

Sarah and Cathy stood silent with shock, Sarah at the effect of her innocent words and Cathy at the suddenness and venom of the quarrel.

Greg and John were both on their feet now, breathing heavily. At John's last words Greg made a lunge towards him with his arm raised. Cathy stepped swiftly between them.

'Greg, John!' she said in horrified tones, then burst into tears and sank on to a chair by the table with her face in her hands.

Sarah plunged to her side and put an arm round her. 'Now look what you've done!' she cried. John snatched up his jacket and dashed out of the house and Greg went to put his arm around Cathy, who shook it away.

'I'm sick of it, sick of it,' she wept. 'I thought all that nonsense was finished.'

'I'm sorry —' Greg began, but she interrupted him.

'And so you should be! You started that.'

'*I* did?' he exclaimed. 'I suppose you think your precious son should air his views about everything and no one must correct him?' Sarah looked from one to the other of their furious faces.

'Would you like a cup of tea?' she said desperately but they ignored her. She went into the back kitchen anyway, but she could still hear them. Her mother seemed to have forgotten her tears and was saying angrily, 'Of course John can't do anything right as far as you're concerned, and don't think I don't know why.'

'And what does that mean?' Greg demanded. 'I know you've got some bee in your bonnet about him and I'd like to know what it is.'

'It's because I brought him up on my own while you were in the Army, and of course you could see all the things I'd done wrong while I didn't have a clever fellow like you to tell me what to do,' Cathy sneered. 'You started finding fault with him as soon as you came home and you've never stopped.'

Greg's face was white and he sat down as though he had received a blow. His anger seemed to have gone, driven away by the shock of her words.

'You can't mean that, Cathy,' he said. 'You're saying it because you're in a temper, but you can't believe it.'

'I do believe it,' she cried. 'You think Mam and Dad and I spoiled him. You never loved him like you loved the others.'

'You think that of me?' Greg said in a dazed voice. 'That I could be so petty and small-minded? That I could love him less . . .' Sarah could see his face as she stood near the door and tears spilled down her cheeks at his expression. She longed to go to him, to put her arms around him and blot out her mother's voice. How could she say such things?

Cathy had raised her head. She looked at Greg's stunned expression. 'There's no need to look so shocked,' she said. 'You've said yourself he's been spoiled and that Dad is a bad influence on him.'

'I didn't say he was a bad influence – I said he didn't allow for John's being so reckless and headstrong. I know your father would teach him nothing but good principles, but John distorts what he's told and goes overboard about everything.'

Cathy was silent, recognizing the truth of what he said

and already regretting some of her remarks.

Greg went on, 'I do think he's spoiled, and I can take the blame for that partly. I should have been firmer with him but – I was afraid to annoy you, I suppose.' Suddenly the gas went out with a plop. Sarah had slipped out of the back door a few seconds earlier and for a moment they sat in the faint light of the fire. Then Cathy stood up.

She had intended to go to put a coin in the meter but had heard the hurt in Greg's voice and instead went to sit beside him on the sofa and put her arms round him. 'Greg, I'm sorry. I shouldn't have said all that.'

He held her close. 'No, Cath, I'm to blame. We should have had this conversation a long time ago.'

'No, it was only a vague idea. It sounded worse than it was when I put it into words. That sounds muddled, but you know what I mean.'

'I do,' he said. They both found it easier to talk freely in the half light.

Cathy said quietly, 'If I face facts, Greg, I *have* always been on the defensive about John, resenting it if you criticized him.'

He kissed her gently. 'And if I face facts, I've got to admit it's not true that I didn't check John for fear of vexing you. It was a much meaner reason, I can see now. I wanted him to love me more than he loved Lawrie.'

'Oh, Greg, he loves both of you,' Cathy said.

'I'm not proud of myself for it, Cath, but it's the truth. That's the real reason I drew back from chastising him, and now we're seeing the fruit of it.'

'I don't think we've anything really to worry about,' Cathy said quietly. 'I don't think there's anything wrong with John that time won't cure.'

'That's true,' he agreed. 'You can't put an old head on young shoulders. What's that quotation? "When a man's sixteen he thinks he knows everything, and when he's thirty he realizes he knows nothing." We'll have to remember that when we're dealing with John.'

The front door crashed back against the wall and they heard Mick's loud voice. 'What's up? Haven't you got a penny for the gas?'

Cathy hastily drew away from Greg and he stood up.

'We were waiting for you to provide it,' he said as Mick appeared in the doorway. The boy grinned.

'Hard lines,' he said cheerfully. 'You'll have to stay in the dark.'

'There's a penny on top of the meter,' Greg said. 'Put it in, Mick, while I light the gas.' He stood in the centre of the kitchen beneath the light fitting, and when the penny had been inserted and the gas came through he lit the gas mantle.

The light dazzled their eyes for a moment. Cathy quickly turned her tear-stained faced away from Mick, but he seemed to notice nothing.

'It was the gear in the club tonight,' he said. 'I won the darts then I won the table tennis match. I saw our John in the gym.' He laughed. 'He wasn't half battering at the punch bag! Good job it wasn't somebody's head.' He went through to the lavatory in the back yard, whistling cheerfully, and Cathy and Greg exchanged a look of relief.

'I'm glad to know where he is,' she said. 'I was worried about him.'

'Thank God for the Boys' Club,' Greg agreed. 'He can work his temper off there.'

Mick had come back and was washing his hands at the sink as Cathy prepared supper. 'No need to drown everyone, Mick,' she exclaimed as he splashed water in all directions, but she looked at him with affection. Thank God for Mick, too, she thought, cheerful uncomplicated Mick. I'm sick of all these complicated people – and yet, perhaps there were hidden depths in Mick too. She would not have suspected that at this stage of their lives she would discover unknown depths in Greg. And in myself too, she admitted honestly, so I can't be sure about Mick.

All the family except Cathy were in bed when John arrived home. She made no reference to what had happened earlier, and neither did John. He seemed a different person, warm and affectionate as he always was with his mother, gently teasing her when he opened a cupboard and several items fell out.

'Didn't you win a prize once for a slogan about tidiness, Mam?'

'I think I won it under false pretences,' she laughed. If only he was always like this, she thought, remembering the surly aggressive boy of a few hours earlier. He'll grow out of these moods though, she told herself with her usual optimism.

Cathy watched her husband and elder son closely during the following weeks and could see that Greg often ignored behaviour by John that could easily have led to a row between them. She realized that Greg was prepared to let some things pass until John learned more sense, and was relieved.

John had managed to avoid his father for a few days after the quarrel about the Doyles, but on the Saturday he was in the kitchen when Greg came downstairs wearing his St Johns Ambulance uniform. He was on duty at the Everton Football Ground and Mick was delighted. 'Hey, Dad, will you look up at the Boys' Pen and wave to me?' he said excitedly.

John looked his father up and down, making no attempt to hide the sneer on his face, but Greg blandly ignored him and smiled at Mick.

'I will, son,' he said. 'And if Everton score, I'll wave twice.'

'They're bound to,' Mick boasted. John would normally have argued with Mick about football, but he turned his head away and took no part in the conversation.

After several attempts to provoke Greg failed, John seemed to realize that his father's attitude was a deliberate ploy and stopped trying to aggravate him.

Occasionally he tried to talk to Mick about politics or the causes he found so interesting, but his brother only grinned. They were in their bedroom one day arguing on the subject when Mick said airily, 'Why worry? All be the same in a hundred years.'

'Yes, it will, if everyone is as selfish as you,' John said in exasperation. 'We should be fighting to make things better for everyone one day, a more equal sharing of the country's wealth.'

Mick only smiled and took a copy of the *Magnet* from beneath his pillow.

'Hey, that's mine, you little turd!' John exclaimed. 'Give it here.' Mick held on to the comic so tightly that it would have been torn if John had tried to pull it away, so he cuffed Mick's head instead. 'Give it here,' he said again.

'Thought you believed in sharing everything,' Mick said cheekily. 'Different when *you've* got to part with something, isn't it?' He suddenly ducked under John's arm and clattered away down the stairs, laughing merrily.

John was fuming, but suddenly he was struck by the justice of his brother's remark and found himself laughing at Mick's cheek.

John tried to arouse Sarah's enthusiasm for his views but she only quoted her grandmother's remark about doing what was next to hand. 'Grandma does that,' she said. 'She helps anybody who needs it. She looks after people when they're sick, and helps people with food and clothes, and looks after families when their mam's sick.'

'That's all right for old people,' John said in unconscious imitation of his mother's response to Sally's views many years before. '*We* should be getting things done, young people like us.'

'Mam always says life will be better when Parliament passes the Family Allowance Bill,' Sarah said.

'But it's only scratching at the problems, not getting to the root of them,' John cried. She stubbornly refused to be convinced.

Christmas 1932 was happy for all the family. For several weeks before Christmas Cathy received at least three "Please be at's" each week, and the extra money provided more food and treats for everyone. She helped Kate make three handkerchiefs for Josh and embroider them with his initial, and the old man was delighted.

John had saved from his pocket money to buy gifts for all the family. A doll in a bath for Kate, a puzzle for Mick, a tiny bottle of scent for Sarah, and five De Reske Minor cigarettes for his father. For his mother he had been paying coppers every week at Clarkson's for a large glittering brooch that cost two shillings. A book for his grandfather and sweets for his grandmother completed his purchases, and he looked forward eagerly to distributing his gifts on Christmas Day.

Sarah had also managed to buy small gifts, mostly sweets, from her pocket money of twopence a week and coppers she had been given for running messages or by her grandma. But she said wistfully to John. 'I wish I could buy proper presents. I can't wait till I leave school this time next year.'

'Don't be in too much of a hurry,' he advised. 'Make the most of this year, Sar. I often wish I was back at school.'

'Yes, but you don't like the office. I'm dying to work at Elsie's.'

Sally and Lawrie were happy because a long letter had arrived from Mary and Sam, with photographs of a luxurious house.

'It's like that feature film me and Peggy saw at the Majestic about film stars' houses,' Sally said.

'Mary sounds made up with the weather there,' Lawrie said. 'And she says the house has all sorts of gadgets.'

'And Sam's working hard,' Sally said. 'He must be to have them back on their feet so quickly.'

'He certainly must, and seeing something for it,' Greg agreed as he looked at the photographs of the house and of Mary lounging on the beach. He sighed.

'I think it's a place where you're right up or right down, lad,' Lawrie said. 'I think we're better off on the middle road, Greg.' He looked at his father-in-law with deep affection.

'Yes, Liverpool suits me,' Cathy agreed. 'I'm glad they're doing so well, but I wouldn't want to change places with them.' She smiled at Greg and he bent and gave her a swift kiss.

Although John had made no friends in the office, he had made many among the office boys who thronged the top floor of Harry Petty's dining room, and had asked them to tell him if they heard of a vacancy anywhere. Early in January one of the boys told him that there would shortly be a vacancy for a junior clerk in the shipping office on the floor below his present employers.

'I'd apply for it myself,' he said, 'but I've got the chance to go into a bicycle shop as a trainee repairer, and that's what I want to do. It's the coming thing. I'll learn to repair motor cars too.'

John immediately applied for the position and was taken on at a wage of twelve shillings a week.

He heard later that his reference from the fruit importer's office was so bad that his new employers suspected that they were unwilling to lose him, so the spitefulness of the senior clerk misfired.

John settled very happily into his new job. He found the work interesting and liked the young men he worked with. Their work often concerned the destination of ships and Lawrie was interested in hearing about it.

'I knew all those ports when I was a seaman,' he told John. 'Mind you, that's all you see of a country when you're a seaman – the ports. I often thought I'd like to get to know the countries, but still – I have through these.' He nodded at the books in the bookcase Greg had made for him.

Most of the books reflected Lawrie's interest in politics and he and John still held discussions on the state of the country, although with less hope than they had previously felt.

'1931 was the watershed, lad,' Lawrie said bitterly. 'The bankers caused that crisis and the government could have sorted it out, but they panicked. Montagu Norman wanting to print ration books in case we had to go back to barter – that's the kind of cool head we had to depend on! Talk like that from the Governor of the Bank of England!'

'Was that because they thought we'd be like Germany, taking wages home in handcarts because money had lost its value?' John asked.

'There's no comparison,' Lawrie said. 'Prices are falling here, not rising like in Germany. And we've got gold in the Bank of England, too.'

'I get fed up sometimes, Grandad,' John said. 'All the talk, but it gets us nowhere. The only real power is with the government.'

'That's true, lad, and that's why I had such hopes of working men in Parliament, a Labour Government. But this so-called crisis – you see what happens. The first thing Parliament thinks of is cuts in unemployment benefit, then cuts in wages.'

'But didn't nine Labour members resign rather than pass them? That's what I heard.'

'And what good did it do? It only brought them down,' Lawrie said. 'And now we've got this National Government, but you notice Ramsey Mac didn't lose his job? Oh, no, he's still Prime Minister, and creeping round the Opposition. That's what makes me lose heart, John, seeing men I've respected looking after number one and to hell with their mates. But I don't want to discourage you, lad. There's plenty of good men too, like Henderson and Clynes.'

They were interrupted by Sally who came in from visiting a sick neighbour. Lawrie winked at John and changed the subject. Sally had only come back for a blanket and when she had gone again, he said quietly, 'I often wish I'd done more – fought harder, you know, John. But when you've got children and a wife to think about, they've got to come first. I remember a lad I worked with when your Aunt Mary was a baby, and I was in a grain warehouse. We wanted to start a union and he said to me he could speak up because he'd given no hostages to fortune. Poor fellow, he was knifed when he was trying to save young lads from going on board ships, but I often think of his words.'

Greg filled in the forms that Mick brought home for the entrance for the scholarship but no one expected him to pass. There was general amazement when he was awarded a place in the College, but Mick took it very calmly.

Cathy was determined that there would be no distinction made between her children, so as when John passed the scholarship there was a family gathering at her parents' house to celebrate Mick's success.

'We're proud of you, lad,' his grandfather told him, and as with John gave him one of his treasured books, suitably inscribed, before they all drank to his success.

'Have you any idea what you want to be?' Josh asked him.

Mick shook his head. 'I'll have to think about it,' he said.

Lawrie laughed heartily. 'I tell you what, the College don't know what they've got in store for them.'

Josh had given Mick half a crown and he was obviously impatient to be off, John and Sarah both wanted to see friends, so the three young people went out together.

'I got the shock of my life when he walked in with the envelope,' Cathy said. 'Not a feather out of him, and when you think how excited we were about John!'

'The first one's always the most exciting,' Sally said.

'Yes, but I'm sure he hasn't done any extra studying,' Cathy said. 'If he had any homework, I never saw him do it. He always said he hadn't got any if we asked him. I think you're right about the College, Dad. I can see us being sent for every five minutes when he starts his capers there.'

'Now don't cross your bridges before you come to them,' Sally said. 'He'll settle down all right.'

'Yes, remember him in hospital?' Greg said. 'You'd think he'd spent half his life there, yet he'd never even seen a doctor before that.'

'I've warned him the grant will only cover one outfit, so if he loses his blazer or cap or tie he'll have to take the consequences,' Cathy said. 'But I don't think he was even listening to me.'

She glanced at the clock. 'I'd better get back. I've got a lot of ironing to do.'

'And I'd better go down to Hammond's. I told Elsie I'd sit with her mother for a while because she's got to go down to the shop.'

'How is she? Mrs Hammond, I mean.'

Sally shook her head and sighed. 'Not well at all, poor soul. I know she's been ill off and on for years but this is different somehow. She's gone away to a shadow.'

'Sarah says Elsie's gone very moody,' Cathy said. 'But I suppose she's got a lot on her mind with her mother so bad. Sarah said Elsie has to keep nipping out of the shop for things or to run home to see her mother, and she asked if she could get Elsie's messages for her. She said Elsie nearly bit her head off.'

They had left the house and Cathy walked with her mother to the Hammonds' house. 'I've told Sarah she mustn't take offence if Elsie shouts at her.'

'No. God help her, poor Elsie's got a lot of worry and no one to share it.'

'Poor Mrs Hammond was very low in spirits last night,' Sally told Cathy the following day. 'She seems to have no will to live. In fact, she said as much to me. I tried to cheer her up but she said, "No, I'll be glad to go from this vale of sorrows." She seems to have turned against Elsie, saying she's brought her nothing but grief and worry.'

'What a shame. Poor Elsie. She's always been such a good daughter.'

'Yes, but people go like that sometimes near the end. I've seen it before and I said to Elsie on the quiet, "If your mam says anything that upsets you, don't take any notice. It's the illness that's causing it." '

159

'Did she know about it? I mean, does Mrs Hammond talk like that to Elsie herself?'

'I don't know. I see what Sarah means though. Elsie turned on me quite sharp, wanting to know exactly what her mother had said. I felt as if I was in the witness box, but I put her mind at rest. I told her the way my poor father went, even using bad language which he'd never have used in his right mind, and turning against your dad who'd been so good to him. Your dad said it was the illness had twisted his mind and I wasn't to worry about it, and I think that comforted Elsie.'

Less than a week later Mrs Hammond died quietly in her sleep, but Cathy was far more distressed to hear of the death of Freda's mother. When she was widowed Freda went to live with her mother, and her unmarried sister went to live with another relative in the street so that Freda could have her children living with her.

This arrangement had done much to comfort Freda. It had also helped her financially. Her widow's pension was ten shillings, with three shillings for each of her five children, and if she had remained in her own house she would have needed to go on the parish.

Moving to her mother's house saved her from that degradation, which she later told Cathy would have been the last straw. Her mother had a pension of ten shillings a week from the brewery where her husband had worked before his death in an accident, and a bachelor son who worked in Lancaster sent her a further ten shillings a week, so with pooled resources they could manage.

It was better for the children, too. In their grandmother's house they were at the centre of a close, loving family life which went a long way towards compensating them for their father's death.

Cathy went to see Freda as soon as she heard the news. There were several women sitting with her, and Freda introduced them as her sisters or sisters-in-law. They all wore black, and their pale faces and eyes red with weeping showed that old Mrs Clancy was sincerely mourned.

Cathy was given a glass of port wine and a piece of fruit cake then taken upstairs by Freda to see Mrs Clancy in her coffin.

White sheets were hung round the walls, covering pictures, and candles and flowers stood on a small table. Mrs Clancy looked dignified and peaceful, and Cathy exclaimed, 'I never realized! You're so like her, Freda.'

'I hope I'll be as good a woman as she was,' Freda said with a sigh. 'And that people will be as sorry when I die. Everyone loved Mam.'

Her tears fell and Cathy put her arm round her.

'Never mind. She went quickly, and that's always better for the one who goes although it's harder for those who are left.'

'I don't know what I'd have done without her when Les died,' Freda wept. 'No one knows. We could always come to Mam. Anything from a splinter in your finger to trouble like mine, she could always make it better.' Cathy wept with her, in sorrow for Freda and her mother, and in terror as she imagined her own mother being lost to her.

Downstairs again Cathy was more practical and offered to look after Freda's children and any others whose mothers would be attending the funeral.

'That'd be a great help,' one of the other women said. 'With us all being related, like, and all at the funeral.'

It was speedily arranged and Cathy left, glancing down Norris Street as she passed. Mrs Parker was at her door as usual and Cathy wondered how many would grieve for *her* when her time came.

She told her mother of the sad scenes in the Clancy house, and added how she felt about Mrs Parker. 'It seems hard that someone like Mrs Clancy must die and someone like Mrs Parker be left.'

'Aye, God's ways are not our ways,' Sally agreed. 'As Mrs Mal used to say, everything that happens is part of a plan. What will Freda do now?'

'I don't know, Mam. It didn't seem the time to ask.'

Eleven children came to stay with Cathy on the day of the funeral. Fortunately it was a fine day and Sally helped her to pack a basket with sandwiches and cake, a can of tea and bottles of lemonade. She also took bats and balls, and they all had a happy day in Newsham Park.

In the middle of a game of rounders, Freda's eldest girl suddenly said to Cathy, 'Should we be laughing, Mrs

Redmond, when our nin is being buried?'

Cathy hugged her. 'What do you think your nin would want, love?' she said gently. 'She always loved to see you enjoying yourselves, didn't she?'

The child nodded and carried on with the game, and Cathy watched her sympathetically. That child, Daisy, would be a comfort to Freda, she thought.

Mrs Hammond's funeral had been a much quieter affair. Apart from Elsie, the only mourners had been an elderly cousin and neighbours, and after the funeral breakfast Elsie said that she would prefer to be alone to mourn her mother. Well-meant offers to stay with her or to send a daughter to sleep in the house with her were brusquely refused and were not repeated by her affronted neighbours.

Sarah still went to the shop and sometimes Elsie seemed quite happy and pleased to have her help, she told Cathy, but at others she was very short-tempered.

'I hope she's not going to be like that when I'm working there, Mam,' Sarah said. 'I'd still like to work there but it was nicer the way Elsie was before.'

'Bereavement takes people different ways,' Cathy said. 'She'll have got over it a bit by the time you go there at Christmas.'

'Only six months now until I leave school and start work,' Sarah said happily.

'Don't be wishing your life away,' Cathy warned. 'And when your summer holiday starts next week, make the most of it. It's the last long holiday you'll have, don't forget.'

Chapter Fourteen

John tried to warn Mick what to expect at the College but his brother was unperturbed.

'I'm just trying to prepare you,' John said. 'I got a hell of a shock when I found out how much homework I was expected to do.'

'I'll just do as much as I can,' Mick said airily.

'Then you'd better harden the palms of your hands,' John said. 'I got plenty of punishments and I was *trying* to do it.'

Later John told Cathy that he had wasted his time trying to advise Mick.

'He just doesn't give a damn, Mam,' he said. 'I wish I could be like that.'

'The calm way he took winning the scholarship!' Cathy said. 'He was far more excited when Everton brought the Cup home.'

'I was excited myself,' John said. 'What a day! I've never seen such crowds, and everyone feeling ten feet high. It was the gear.'

'Well, you've done your best to tell him what to expect, John,' his mother said. 'We'll have to wait and see. He'll probably fall on his feet. He usually does.'

Cathy went again to see Freda and to take some of Kate's outgrown clothes for her youngest child. She found her friend still sad but busy reorganizing the bedrooms. The unmarried sister who had moved out to make room for Freda and her children was going to come back there to live.

'Our Margaret was awful good moving out for us, you know, Cath,' Freda said. 'She had her own bedroom here and everything lovely in it, but she never hesitated. She arranged to go to our Clara's although she knew she'd have to share a bedroom with the girls.' She sighed. 'I wish there was a different reason for her coming back.'

'Still, it means you'll be able to manage, doesn't it?' Cathy said. 'And you get on well with Margaret. Will Clara mind?'

'No. It was a crush for them with Margie there, but Clara's husband's the only one working so that was the only place she could go.'

'But why—?' Cathy began.

Freda lowered her voice. 'Because the others are on the parish. They all worked at Allen's, you see, so when Allen's closed down the five of them went on the dole at once. Only Clara's husband got another job. The dole finished for the others and they had to go on the parish. They'd lose it if Margie lived there.'

'I didn't know,' Cathy said. 'But there's plenty in the same boat, aren't there? Peggy Burns was crying in Mam's one night about what her daughters have had to put up with. Pawning or selling everything, and snoopers coming round all the time. One fellow even told Peggy's daughter she had to sell her plant stand and aspidistra or lose her benefit, because it was a luxury.'

'I could tell you some tales of what ours have had to put up with,' Freda said. 'They even came here in case my sisters had hidden anything. Mam was quiet but she sent *them* off with a flea in their ears. Told them it was a pity our lads killed Germans in the war because the Germans sounded more decent than they were.'

Cathy walked home, thinking how fortunate she was in comparison with others. Her husband and son both working, a job promised to Sarah, and even being able to bring money into the house herself with her waiting-on job which she enjoyed.

She had begun to save a little. At first she had a pot on the mantelpiece like her mother's handleless teapot in which she had saved for so many years, but Cathy was not as strong-minded as her mother and as soon as the money mounted a little she took some of it for something which seemed absolutely essential at the time.

'I'm hopeless, Mam,' she told Sally. 'If the money wasn't there, I know I'd manage without it but while it is—' she shrugged.

'Then give it to me and I'll save it for you,' her mother

said. 'But I warn you, I won't give it to you until Christmas or whatever you're saving for.'

Cathy was delighted with the arrangement and now every Saturday morning she gave her mother three shillings to save for her. Without telling anybody she also saved a shilling out of every four she received for a job, and so far she had resisted the temptation to use the money.

I feel almost ashamed that everything is going so well for me, she thought. Dad seems so much better, and Greg and I have such a good life with the dances and everything. No trouble between him and John now either. She touched the wood of a doorpost superstitiously.

When she reached home Sarah was back from school and told her excitedly that the Doyles now had a new house.

'It's not far from Alder Hey Hospital where their Martin is,' Sarah said. 'Maisie says it's lovely. There's a big garden, and a bathroom and lavvie upstairs, and three big bedrooms. The garden's at the front and the back. They went to see it on Sunday and they're moving on Saturday.'

'I'm very glad,' Cathy said. 'Poor Mrs Doyle, it's been a struggle for her trying to bring up a healthy family, but they should all be better now. Imagine, a bathroom and lavatory upstairs.'

Sarah went less often to the florist's shop now, partly because she heeded her mother's words about enjoying her last long holiday and partly because Elsie was still so moody.

Twice she took the tram out to Dovecote where the Doyles' new house was situated. She came home impressed and envious. 'It's *lovely*, Mam,' she said. 'You should see the gardens. They've got grass and flowers round it in the front, and Mr Doyle's growing vegetables in the back.'

'What's the house like?'

'It's lovely too. There's a big room with a bay window and cupboards and shelves in the corner. The grate isn't like this. It's black with an oven beside the fire, but it's flat on top and there's little lids that you lift out to put pans on, and a kind of rail thing over it where Mrs Doyle warms the nightdresses and other clothes. There's a *gas* boiler there for boiling the clothes too, and Mrs Doyle said they dry in no time, hanging out in the back garden.'

The first time Sarah had been unable to see the bathrooom as Vera was having a bath, but after her second visit she came home ecstatic.

'I had a bath, Mam,' she said. 'Maisie filled the bath right up and pinched some of their Vera's bath salts for me. It was yummy.'

'Did Mrs Doyle know?' Cathy exclaimed.

'Yes. She said it was about the first time this week the bath had been empty so I was in luck. She said their family had never been so clean, and their Vera'd wash herself away if she wasn't careful.'

'I suppose you'd like to live there?'

'No. I'd like the bath and the garden but I wouldn't like to be so far away from Grandma and Grandad,' Sarah said.

Cathy hugged her. 'That's why I wouldn't like to move out there,' she said. 'And you'd be a long way away from Elsie's shop too.'

When John came in Sarah began to tell him about the Doyles' house, but his face clouded and she remembered the quarrel about them before and swiftly changed the subject.

John had so many interests now that politics and causes were taking a back seat to them although he still spent time with his grandfather and discussed with him the burning questions of the Means Test and the cuts in wages and benefits.

A new type of chocolate bar was in the shops, milk chocolate upon dark, and John sometimes thought that his mind was like that: the milk chocolate representing his membership of the Young Men's Club and his cycling and billiards playing, and the dark chocolate the bitter anger he felt at the injustice and misery he saw around him.

He rarely went to the open air meetings now as he felt helpless to do anything about the wrongs that were aired there.

The clerks he worked with were a light-hearted group and John was happy in the shipping office. The fruit importer's office had been in Mathew Street, a lane so narrow it was dark even on the brightest day. The shipping office was in Oldhall Street, wide and with solidly built offices with large windows, and the firm were good employers. There was great excitement in the office when the staff were told that senior clerks and those with over fifteen years' service were to be given a week's holiday with pay, and that the scheme might be extended to include those with less service at a later date.

'You see, things *are* getting better,' one of the clerks who knew John's views said to him.

'For some people,' he agreed.

A few weeks later he was walking through Dale Street when he met Gerry and Peter who had been in his form at school. They had stayed on to take the Higher School Certificate and John had not seen either of them since, but they seemed pleased to see him and they all went into Rigby's Pub for a drink.

'My brother Henry asked about you. He's home for the Long Vac,' Peter Vaughan said. 'You remember he met you when he was home from Cambridge some years ago? He wondered if you'd kept up your interest in politics.'

'I have,' John said, 'but it all seems a bit hopeless. My grandfather always pinned his hopes on working men in Parliament, but even he gets a bit discouraged. Do you think having Roosevelt as President of America will make any difference?'

'None,' Peter said decisively.

'But he seems to have a more open mind about the War Debt,' John argued.

'No, no. A corrupt Capitalist society —"Devil take the hindmost." "Brother, can you spare a dime?" That's America,' Peter said. His voice had risen, and Gerry nudged him.

The barman seemed to be watching them and Gerry said urgently, 'Drink up. Let's talk outside.' They left the pub and walked towards home.

'No use looking towards America, John,' Gerry said. 'Russia is the place. They threw off the shackles of centuries and so can we. It's the old men who hold us back.'

John was excited by the talk and eagerly agreed to go to a meeting at Gerry's house.

'Won't your father object?' John asked.

Gerry said bitterly, 'No, he doesn't care what I do. He has other interests.' And John said no more.

He dressed carefully in his best clothes to go to the meeting at the doctor's house, but found that the dozen or so young men there were dressed in a Bohemian fashion that made him feel out of place. Several of them were Cambridge undergraduates, friends of Peter's brother, but they made John welcome and he was flattered when they seemed to listen attentively to his views.

Always confident, John spoke freely about conditions in Liverpool and the state of local politics, but he soon realized that they were drawing him out to talk because he was so different from them.

His Liverpool accent was not strong, partly because since childhood he had unconsciously imitated his father's pleasant tones although he would hotly have denied this, but he became aware of the fact that his speech was very different to the drawling tones of the Varsity men, and fell silent.

He had just decided that he would never return when a maid appeared with coffee and sandwiches and the men broke into small groups. A friend of Henry Vaughan's, who had been introduced to John as Richard Allen, sat down beside him.

'I was interested in your comment that religion was the cause of division in Liverpool,' he said. 'Is sectarianism so rife?'

'It is indeed,' John said. 'It's what's holding back reforms that could give a lot of people a better life. My grandfather says that if only working people would stick together they could change their lives, but they'll never do it while they're fighting among themselves about religion.'

'Your grandfather sounds an intelligent man,' Richard Allen commented.

John's face coloured with pleasure and he said eagerly, 'He is. He can talk about anything, and he always talks sense.'

'What does he do?' asked Richard.

'He's a checker in a railway yard. His health isn't good now but he still does a lot to help people. He's treasurer of his union, and he writes letters for people and goes with them to see the relieving officer, or asks Councillors he knows to have cases reviewed.'

'Yes, I admire him for that, but it's only dealing with the effects of the system, isn't it? We need to get at the root cause.'

'My grandfather *has* dealt with the roots, and suffered for it,' John said, quick to resent any criticism of Lawrie, however mild. 'When he was a young man he tried to form a union in a warehouse where he worked, because the men were so badly treated. He got sacked for it.'

Henry Vaughan was lounging against the mantelpiece. Now he came over and gave Richard a warning glance. 'John's grandfather is one of the unsung heroes of the early days,' he said. 'They broke the ground for us.'

John turned to him gratefully. 'That's true,' he said. 'And he didn't just try to organize men and fight for better conditions. He took soup out with the Lee Jones for men sleeping rough. He's not a churchgoer but he worked with a clergyman running a shelter for destitute children, and mended boots for them. He's very tolerant as well as being a fighter.'

'That was right for his times, John, but tolerance isn't a virtue now. We're the new generation and we won't tolerate the old system.'

'It makes me mad,' John said, 'when I see women and children in Liverpool hungry and ragged because the men can't find work. And instead of offering sympathy and help, the government behaves as though poverty's a crime. As though the poor are to blame instead of being victims.'

'Hear, hear,' Gerry said. He came over to join their group. 'It's not only the government. You only have to open any newspaper to see some pot-bellied businessman saying the same thing. Did anyone see that cartoon about a man on relief lounging back with a cigar in his mouth, saying, "Why work?" My God, when you look round the queues four deep at such places, and their tatty clothes and broken boots.'

'Nothing will change under Capitalism,' Richard Allen declared. 'Communism is the answer. One for all and all for one. Sweep away the whole rotten system.' Again Henry Vaughan gave Richard a warning glance. There was a general shift round of the groups and John found himself standing by Peter.

'My brother says a lot of Varsity men feel as he does,' Peter said. 'They tried to help the hunger marchers, and some of them work in East End settlements in London in the Vac, and try to organize discussion groups there. Some of them belong to the Fabian Society but Henry says they're talkers not doers.'

John was sorry when the meeting ended. Henry Vaughan walked with him to the tram stop. 'I was very pleased to see you at the meeting,' he said. 'You and Gerry are what we need. Intelligent young men who know the local conditions.' The tram was approaching and Henry shook hands with John. 'I'll look forward to seeing you at the next,' he said.

John returned home feeling as though he was walking on air. To have made friends with a group like that, in sympathy with all he had discussed with his grandfather, was like finding a crock of gold.

He went straight up to his bedroom, refusing supper, to lie awake going over and over all that had happened that night, particularly Henry Vaughan's words to him at the tram stop.

It was obvious to the family that something had happened to him because he was so excited and happy during the following few days, but he said nothing about the meeting at home. He had no opportunity to speak privately to his grandfather and he was determined to say nothing to anyone else in case anything derogatory was said.

His mother and grandmother thought he had met a girl and waited for him to tell them about her, but they waited in vain.

Finally he was able to talk to his grandfather alone, but to his surprise Lawrie advised caution. 'You'll hear a lot of hot air from those fellers, lad. You say one of them was talking about Communism. I remember when you went there years ago there was someone running down the Jews in Germany. That sounds more like Mosley's lot to me. Listen and weigh them all up. Find out what they're up to before you say much there.'

For almost the first time John found himself thinking

that his grandfather was too old to understand. He was too naive to realize that the comments at the meeting had been intended to distance him from his grandfather's moderate views.

He realized that Lawrie must have mentioned the meeting to his mother when a few days later she said innocently, 'I didn't know you'd met Doctor Hanson's son again, John. He's still at school, isn't he?'

'Yes, he's taking the Higher School Cert,' John said gruffly.

Greg looked up. 'Was that where you went on Wednesday? To his house?'

'Yes. Why not?' John said insolently. 'We had a very interesting meeting.'

His father looked grim. 'No doubt you set the world to rights, but see that it remains just talk. Don't get involved in skirmishes with the police, breaking up meetings just because you don't agree with the speakers. I've heard of the activities of that group.'

'I don't believe it,' John said, jumping to his feet. 'They were nearly all Varsity men on their Long Vac.'

He felt very sophisticated and superior as he used these terms, but his father was unimpressed.

'I'm not going to dictate to you about your friends, John,' he said quietly. 'I just ask you to use your commonsense and not to get carried away by wild talk. And certainly don't get involved in any of these madcap schemes for going in gangs to break up meetings. You're supposed to believe in free speech, remember?'

'I'm going out,' John said, snatching up his cap. Cathy started forward but Greg shook his head at her.

'Let him go,' he said as the front door closed with a crash. 'Perhaps he'll walk off his temper and think about what I've said.'

'But are you sure it's true?' Cathy said. 'A respectable family like Doctor Hanson's.'

'That's the trouble, I'm afraid,' Greg said. 'Doctor Hanson is having an affair with another woman, and Mrs Hanson has left home. I don't blame his boy for kicking over the traces but I won't have John involved.'

The day after the argument with his father John spoke

about Gerry in the office and one of the other clerks told him about Doctor Hanson's affair. So that is how they're able to have the meetings, John thought, and felt self-conscious when he met Gerry as he walked home from the office.

To cover his confusion he asked about Richard Allen.

'He's a friend of Henry Vaughan's,' Gerry said. 'They were at Cambridge together, although Henry's left now and joined his father's firm. You know the Vaughans live on the Wirral now, and the firm is Vaughan and Hoslin's of Chester?'

'Did Henry want to do that? Is he happy there?' John asked.

'No, but his father insisted. Wouldn't let him stay on to do post-graduate work. Peter says Henry hates the office. His father's a terrific snob. He just wanted to be able to say he had a son at Cambridge – didn't care what Henry wanted to do really.' His face clouded and John guessed that Gerry was thinking of his own father and hastily changed the subject.

Later, when they parted, John walked along scowling. Fathers, he thought. They were all the same. Gerry's father embarrassing him by having an affair, Henry's father a snob, and his own father . . . Criticizing everything he did, yet doing nothing himself. Believing in the League of Nations and the Peace Pledge Union, and thinking that men in power were honestly trying to solve the problems of destitution. He was a fool, John decided.

He continued to go every Wednesday to Gerry's house but the Cambridge men had returned to the university and Henry Vaughan was not often there, so he found the meetings less exciting than the first one, although Henry continued to single him out when he did attend. John's interest in politics revived.

Lawrie rarely went to meetings now but John attended every one he could find time for. Every shade of opinion was aired by the soap box orators at the Pier Head, and John was always ready to put questions and to argue with the speakers. He joined a club whose banner read "Workers of the World, Unite", and where he often heard the phrase "The Brotherhood of Man".

John was now eighteen, tall and well built, with grey eyes, a cleft chin and thick dark hair. There were few girls in the shipping office but there were many working in the same building who were interested in him.

They contrived to leave the building at the same time as John, but he only greeted them cheerfully and strode away, his head too full of dreams of becoming an orator to leave any room for romance.

Chapter Fifteen

When Sarah returned to school after the summer holidays she went frequently to Elsie's shop but found her old friend's behaviour still very odd. Sometimes she would welcome Sarah and tell her to make a frame and deal with any customers who came in while she slipped out for a message, and at other times she would say brusquely that there was nothing for Sarah to do.

Nellie, the apprentice, told Sarah while Elsie was out one day that she was always bobbing in and out of the shop.

'She's turning away orders too,' Nellie said. 'And I can't do nothing right for her.' It was true that the shop, once filled with flowers for sale, and elaborate wreaths made to order, now looked quite bare.

'My mam says if she goes on turning people away they'll stop coming altogether,' Nellie said.

'Perhaps it's because she's so upset about losing her mother,' Sarah suggested, but Nellie was unconvinced.

'I think she was made up when her mam died,' she said. 'She seemed more excited than cut up about it.'

Their conversation ceased abruptly when Elsie returned. She breezed in, her eyes bright and cheeks pink. 'That's good, girls,' she exclaimed, looking at the frames they had made. 'That's enough for now.' She took two pennies from the drawer and gave them one each. 'Go and get an ice cream and then you can go home.'

The two girls ran through to Fusco's for the ice cream, both mystified at the sudden gift.

'I told you. You never know what's going to happen next with her,' Nellie said. 'And you never know when you're doing right. She's so up and down.'

Sarah told her mother what Nellie had said and about Elsie's strange behaviour. Cathy looked thoughtful but to

Sarah she said only that Elsie might be upset at the loss of her mother. Later to Greg, when she told him the tale, she said, 'I wonder if she's taken to drink? Going out low in spirits and coming back cheerful, the way Sarah described her today. It seems likely, doesn't it?'

He agreed and Cathy remarked, 'I hope it's just because she's grieving for her mother, and she gets over it before Sarah starts in the shop. I hope the shop doesn't go down too much either.'

'There's a few months yet before Sarah'll be going there,' Greg said. 'Elsie seems a sensible woman. I'm sure she'll pull herself together.'

A few days later Cathy went to her mother's house shortly after the children had left for school. They had started work on the brasses when there was a call from the lobby. It was Peggy Burns, calling, 'Sally, are you there?' in an excited voice. Before Cathy could open the door into the lobby, Peggy burst in.

'Sally, Cathy,' she said breathlessly, 'I've just been to the shop and they're all talking about it. Elsie Hammond's run off with Bella Menzie's husband.'

'*Elsie*?' Cathy exclaimed incredulously.

Sally said, 'Bella Menzies? Used to live in Aber Street? But they've got young children.'

'Five,' Peggy declared. 'The youngest two and a half and the eldest ten. Poor Bella's out of her mind.'

'I can't believe it,' Cathy exclaimed. 'Not Elsie. The fellow might have gone but it doesn't mean Elsie's gone with him. She might be ill in bed.' Or drunk, she thought to herself, but Peggy swept on.

'No, someone saw them at the station – Lime Street – last night, but not together. Never thought nothing of it at the time.'

'But is Bella sure?' Sally said. 'Elsie . . . a decent girl like that.' Her eyes were wide with shock and she sat down heavily. 'I thought I knew her. There with her when her mam was ill, and when she died –'

'That's all they've been waiting for, Bella says. For the old lady to die. She says it's gone on for over a year.'

'I can't believe *that*,' Cathy exclaimed.

Sally said quietly, 'But why hasn't Bella said something? How has it been kept quiet?'

'She says she didn't know about Elsie at first but about a year ago Luke started going funny with her, never speaking and coming home all hours from work. She thought he was gambling because he was always short of money, and then he started saying it wasn't right about the lads and girls sleeping together – they've only got two bedrooms – so he slept with the lads and she slept with the girls. She says she thought the kids were young for him to start fussing about them sleeping together, but she was glad because she didn't want no more. But now she can see his game.'

Peggy stopped for breath and Sally said in a low voice, 'God forgive her if it's true. To take a father from young children like them.'

'I don't think it is true,' Cathy declared. 'I think Bella Menzies is jumping to conclusions. Maybe her husband's scarpered but it doesn't mean Elsie's with him. *Someone* would have suspected something before now.' She suddenly thought of Elsie's strange behaviour and fell silent.

Her mother said quietly, 'Put the kettle on, Cath. Have a cup of tea, Peggy?'

She stood up. 'No thanks. I'll have to go back to the shop. I forgot to get my messages with the excitement.'

'She's afraid of missing something,' Cathy said as Peggy dashed away, but she spoke absently. She looked at her mother. The same thought was in both their minds. What about Sarah?

'Do you think it's true, Mam?' Cathy said. 'She *has* been acting queer lately.'

'I wouldn't have thought it of her,' Sally said. 'But Bella Menzies must have more to go on than them being seen at Lime Street. I know I should be thinking of Bella and her children, Cath, but it's Sarah I'm worrying about.'

'Me too,' Cathy said. 'But surely Elsie wouldn't let her down after promising so long ago?'

'If Bella's right, letting Sarah down will be the last thing Elsie's worrying about,' Sally said dryly. 'If she can take a father from his children—'

'I'm going to take a walk down to the shop,' Cathy said

decisively. 'It might all be just a rumour.'

'I'll come with you,' Sally said, and within a few minutes they were walking down Plumpton Street. It was a time when women would normally be busy indoors but little knots of them stood about, talking eagerly.

'It looks all too true,' Sally said, as they hurried along past the gossiping women until they reached the shop.

The door was closed and when they looked through the window they could see that there were no flowers, only a tea chest containing moss and wires and a few vases.

Mrs Gorman from the fruit shop next door came out.

'Hello, are you looking for Elsie?' she asked. 'She wasn't here yesterday either, and I'm told she's run off with a married man, a feller with five young children. Would you credit it? Mind you, she's been awful funny with people these last few weeks.' She came and stood beside them, looking through the shop window.

'She buys her flowers every morning, so there's no stock to worry about, only the moss for the frames, and it's a lock-up rented shop. I think we've seen the last of her,' Mrs Gorman said.

'What about Nellie the apprentice?' Cathy asked.

'She give her the sack the night before last,' Mrs Gorman said. 'I seen her going home crying. I'd heard things, mind you, but I never put two and two together. Our Jinny saw Elsie sloping through the back entries to Brunswick Road a couple of times, and I got told this morning the feller worked there.'

Cathy and Sally walked away from the shop, wondering how they would tell Sarah.

When she arrived home at lunch time it was clear by her white face that she had already heard the news. 'Never mind, love,' Cathy comforted her. 'You remember Mrs Malloy I often tell you about? She always used to say God never closes one door without He opens another, and it's true. Something else will turn up for you, pet.'

'No wonder Elsie was so queer lately,' Sarah said. 'I suppose it was a guilty conscience.' Cathy was not so sure but she only told Sarah about Nellie's being sacked.

'It could have been worse. You could have started work there,' she said.

A few weeks later Peggy told them that the Hammond house had been cleared. 'I seen the door open,' she said. 'So I went in because it might have been someone robbing the place.'

'Oh, Peggy,' Sally said, laughing. 'You went in to nose.'

'Anyway,' Peggy said, 'some fellers were packing things up and I said to them: "What are you doing with Miss Hammond's stuff?" They said it was all right then this posh feller come out of the parlour and told me Miss Hammond had instructed them to clear the house, so there was nothing for me to worry about. Did you ever hear the like? That wasn't no sudden thing, running off like that. She had it all planned, the crafty bitch.'

'Poor Mrs Hammond,' Sally said with a sigh. 'I can see now why she had no heart to live. She must have known what was going on.'

'Trust Peggy to go nosing in,' Cathy said when her mother told her what she had learnt. 'She's enjoying this. It's a bit of excitement, as far as she's concerned.'

'Don't begrudge it to her, love,' Sally said quietly. 'If it can take her mind off her worries.'

'Yes. I suppose you're right, Mam,' Cathy said, looking shamefaced.

Peggy had many worries. Several of her sons and sons-in-law were out of work and had been for some time. Michael, the only son still at home, had always been delicate, but in desperation had taken a job in a foundry. He came home every night exhausted by the long hours of work and the heat, and with small burns caused by the splashing of molten metal.

'I wouldn't let the wind blow on him when he was little,' Peggy mourned to Sally. 'This'll kill him but he's determined to keep the job. Mind you, our Robbie or Chrissie's husband would give their right arms for the chance of a job there, bad as it is.'

Chrissie came often to her mother's with her thin, poorly dressed children, and Peggy did her best to provide a good meal for them every time they came, and a parcel of food to take home. Although only in her thirties Chrissie, thin and haggard, looked more like a woman of fifty. She had two sets of twins and four other children. Sally bought clothes from the wardrobe dealer she had dealt with when Cathy's children were younger, and between them she and Cathy unpicked the clothes and made dresses for Chrissie's girls and trousers for the boys. Peggy paid two shillings a week clothing club for Chrissie to buy shoes for the family, but the money was unobtrusively given to Peggy by Sally.

Peggy herself had little money to spare. Her husband Jimmie worked in the same yard as Lawrie, but he had never given all of his wages to his wife as Lawrie had done, or shared Peggy's burdens as Lawrie shared Sally's. He loved his wife and children, though, and Lawrie always declared, 'Jimmie Burns is a good fellow. He's as good a husband as he knows how to be, only he copies how his father was.'

Jimmie had injured his back at work and although he could still walk was in constant pain. He went doggedly to work but every night went straight to the nearest public house and drank brandy to dull the pain.

'I sometimes think I'd be better off if he gave up work,' Peggy said bitterly to Sally. 'For all that's left of his wages after the brandy's paid for.'

'But he might still need it if he was at home,' Sally pointed out. 'And you'd have to feed him all day.'

Although Peggy worried so much about Michael, she knew she could not have managed without his wages, especially as she had her orphaned grand-daughter to keep.

Peggy had other worries too. Her son Rob had been out of work and receiving relief for several years when his only child left school and managed to obtain a job in the doll factory.

'She'll get nine shillings a week and Rob's been getting thirteen shillings and sixpence to keep the three of them. They're desperate, Sal, and they thought the girl's money would be the salvation of them.' Peggy started to cry. 'Poor Molly has tried. She got flour sacks and she's used them for everything. Towels, teatowels, even underclothes.'

'I know Mollie's a good girl,' Sally said. 'I remember when her and Rob got married I told him he was a lucky lad, because she'd make him a good wife.'

'And she has, but God knows it's been hard going for them. And now this. They were made up when young Esther got the job but when Molly went for the relief they told her it was cut to five and six a week,' Peggy said. 'They took eight shillings off them because of Esther's wages.'

'But the girl's going to need fares and carry out and something in her pocket.'

'Molly said that, but the woman on the committee said she could walk to work, and she shouldn't expect pocket money. It was her duty to give all her wages to her parents. Old cow! The bloody women on them committees are worse than the men,' said Peggy. 'This one had an answer for everything. Molly said Esther couldn't walk to the South End to the job because her shoes were so bad, and she couldn't go to work in the poor clothes that were all she had."

Peggy wept again and Sally said indignantly. 'Surely they could see the point of that? Thirteen and six would only keep them alive. It wouldn't leave anything for clothes.'

'The old cow said Molly would have an extra shilling with the five and six and Esther's nine shillings and she could buy clothes with that. Molly said she sneered and told her: "And as for carry out, as you call it, give her what she would have eaten at home." And she smirked round at the fellers on the bench.'

'God forgive her!' Sally said. 'Never mind, Peg, I got a lovely dress and bolero from the wardrobe dealer. Me and Cathy'll make something nice for young Esther. And, listen – I'll mug her to a pair of shoes to start work, but you tell her you bought them for her.'

'But it doesn't seem right. You should get the credit for it,' Peggy protested.

'I don't want the credit, I'm glad to help,' Sally said. 'I know what she's going through – Molly, I mean. I had a bit of that myself when the girls were young, and Mrs Malloy helped me out, so that's the way it goes. We all take our turn.'

'I've never been able to do much for anyone,' Peggy said with a sigh.

'Don't be daft,' Sally said. 'Look what you did for your

Mabel, and then you took the baby when her and Sidney died, and Meg's had every care. Anyway, Peg, with the houseful you had there was never anything to spare.'

'You spoke a true word there,' Peggy said. 'I was just getting on me feet with a few of them working when the war came, and the next thing they all got married and the house cleared out. You were lucky you only had the two.'

Sally turned away and fiddled with the fire irons, then said in a low voice, 'I don't know about lucky, Peg. I'd have given anything if only my little lad had lived.'

'Oh, God, I'm sorry, Sally,' Peggy exclaimed. 'Me and my big mouth. I'd forgotten about the stillborn lad you had.'

'Well, it was all a long time ago, even before you came to live here, so I wouldn't expect you to remember. Now, thank God, I've got Greg. He's like a son to me, and I'm sure Sam would be as thoughtful if he lived near.'

'Yes, your girls both fell on their feet, didn't they?' Peggy said wistfully.

Sally lifted down the handleless teapot from the mantelpiece and took five shillings from it. 'Get Esther's shoes with that, Peg,' she said. 'But mum's the word. Will you have another cup of tea?'

'No thanks, I'd better get back and get my curtains up in the parlour,' Peggy said. She began to laugh.

'You know I put newspapers up to the windows while the curtains were down. When Sarah came with that dish, she was very nearly standing on her head trying to read the paper while she was waiting on the step.'

'That child would read tissue paper if there was nothing else,' Sally said. 'Lawrie and Cathy and Greg are all fond of reading but I've never seen anything like Sarah. Always got her head in a book.'

It was true that Sarah was reading more than ever since her hopes of becoming a florist had been dashed because with a book she could escape to another world and forget her disappointment. The shop stood empty and abandoned, until just before Sarah left school at Christmas it was let again to a cobbler. Elsie seemed to have disappeared without trace.

Josie was inclined to think that her flight could prove an

advantage for Cathy. 'Your Sarah can get a job and bring something in when she leaves school at Christmas,' she said. 'I always thought you'd have been mad to let her work for nothing.'

'But she'd have been trained,' Cathy said. 'If she'd passed the scholarship we'd have had nothing from her until she was sixteen anyway.'

'You want to get her in a factory,' Josie advised. 'That's what I'm going to do with our Edie. I've asked Betty Ashcroft about Crawford's because I know she's spoken for their Lucy there.'

'Betty seems to like it there, doesn't she?' Cathy said. 'I know she gets broken biscuits for Mam and Peggy Burns, and Mam told me Betty was in a netball team there.'

'She told me to tell Edie to write in and ask if there were any vacancies, and said she would mention her name,' Josie said. 'You want to get Sarah to do the same.'

'I'd like to get her into another florist's like Fishlock's but I don't think we'll be able to,' Cathy said. 'Elsie told me they all want premiums, but she'd take Sarah for nothing.'

'I wouldn't take much notice to what she told you, the sly faggot,' Josie said. 'All that going on, and us feeling sorry for her because she was on her own without her mam.'

'Greg blames the man, Luke Menzies,' said Cathy. 'He says he was the one who had responsibilities and should have honoured them. He says he was trying to have his cake and eat it.'

'Walter's just the opposite,' Josie said. 'He says it's always the woman to blame, like in the Bible it says "The woman tempted me".'

'That always seemed wrong to me,' Cathy argued. 'Adam blaming Eve. He didn't *have* to eat the apple.'

Josie laughed aloud. 'Just listen to us,' she said. 'Picking faults with the Bible.'

Cathy laughed too but then she said more seriously, 'Greg was defending Elsie. I was so mad for Sarah's sake I was calling her for everything, and he said that Luke Menzies must have asked her to run away with him when she was feeling low after her mother's death.'

'Like you said about Adam, she didn't have to do it,' Josie declared. 'No, I blame her.'

'Well, whoever's to blame, poor Bella's left with all the problems and Sarah's been let down,' Cathy said. 'I only hope they think it's worth all the trouble they've caused.'

Sarah's teacher knew of her disappointment and promised to give her a letter of introduction to another florist's shop nearby. A few days after leaving school Sarah went into the shop and, too shy and nervous to speak, handed the letter to one of the assistants who brought the manageress.

She read the letter then called Sarah to the end of the counter. 'This is a good recommendation, love,' she said kindly. 'I see you were hoping to work for Elsie Hammond and that you can make frames and wire flowers. I'd like to take you but we just haven't got a vacancy, you see, but I'll keep this letter and keep you in mind.'

'Thank you,' Sarah whispered, not really surprised at being refused. She had sent applications to several places, including Crawford's. A reply came from the biscuit factory acknowledging her application and promising to file it.

'That means they'll call you for interview when there's a vacancy,' Edie told her. She had been accepted and was now the proud owner of a bicycle paid for at one shilling a week on which she rode to the factory in Edge Lane every day.

'I hope you get in,' she told Sarah. 'The money's good and the work's nice and clean. I'm making cartons for cream crackers, but when I'm older I'll go on the web on piece work and earn more.'

'The web?' echoed Sarah, looking puzzled.

'The conveyor belt,' Edie said impatiently. 'It's a sort of canvas belt that goes past the tables where the girls work. There's tables down each side of it with three girls to each table. The crackers come past on the web and one girl takes some off and weighs them, then she puts them in a sort of tin thing with four spaces and the other two girls take them off and wrap them.'

'How many tables?' Sarah asked.

'About eight each side,' Edie said. 'The girls are real quick and they don't half make good money. We've got to be quick with the cartons and all to keep up with them. There's hundreds altogether in the packing room and there's always something going on. I love it.'

Sarah looked doubtfully at Edie. It all sounded rather daunting to her although she could believe that Edie, big and self-confident, enjoyed it.

Cathy shared Sarah's doubts. 'I'd worry about Sarah in a big crowd of girls like that,' she told her mother. 'She's so shy.'

Sarah's name was also on a waiting list at the pen works, as the fountain pen factory near Hope Street was known locally, but before she was called to either place she had been offered a job in a bread and cake shop where the manageress was a friend of her grandmother.

'Mam cast her bread on the water by helping Mabel when her husband died,' Cathy said to Josie, 'and it's come back in the form of a job for Sarah.'

'She'd have been better waiting for Crawford's,' Josie said. 'The money won't be as good in a shop.'

'No, but she won't have any fares to pay and she'll be able to come home for her dinner,' Cathy said. She said nothing to Josie about her doubts about Sarah working in a crowd.

Sarah was happy from the start in the cake shop. The manageress, Mabel Burroughs, was a plain woman, tall and angular, with large hands and feet, but she had a sweet smile and a pleasant manner, and was kind and encouraging towards Sarah.

The owner and his wife ran the bakery behind the scenes but in the shop Mabel ruled supreme.

'I'm pleased with Sarah,' she told the owner in Sarah's hearing. 'She's a good little girl, very quick and willing to learn, and she's polite to the customers.'

'If she suits you, Mabel, that's all right,' Mrs Dyson said. 'Me and Albert have got enough to do in the bakehouse without worrying about out here.'

On the first Saturday of her working life Sarah came home at seven o'clock and proudly handed her mother her wages of twelve shillings, a box of cakes and two loaves.

'Mrs Dyson gave me them,' she said. 'She thinks I'm making a good shape, and if I work hard I'll do well.'

Cathy hugged her. 'I'm proud of you, love,' she said. 'This is going to be a good help to me, and I'm sure you're going to be happy there.'

'I am, Mam,' Sarah said eagerly. 'I like the shop and the customers, and Mabel's awful nice and so is Mrs Dyson.'

Cathy handed Sarah two shillings for her pocket money and then took another florin from the packet.

'Grandma got you the job, love, so run down to the shop and get some sweets for her, just to say thank you.'

'I'll get them from my own money, Mam,' Sarah said. 'I'd rather do that, honest.' Her mother agreed and Sarah dashed down to the sweet shop.

She bought half a pound of Sally's favourite peanut toffee, a quarter of sugared almonds for her mother, a pennyworth of stickjaw toffee for Mick, and a sherbet dab for Kate. She added five De Reske Minor cigarettes for her father and a quarter of mint imperials for John and a bar of chocolate for her grandfather.

'You'll have nothing left of your pocket money, love,' Cathy said, noting that Sarah had bought nothing for herself and smiling at her fondly.

'I've still got sixpence ha'penny left,' Sarah said. 'And I've got no fares or anything.'

'Take some of these cakes over to Grandma's, too,' Cathy said. 'She won't want any bread. She baked this morning.'

The shop was a busy one, especially at lunch time when people from other shops and offices, as well as housewives, came in for the succulent meat pies for which the shop was famous. They were brought through on trays by the bakehouse lads and placed piping hot on a side counter. Soon Sarah took responsibility for serving the continuous stream of pie customers while Mabel dealt with the customers for bread and cakes.

'We make a good team, don't we?' she said one day when Mrs Dyson came through from the bakehouse and stood watching for a while.

'You do,' the owner agreed. 'Whose idea was it to hang bags by the pie counter instead of coming round for them every time?'

'It was Sarah's,' Mabel said generously. 'I told you she'd got a good head on her.'

In this encouraging atmosphere Sarah's confidence grew. She had grown tall and slim, and had managed to coax a wave into her shining chestnut hair. Her blue eyes, clear skin and quick, shy smile made her very attractive, and the young men who came to the counter all tried to flirt with her.

She soon learned to look out for one in particular, a bank clerk who always let others be served before him so that he could spend more time looking at Sarah, smiling at her whenever their glances met. He always held her hand as he gave her his money, and again when she gave him change, and the other young men soon realized what was happening.

'Don't trust him. He's got a girl in every shop,' one said, and another told her that he was only flirting because the bank wouldn't allow him to marry until he was twenty-six.

'You'd be far better with a well set up fellow like me who can please himself,' he told her, and young men from other shops and offices told her the same. It was all lighthearted and Sarah only smiled and blushed, but when Dennis from the bank had finally gone she happily wove dreams about him as she worked.

To Sarah, everyone seemed happier at this time. Peggy's daughter Chrissie certainly was. Her twin sons left school at Christmas and both obtained jobs, Jimmie delivering bread from a handcart and Johnny in a butcher's shop.

'Best of all though,' Chrissie told Sally, 'Arthur's got a job labouring so we'll feel the benefit of the lads' money. If we were still on relief, they'd have taken off as much as the lads earned.'

Peggy's daughter-in-law Molly had obtained work at Tate and Lyle sugar works so she was now spared the weekly ordeal of applying for relief.

'Things are better for everyone, aren't they?' Sarah said happily to her grandmother. Sally smiled but said nothing to spoil Sarah's happiness, and lost in her dreams the girl failed to realize how worried her parents and grandmother were about her grandfather's health.

The winter had been a bad one with snow falling at Christmas and bleak days to follow. Lawrie's bout of bronchitis in early January was a slight one, but although he was quickly back at work and as cheerful as ever, it was clear that much of his strength had gone.

When he reached home after work he seemed thankful just to sit in his chair for a while and recover from the effort of walking home. He worked days now so Josh reached home at the same time, and Sally had a quiet word with the old man.

He readily agreed to wait for half an hour for his meal and sit chatting to Lawrie while he gathered his strength.

After the meal Lawrie would sit and read the newspaper for a while, but he was rarely without a visitor. Greg came often to talk about the allotment and about current affairs, and Cathy and the children came every night to see him briefly, but the visits that meant most to him were from John.

John never failed to call in to see him, even if it was late and Lawrie was already in bed. They were as close as ever and Lawrie enjoyed hearing the news of meetings and deputations that John brought him.

Chapter Sixteen

John carefully edited the news he gave to his grandfather, and told him nothing about the revolutionary views of some of his new friends or the times when they disrupted meetings by political opponents, in case he worried.

Grandad would do this sort of thing if he was younger, John told himself. He's just too old to realize that this is what's needed now.

At half-past ten Sally always came up with a cup of cocoa for Lawrie and a shovelful of slack to damp down the fire.

'Five more minutes,' Lawrie would plead jokingly, but Sally was always adamant. 'No, you need your rest. Your cocoa is ready downstairs, John.'

'I won't get a fire in the room if I don't do as I'm told,' Lawrie joked, but he always drank the cocoa obediently, knowing that it was partly Sally's care for him that kept him alive.

One fine day in April Greg hired a taxicab to take Sally and Lawrie, Cathy, Sarah and Kate to the allotment. He was there waiting when they arrived. He had placed some chairs in a patch of sunlight and told Lawrie that he needed his advice.

It was his first visit to the allotment for several months and he was delighted to see it looking so well.

'You've worked hard, lad,' he said to Greg.

'Mick helped with the digging,' Greg said. 'And Sarah's been a good help too. She's inherited your green fingers but we need some advice about crops now, don't we, Sass?'

'*I* pulled up some weeds,' Kate said.

'Yes, you did, love,' Greg said. 'Everyone helped.'

Everyone but John, Cathy thought. He took no interest

in the allotment now that his father was in charge of it, so they were all surprised when he suddenly appeared some hours later.

He was carrying the Brownie camera which had been his present from his parents on his eighteenth birthday.

'You were saying you'd like to send some snapshots to Auntie Mary, Grandad,' he said. 'I thought this might be a good occasion to get some of all the family. Here's Mick. I told him to meet us here.'

'Look at the state of him,' Cathy exclaimed. 'Oh, John, why didn't you tell us? We could have put our best clothes on.'

'That's why I didn't tell you. It's much better like this,' he said.

He took photographs of his grandparents sitting side by side on the chairs, after Sarah had objected when Lawrie sat on a chair and Sally stood beside him with her hand on his shoulder.

'That's old-fashioned, Gran,' she said. 'Now the lady sits down and the man stands beside her.'

'Votes for Women,' Lawrie laughed. 'Has your mam been getting at you, Sarah?' But Greg placed the other chair beside Lawrie. A man from another allotment came and offered to take all the family together, then John took several other snapshots and Greg took one of John and Lawrie standing together.

All the snapshots were clear and John was delighted that they had all come out, but Cathy was struck to the heart at the appearance of her father in them. She sat looking at them again when she and Greg were alone.

'I never realized,' she said in a low voice, 'Dad – he looks so frail. Seeing him every day—'

'They might be a shock to Mary and Sam,' Greg agreed. 'Do you think it would be wise to send them?'

'I don't know.' Cathy looked again, not at the family group but at the picture of Lawrie and Sally. In their youth sitters had not been allowed to smile while their photograph was being taken. They were both staring fixedly into the camera.

Sally's shoulders were stooped. Her face bore a look of anxiety and lines from the pain she suffered from arthritis.

Lawrie's face looked gaunt, his eyes sunk deep in hollow sockets. His thin shoulders were bowed as though with weariness, and his hands on his knees looked transparent.

In the second photograph John had urged them to smile and they both looked better, although old and worn.

The snapshot of John and his grandfather was the one that upset Cathy most. The contrast between John, young and strong, shoulders back and head high as he smiled confidently at the camera, and the figure of his grandfather, smiling bravely but looking bent and old, made her tears flow.

'I never realized – I always thought of Dad as looking like that, like John is,' she wept. 'He looks a frail old man.'

'It was just a bad time to take the snapshots,' Greg consoled her. 'He was tired after being there for a couple of hours. John should have warned us and we'd have arranged things differently.'

Cathy put the snapshots together and stood up. 'John did it on an impulse when he remembered what Dad said about sending some to Mary,' she said stiffly. 'Dad's pleased with them anyway.' Greg's lips tightened but he said no more.

The day at the allotment seemed to have been good for Lawrie and with the coming of summer his health gradually improved, but in June the whole family was shocked by the sudden death of Jimmie Burns.

He had continued to work and to drink brandy to dull the pain in his back. Coming home late from the public house one night, he fell and damaged his ribs. He was helped home by a passer-by and Peggy put him to bed and called the doctor.

'He should have been going to the doctor for the pain,' Michael Burns said to Sally. 'He's on the panel being as he's working, and it would have cost him nothing, but it suited him better to drink brandy for it.'

'Your mam's the one who should go to the doctor,' Sally said, deciding to ignore his comments about Jimmie. 'She's taking bicarbonate of soda by the minute for her bad stomach. I'm sure it's not good for her, Michael.'

'Women and children should be able to go to the doctor

free as well as men,' Lawrie said. 'Not be dosing themselves because they can't afford to pay the money.'

'That'd be the day, Mr Ward,' Michael said. 'Where would the money come from?'

'From what they're saving on defence, if they're telling the truth about Disarmament,' Lawrie replied. Michael looked at Sally and shrugged eloquently. When he had gone, Lawrie smiled at her.

'That lad thinks I'm soft in the head,' he said. 'But all these things will come, Sal. The trouble is, they're not coming quick enough.'

'Well, widows' pensions have come, and old age pensions and sick pay,' she said. 'You've got some of what you've fought for, lad.'

'Aye, and John and lads like him will carry it on,' Lawrie said. 'That's been my greatest happiness, Sal, having John growing up like he has.' He leaned over and patted her knee and winked at her. 'Barring times only we know about, eh, girl?'

'Go on with you,' she said, blushing and bending her head over her knitting.

Only a few days later Jimmie developed pneumonia, and within two weeks he was dead.

Rob, as the eldest son, took charge, helped and advised by Sally and Lawrie. Cathy had taken Meg to stay with her while Peggy's house was full of mourning relatives. Her respect for Peggy grew as she took her turn to struggle with Meg's wild swings of mood and sudden tantrums, when she lay on the floor and refused to move except to drum her heels and bang her hands on the floor.

Cathy was relieved when Sarah and John returned from work in the evenings. Meg would do anything for John, and Sarah could make her go to bed by promising to go with her.

During the days after Jimmie's death Peggy had clung to Sally, but after the funeral she recovered her strength and courage. 'Our Michael's the one who'll take it hardest,' she told Sally. 'I never let on to anyone but he hasn't spoken a civil word to Jimmie for months. You know he's always been the one closest to me, our Michael, and he thought Jimmie wasn't treating me right, spending on the brandy.'

'The young ones don't understand,' Sally said. 'Jimmie was trying to manage the pain the best way he knew and didn't realize it was leaving you short, he was that muddled with the pain and the brandy.'

'He done his best. Our Robbie said after the funeral, when he was young he thought Jimmie never had no feeling for them when they were kids, but now he's a father himself he sees it different. Jimmie fed and clothed them and gave them their Saturday penny, and now Robbie said he appreciates that Jimmie was hard with himself as well.'

'It's the times we've lived through, Peggy,' Sally said. 'Jimmie and Lawrie – they'd go to their work sick or well. I'm worried to death about Lawrie very often, going back to work when he's hardly able to stand up, but he won't be told. He seems easy going but about that he's so stubborn.'

'It's their pride,' Peggy said.

Sally looked at her in surprise and Peggy said bitterly, 'They take a pride in keeping their families and being someone in their own house, because to anyone else they don't count.'

Tears ran down her face and she wiped them away. 'I wasn't going to tell anyone but a fellow came from the Railway. He hummed and hawed and beat round the bush, then he said what he'd come for.'

Peggy's tears flowed again and Sally patted her hand in silent sympathy.

'You know it was a Friday night Jimmie fell?' Peggy said. 'He'd been paid, and so he'd got the Saturday morning he wasn't in. This fellow come to ask for it back. Four shillings and threepence, Sally.'

'Never!' she exclaimed.

'As true as I'm sitting here. The years he worked for the Railway, and hurt his back there, and still dragged himself there, and that's how much respect they had for him. To send while he lay in his coffin for four and threepence overpaid.'

'My God,' Sally said. 'Listen, Peggy, that didn't make any the less of Jimmie, that they behaved like that.'

'It wasn't the money, Sally. It was – they thought so little of him that they'd do such a thing. He wasn't a man to them, just a number on a time sheet,' Peggy wept.

'Then that shows what they are, not fit to lick Jimmie's shoes!' Sally exclaimed. 'The man that worked it out and the creature that came for it, they're not worth another thought, Peg. Try and put the whole thing out of your mind. Jimmie had a family and plenty of friends who respected him, so you don't have to worry about creatures like that.'

'Don't tell anyone, will you?' Peggy said, drying her eyes. 'I'm glad I told you but I wouldn't want anyone else to know.' She tucked her handkerchief away and gave Sally a ghost of a smile. 'I'm glad I've got you for a neighbour, Sally. You've been a good friend to me always.'

'And you have to me, Peg,' Sally said. 'I don't make friends easily. All these years you've been my only real friend, and a good one.'

'Nearly twenty-four years since we came to this house and never a wrong word between us,' Peggy said.

In all their long friendship they had never spoken so freely before and were both suddenly self-conscious, but Sally said with a laugh, 'I had plenty of wrong words with Mrs Kilgannon who was there before you. She was a right faggot. The trouble she caused here, and then at the finish she went queer, running round the streets naked, so her daughter took her to live with her.'

'I hope we don't go like that,' Peggy said. She glanced down at herself. 'You wouldn't look so bad, being thin, but me! I'm like a cottage loaf. I'd soon collect a crowd.'

Sally wondered how Peggy would manage without Jimmie, but she surprised everyone with her energy and resourcefulness. She cleaned through her house like a whirlwind and reorganized the sleeping arrangements. Michael was moved into the third bedroom formerly occupied by Meg, Peggy and Meg moved into the second bedroom, and Peggy prepared the main bedroom and the parlour for a lodger.

'I shouldn't be surprised really,' Sally said to Cathy. 'Peggy has always been one for hard work. Dad says this is her way of managing the shock of losing Jimmie.'

'Greg says he should have had compensation because he

injured his back at work,' Cathy said.

'Dad told him that but it seems he didn't report it right away,' Sally said. 'Anyway, it's too late to worry now.'

Peggy soon found her lodgers. 'Two brothers, respectable lads. Their mam and dad are dead and a sister's been looking after them, but she's getting married and going to live in Manchester,' she told Sally. 'They'll suit me down to the ground. I didn't want girls who'd be in and out of my kitchen, or a young couple, but the lads will have their meals with us and I'll do their washing.'

'That's worked well for us with Josh,' Sally said. 'I hope these lads are as easy as he is.'

'I don't think our Michael likes the idea but he's very meek these days,' Peggy said. 'He's upset because he fell out with Jimmie so often, but I told him lads often fall out with their fathers. It's usually eldest sons, like with Greg and John, but Michael's the eldest one here now.'

Sally said nothing but later she told Lawrie about the conversation. 'I got the shock of my life,' she said, 'but Peggy just rattled on as if it was something everyone knew – that John and Greg are at odds sometimes. I'm sure I've never said anything to her, Lawrie.'

'You know Peggy,' Lawrie said easily. 'She knows everyone's business, but there's no harm in her.'

'I know, but it was just a shock to hear her say it, so matter of fact.'

'Did you send those snaps John gave us to Mary?' Lawrie asked.

'Cathy sent hers. She said we can keep ours,' Sally said.

Cathy had been unsure about sending the snaps to Mary but had soon realized that her parents would wonder why she made no mention of them if they were not sent.

An answer to her letter to Mary enclosing the snapshots came almost by return of post from America. Mary's letter was tear-stained and almost incoherent from anger and distress.

Why didn't you tell me? How could you let them get like this? Mam looks so old, and Dad – he's like a frail old man. Why haven't you looked after them? Wrapped up in your precious husband and your flaming family, I suppose. I'll never forgive you for letting this happen.

Cathy was furious. She flung the letter to the back of the dresser and began to work off her rage by fiercely scrubbing floors and paintwork, and polishing linoleum, until she felt exhausted.

She had calmed down, washed and changed and just made tea, when the four o'clock post came.

'Another letter from America,' the postman said. 'You're doing well.'

She's had second thoughts, Cathy thought grimly, but this letter was from Sam.

> I know that Mary has written to you, Cathy, and she was so upset that I think she might have said something to hurt you. If so, I'm very sorry. It has been a comfort to Mary and me all these years to know that you and Greg and your family are living so near to your parents, and I know from what they write how much you all do for them and how much happiness you have brought them.
>
> I hope you can understand, Cathy, why the snapshots were such a shock to us. You see your mam and dad every day so the change in them has come to you gradually, but we haven't seen them since 1926 and nine years is a long time.
>
> I think Mary's mental picture of them went even further back than that. I think she pictured her mam and dad as they were when she was a girl at home, so you understand what a shock she got at the difference in them now.
>
> I think, too, Mary feels guilty because we haven't been able to help them and that's why she must blame someone, so again, Cathy, if she has said anything hurtful please overlook it. You know it's just shock because she loves her mam and dad so much, and when she calms down she'll be truly sorry.
>
> The only way I can console her is to bring her over to see them, and I'm working out how to do it. I've got some good men here and as soon as I can fix things

up we'll travel home. Probably late summer, certainly no later than the fall of this year.

Our love to you and Greg and the children, and thanks for everything, Cath.

Yours affectionately,
Sam

Cathy retrieved Mary's letter from where she had flung it, and folded it up inside Sam's. I'll show them to Greg, she decided, but I won't let Mam or anyone else see them.

Cathy waited until the evening meal was over and the family dispersed before she showed Greg the letters.

'Read that one from Mary first, then the one from Sam,' she said. Greg read Mary's letter then looked at Cathy with raised eyebrows.

'Quite a tirade,' he said. 'But you're not going to let it upset you, are you, Cath? You know what she's like. The snaps must have been a shock to her. Remember they were a shock to you.'

'Yes, but I didn't write to her spouting about it being her fault, did I? Her letter *did* upset me, but anyway, read Sam's letter, Greg.'

She watched his face as he read Sam's long letter, then he looked up. 'Sam certainly understands Mary,' he said. 'She's upset and feels guilty so she has to blame somebody else.'

'Yes, but he still idolizes her and makes excuses for her,' Cathy said bitterly. 'She's a selfish, thoughtless bitch! She must know I'm upset too yet she writes to me like that. I'll never forgive her.' But even as she spoke Cathy knew that although she was bitterly angry now with her sister, if she saw Mary all the old feelings of love and admiration for her would come surging back.

'Sam's a good fellow,' Greg said. 'One in a thousand. He's a busy man yet he's taken the trouble to write a long letter like that in case your feelings are hurt.'

'Too good for our Mary,' Cathy said.

'I'm sure she regretted sending that letter as soon as it was posted,' Greg said soothingly. 'She just got a shock and wrote on impulse. She didn't really mean those things.'

'Indeed,' Cathy said shortly. Greg, too, she thought, making excuses for her. Mary was very well able to look after her own interests yet she aroused a protective instinct in every man she met. She stood up and began to sort through her mending basket and Greg glanced at her face and decided to say no more.

Later she said that she would burn the letters.

'I'll tell Mam that I burned a letter from Mary by mistake or she'll wonder why I don't show it to her,' she said. 'I won't say anything about them coming in case Sam can't fix it.'

'Just say it was a short note acknowledging the snaps,' Greg suggested. 'Sam and Mary are bound to write to them soon to tell them of their plans.'

Ten days later a letter arrived from Mary to her parents, telling them that she and Sam would be visiting Liverpool in August.

"We will be staying at the Adelphi for two weeks," she wrote, "and we'll spend every waking minute with you. I can't wait to see you both, and Cathy and her family of course."

Sally immediately decided that the house must be redecorated. 'But they won't be staying here, Gran,' John protested. 'Do you need to have the bedrooms done as well?'

'I'll feel better if they are,' Sally said firmly. 'I know you and your dad are willing to do them, John, but I'll get Ben Burns in. He can work at them all day and he'll be glad of the few shillings.'

Josh said he was satisfied with his rooms as they were so Sally arranged for Ben to paper the front bedroom and smallest bedroom, and the kitchen/living room, and paint the lobby and the back kitchen. While this was taking place Lawrie slept in John's bed on the insistence of both Sally and Cathy, in case the paint got on his chest.

John slept in Sally's third bedroom which Ben had finished in one day, and painted the outside woodwork of the house and the railings. After his initial protest no one had commented on the extent of Sally's preparations because Cathy had told them firmly that she understood how her mother felt, and because it was obvious that Sally was taking pleasure in preparing for her visitors.

The family had all enjoyed having Lawrie staying with them, and Sally and Josh coming for meals while the upheaval took place, and Sarah in particular had appreciated her grandfather's company. Lawrie never discussed politics with her but they talked of books which they both enjoyed, and of poetry which they loved.

Sarah had never been a Girl Guide but she bought a *Guides' Handbook* for a penny, and discovered at the end of an article on the hiker's badge a few lines of poetry quoted. She read them aloud to Lawrie.

> ' "I watched the sorrow of the evening sky
> And smelt the sea and earth and the warm clover,
> And heard the waves and the seagull's mocking cry
> I saw the pines against the white north sky
> Very beautiful and still and bending over
> Their sharp black heads against a quiet sky
> And there was peace in them." '

They were silent for a moment then Sarah said softly, 'Isn't that lovely, Grandad? I felt as though I was there. Sitting on a grassy headland, with the scent of the clover, and looking at the sea and the white sky and the pine trees.' Her eyes were shining as she looked up at him. Lawrie gently smoothed back her hair.

'Yes, it's beautiful, love,' he said. 'Remember the line from Keats' poem: "A thing of beauty is a joy for ever"? If words have painted a picture for you to remember it's the same as remembering a lovely thing you've seen, like Keats did. You can always call it up in your mind.'

'I don't know who wrote that,' Sarah said. 'It didn't say.'

'I think it was Rupert Brooke,' said Lawrie. 'The man who wrote the war poem "If I should die think only this of me". He did die, poor lad, and was buried in foreign soil, but not in France. He died on the way to the Dardenelles and was buried on an island called Skyros. He was only twenty-eight, I think. I read an article about him not long ago.'

'And the place where he wrote that about the pine trees, I suppose that's still there while he's dead and can't see it,' she said thoughtfully.

'That's the way it is,' her grandfather said. 'The places are there for each generation to enjoy, unless someone spoils them.'

'But it seems hard,' she said. 'I mean, Grandad, it's like when Mr Burns died. It was the Jubilee and everyone was enjoying themselves, the streets all decorated and street parties and everything. We even had one in Egremont Street, but they kept it up the other end.'

'Mrs Burns wouldn't have expected them to cancel it, love.'

'No, but – I went with Edie Meadows to see the decorations in Pitt Street. You know, the tenements were lovely. They had gold and red paper made into flowers and all wound round the posts on the landings, and crowds were there to see them. We were looking in the windows of the little Chinese shops and there were back scratchers there, like little curved hands on bamboo poles. We were laughing and then I thought about Mr Burns.

'I liked him, Grandad. He always bought sweets for me when he bought them for Meg, and one time when I showed her how to use a stencil set he gave me a threepenny bit and said I was patient like my grandma. He was dead and yet I was laughing.'

'And why not?' Lawrie said. 'It's a trite saying, Sarah, but a true one just the same – life must go on. Mr and Mrs Burns, and Grandma and I – we've all had a good innings, love. Jimmie didn't die out of his time, like Rupert Brooke. My father's generation didn't reckon to live much over fifty, if they were lucky. So you see, love, we've done well. Turned sixty and still going strong.'

He smiled at Sarah and she tried to smile back but she felt as though cold water trickled down her spine. Grandad was trying to warn her, to prepare her, she felt sure.

'Lucy Ashcroft's great-grandma is seventy-eight,' she said.

'There you are. No one goes till their time comes,' Lawrie said. 'But if you've had a good lifespan like Jimmie, people shouldn't get too upset. Just remember that he had a good life, some good times and some bad, but he enjoyed himself and wouldn't want anyone to get upset over him.'

'We couldn't help it, Grandad,' Sarah said, her eyes filling with tears, not for Jimmie Burns but at the thought of what her grandfather was trying to tell her.

'Well, yes, love,' he said, 'but remember it is something that must come to everyone. It's what they call the "natural order" of things. After all, if no one ever died, what about the people who are being born? The earth would be so over-crowded we'd all be slipping off the edge.'

Sarah smiled as he intended, and conscious that he was trying to strike a more light-hearted note, asked if he had seen the Jubilee decorations in Pitt Street.

'No, not Pitt Street, but I saw a lot in the other streets, and the pavements all scrubbed and whitened,' he said. 'It was a chance of some jollification for people.'

'The decorations were made out of Crawford's labels, Edie told me,' said Sarah. 'All the bits round the edge when the labels are stamped out, and yet they looked the gear. She got five shillings from Mr Crawford for the Jubilee. They all did.'

'That'd be a nice little lift for her.'

'Her mam let her keep it but she said she had to buy a hat. Edie got a hat for two and eleven and treated me out the rest.' Sarah stood up. 'I've promised to help Grandma turn out a cupboard, Grandad. I'd better go.'

'I'll look for that article for you, love,' Lawrie said. 'That's if Grandma hasn't thrown it out. Nothing's safe now while the cleaning's on.'

'I'll save your magazines,' she promised, smiling at him like a conspirator.

Chapter Seventeen

When the decorating was finished in Sally's house, the curtains had been washed and re-hung by Cathy and the cupboards turned out, she attacked her own house.

Lawrie had returned home to sleep so Cathy and Greg, helped by the younger members of the family, painted and papered the rooms, and the outside of their house. The tennis season had started and Cathy received several "Please be at's" each week.

Although her afternoons were precious while there was so much to be done in the house, she welcomed the extra money to buy new curtains and china, and fresh coconut matting for the kitchen floor.

She also enjoyed the change of scene and the company of the other women, and Cissie's exploits were a constant source of amusement.

'She doesn't care a button for anyone,' Cathy told Greg, laughing heartily at the memory. 'We were putting the strawberries ready when this crowd of boys came into the marquee. Public schoolboys home on holiday, but they were a disgrace. Jostling us and snatching strawberries and giving these stupid neighing laughs.'

'Probably thought it was a big joke,' Greg said.

'Cissie didn't. She picked up a knife and said to one of them, "Have you been circumzised, lad?" And he said all haughty, "*No*, indeed." And she said, "Put them strawberries down or you soon will be.' Mrs Nuttall had dashed off to get the man who owned the place and he came back with her but the boys had all run away by then.'

'Because of Cissie's knife?' Greg asked, laughing.

'Probably. I think she might have done it, too. The man was saying boys would be boys, and Mrs Nuttall was all smiles because he gave her ten bob for the extra work, but

Cissie was fuming. She was saying, "Boys! They'll never be bloody men if they come near me again." She's a case.'

One of the women had found a full-time job, so Cathy "spoke" for Freda for the vacancy. Cathy was a favourite with Mrs Nuttall. Now she asked if any jobs that came for her while Mary was home could be passed to Freda, and Mrs Nuttall agreed.

Cathy felt that she had made all possible preparations for her sister's visit, and looked forward eagerly to it, and to showing Mary and Sam her children.

John and Sarah were both settled and happy in their jobs, and Mick was very successful at school. His yearly report showed him to be top of his form and first in almost every subject. He won numerous prizes but remained unconcerned, and seemed to spend little time on study.

'I don't understand it,' Cathy said to Greg. 'When you think how hard John worked. He did well but nothing like this.'

Greg discovered the reason when he was asked to see the headmaster. 'I didn't know what to expect,' he told Cathy. 'He looked so severe, but he said Mick has a most unusual gift, a photographic memory. He said he'd only ever known one other person with it, a student at Stonyhurst when he was there.'

'What does it mean?'

'The headmaster said the boy he knew could look at a page of Greek, then close the book and write out the page without a single fault. Mick's the same.'

'No wonder everything's been so easy for him!' Cathy exclaimed.

Greg smiled. 'The headmaster told me the name of the other boy, and I'd heard it but forget it now. He said he was very eminent in the Church and a famous preacher. I said I couldn't really see Mick doing anything like that, but he said we must give serious consideration to Michael's future. The gift must not be wasted.'

'I can't get over it,' said Cathy. 'And Mick's never said anything about it.'

'I said that, but the headmaster said he just takes it for granted. Until they spoke about it, he thought it was the same for everyone.'

Kate was looking forward to seeing her aunt because several people had told her that she was growing like her Aunt Mary.

'Mrs Briggs said I'm going to be like Auntie Mary, and she was beautiful,' she announced to her mother.

'Mrs Briggs only came to the street after Auntie Mary was married,' Cathy said. 'She hardly knew her. You're not like her. She had blue eyes and red hair. Still has, I suppose.'

'Mrs Burns said to Grandma I was the model of Mary except for my colouring,' Kate insisted.

'I suppose you'd been throwing a tantrum,' her mother said. 'You're like her in that way.

'Kate's growing a vain little madam,' she said to Greg later. 'Bragging about being like Mary, and someone told her Mary was beautiful. Do *you* think she's like Mary?'

'She is in features, I think, but of course Kate's eyes are brown. Strange that when her hair came out after the scarlet fever it grew in fair again, because she was as dark as you at first, wasn't she? I think she's a beautiful child, though.'

'So do I but we would, wouldn't we?' Cathy said. 'I just hope Kate doesn't bring us as much heartbreak as Mary brought Mam and Dad – or bring as much trouble on herself as our Mary did.'

'Yes. Mary was her own worst enemy in many ways,' Greg agreed. 'Beauty isn't always an advantage for a girl.'

Cathy glanced at him and he said hastily, 'She was lucky that she met up with Sam again. He'll keep her on the right path and look after her.'

"Quite an authority on Mary, aren't you?" Cathy was tempted to say, but managed to keep back the words. Instead she said firmly, 'We know what *can* happen so we'll guard Kate against it.'

They had all been so busy with preparations for the visit that the weeks which they had expected to drag by seemed to pass in a flash. The neighbours who had known Mary were all waiting eagerly to see her; some of them, Cathy felt, half hoping to see her looking very different from the beautiful, well-dressed girl they remembered.

She said so to Josie, who laughed. 'My mam is,' she said frankly. 'She said she thinks Mary's been codding your mam about the money she's got and the cars and everything.'

'You don't think that, do you?' Cathy exclaimed.

'No, but I might as well admit, Cathy, I hope she *hasn't* stayed the same, while we've all got the worse for wear,' Josie said, laughing, and Cathy laughed with her.

Later she told her mother what Josie had said, although she said nothing of Mrs Mellor's words.

'Mary won't care anyway. She'll only want to see how you and Dad look, and he looks better, doesn't he?'

'Yes, Peggy said that,' Sally agreed. 'She said his face had filled out. Of course, the summer's always the best time for him. If only we didn't have fog. He can stand the cold and the frost.'

'Greg hates fog,' Cathy said. 'I don't mean it makes him ill or he doesn't like the inconvenience. He just *hates* it.'

'Perhaps it reminds him of the gas attacks in France?' Sally suggested.

'Maybe. I don't remember him being like this about it before the war.'

It was the sunniest August for many years and Sally and Lawrie spent each Sunday at the allotment, usually joined there by Cathy and Kate and sometimes Mick or Sarah. Greg was always there when they arrived, and Lawrie's health visibly improved as he pottered about helping Greg or sat in the sunshine with Sally.

'They both look so much better, thank God,' Cathy said to Greg. 'Mam doesn't look so strained and they both have a good colour with the sun.'

'It will be a relief to Sam and Mary to see them looking so well,' he said. 'It's certainly a relief to us, isn't it?'

At last the day arrived when Mary and Sam were due. The family were ready from early morning, dressed in their best clothes. Lawrie had obtained a day's leave of absence from work, and Mick and Kate were on holiday from school, but Greg, Sarah, and John were at work during the day.

The rest of the family were waiting when a large hired car

drew up outside the house and Sam stepped from the driving seat. He wore a pale grey suit with a wide silk tie and a light grey Homburg hat, but he received only a glance from the neighbours peeping from behind their curtains.

They watched eagerly as Sam walked round the car and handed Mary from it as though she was Royalty. She was a vision of loveliness, wearing a floral chiffon dress and bolero, with white gloves and a small white hat tipped over her right eye, and her red-gold hair curling up around it.

In her high-heeled white shoes, she came up to Sam's shoulder, tall though he was. She laid her hand on his arm and began to walk gracefully towards the house. The front door was flung open and Sally and Lawrie appeared. Immediately Mary dropped Sam's arm and ran forward to fling her arms around both of them. Sam followed, smiling broadly.

Mary released her parents briefly while Sam greeted them, but when they had all gone down the narrow lobby into the kitchen she hugged them again, all of them laughing and crying at once. Sam had kissed Cathy and lifted Kate to kiss her, then shaken hands with Mick before Mary turned from her parents to greet Cathy.

As she had expected, all feelings of bitterness towards Mary vanished as soon as she saw her. Cathy hugged and kissed her sister with warm affection.

'I'm sorry about that letter,' Mary said. 'I didn't mean it. I was just so upset.'

Cathy was aware that her mother's sharp ear had caught the words and murmured to Mary, 'I burnt it. Didn't show it to Mam or anyone.' She drew Kate forward. 'John and Sarah are at work, and Greg of course, but this is Kate.'

'Why, you're a little beauty! Real cute,' Mary exclaimed. 'How old are you, Kate?'

'I'm nine,' Kate said, preening herself.

'And this is Mick,' Cathy said hastily. 'Scarface.'

The scars of Mick's many mishaps had faded and Mary looked at him admiringly. 'I wouldn't have that label, Mick,' she said in her husky voice, holding his hand and smiling at him. 'I think you're real handsome.'

She's flirting with *Mick*, Cathy thought in amazement, but he only said calmly, 'You're quite good-looking yourself.'

They all exploded with laughter but Mick was unabashed. He turned to Sam and asked if he might look at his motor.

'He's a case,' Lawrie said as Mick dashed off down the lobby. 'Life's never dull with him around.'

Kate was pouting at being ignored but when they were all settled down, with Mary and Sam sitting on the sofa, Mary drew the little girl down beside her.

'You were just a tiny baby when I last saw you,' she said. 'You looked very like your mam then, with your dark hair.'

'Her hair came out after the scarlet fever, and it grew again that colour,' Cathy said. 'Not as blonde as Mick but quite fair. I thought I told you in a letter.'

'You probably did, but it doesn't seem real until you see these things,' Mary said. She smiled at Kate. 'It's certainly very attractive now, the fair curls and the brown eyes.' She ran her hand over the curls which clustered over Kate's head. 'You look just like Shirley Temple.'

Kate snuggled closer to her, smiling up at her with delight. 'Mrs Briggs said I'm going to be a beauty like you,' she announced.

Cathy and Sally exchanged a wry glance but Mary looked pleased. 'Who's Mrs Briggs?'

'A new neighbour. I don't think she's ever seen you,' Sally said.

'She saw Auntie Mary the year I was born, Gran,' Kate piped up, but Sally turned to Cathy.

'Put the kettle on, please, love.'

'We've just had —' Mary began, but Sam nudged her and she hastily amended it to, 'We've just had a meal but I'm dying for a cup of your tea, Mam. Tea never tastes the same anywhere else.' Sally looked pleased and followed Cathy into the back kitchen where the best china had been laid out.

Mary took a wooden stool beside Lawrie's Windsor armchair so that she could sit beside him and put her arms round his neck and her head on his shoulder.

'I've missed you terribly, Dada,' she whispered. 'It's lovely to see you again.'

Kate moved up beside Sam and he put his arm round her and talked to her, so for a while Mary and Lawrie were in a world apart.

In the back kitchen Sally said quietly to Cathy, 'What was Mary saying about a letter and being upset?'

'You know Mary,' Cathy said. 'She spouts first and thinks afterwards.' She tried to speak lightly but her mother glanced at her and laid her hand on her arm.

'It was when you sent the snaps, wasn't it? The letter you told me you'd burned?' Cathy nodded, and her mother said gently, 'You have to understand, love, to see your family growing up around you, and her and Sam with no sign of a child – it must have upset her.'

Cathy was silent with amazement. Her mother went on, 'Make allowances, Cath. You're very lucky to have such a lovely family, so don't bear a grudge, love.'

'I don't, Mam, honestly,' she said. 'If I had I'd have to forget it when I saw her, anyway. They both look marvellous, don't they?'

Sally smiled proudly and carried a plate of fruit cake into the kitchen, followed by Cathy with the tray of teacups.

Sam drank his tea quickly and went out to check on the car. A crowd of children stood at a respectful distance around it, and Mick had opened the bonnet and was examining the engine. He questioned his uncle eagerly about the car's performance but Sam told him he had only hired it a few hours earlier.

'What about your own cars – the ones you have in America?' Mick asked, and Sam tried to answer his questions. Mick had brought out a sheet of plywood from their house and now he asked if he could go beneath the car to examine it.

'Sure, son, sure,' Sam agreed thankfully. Mick lay down on the plywood and propelled himself beneath the car while Sam went back into the house, wiping his brow.

'Any more tea, please, Cathy?' he asked. 'I need reviving.'

She started forward in alarm. 'What's he done?' she exclaimed.

'Nothing,' Sam said hastily. 'He's kept the kids away from the car, but he's made a monkey out of me with his questions. Where did he learn about engines?'

'I didn't know he knew anything about them,' she said.

'He had the hood up when I went out and he asked me dozens of questions. I could hardly answer one! I told him the car was only hired a few hours ago, so then he asked me about the cars back home. Gee, Cathy, all I knew was the make and the horsepower, but you'd think the kid had been around them for years.'

'He likes messing with machinery,' Cathy said. Mindful of her mother's words about her good fortune in having a family, she said nothing about Mick's strange gift but only asked if he was coming in for tea.

'He's lying under the car,' Sam said. 'On a piece of plywood,' he added hastily. 'I guess he's not worried about tea.'

While Sam talked to Sally and Lawrie about America and his new business, Mary and Cathy had the chance of a few quiet words.

'I think Mam and Dad look real well,' Mary said. 'Older, but Sam said I should expect that. Not a bit like those snapshots.'

'Dad's always better in the summer,' Cathy said. 'So of course Mam's not so worried. Then Dad's always laughing and talking and cracking jokes so you don't notice that he looks ill. He only lost his spirits once after he had shingles, but that was unusual. The snaps looked worse because he was still, for once.'

'Sam said they say the camera cannot lie but we know different! Some of those glamorous film stars in real life . . . you'd never believe,' said Mary.

'You know that Jimmie Burns from next door died?' Cathy said. 'That upset them because they'd been friends for a long time.' But Mary was not interested.

'I was *so* upset when those snaps came,' she said. 'I just cried and cried. Sam was distraught. He didn't know what to do to comfort me, and then he thought of coming home for a visit. It wasn't easy for him to get away, but he'd do just anything to make me happy.'

She patted her hair complacently, and Cathy said shortly, 'You've come at the right time to see them both looking well after the good weather we've had.'

'I suppose the thought of my visit has been good for them,' Mary said. 'Given them something to look forward to.'

'I suppose so,' Cathy said, trying to hide her irritation, and resisting the temptation to tell Mary that her parents' interest in their grandchildren gave them plenty to fill their lives.

'I wish we could take them back with us,' Mary said. 'We take good weather for granted, and I'd like to show them a bit of luxury.' She glanced disparagingly about the kitchen of which Sally was so proud. 'I'm going to hate to go home and leave them in this place.'

Cathy's face grew red with anger. 'Mam and Dad are very happy in *this place*,' she said furiously, 'and so are we, Greg and I and our family.'

Mary put her arm round her and kissed her. 'Of course, Cath,' she said. 'And so would I have been if I'd never seen anything different. But just think, if I could take them there to lie in the garden beside a swimming pool all day, with a long cool drink and nothing at all to do . . .'

'It'd drive Mam crackers, having nothing to do,' Cathy said bluntly.

'You haven't changed,' Mary laughed. 'Still the same little firebrand and straight talker.'

Sam appeared beside them. 'We'll have to be going, honey,' he said to Mary. Then as she moved away to her parents, he kissed Cathy's cheek. 'You've got two great kids here, Cath,' he said. 'Mick's a real character and Kate's certainly a pretty little girl.'

'Yes, and doesn't she know it?' Cathy said ruefully, smiling at him.

'Still, she hasn't inherited your dimples,' he said. 'Has Sarah?'

'No. She hasn't got a round face like me, luckily.'

Mary was telling her parents that Sam had ordered an early dinner in their suite so that they would be able to come back for the evening, and Cathy said to him, 'Will you come to our house when you come back? There's a bit more room for all of us in our parlour.'

'Of course. How's the old man who lives here?'

'Josh Adamson. He's fine. He eats proper food now,

and he's fat again, but he's happy.'

'I'll bet he is,' Sam said with a grin. 'I remember the Sunday teas here when I was trying to court Mary. I didn't get many, mind you. She always seemed to cast me off before the weekend.' They both laughed at the memory, then Mary and Sam left. Sam opened the door of the car, but Mary stood looking about her for a moment, giving everyone a chance to admire her, before she slipped into her seat.

'It seems terrible,' Sally sighed as they drove away. 'My own daughter and I can't do a meal for her. This is where I miss having the parlour to myself, Cath.'

'It wouldn't make any difference, Mam,' she said. 'They're just used to a different way of life now. I don't suppose they ask people round for spareribs and cabbage when they're at home.' Sally smiled and agreed.

'You've got a nice parlour now to entertain,' she said.

Cathy was proud of her parlour. Over the years she and Greg had managed to furnish it with a green moquette suite and two fireside chairs in matching material, and a black rug before the fire. The cabinet gramophone had a record cabinet beside it, made by Greg, and they had recently acquired an upright piano. Most of the furniture had been paid for by hire purchase, but with Cathy's extra money and John and Sarah's wages the debt had been quickly paid.

It was a lively gathering there when Mary and Sam returned. Mary had changed into a deceptively simple dress of pale green marocain, calf-length and showing her figure to perfection. With it she wore only a plain gold locket and gold earrings. Only Cathy and Sarah realized how the skilful use of cosmetics had heightened Mary's beauty, and how expensive was her perfume, but Sarah was not overawed.

She had a new dress for the occasion, made by her mother, of cream linen with a square neckline and box pleats. It fitted her perfectly, and her mother had given her a dab of the Evening in Paris perfume that had been a present from Greg.

She stood waiting with her father and John to welcome Mary and Sam, who had gone first to kiss Sally and Lawrie.

'This is Sarah,' Cathy said, but Mary only smiled at her briefly, then her eyes went to John who stood beside his sister.

Mary was wearing Louis-heeled shoes and John, tall and broad-shouldered, seemed to tower over her. She took his outstretched hand and smiled up into his face. John, seeming dazzled by her beauty, stood tongue-tied and motionless until she said huskily, 'Don't I get a kiss, John?'

He woke from his trance, and smiled and kissed her. She patted his cheek before turning to where Greg, as tall but thinner than John, stood obscured by him. Sam was shaking hands with John and Cathy had gone to put a cushion at her mother's back when Mary stood before Greg and held out both her hands.

'Hello, Mary,' he said quietly, smiling at her. She drew in her breath at that remembered smile. Her hands gripped his as he bent, intending a light brotherly kiss, but Mary pressed her lips hungrily on his and her body close to him.

Surprised, and unwilling to hurt her by rejection, Greg prolonged the kiss for a moment then drew gently away and said with an effort, 'You look very well, Mary.' She was trembling and her breathing was quick and shallow, but Greg turned so that she was shielded from sight as he shook hands with Sam.

Anger was replacing shock in Greg's mind as he looked at Sam's honest face, and thought of Mary's behaviour. So she's still at that game, he thought, and having the damn cheek to do it in my own house, with my wife and her husband here.

Greg would have been surprised to know that Mary's behaviour had been as much a shock to herself as to him. She was a faithful wife to Sam in spite of many temptations to be otherwise in the circles in which they moved, and she was horrified that her love for Greg could be so quickly revived.

I thought I was over all that, she thought in distress, but he only has to smile at me. Oh God, how am I going to get through these weeks? And he doesn't even realize!

She quickly recovered her bright smile and teasing manner, and no one suspected the turmoil within her as she joked with her father and talked about the other passengers on the liner they had sailed in.

She and Greg were both confident that they had been unobserved. Sam had been engrossed in his conversation with John and Cathy had been busy making her parents comfortable, placing a stool for Sally's feet and a small table beside her father for his tobacco.

They had both overlooked Sarah who had moved away from the group and was the unwilling observer of the passionate kiss. She saw the shock on her father's face and decided that Mary was to blame. But why hadn't he pushed her away immediately? she wondered. For a moment her faith in her beloved father wavered, then she decided that he was unwilling to cause a fuss and upset her mother.

She watched Mary with dislike and contempt, noting her successful efforts to charm everyone and deciding that *she* would never be charmed by her. She would ignore her aunt as far as possible during the rest of her stay.

Cathy and Greg were handing round drinks from a tray which stood on the record cabinet, and contained whisky, rum, port, a bottle of John Collins cocktail and one of crème de menthe. There was also a dish of cheese straws and Cathy felt proudly that Mary and Sam would see that she and Greg knew what was right for an evening party.

The crème de menthe and the cocktails had arrived in Cathy's case after a job, via the poacher's pocket beneath Cissie's apron.

'Ee are, girl, for your next "do",' she had said. 'Don't feel nothing about taking them from this lot. It's been a bloody pig of a job and they owe us this and more.'

'But can't you use them, Cissie?' Cathy said.

'No, girl, my fella wouldn't drink this foreign muck. He'd rather have Red Biddy, but youse young ones are different.'

'I don't feel guilty about taking them,' Cathy told Greg. 'And I'm not going to tell it in Confession because I don't think I've done anything wrong. Everywhere was filthy and we had to clean for nearly an hour before we could start to lay up. Mr Owen said he couldn't pay extra because it wasn't the responsibility of the firm to have a clean hall and kitchen, and the people who booked us didn't even thank us for the cleaning.'

Greg agreed that the women were entitled to take the money owed to them in kind, and they laughed together about Cissie's words. They exchanged smiles, too, when Mary said, 'How sophisticated! John Collins and my favourite crème de menthe.'

'We got it to match your dress,' Greg said, winking at Cathy.

Chapter Eighteen

Sarah was relieved to see her parents joking together but it did nothing to change her feelings towards Mary. Later in the evening her aunt commented on Sarah's cream linen dress and the alice band which held back her hair, but Sarah looked at her unsmilingly, without speaking, and Mary decided she was gauche and turned back to charming the boys and Kate.

For the rest of the visit Kate hung round her at every possible moment, and Mary was flattered and pleased by the little girl's devotion to her.

'You'll have to come and visit with us when you're a little older,' she told Kate, and the child was even more enchanted.

John also fell victim to Mary's charm, and spent as much time as possible in her company, and Cathy and her parents poured out their affection for her unstintingly. This compensated Mary a little for the fact that Greg was avoiding her, and for the disconcertingly hostile glances she received from Sarah, but Sam was a favourite with everyone and he and Greg became firm friends.

Only once did Greg speak to Mary alone, and that was for a special reason. They had all gathered as usual in Cathy's parlour, and talk had turned to Lawrie's health and to how much it had improved.

'As long as we don't have fog,' Cathy said. 'Fog always causes trouble.' She happened to glance at Mary as she spoke, and was amazed to see Mary dart an angry glance at Greg.

Cathy was unaware that when Greg was returning home after demobolization at the end of the war, he had been stranded in a London 'pea soup' fog and Mary had tried unsuccessfully to seduce him. Now she evidently thought that Cathy knew of the incident and was making an oblique reference to it.

Greg's face coloured but he said hurriedly, 'We may have a mild winter. We're due one.'

'Aye, we've had enough bad ones the last few years,' Lawrie said. 'But the way I feel now, I could deal with anything, even fog.'

'We'll drink to that, Grandad,' John said, raising his glass, and the awkward moment passed, but Mary remained unusually silent for some time.

The memory of her humiliation was like a sore in her mind, which she had covered by telling herself that Greg was impossibly provincial and by all the success she had enjoyed since then. But the thought that Cathy knew of it was unbearable to her.

The memory of that night, her love for Greg, and the thought that he had betrayed her to Cathy, all churned in her mind and filled her with bitterness and regret. For once she was unable to join in the merry conversation. Sam sat down beside her. 'All right, honey?' he asked, and she raised her head and forced a smile.

'Of course,' she said. 'A bit tired, that's all.'

'We'll leave early then,' he said. 'Have an early bedtime.'

Dear Sam, she thought. Always watching out for her. She was very fond of Sam – she *loved* him. This crazy feeling for Greg was a kind of madness in her blood; once she was away from him she could forget him.

But she knew in her heart that, madness or not, it was with her until the day she died.

And he was Cathy's husband! She watched with bitterness as Greg took a glass from her and they stood smiling at each other.

A little later Cathy and Sarah went out to prepare supper, and then while Sam and John and Lawrie discussed Roosevelt and Sally listened placidly, Greg drew Mary to the other end of the room.

'Cathy knows nothing of the fog in London,' he said quietly. 'She thinks I met you briefly on the station and tried to persuade you to come home, but you wouldn't come. That's all.'

'It's a wonder you mentioned me at all,' she said,

an angry colour in her cheeks.

'I had to tell your parents you were alive and well. They were so worried about you,' he said. 'I said at first that I saw you from the train but then I had to admit I'd spoken to you. I'm a poor liar, Mary, and I *hated* deceiving Cathy, but I thought it was better all round.'

'Why did she say that about fog?' Mary demanded.

'Because it's the truth. It does upset your dad. Anyway, Cathy wouldn't go that way about it if she knew anything. She's too straight.'

'Quite perfect,' Mary sneered, turning away to sit by her father and be comforted by his abundant, uncritical love.

When everyone had gone home, and Cathy and Greg were preparing for bed, she asked him about the glance from her sister. 'Why did Mary give you that dirty look tonight?' she asked.

'I don't know. I was surprised,' he said.

'What were you doing? I had my back to you when I saw her look daggers at you. There must have been some reason.'

'I was only giving Kate some dandelion and burdock,' he said. 'And I looked up and got that look. Who knows with Mary?'

Cathy looked thoughtful. 'I wonder,' she said. 'You know, Mam got hold of the wrong end of the stick about that letter. She thought it was because Mary was upset to see our family. Well, we know that wasn't the reason that time, but I wonder if she does feel a bit jealous, and now and again she can't help showing it?'

'Perhaps,' Greg said. 'But we can't keep the kids locked away.' He gave a sigh of relief then said quickly, 'I don't envy Sam, dealing with her moods.'

'Sam's well able to,' Cathy said. 'He's a good husband, the way he took her home early because she was tired. I was going to suggest having a dance to the records but perhaps we can do that tomorrow night.' She kissed him and said goodnight, but Greg lay awake for a while thinking of his narrow escape. Blast Mary, he thought. I never wanted to deceive Cathy about that business and now I've had to compound it by deceiving her again. I'll be glad when Mary goes back and I don't care if I never see her again. She's nothing but trouble. Sam deserves better than a wife who flirts with every man she sees.

Greg was still unaware of the depth of Mary's feeling for him and that he was the only one who could arouse such a response from her.

The following night Mick was enlisted to wind the gramophone, and Mary and Sam, Cathy and Greg, and John and Sarah all danced to the records of Jack Hylton and Henry Hall. Cathy danced several times with Sam and there was much laughter when they danced an "exhibition tango", but Greg was careful to dance only once with Mary, and then she danced chiefly with John.

Cathy and Greg had talked about their visits to the Grafton Rooms and Sam suggested that they should make up a foursome to go there on Thursday night.

'We'll have to ask Josie and Walter,' Greg said firmly. 'We go with them every week.'

'That scatty girl!' Mary exclaimed.

'She's not scatty now,' said Cathy. 'She lost four brothers during the war, including Frank.' She looked challengingly at Mary. 'We're very good friends.'

'Josie got the waitress job for Cathy,' Sally said.

Greg was determined to include Josie and Walter in the party, and not to be part of a foursome which would mean dancing frequently with Mary. Even when dancing in the parlour she had pressed herself close to him, and he felt that in the crowded ballroom she would be even more blatant. He was not flattered by her behaviour, remembering Mary in her youth and the constant succession of young men around her, and believing that she still craved for that adulation from any available man. She can do what she likes in America, he thought grimly, but she's not going to do anything here to hurt Cathy.

Josie was reluctant at first, urging Cathy to go just with Mary and Sam, but finally she was persuaded.

The evening was surprisingly successful. Walter was shy and tongue-tied at first but as they sat down round a table on the balcony, Mary said patronizingly, 'Do you dance, Walter?'

Her tone aroused his native independence and he said straight-faced, 'No, I come because the chair's comfortable.'

Sam gave a shout of laughter and Mary had the grace to smile, then Walter stood up and asked her to dance.

It was a tango at which Walter excelled and he swung Mary around and bent her back almost to the floor. She entered into the spirit of it and made her movements as exaggerated as his, and they came back to the table flushed and laughing.

That seemed to set the tone for the evening, and everything that happened seemed to be cause for laughter. Greg danced once with Mary. When they returned to the table, a man they knew slightly approached them.

'Oh, God, here's the lounge lizard,' Josie whispered. He was a slim man, with dark hair plastered to his head with brilliantine, and a pencil-thin moustache. He spoke as though they were close friends. Greg was compelled to introduce Mary and Sam, and immediately he asked Mary to dance.

'Looks a bit of a dago. Is he all right?' Sam asked as Mary went to the dance floor with the man.

'He's harmless,' Cathy assured him. 'He just thinks he's God's gift to women.'

'And Mary thinks she's God's gift to men,' Josie laughed. 'This should be good.'

Cathy glanced quickly at Sam, but he was laughing at Josie's bluntness and asked her to dance. Walter claimed Cathy, and Greg sat back and watched the dancers. The lounge lizard brought Mary back after the dance and left after a deep bow. She sat down, fanning herself.

'Phew. Isn't he *incredible*? Why didn't you rescue me?' she challenged Greg. 'I thought you'd come and excuse me.'

'I couldn't have caught you,' he said. 'The way you were swooping through the crowd.'

Mary laughed. 'Watch out for him,' she said. 'I'm afraid he'll be back.' But when the next dance was announced and the man approached their table, they all quickly stood up and moved on to the dance floor.

Time flew and they were amazed when the Last Waltz was announced. They each danced with their own partner. The dance floor was crowded with couples but at one point Mary and Sam found themselves close to Cathy and Greg.

The music was soft and romantic and the lights were low.

Oblivious to the couples around them, Greg and Cathy danced cheek to cheek, holding each other close. Involuntarily Mary drew in her breath and her hand tightened on Sam's shoulder.

He steered her away and looked down at her. 'Remember the ship's ballroom where we met again, honey?' he said. 'I looked across the room and there you were. I know what they mean when they say "My heart stood still".'

Mary smiled. 'I was so unhappy, Sam,' she said softly, 'and you made everything right for me.'

'I always will, honey,' he promised.

The dance ended and the lights went up, and everyone stood applauding the band and looking about them self-consciously.

That evening at the Grafton Rooms was the only time that Mary spent away from her parents, except for the necessary time at the hotel, but the weather continued fine and Sam arranged several outings.

He hired a large car and drove Mary and Cathy, Sally, Lawrie and Kate, to Southport where they had tea in the Palm Room of one of the large hotels.

Afterwards Mary decided that she and Sam would take Kate to look at the shops and more tea was ordered for Cathy, Sally and Lawrie. When the tea was brought Cathy chatted to the elderly waitress, telling her about her own job with the catering firm.

When the waitress moved away, Sally sighed. 'I wish I could be more at ease in these places,' she said. 'But I can't. It's silly at my age.'

'There's nobody any better than us here, Sal,' Lawrie said sturdily. 'Hold your head up, girl.'

'I always do,' she said tartly.

Cathy said quickly. 'I like Southport. I always enjoyed a day on the shore here when the children were small.'

'Our poor Emily was here, remember? I wonder, is that nursing home far away?' Sally asked. 'Not that I want to go there,' she added quickly. Her face was sad and Lawrie put his hand over hers.

'Emily was happy here, love,' he said, 'and she had a happy death.'

Sally smiled at him and Cathy watched them with

affection. How easily Dad can find the right words of comfort, especially for Mam, she thought. A moment later Mary and Sam arrived, laden with gifts for the family.

Kate had a heart-shaped little locket on a fine chain and a brooch in the shape of a dog. She wanted to show these to her mother right away, but the other gifts were left in their wrappings until later. They left the hotel and Cathy hung back to say goodbye to the waitress.

'Cathy's made a friend,' Lawrie said with a grin. 'She does that everywhere she goes.'

'She's not as shy as she used to be then,' Sam said.

'No. But, mind you, she was always friendly for all she was so shy,' Sally said. 'I think this job's brought her out of her shell a bit.'

They walked down through the flower gardens to the Pier and Sally told everyone to breathe deeply.

'This ozone is very good for you,' she told them. They all looked well, slightly sunburned, and in Cathy's case wind-blow too. Her hat had blown off twice and her hair was untidy. She looked at Mary and Kate and marvelled that they both looked as neat as when they set out.

Mary was wearing blue chiffon with a blue fur cape and a tiny pillbox hat in blue fur tilted over her right eye. Even her red-gold hair curling around it seemed undisturbed. I'm just naturally untidy, Cathy concluded ruefully.

They had a day trip on the Isle of Man boat, and another on the boat to Eastham. As they walked along from the boat, Cathy noticed that her mother's arm was linked in her father's and that they were holding hands, as they strolled slowly along.

She remembered then that their brief honeymoon had been spent at Eastham, and tactfully fell back to ask Sam to lift Kate up to see a liner in the river. They stood for a few moments, talking about the ships, until Kate exclaimed, 'We've lost Grandma.'

'We'll soon catch them up,' Cathy said, and they all ambled along until they came upon Lawrie and Sally looking into a small wood.

'We'll go up to the hotel when you're ready,' Sam said.

Sally said wistfully, 'We were looking about for a little cottage that used to serve teas, but we can't see it.'

'It was a long time ago, girl,' Lawrie said gently. 'Forty-four years in October.' They smiled at each other and Kate put her hand in Sally's.

'We thought we'd lost you, Gran,' she said.

Kate was delighted with the tiny cucumber sandwiches and the dainty cakes served at the hotel, but before they reached the boat again she announced that she was hungry.

'You've got to get used to that if you want to be a lady,' Sam told her solemnly. 'Did you know about Kate's plans, Grandma?' he said to Sally.

'Hmm, we're all as God made us,' she said, with a glance at Mary.

Sally was nervous in motor cars and enjoyed the trips by train or boat more; but even on the train Sam booked first-class and they went to a luxury hotel in Morecambe for tea. 'I'm too old a dog to learn new tricks,' Sally told Cathy. 'I enjoy the evenings in your parlour most of all.'

Lawrie was due to retire at the end of the month and the yard manager had told him that he would turn a blind eye if he took time off while his daughter was home, so he was able to go on these trips. But Cathy hinted to Sam that they were tiring for him, and most of the time was spent at home.

The gifts from Southport had pleased everyone. Sally received a sapphire and diamond brooch, Cathy a gold bracelet and Sarah a gold locket. For Greg they had bought a silver cigarette case and for Lawrie a leatherbound set of the works of Charles Dickens. John and Mick both received silver-backed hairbrushes, and before they left Mary tried to persuade Cathy to have some of her clothes, but she refused.

'They'd be wasted on me, Mary,' she said. 'I wouldn't have the opportunity to wear them, and they wouldn't look the same on me anyway.'

'You're just too independent, that's what it is,' Mary said. 'You're as bad as Dad.'

It was nearly time for Mary and Sam to leave but before that they had a serious talk with Sally and Lawrie.

'We want to talk about money, Mr Ward,' Sam said. 'The last time we did that it had to be by letter and I don't think I was able to tell you how much we appreciated your offer to send that money. Well, we've been damn' lucky and we're on our feet again now. I'd like to – well, open up again on that, now you're due to retire.'

'We're all right, lad. Don't worry about us,' Lawrie said hastily.

'It's ourselves we're thinking about really, isn't that so, Mary?' Sam said. 'You know it says in the Bible "Honour thy father and thy mother," and this is the only way we can do it. If you'll let us send something, not to keep you, just to put a bit of jam on the bread if you like, it'd ease our minds no end, wouldn't it, Mary?

She slipped her arm through Lawrie's. 'Let Sam do it, Dada,' she pleaded. 'It's the only way we can help. I can't clean your windows or anything like Cathy does.'

'And I can't put up a shelf like Greg,' Sam said. 'But we want to be part of the family.'

'You are, lad, you are,' Sally and Lawrie both protested.

'I'd feel I was if you'd let us do this,' he said. 'I'm sure my parents would take it if they were still alive.'

Lawrie and Sally looked at each other and Lawrie said, 'I get your point, Sam, and you know I believe that children should look after their parents if they're in need, but me and Mam have always managed all right for money.'

He caught an ironic glance from Sally and chuckled. 'I'd better amend that. Your mam has always managed all right for money. I'm hopeless with it as you well know, Mary.'

'So will you take it, *please*, Dada?' she coaxed him, and Sam put his hand on Sally's.

'Will you, Mrs Ward?' he asked. She looked at Lawrie and gave a slight nod.

He said cheerfully, 'Yes, we will, and thanks very much. I never heard of anyone pleading to give money away before.'

'You're good children to us and we're very grateful to you,' Sally said quietly.

The next morning Sam told them that it was all settled. 'It'll be in the form of an annuity,' he said. 'So you'll receive a draft each month starting the beginning of September.'

'That was quick work!' Lawrie exclaimed.

'I might as well tell you, I had it all worked out,' Sam said. 'I just needed your say so.'

Mary and Sam were due to leave the following day and

although Cathy had sometimes been irritated by Mary, when the time came she wept bitterly at the thought that her sister was leaving, and that she might not see her again for years, and Lawrie wept with Mary as she clung to him.

Sally hid her feelings behind a stony expression until the last moment, when she too broke down and cried. Kate wept and asked if she could go with them, but Mary promised that she would send for her one day.

Mary had asked if they could say goodbye at home but Kate pleaded to go to see them off on the boat and Mick was looking hopefully at Sam. In the end it was decided that John would take Mick and Kate to wait at the Landing Stage to wave them off, but the other goodbyes were said at home.

When they had all departed, Sarah made a pot of tea for her parents and grandparents. She had expressed no wish to go to the Pier Head, and no one had pressed her.

She liked Sam and was sorry to see him go, but the episode on the first night had given her a deep distrust of Mary, and her young intolerance could see no redeeming feature in a woman who had behaved so with her father. Mary was aware of her animosity and had not bothered to try to charm her, and they parted with no regret on either side.

Chapter Nineteen

Before Mary and Sam had even reached America, life had settled back to normal for their relations in Liverpool. Everyone was pleased that Lawrie had now reached retirement age, and Sally was pleased to have him home all day.

'I won't have to worry now when the weather's bad, because he won't have to go out in it,' she told Cathy.

Mary's visit seemed to have completed the improvement in Lawrie's health and he was fitter and stronger than he had been for years.

'I feel a fraud, retiring now,' he told John. 'I seem to have got a second wind.'

'But you didn't retire because of your health,' John said. 'You'd reached retirement age.'

Lawrie had resigned as treasurer of his union, but was still organizing committees and deputations, working hard for better wages and conditions.

'It's all so *slow*, Grandad,' John said impatiently.

'Yes, but steady, lad. There's a poem I often thought of when things seemed at a standstill and I was young and impatient like you. It's by a Liverpool man, too, Arthur Hugh Clough:

> "Say not the struggle naught availeth,
> The labour and the wounds are vain,
> The enemy faints not nor Faileth,
> And as things have been things remain.
> For while the tired waves, vainly breaking
> Seem here no painful inch to gain,
> Far back through creeks and inlet making,
> Comes silent, flooding in the main."

'Think of that, John, when you feel things are too slow. Quietly and steadily we're making ground, lad. Some of the things I've fought for have come, and more will yet.'

John was not convinced. 'I don't think we can afford to wait, Grandad,' he said. 'Peter's brother was in London last week and he said the Fascists are strutting round as large as life. I saw one here in Sheil Park in jackboots and a blackshirt. Gerry and I chased him, and Gerry said: "He'll have brown trousers now as well as a black shirt." '

Lawrie looked troubled. 'Those lads are a bit wild, aren't they, John?'

'No, we just meet and talk usually, but we're worried about what's happening in Abyssinia.'

'Aye, but it's been referred to the League of Nations,' Lawrie said. 'They'll make this Signor Mussolini toe the line.'

'I don't know,' John said. 'Dad believes in the League and the Peace Pledge people, but I don't think Signor Mussolini or Herr Hitler cares about them.'

John felt that he had been proved right when Italy invaded Abyssinia on October the third, and all the news reels showed the sad figure of the tiny Emperor Haile Selassie.

'He looks romantic and dignified in that cloak, doesn't he, even though he's so small?' Sarah's friend Eileen whispered to her. 'I like tall men really, though.'

Sarah knew that the tall man who interested Eileen most was John, but she had warned her that he was too busy with politics to bother about girls.

'He'll soon get fed up with them,' Eileen said confidently, but Sarah was not so sure.

Sarah was desperately in love at this time, but not with a real person, and not even with one man but with two.

Her grandfather had found the article about Rupert Brooke which carried a picture of the poet. His large eyes looked out from a handsome face, his chin resting on his hand and dark hair falling in waves above his brow. He wore a loose shirt and a broad tie, with the deep cuffs on his shirt turned back. 'He looks like a poet, doesn't he, Grandad?' Sarah sighed. 'He seems to be looking right at you too.'

She had framed the picture in passe partout and hung it above her bed, but now it had been joined by another picture, that of the actor Hugh Williams. He too looked unsmilingly from the picture and had large dark eyes and sensitive features, and Sarah found it hard to decide which photograph appealed to her most.

She took Eileen Reddy up to see them, and Eileen assured her that it was possible to be in love with two men at once. 'It said so in *Peg's Paper,*' she told Sarah. She also said that she thought that both men were like Sarah's dad, but Sarah disagreed with her.

'For one thing Dad's quite old,' she said, but her real reason was that it seemed wrong to feel as she did when she looked into the eyes in the pictures if they were linked by a resemblance to her father. Sarah knew exactly how she felt but would have been unable to explain her feelings to anyone else, although sometimes her grandfather seemed to understand her.

He had found a copy of the poems of Rupert Brooke in the Library, and she had been amazed to find that lines had been taken from a longer poem and put together to form the short poem she had seen in the *Guides' Handbook*. She also learned that the poem had been written in Lulworth Cove, and Lawrie said that she might go there one day.

'I wouldn't want to, Grandad,' she said.

He looked surprised. 'You wouldn't, love? Why not?'

'Because I – I have a picture of it in my mind,' she said. 'If I go there it might not be the same, and it would spoil the poem.'

Her grandfather had not laughed, Sarah thought later with gratitude, only kissed her gently and said, 'Oh, wise young bird. You're right, love. Don't ever change, Sarah.'

Lawrie was enjoying his retirement. The extra money from Sam meant that they could live comfortably without drawing on their savings, and he enjoyed pottering round the second-hand book shop in Brunswick Road while Sally shopped for food, then meeting her to sit in the herb shop and drink a mug of Bovril before walking home arm in arm.

Most of the crops had been cleared from the allotment, and Greg spent only a couple of hours there at the weekend but he and Lawrie enjoyed planning for the following year, reading through catalogues and making scale drawings of the plot.

John still held long discussions about local politics with his grandfather, but he said nothing about his activities with Gerry and his group.

One night when Cathy was out late at a job, Greg heard a noise in the lobby and went to investigate. John was leaning against the wall, breathing heavily. His coat was torn and there was mud on his face and blood from a cut above his eye. He straightened up when he saw Greg and tried to push past him but his father blocked his way.

'What's this?' he said. 'Breaking up meetings?'

'No. Someone trying to break up ours,' John said in an insolent voice. 'But they didn't succeed, you'll be sorry to hear.'

Greg had been about to offer to treat the cut, but he lost his temper at John's tone.

'Don't speak to me like that,' he said furiously. 'You're not with your roughneck friends now, and by God you'll behave civilly in this house.'

'Do you call that civil? Insulting my friends,' John said hotly. 'I'll do what I like. It's my life.'

Greg stood back and gestured towards the kitchen. 'Go and clean yourself up before your mother sees you,' he said with icy contempt. He went back to his chair and tried to read but found he was reading the same lines over and over as he strained his ears to listen for Cathy above the noise of splashing from the kitchen.

Finally he put the book aside and went to the door of the back kitchen. John's torn jacket lay on the chair and he had washed his face but blood still trickled from the cut.

'Sit down. I'll dress that,' Greg said quietly. As John began to refuse, he added, 'Your mother will be here at any moment.'

John sat down on the chair without a word and Greg quickly and skilfully dressed the cut.

'You'd better go up to bed and take that jacket before she comes. I'll bring you a cup of tea.'

'I don't want—' John began.

Greg said firmly, 'Treatment for shock. Very necessary.'

John was cold and trembling with the shock of the sudden

attack, and he knew that his father was right. Although he would have liked to refuse help, he was glad to accept the mug of hot tea and the aspirins his father brought up when he was in bed.

When Greg bent over him and put the aspirins in his hand John felt a sudden urge to cry and cling to his father, but Greg spoke and the moment passed.

'I'm not going to ask you any questions now,' he said, 'but I expect you to tell me tomorrow what happened. I'm sure you'll be able to think of a convincing lie for your mother about that cut.' He hesitated, but John said nothing and kept his eyes lowered. Greg went out of the room.

Sarcastic swine! thought John. He regretted his moment of weakness and was glad that he had not given way to it.

The next morning John told his father briefly that he and Gerry had gone to a meeting in the park, and had been standing at the back when a crowd of hooligans had suddenly attacked them. John had been hit by a stick and knocked to the ground, and Gerry had pulled him up and away from the crowd.

To his mother he explained that the cut over his eye had been caused when he and Gerry had been "horsing around" in his friend's bedroom and he had fallen against the furniture. Thanks to Greg's treatment the cut was healing and looked insignificant, and Cathy was less interested in it than in the fact that it had been acquired in the doctor's house. She was innocently pleased that John had taken up again with such "nice" friends, and told her mother about it later.

Lawrie looked up and frowned. 'I don't like him going round with that lad, Cathy. He's very wild.'

'John said he used to be but he's not now,' Cathy replied.

Sally said, 'Peggy says the doctor and his wife have patched things up so maybe that's had some effect on the lad.'

John talked to his grandfather later about the fracas.

'It was unprovoked, Grandad,' he insisted. 'The speaker *was* a Communist, and Gerry and I had gone along to listen, but those louts attacked the crowd for no reason. They weren't in uniform but I'm sure they were Blackshirts.'

'I'd give the whole lot a wide berth if I was you, lad,'

Lawrie said. 'There's better ways of going about things. Your mam told us about the fall but I thought it sounded a bit fishy. She and your gran believed it, though.'

'I could have told Mum the truth and she'd have understood,' John said angrily. 'But *my father* told me to tell her a lie.'

Lawrie looked surprised at the way John spat out the words "my father" and said quietly, 'Don't underestimate your dad, John. He'll do anything to shield your mam from worry. He might have a quiet manner, lad, but underneath that he can be very hard where she's concerned. He won't let her be hurt.'

'You mean, he'll ditch his conscience and tell me to lie?' John said.

'I mean he won't let anyone upset your mam, John, not even you.'

'But I wouldn't upset her,' protested John.

'Not intentionally,' Lawrie said. 'But just watch yourself, lad, and try and see why your dad gets narked sometimes.'

Although John felt sometimes that his grandfather's views were out of date, he still had a great respect for him and stored up his words in his mind.

There was a spatter of hail against the window as Sally came in from the parlour where she had been making up the fire for Josh.

'Will you listen to that?' she exclaimed. 'I hope Josh waits for it to go off but I don't suppose he will. He goes out and comes back at the same time every night, no matter what.'

'I see that fellow in Birkdale forecasts a hard winter,' Lawrie said. 'Well, he's been right before. We're having freak weather all right. Snow in May.'

'It's these aeroplanes, I'm sure, disturbing the heavens,' Sally said. 'If God meant people to fly, he'd have given them wings.'

'Better not let Mick hear you, Gran,' John said, grinning. 'He's determined to have a flight soon. He wanted to go up when they went to Blackpool but he hadn't enough money. He'll do it though. You know how determined he is.'

'And the first thing he'd do would be fall out of it,' Sally exclaimed. 'Surely your mam won't let him?'

'No. He hangs round Speke at the new Airport but he only talks to mechanics. You need money to fly, Gran.'

Since his retirement Lawrie had visited old workmates who were ill in hospital and without family to visit them, and one day at the beginning of December he visited an old man in the Southern Hospital and took him some sweets and some of Sally's cakes.

The day had been fine but rain began to fall as Lawrie waited for the tram home. When it came, it was crowded. The conductor allowed four people on but put his arm across as Lawrie and an old woman attempted to board it.

The old woman was a "Mary Ellen" wearing voluminous skirts and a black shawl. She said civilly to the conductor, 'How long'll the next tram be, Mister?'

'The same length as this one, Missis,' he said loudly, guffawing at his own wit.

Quick as a flash the woman shouted, 'An' will it 'ave a gobshite like you on the back too?'

The smile was wiped from the conductor's face and Lawrie stood helpless with laughter at the expression on the man's face as the tram moved off. He was so tickled by the incident that it seemed no time to him before the next tram came, but it was nearly fifteen minutes and he was thoroughly soaked when he arrived home.

He tried to tell Sally about the incident at the tram stop but she bundled him upstairs. 'Go and get those wet clothes off. When are you going to learn sense, Lawrie?'

She had a hot drink ready for him and a mustard bath for his feet when he came downstairs, but in spite of her remedies Lawrie developed a cold which soon became a bout of bronchitis.

Fortunately the attack was slight, but all the family regarded it as a warning that he was still vulnerable and Lawrie promised to be more careful in future.

'I don't know what I'm supposed to do,' he said to Greg when they were alone. 'Sally'd like to keep me in this kitchen for the whole of the winter, as if I was hibernating. I can't let people down when they're waiting for a visitor.' Greg agreed but said he understood why Sally was so worried.

'She said she could wring the water out of your cap,' he said. 'I don't think you can stay in all the time but you should be ready for our English weather. Wear a raincoat and carry a spare cap in your pocket.'

'That's sensible talk, lad,' Lawrie said. He grinned. 'You don't mind if I put it to Sally as my own idea? I've got to convince her I'm sensible, safe to be let out.'

Before Christmas Lawrie was able to visit the hospitals again, carrying a raincoat and a spare cap, and bearing small gifts to make the holiday more cheerful for his old workmates. Sally had been impressed by the idea of his carrying a spare cap, as she was convinced that Lawrie's cold had been caused by the fact that he had worn his wet cap while travelling home on the tram.

It was a happy Christmas for all the family. Money was more plentiful and Cathy and Sally were able to spend freely on extra food and small luxuries. As usual each family had the Christmas dinner at home then all went to the grand-parents' house for tea.

Sally had the usual leg of pork for dinner, supplemented this year by a sirloin of beef provided by Josh. He had also bought one for the Redmond family. This year for the first time they also had a turkey for the Christmas dinner.

Cathy felt proud as she looked around the table at her well-fed, well-dressed family. The scrubbed kitchen table and dresser had recently been replaced with a square dining table and chairs with seats covered in rexine, and a highly polished sideboard. A large bowl of fruit and dishes of sweets and nuts stood on the sideboard, and the table was filled with the turkey and beef and tureens of vegetables. There were also, for the first time, two bottles of wine provided by John. He had bought a sweet white wine for his mother and Sarah, and a Burgundy which he knew his father would enjoy.

John was on better terms with his father now. Gerry's father had been told by a patient about the trouble at the meeting, and in the ensuing row had hit Gerry several times with his walking stick and told him that if there was any more trouble he could get out of the house.

'He knows damn' well that I've got nowhere else to go, otherwise I wouldn't stay there,' Gerry told John gloomily. 'For two pins I'd chuck the quantity surveying and go to sea.'

'You'd never get a ship,' John said. 'Look at the experienced seamen in the club who are ashore for months.'

'That's all that's stopping me,' Gerry said quickly, but John felt that he had seized on the excuse. He's a bit of a windbag, he thought. He felt so even more strongly when they arrived at the Club.

There were several groups within the Club. The one in which Gerry and John moved was of young men like themselves, enthusiastic but inexperienced, idealistic but not yet sure how to attain their goal of a better world for the mass of suffering humanity they saw around them.

There was another group of older men who had been imprisoned for leading demonstrations or heading hunger marches, including one who belonged to the International Workers of the World, a man who had been a police striker, and several seamen who knew something of conditions in America.

These men held themselves aloof but there was one whom John particularly admired. He was a quietly spoken man who reminded John of his grandfather. He was a speaker at one meeting when a man had complained about the apathy of working men and said they were not worth fighting for.

The speaker had said instantly, 'Don't ever say that. These men are your brothers. You've got to find the cause of the apathy. For every man who just can't be bothered, there's another who longs to fight but whose hands are tied because he has a wife and a crowd of children to keep. His day will come, though.'

'That's tosh,' Gerry whispered to John, who disagreed.

'No, it isn't. He always talks sense, like my grandad.'

Gerry sniggered. 'I'd better not say any more about him then,' he said.

When they entered the Club on the night after John had been injured, the quiet man, George, came to speak to him and ask about the meeting. Gerry kept close to John, and when the older men crowded round implied that the bruises on his face caused by his father's stick had been received at the meeting.

John was disgusted by his boasting, especially when he remembered him pleading, 'Don't hit me, don't hit me,' to the youths, and using John's injury as an excuse to dash away from the meeting. He said nothing about this however as they walked home, but only commented on the toughness of the older men and all they had endured.

'My old man would be a match for any of them,' Gerry boasted. 'Not like yours.'

'What do you mean?' John demanded.

'Well, he's a bit of a wet Echo, isn't he?' Gerry laughed. 'Too meek to raise his voice, never mind his hand.'

'That's where you're wrong,' John said angrily. 'Just because he doesn't shout and bluster doesn't mean that he's soft. Just the opposite, in fact.' He was amazed to find himself defending his father, but they had reached the corner by then. He parted from Gerry and walked away, still angry.

The cheek of him to criticize my father! he thought. Suggesting that he's inferior to old Hanson. He told me himself that his mother was screaming at his father to stop hitting him, and his father ignored her. Dad's only concern was to stop Mum being upset about my cut. And to imply that Dad's soft! He's stronger than the doctor, and with a damn sight more principle too. He'd never look at another woman.

John was still in this mood when he was given a Christmas bonus at work. He decided to buy wine for the Christmas dinner, and chose the Burgundy for his father. Now, as he surveyed the table, he felt proud of his contribution to it and thought the wine bottles lent an air of sophistication.

Of all the people sitting around the table, Sarah was the happiest, but her emotion had nothing to do with the array of good things. She was in the throes of first love for a real person, a young man who came every day to the shop.

He was tall, with blue eyes and dark hair growing in a "widow's peak", and Sarah fell in love with him as soon as she saw him. Mabel, who carried a store of lines of poetry in her mind and always attributed them to the Bible, told Sarah that this was the real thing. 'As it says in the Bible,' she said, ' "He never loved who loved not at first sight." '

It was Mabel who found that he worked in the office of an engineering works and that his name was Michael Rourke. Sarah was happy just to think about him all the time, and to pick out the largest and best pie for him, smiling at him in a bemused way as she handed it to him and their hands met. He seemed as shy as her and they might have gone on like this for months if Mabel had not given matters a push.

She bustled round when he came in the shop and took over the pie queue as soon as Sarah began to serve him, so that they were free to exchange a few words. Michael mentioned that he had seen the film *Naughty Marietta*, and Mabel immediately joined in, gushing about the singing of Jeanette Macdonald and Nelson Eddy.

Sarah was ready to resent Mabel's taking up Michael's attention until she suddenly found that he was asking her out.

'It's on all week at the Regent in Crosby,' he said. 'Would you like to see it?'

'But you've already seen it,' she said.

He smiled at her. 'I don't mind seeing it again. It's very good.'

Sarah could remember very little about the film. She sat all the time in a happy dream, stealing glances at Michael in the dim glow of the screen, flattered to realize that he was doing the same to her. She wondered whether he would ask to kiss her good night or simply do it.

Eileen Reddy had told her that it said in *Peg's Paper* that a girl should not allow a man to kiss her on a first date. It made her look cheap, and kisses should be kept for the one you really loved. Sarah had agreed at the time but now she knew that she wanted Michael to kiss her, and hoped that he would not think her cheap if she allowed it.

She need not have worried. They sat close together on the tram home, but when they reached Egremont Street Michael held out his hand. 'Goodnight, Sarah,' he said. 'Thank you for your company.'

'Goodnight, and thank you,' she said. Michael held her hand for a moment longer and smiled at her, looking deeply into her eyes. Then, as a woman approached, he said goodnight again and turned away.

Sarah went up the steps to her house, thinking with a touch of her grandmother's dry humour that perhaps Michael read *Peg's Paper* too.

The shop had grown busier as Christmas approached and another assistant had been engaged, named Anne Fitzgerald. Sarah liked her immediately. They were almost the same age and Anne had been working in another cake shop for a few months.

'It was awful,' she told Sarah and Mabel. 'The owner was an Australian. He made lovely fruit cake, but what a bully! He thought he was dealing with kangaroos. All we ever heard out of him was: "Jump to it." '

'You won't get any bullying from Mr and Mrs Dyson,' Mabel told her, 'but you have to pull your weight like Sarah's done since she started.'

Anne was fascinated by Sarah's account of her night out with Michael, and commented that she would have expected a fellow with looks like that to be more experienced.

He still came in the shop every day, but made no attempt to ask Sarah out again. Mabel told her she should encourage him. 'He's shy,' she said. 'You'd never have had that date if I hadn't helped things along. I asked that woman if she'd seen *Naughty Marietta*, and then he said he'd seen it too, so I gave him the wink to ask you.'

'Oh, Mabel, I'd never have gone if I'd known,' she exclaimed. 'I suppose that's why you sent me round to serve that loaf, so I wouldn't hear you.'

'You enjoyed yourself, didn't you?' Mabel demanded.

'Yes, but I'd rather have gone out with him because *he* wanted to ask me.'

'But he does! He's just too shy to get round to it, that's all. Tell him you like George Raft. *Rumba*'s on in Crosby this week, and he can take you.'

'I couldn't,' Sarah gasped.

'You're as bad as he is,' Mabel said. 'You'd ask him, wouldn't you, Anne?'

'No, I wouldn't,' she said. 'I think if he wants to ask Sarah out, he should conquer his shyness and do it.'

'You two are living in a dream world,' Mabel said. 'You'll learn.' But in spite of her irritation with them she spoke to Michael about the film and told him that Sarah liked George Raft.

Sarah was unaware of this and was surprised and pleased when Michael asked her to go to the pictures with him again.

This time he held her hand during the film but when they returned home, instead of the kiss she expected, he shook hands with her and wished her goodnight. Sarah told herself loyally that she preferred a shy boy rather than a pushy type, but wondered how long it would be before Michael managed to kiss her.

It was now nearly Christmas and he had said nothing about seeing her again, but on Christmas Eve when he came to the counter he slipped an envelope into her hand.

Inside the envelope was a Christmas card which simply said, 'Christmas Greetings from Michael', but there was also a very pretty topaz brooch wrapped in tissue paper.

Sarah's first impulse of pleasure was quickly clouded by the thought that she had not bought him a present.

'I thought of it but I didn't want to seem forward. If I'd only known he was going to give me one,' she said.

'It's a pity he didn't have the nous to give it to her yesterday,' Mabel said to Anne. 'I think Sarah's going to have an uphill struggle with this fellow.'

Sarah was delighted with the brooch and the thought that Michael had chosen it especially for her, and as she sat at the Christmas dinner table her hand kept straying up to touch it, or she glanced down at it and smiled blissfully.

The family knew all about Michael, both from Sarah's account of her visits to the cinema with him and from Mabel who had met Sally and told her about him.

'He's a bit backward in coming forward, if you know what I mean,' she said. 'But better that than the other way,' unconsciously echoing Sarah's thought on the subject.

Kate and Mick were happy too, Mick because he had received a Meccano set for Christmas and Kate because her mother had made her a brown velvet dress, and a coat and a bonnet-shaped hat trimmed with some of the brown velvet.

When she came out of church with her parents, several people had told her how pretty she looked, and now as she sat at the table she could see her reflection in the mirror above the sideboard.

John had poured white wine for Cathy and Sarah, and cherry wine for Mick and Kate, and Greg drew the cork of the Burgundy. He held the bottle above John's glass and looked at him inquiringly.

'Just a little, please, Dad. It may be too dry for me,' John said with a worldly air.

Greg guessed that he was quoting the wine merchant, but only said quietly, 'There's a little to try. It's a good wine but tastes vary.'

He put the bottle down and began to carve the turkey and the beef, and the tureens were uncovered and passed round the table which had been extended so that Cathy was further away from Greg than usual. But she smiled at him, a smile of such pure happiness that Greg stood holding the carving knife and smiling back at her as though they were alone in the room.

'Oy, more turkey please,' Mick said, and Greg hastily began to carve again.

How lucky I am, Cathy thought, looking around her, Greg for my husband and these good children. Life was perfect now all her worries were over. No money worries, her father's health better, and most of all Greg and John good friends.

She felt a rush of pride and tenderness as she looked at John. He was a son any mother would be proud of, she thought. Greg hadn't liked his being friendly with Gerry, but they seemed to have quarrelled and John spent his time now with friends from the office or with his grandfather, and the discord between him and his father seemed to be a thing of the past.

She suddenly realised that Sarah and Mick had filled her plate and Mick was pushing the gravy boat to her and saying loudly, 'Oy, wake up at the back there.'

'I was miles away,' Cathy said, laughing.

When the meal was over and cleared away, they gathered up their gifts for Lawrie and Sally and Josh, and went over to their house. Everything was ready there with the meal cleared away, and the sofa and chairs and stool arranged in a semi-circle round the fire.

There had been a vague suggestion that it might be better to meet in Cathy's parlour where there was more room, but no one wanted to break with the tradition of Christmas Day at the old home. Everyone had spent a great deal of thought on the presents they had chosen and everyone had money to buy them this year.

Even Mick had a paper boy's round now, so Kate was the only one who was unable to buy gifts, but she was more interested in receiving than in giving, and quite happy to distribute the presents that her mother provided for her.

There were cries of delight and "Just what I wanted" as the presents were opened, then Kate played with her dolls' sweet shop and other toys and Mick read a *Beano Annual*, while the rest of the family sat around the fire and talked. Josh's armchair had been brought in and he sat puffing his pipe. Greg and Cathy sat together on the sofa. Sarah had put her stool close to her grandma and linked her arm through Sally's, and John sat close to his grandfather.

The talk was all of old times which the older people were happy to recall and the younger ones loved to hear about, and Sally recalled the Christmases when she and Lawrie were young, spent with their neighbour Mrs Malloy and her lodger Paddy.

'Remember Paddy's fiddle?' Lawrie said. 'He could make it sing.'

'And Mrs Mal's tales of her days in service,' Sally said. Cathy had heard the tales as a child and repeated them to Greg and her children, and they all smiled as they remembered them.

'Remember Paddy's suit and his shoes?' Lawrie said suddenly. 'God bless him and Mrs Mal. They helped us to weather the storm.'

'Aye, she helped me all my life,' Sally said simply. 'But never more than then. God rest them both.'

'Hard times, girl,' Lawrie said. 'But we had each other and we got through.' They smiled at each other and Sarah felt her eyes filling with tears, but she gripped her grandmother's arm and blinked them away. Greg stood up and refilled the glasses and Mick produced his mouth organ and suggested that they sang Christmas carols which he would accompany on the mouth organ.

They had a hilarious time as Mick's accompaniment raced ahead of them or fell behind, and they all laughed too much to finish the carol.

After tea they drew around the fire again and Kate sat on her father's knee and Mick on the rag rug with his head against Cathy's knee. Josh volunteered to recite a monologue then Lawrie told a ghost story of a phantom ship and Greg one about a haunted house which made Kate cling to him, and Sarah and her grandmother draw close together. They had turned out the gas and sat in the flickering light of the fire. When they lit the gas again, Cathy looked round the circle as they all blinked their eyes.

She smiled. 'It's been a lovely Christmas, hasn't it?'

They all agreed and Lawrie said cheerfully, 'Aye, the best yet.'

None of the family realized then what a milestone in their lives that Christmas would be, and how often every detail of that happy time would be recalled by each of them throughout the rest of their lives.

Chapter Twenty

After Christmas the weather became even worse, bitterly cold with high winds and torrential rain. Lawrie scarcely went out except to visit old friends who lived alone in nearby streets, and once to visit an old workmate who was in the Royal Infirmary.

It was a short journey and the day was dry, so even to Sally's anxious eyes, he seemed unaffected by his outing.

New Year's Eve was piercingly cold but Lawrie and Greg went out into Egremont Street before twelve o'clock. The tradition was that the man of the house was the first to enter after twelve to 'bring in the New Year', carrying bread and coal as a token of prosperity. They met Walter and other men waiting outside.

On the stroke of twelve the sounds of hooters and sirens from the many ships in the Mersey filled the air, with church bells and even fog horns adding to the noise. The men wished each other Happy New Year then each went into his own house to be greeted by wife and family, before everyone poured out into the street again to exchange greetings and good wishes.

Cathy hugged and kissed her mother then turned to her father. 'A Happy New Year, Dad,' she said.

'Happy New Year, love,' he said, hugging and kissing her. 'Happy times now, eh, Cathy pet?'

'And even happier to come, Dad,' she said. Lawrie turned to kiss Sarah and Josie swooped down on Cathy.

'Happy New Year, Cath,' she shouted exuberantly. 'With plenty of "please be at's", we hope.'

The noise was deafening, with the sound of a drum being beaten and someone playing a saxophone to add to the sound of bells and the ships' hooters. Everyone seemed to want to greet Lawrie, but before long Sally spoke to John who touched his grandfather's arm.

'I think Grandma wants you,' he said. 'She says the table's laid.'

'Right, lad,' Lawrie said immediately, and followed the family into his house. The table was laid with spareribs, bunloaf and mince pies, and Mick and John started to eat even before Greg and Lawrie had poured drinks. They all drank to the New Year but before long Kate was falling asleep on Greg's knee and they took her home to bed.

John and Mick and Sarah went to join the merrymakers at the other end of Egremont Street, and Sally and Lawrie went to bed.

A few hours later Sally woke to hear the sound she dreaded, of Lawrie coughing and wheezing as he drew breath. With the speed of long practice she immediately did everything possible to bring him relief. More pillows to prop him higher in the bed, a dose of her home-made cough mixture to soothe his cough, and a fire lit in the bedroom grate.

'I'm sorry, Sal,' he wheezed. 'I didn't want to disturb you, girl.'

'Don't be daft, Lol,' she said. 'Keep that blanket up round you.'

'Come back to bed then,' he pleaded. 'I'm fine now.'

'I'll make a hot drink for both of us, then I'll come,' she promised.

When Cathy came over at nine o'clock she was surprised to hear her father coughing and to find him propped up in bed. 'What's happened, Mam?' she asked. 'He seemed all right last night, but that cough sounds awful, doesn't it?'

'He's better than he was a few hours ago,' Sally said. 'He must have caught cold last night but I think I've caught it in time.'

She looked pale and tired and Cathy insisted that she must go to bed for a few hours. 'I'll put the hot water bottle in the bed in the little room,' she said. 'Don't worry, Mam, I'll keep up the fire in Dad's room and stay here to look after him.'

Lawrie had fallen asleep, and Sally sat by the fire and sipped a cup of tea until the hot water bottle had warmed the bed in the small bedroom.

'Pity there's no grate in that room,' Cathy said when she came downstairs. 'There's ice on the inside of the window.'

'Josh said he'd have a lie in. He's not working today but I'll have to do his breakfast when he gets up,' Sally said wearily.

'I'll see to that,' Cathy said. 'You just settle down in bed and have a good sleep. You've got nothing to worry about, honestly.'

Sally smiled at her. 'You're a good girl, Cathy,' she said. 'What would I do without you?'

She went to bed and Cathy did the housework quietly and cooked breakfast for Josh when he came downstairs. From time to time she peeped in at her father but he still slept and she thought his breathing seemed easier.

She put the meat and vegetables on for barley broth then took a bucket of coal upstairs, but she was alarmed to find that her father had slipped down in the bed. The sound of his wheezing filled the room.

Cathy tried to lift him higher on the pillows and he woke and looked at her blankly, then smiled.

'Hello, love,' he gasped. 'Where's Mam?'

'She's lying down, Dad,' Cathy said. 'I put the hot water bottle in the bed in the little room and she's asleep now.'

'That's good. I disturbed her last night, Cath, and we were late getting to bed anyway,' Lawrie said. His breathing seemed easier while he was sitting upright, but his voice was hoarse and Cathy suggested another dose of her mother's cough mixture.

They spoke quietly, but the next moment the door opened and Sally appeared.

'Oh, Mam, I thought you'd have a good few hours,' Cathy exclaimed.

'I've had a good rest, love,' Sally said. 'The bed was lovely and warm although that room's like an ice house. How do you feel now, Lol?'

'I'm fine, Sal, fine,' he assured her. She looked at him critically, at his flushed cheeks and over-bright eyes, and put her hand on his forehead. 'You're still very hot,' she said.

'No wonder, girl, with the blankets you've got on me and the hot water bottle burning my toes.'

'Well, you know you've got to sweat it out of you. Keep that blanket up round you.'

'Don't grumble about being too hot, Dad,' Cathy said. 'Not many people are in this weather, believe me.'

'Aye, I only worked this to dodge the bad weather,' Lawrie said, winking at her.

Cathy replenished the fires and then went home to attend to her own house, and when she came back her father was asleep again. 'It'll do him good,' her mother said. 'Sleep and warmth are what he needs now.'

While Cathy was there to watch over Lawrie, Sally took the opportunity to go in to help Peggy Burns.

'Poor Peggy,' she said when she returned. 'She's worried to death about Meg. She's started running after lads now and she throws these terrible tantrums if Peggy tries to stop her. Anything could happen to her, though.'

'Why is Meg like that, Mam?' Cathy asked. 'She doesn't look different, like Joe Angus or Philomena M'Quade.'

'I think she was damaged at birth,' Sally said. 'Mabel was on her own when Meg was born. She'd asked that ne'er-do-well husband of hers to go for the midwife but it was raining heavy and he wouldn't go till it went off. When he got back with the midwife, Mabel was lying on the floor and the baby was born. That's when the damage was done, I think.'

'It's a terrible worry for Peggy,' Cathy said. 'And Meg's so big and strong. I could hardly manage her when she came to me while Jimmie's funeral was on. Makes you realize how lucky we are that our kids are all healthy.'

Lawrie's cough seemed easier although he still seemed weak and slept for most of the day. The family were convinced that Sally's prompt treatment had saved him from another severe bout of bronchitis.

'It's Sally's cough mixture that's cured you,' Peggy Burns said when she came upstairs to see him. 'It's better than the chemist's stuff any day, although Mr Norton's very clever. He only failed his last exam, or he'd have been a doctor.'

'That last exam must be tough,' Lawrie teased her. 'I've heard that about every chemist in Liverpool. None of them can beat Sally's jollop though. I think she puts knock-out drops in it. I've done nothing but sleep.'

'It's well for you,' Peggy said. 'Lying there nice and warm

and sleeping all day. It's not fit for a dog to be out in this weather.'

After a few days Lawrie spoke about getting up, but Sally insisted that he stay in bed. Cathy urged caution too. 'No sense in getting up and getting a fresh cold, Dad,' she said. 'You couldn't go out in this weather, and you'd only be reading. You can do that just as well in bed, in warmth and comfort.'

'I don't want Mam up and down the stairs running after me, though, Cath,' he said. 'She's not fit for it.'

'I can do all the running round that's needed,' Cathy said firmly. 'There's nothing to stop Mam sitting by the fire up here and keeping you company. Why don't you tell her that you want to get up because you're fed up being up here on your own, then she'll stay up here to keep you in bed.'

'Cathy, I didn't think you could be so devious,' Lawrie exclaimed. 'There's crafty, as the Welshmen say.'

She blushed. 'I've got to do something to make her take more care of herself,' she defended herself. She was beside the bed, plumping up Lawrie's pillows, and he took her hand.

'You're a good daughter, Cathy,' he said. 'It's made all the difference to me and Mam having all of you so close. Taken a weight off me, girl, knowing you and Greg are there to look after her.'

Cathy's head jerked up and she looked at him in wide-eyed alarm, but he was smiling cheerfully and before she could answer him there was a knock on the bedroom door and Josh came puffing in.

'How're you doing, Lawrie?' he panted.

'I'm fine, Josh,' Lawrie said. He still wheezed as he spoke and now he laughed. 'We make a good pair, I think, with bellows to mend.'

'It's the weight with me,' Josh said. 'Sally looks after me too well.'

'She has a talent for it,' Lawrie said. 'And here's another one. Our Cathy. Waits on me hand and foot.'

'Aye. Your mam said you did the fire in me bedroom,' Josh panted. 'Thanks, Cathy. Makes a difference these nights, I can tell you. I reckon I'm very lucky, Lawrie.'

Cathy left the two men to talk and went downstairs. She

told her mother what Josh had said, and Sally replied, 'I don't mind what I do for Josh because he appreciates it, and he tries to save me trouble as much as he can. That reminds me, though, I'll have to listen out for a coalman.'

With fires now burning in both bedrooms and in the kitchen and parlour downstairs, Sally's stock of coal had been quickly depleted, but she stopped a passing coalman and had the coal place filled again.

'This is where I feel the benefit of that money from Sam,' she told Cathy. 'I can buy the extra coal without worrying about the money for it.'

'Well, that's what he sends the money for, isn't it?' Cathy said. 'I wrote to our Mary last night and told her Dad has had another bout but is getting over it. Can you imagine them sitting in sunshine when you look at our weather? It seems to be getting worse.'

Cathy was not sure whether Lawrie tried her suggestion, but her mother began to spend more and more time sitting by the fire in the bedroom, and gradually the heart of the house seemed to move from the kitchen to Lawrie's room. His cough and his breathing seemed easier but he said no more about getting up, and seemed content to lie in bed, dozing and waking throughout the day.

Kate and Mick called in to see him after school every day, and Sarah and Greg came over every evening. The visits were usually fairly brief but John spent every evening sitting with his grandfather, and Sally often left them together to go downstairs to potter about and talk to Josh. John always carried buckets of coal up to both bedrooms, and filled the two coal scuttles downstairs before he left, and Sally never hurried him away but left him to talk to his grandfather for as long as he liked.

John and Lawrie usually talked about local politics or items in the newspaper, but often they spoke about the dreams they shared of a better future for the poor and deprived.

'It'll come, lad,' Lawrie said one night. 'Some time there'll be no one hungry or homeless, and you'll never see a barefoot child.'

'We'll see that that day comes, and soon,' John declared. 'We won't beg for justice, we'll *demand* it.'

Lawrie smiled at him fondly. 'Aye, I think you will, lad. You've got the education, y'see, and the confidence. I've struggled for better times all my life very near, but there's not much to show for it.' He sighed. 'A bit better, but not much for all the effort.'

'But it's happening. Remember that poem you told me? Anyway, we're only building on what you and your generation have done, Grandad. You laid the foundations for us, and you taught me what needs doing.'

'Aye, and that means everything to me. Having you to talk to and to know you understand and will carry on the fight.'

They sat in silence for a while with John gripping his grandfather's hand, then Lawrie said suddenly, 'We had a little lad, you know, John. Stillborn. But I've had you, lad. We've been good pals, haven't we?'

'The best, Grandad,' John said huskily. He blinked rapidly and swallowed, unable to say any more, and Lawrie lay with his eyes closed and a smile on his face.

He opened his eyes. 'Remember when you were little, John? You recited "Kick the Kaiser up the Bum".'

'No, I don't remember,' John said in mock indignation.

'Aye. Your mam and your grandma went mad and told me off for laughing at you,' Lawrie said. 'Your dad had just come home from the war and they'd taught you a poem to recite for him, but you said that instead.' He laughed. 'You were an independent little beggar even then.'

'That's right. I vaguely remember something about that day,' John said, 'but no details.'

'Poor Greg,' Lawrie said with a sigh. 'He missed the best of you. We were the gainers, having you living with us, but he was the loser, like a lot of fellows then. Your mam had your photograph taken and sent it to him, but it wasn't like seeing the real thing.'

'I've seen that photo,' John said.

'Your dad was made up with it. Your mam carried the letter he sent her around with her until it fell to pieces very near. Poor Cathy, it was hard for her too. War's hard on everyone, except the ones that start it.'

'Do you think there'll be another war, Grandad?'

'No, because with aeroplanes and bombs and the guns

they've got now, nations can destroy each other's countries, and the fellows who make armaments are as likely to be killed as an ordinary soldier,' Lawrie said.

'You're a cynic, Grandad,' John said. 'Dad believed in the League of Nations but I think that's been useless. The Japanese invaded Manchuria and China, and the Italians went into Abyssinia while they were still members of the League, didn't they?'

'Yes, and when Germany pulled out of the League in 1933 that finished it, I think,' Lawrie said. 'Herr Hitler's the fellow they need to watch.'

'But I thought you admired him,' John said.

'He's done well for Germany. Pulled them up by their bootstraps and given them hope and confidence in themselves, lad, and if he sticks to his own country he'll be all right. I think he's getting big ideas, though, and I don't like the way he deals with people who oppose him in Germany.'

'Two of the lads from the office went on a walking holiday in the Black Forest and they said the German people idolize him.'

'Aye, well, his mate Herr Krupp is as likely to be flattened as anyone else if there's a war, so I think they'll all make a lot of noise but every country will think twice before they start anything. "Sabre rattling" they used to call it, but nothing will come of it.'

'Wouldn't be much sense if it finished with every country destroyed,' John said.

There was a knock on the front door and the sound of someone entering the house. 'That'll be your dad,' Lawrie said. 'I told him I was worried about old Fred in the Royal and he said he'd go and see him for me. He's a good lad.' The next moment Greg came upstairs and into the bedroom. He greeted them and told Lawrie about the old man and his pleasure at the gifts Greg had taken him.

'He ate the Cornish pasty right away,' Greg said. 'And I put the bunloaf and mince pies handy for him. They'll be gone by now, I'm sure.'

They all smiled and Lawrie said cheerfully, 'Thanks, lad. Did you tell him I'll get to see him as soon as I'm able?'

'Yes. I explained to him and he sent his regards. I'll go

again next week if the weather's not fit for you,' Greg said.

John noticed that his father looked intently at Lawrie's hands, and a little later he said he would go and leave him to rest. The hint to John was plain and he soon followed his father downstairs. They had a cup of cocoa with Sally, and before they left Greg said quietly, 'I think it might be wise to call the doctor tomorrow, Mam.'

John expected his grandmother to protest, but she only said as quietly, 'If you think so, Greg. You know what you're talking about.'

'I know you've done wonders for him,' Greg said, 'but a doctor might be able to give him something different, some drugs that might help him.'

'I'll do it first thing in the morning,' she said. 'Thanks, lad.'

She kissed Greg and he said gently, 'Don't worry too much. He's got a fighting spirit. That's better than anything.'

'Yes, and he'll fight the idea of the doctor but he's having him,' Sally said firmly.

John was silent with shock, but as they stepped out of the house he gripped his father's arm. 'Why do you think he needs a doctor? I thought he was getting better?'

'He's getting over this, but every attack weakens him and I think a doctor might help him, that's all,' said Greg.

'But you must have some reason for thinking that. I saw you look at his hands,' John said.

Greg hesitated, then said, 'I looked at his nails, John. There was a tinge of blue in them, and in his lips. That means the bronchitis has weakened his heart. The doctor could give him some drugs to help that.'

'Then he's very ill,' John exclaimed, looking stricken.

'He needs help, son, but as I said to Grandma, his fighting spirit is his biggest asset, so don't worry too much.'

They had reached their own house and Greg muttered, 'Don't say anything to your mother. She'd worry all night. I'll tell her tomorrow morning about the doctor before I go to work.'

They went in and Greg spoke again about old Fred's pleasure in the food he had taken to the hospital. 'He ate your Cornish pasty, and Mam's bunloaf and mince pies would be eaten tonight, I think, but I left him some sweets and a few Woodbines and matches. He's up now so he can smoke in the lavatory.'

'I hope Dad doesn't want to go there as soon as he's up,' Cathy said. 'In this weather.'

Greg and John glanced at each other and Greg said easily, 'No. I've told Dad I'll go again next week.'

They went to bed a little later but John lay awake for a long time, thinking over all that had been said that evening. He tried to remember his grandfather's hand as it had lain on the coverlet. It had looked just the same to him, the hand of a working man, broad and capable with spatulate fingers, but his father's trained eye had seen the warning signs.

John thought with a glow of happiness about his grandfather's comments on how much he had meant to him, and then about his reminiscences of John's childhood, and his words about what his father had missed. He tried to recall that time but could only remember what had seemed to him an immensely tall man with rough-textured trousers kissing his mother. He could remember pushing between them, shouting, "She's *my* mama," but nothing after that except a vague idea that the man had taken his place in his mother's bed, and he had to sleep alone.

He could remember quite clearly the time he had spent with his grandfather: at the Landing Stage looking at ships, at the allotment, or going with him to see people who cried and were comforted by Lawrie, or angry men that his grandfather had talked to and calmed down.

John's thoughts returned to his father. Grandma and Grandad seem to be very fond of him, and it was hard on him missing seeing me as a baby, he thought. John was unwilling to admit that he had been wrong about his father, but decided that his father had changed.

He did that well about calling the doctor, he thought, without frightening Grandma too much, and he knows what he's talking about. This made him think of Lawrie and revived his fears, but fortunately sleep soon overcame him.

Cathy was alarmed when Greg told her that he had advised calling the doctor, but he told her it was just a precaution and that the doctor might have drugs to help her father to recover.

She found her mother quite calm about the idea. 'I'm glad Greg suggested it,' she said. 'I've been wondering, but I don't want old Hanson. I'll try that new fellow in Mill Road.'

The doctor was a keen and conscientious young man with a pleasant manner. He examined Lawrie thoroughly and complimented Sally on her nursing, then told her that the medicine he would prescribe was similar to one he prescribed for babies with croup, but stronger.

'Your cough mixture has been soothing, but I'd like him to take this and these tablets three times a day.' He turned to Lawrie. 'We'll soon have you right, Mr Ward,' he said cheerfully.

Downstairs he spoke to Cathy and Sally together. 'The coughing has placed some strain on his heart,' he said. 'I've prescribed digitalis, and that should help him. All the right things have been done for him, the warmth, the extra pillows and light diet. Now he must rest and wait for nature and the medication to act.'

'What a nice man,' Cathy said when he had gone. 'If they tell you what's wrong and what they're doing, you don't worry half as much, do you?'

She spoke cheerfully but the doctor's words about her father's heart had terrified her. Her mother said calmly, 'Yes, I'd trust that man. Old Hanson would tell you nothing, half the time because he didn't know himself.'

They went up to Lawrie and found him cheerful and just as impressed with the young doctor. 'That's what Greg should be doing, Cath,' he said. She shrugged.

'Yes, but it wasn't to be, and he enjoys the St Johns Ambulance work anyway.'

Cathy wept when she told Greg of the doctor's words.

'I thought Dad was getting better,' she said. 'I'd no idea there was anything else wrong.'

'He's getting treatment for it now,' Greg comforted her. 'And don't forget, Cath, your dad has a wonderful fighting spirit.'

'He has,' she agreed, wiping away her tears and smiling again.

Later Greg spoke to John. 'Grandad needs rest. I know I don't need to tell you, John, but you should avoid talking about anything that might excite him. He'll still need your company, though.'

A few months earlier John would have resented even this mild advice, but now he agreed and promised to be careful in his choice of topics.

They were all relieved to see an improvement in Lawrie's health and he began to talk about getting up, but Sally would only say, 'We'll see.' She rarely left the bedroom now except to serve meals for Josh and eat with him. Cathy looked after the house and after Josh, who was anxious to be as little trouble as possible.

'D'you think your mam would like me to get a room somewhere until your dad's better?' he asked Cathy. 'I don't want to give her more worry. She's been so good to me.'

'No, Mam would go mad at the idea,' Cathy said. 'This is your home, Josh. I'll see to all that's needed.' The old man heaved a sigh of relief. He had retired at Christmas and was happy to sit reading all day beside his fire.

Chapter Twenty-One

On the tenth of January there was the worst storm for many years. The wind howled round the house as Sally and John sat with Lawrie, John beside the bed and Sally sitting by the fire. She jumped back in fright as pieces of brick rattled down on to the bedroom hearth.

Bits of brick and slate continued to fall but Sally tried to ignore them until Lawrie said, 'Sounds as though the chimney stack's going, girl.'

'Don't worry. It's only plaster,' she forced herself to say calmly.

The curtains billowed out as the wind found every tiny crack in the window frame and the noise of it and of falling slates and bricks was deafening. Sally had to raise her voice to say to Lawrie, 'Keep under the clothes. We can't keep draughts out tonight.'

'God help sailors,' he said. 'There'll be ships and men lost tonight, Sal.'

He looked troubled and she said, 'Perhaps it sounds worse than it is. It often does inside the house,' but Lawrie still looked worried.

'Would you like me to stay the night, Grandma?' John asked.

'No thanks, John. We'll be all right and you've got your work to go to tomorrow. I'll get to bed myself soon.'

John replenished the coal buckets and damped down the kitchen fire with slack before he went home. Sally went to bed. She lay for a while unable to sleep, listening to Lawrie's uneven breathing and the pandemonium outside.

She knew that Lawrie was still awake and after a while she said quietly, 'Can't you catch your sleep, Lol?'

'No. I keep thinking of seamen in this,' he said.

'Put it out of your mind,' she urged him. 'We can't do

anything and it's time enough to worry when we hear of lost ships.'

'You're right, Sal. You go to sleep now, girl,' he said. She fell asleep but as always slept lightly. She woke when Lawrie moved to put his legs over the side of the bed.

'What are you doing?' she cried in alarm, jumping up and going round to stand beside him. He was sitting with his legs over the side of the bed, gasping for breath.

'You'll get your death,' she exclaimed, trying to lift his legs back on to the bed, but he gestured weakly to let them remain as they were. Sally put her arm round him to support him and he gripped her hand.

After a few minutes his breath became less laboured, and he allowed her to lift his legs back on to the bed and pull the bedclothes over him.

'I'm sorry, girl,' he said weakly, lying back on the pillows as though exhausted. He was shaking and Sally pulled the hot water bottle from the bed. 'Will you be all right while I fill this, Lol?' she asked anxiously. He nodded, unable to speak.

He seemed a little better when she returned with the bottle, and worried that she would catch cold. 'Get back into bed, Sal,' he urged. 'You must be freezing.'

'I'll make you a hot drink,' she offered.

But he said, 'No, Sal. Get into bed.' To satisfy him she climbed back in, and he tried to pull the bedclothes around her shoulders.

'Lawrie, lie still,' she exclaimed. He smiled and lay back.

She dozed off again, but was wakened by his coughing. She went round to support him so that his body was not so shaken. He coughed almost continuously throughout the night and on two occasions had to sit with his legs out of bed, struggling for breath before falling back exhausted on the pillows.

They were both glad when daylight came, but Sally had to suppress a cry of horror when she opened the curtains and looked down into the street. It was filled with the debris of the storm, slates and bricks and branches of trees and rubbish of all kinds. Several houses had slates and chimney pots missing. She was relieved to see that Cathy's house was undamaged except for missing slates.

She turned back to the bed without comment. Lawrie looked dreadful in the grey morning light, with patches of red on his sunken cheeks, and grey and hollow-eyed with exhaustion. She stirred the fire into a blaze and tucked the bedclothes firmly round him, then went downstairs and quietly opened the front door. She hurried across the road.

Greg opened the door and drew her inside. 'I'll have to get back,' she said, 'but he'll have to have the doctor, Greg.'

Cathy had appeared on the stairs and he said briefly, 'Dad's not well, love. I'm going for the doctor.'

Cathy ran downstairs. 'Is he very bad, Mam?' she asked, putting her arms round her mother.

'He's had a bad night, love,' she said. Greg had pulled on his coat and now he took Sally's arm.

'I'll take you back and then I'll go right away for the doctor,' he said. Cathy said that she would dress immediately and follow them.

Lawrie was lying quietly with his eyes closed, but he opened them and smiled at Greg. 'All right, lad?'

'Yes, Dad. The storm's died down now. Cathy's coming over to keep Mam company.'

Sally followed him out of the room. 'He'll be all right. Don't worry,' he said before he set off for the doctor.

Cathy came over within minutes and settled her mother by a bright fire in the bedroom, with a cup of tea and some toast beside her. Her father had fallen asleep again, but she refilled his hot water bottle and kept the kettle on for a drink when he woke.

The doctor came back with Greg and Sally described what had happened during the night. When she spoke of Lawrie putting his legs out of bed, he nodded.

'Can you think of any reason for the attacks?' he asked. 'Any exertion or distress?'

'He was worried about the storm, about sailors,' Sally said. 'He was a seaman when he was young.'

'I see. I'll increase the tablets. Just keep him warm and quiet and I'll look in again tomorrow,' he said.

When he had gone Sally began to worry about Cathy's family. 'Go and see to them, love,' she urged. 'I'll be all right now.'

'I woke Sarah, Mam, and she's going to see to things,'

Cathy said. 'It doesn't matter if they all go in late after a night like that anyway.'

'I wouldn't like another like it,' Sally said. 'I was so worried about Dad and it sounded like all the demons of Hell let loose outside. Thank God I had Greg to turn to – and you as well, love.'

'You should have knocked sooner. To think of you going through all that on your own, and us just across the road! I've put the hot water bottle in the bed in the little room. Go and have a few hours' rest now, Mam, while Dad's asleep.'

Sally went to bed, and Sarah and John both called before they left for work. They went up to see their grandfather but he was peacefully asleep and they went away feeling happier about him. Cathy swept the hearth in the bedroom and kitchen, and tidied up, but she felt too restless and agitated to rest, so she took out flour and yeast and made bread. The mixing and kneading seemed to calm her nerves.

Lawrie drifted in and out of sleep all day. Sally was up again and she gave him some beef tea from a feeding cup but he refused the baked custard she had made. Cathy put a hotpot in the oven in her own house and made a meat and potato pie for her mother and Josh.

'You've got to eat, Mam,' she told her mother. 'If only to keep the cold out, and keep Josh company.'

Throughout the afternoon Cathy and Sally sat in the bedroom with Lawrie. The storm had died away and it was quiet and peaceful in the warm bedroom, lit only by the light from the fire and a shaded lamp. Lawrie woke from time to time and they talked quietly to him. The smell of the baking bread had filled the house, and Lawrie breathed it in. 'Ah, bread baking. I love that smell,' he said. It's one of the first things I remember – my mother taking bread out of the oven.'

Kate and Mick arrived home from school and came up to see their grandfather, then Kate went down to Josh and Mick went home to do homework.

Later Cathy went home to attend to the family's meal, then they all came back again. Sally had moved from the fire and was sitting holding Lawrie's hand. His breathing was more even and he smiled at them as they each kissed him.

'I've picked the best spec, haven't I?' he said cheerfully. 'I'm even better off than our Mary.'

A letter from Mary and Sam had arrived, in which they said they were glad to know that Lawrie's cough was better, and spoke about swimming in their pool and having beach parties. Lawrie referred several times to the letter.

A little later Peggy came in and crept upstairs to offer to take Kate to sleep with Meg. Greg lifted Kate to kiss her grandfather, then Peggy took her away.

As midnight approached Mick became sleepy and Cathy told him to go to sleep in the bed in the small bedroom.

'Say goodbye to Grandad, Mick,' Greg said quietly. Mick gasped and opened his eyes wide, but he gave no other sign, only bent over Lawrie and kissed him gently.

'Goodnight, Grandad,' he whispered.

'Goodnight, lad. Clever lad, Mick – go far,' Lawrie murmured.

John had moved to allow Mick nearer the bed, but as his brother moved away John hesitated and glanced at his mother. 'Mum?' he said.

She said gently, 'Stay there, son,' and he sat down again beside his grandfather and took his left hand.

Lawrie's breathing was again shallow and uneven, and even the slight effort of speaking to Mick seemed to have exhausted him. He lay back on his pillows with closed eyes and Sally and John sat on either side of him, holding his hands. Greg stood between Cathy and Sarah beside the bed, with an arm round each of them.

Sally's head was on the pillow beside Lawrie's and he turned his face to hers. She kissed him and laid her free hand on his cheek. 'Rest now, lad,' she said.

He opened his eyes and looked around his family.

'Your bodyguard, Sal,' he gasped. 'I won't worry about you, girl.'

John gripped his hand tightly and Lawrie looked at him and tried to smile. ' "Falling fling the torch behind," eh, lad?' he said faintly. He smiled again and closed his eyes, and the only sound in the room was his rapid shallow breathing.

Nearly an hour passed then Lawrie stirred again. 'What time is it?' he murmured.

'Nearly half-past one, Dad,' Cathy said. He still lay with his eyes closed but moved his face against Sally's.

'I'll go out on the tide, girl,' he said, his voice almost inaudible. He opened his eyes and smiled at her, the same happy smile he had given her the first time they met, then he closed his eyes and seemed to drift off to sleep again.

He lay quietly, his breathing so gentle and faint that no one realized that it had stopped until Sally stood up and bent to kiss him.

As quietly and tenderly as she had done they each kissed him in turn, then Cathy turned into her mother's arms. 'Oh Mam, Mam,' she cried. Greg held Sarah, but John stayed holding his grandfather's hand and staring at his beloved face, as rigid as though his own life had ceased with his grandfather's.

Chapter Twenty-Two

Later Sally said quietly to Cathy, 'Will you help me, love? I don't want anyone else to do the laying out.'

They went upstairs and Sally took some fine linen sheets from the cupboard on the landing. 'I put these ready for whichever of us went first,' she said. 'I'm glad your dad went before me, Cath.'

'Yes. He'd have been lost without you, Mam,' Cathy said, putting her arm around her mother. Gently and tenderly they performed the last sad rites for Lawrie, then Greg took charge of all the arrangements. Cathy and her mother sat close together by the kitchen fire, drawing comfort from each other.

The weather was too bitterly cold for the kitchen fire to remain unlit, so it was arranged that Lawrie's coffin should lie in the bedroom. The undertaker's men helped Greg to move furniture from the bedroom into the small bedroom and reorganize the room.

Sally looked exhausted and Cathy persuaded her to lie down on the sofa, where she fell asleep. By the time she awoke, everything had been done and the men had gone.

The bed had been pushed against the wall and the pictures covered in white cloths. In the centre of the room Lawrie lay in his coffin, with candles burning at his head and feet.

'Do you want to go up now, Mam?' Cathy asked gently. When Sally said that she would, Cathy said that she and Greg would follow her a few minutes later.

They left Sally alone with her husband for a while then followed her upstairs. Lawrie's face looked young and peaceful, and Sally stood looking at him with no sign of distress. Cathy struggled to suppress her own tears, ashamed to weep while her mother showed such stoicism, but her voice shook as she said, 'It seems strange not to see him laughing.'

Sally put her hands to her face and began to weep. Cathy swiftly moved to comfort her. 'He looks so young,' Sally wept. 'Like he was before any of this.' They clung together and Greg put his arms around both of them.

Later they were glad that they had this quiet time with Lawrie, as the news of his death spread like wildfire and there was a constant stream of people coming to pay their respects.

A diversity of people came during the following days. The family had known that he was well known and well liked but were amazed at the number and variety of people who came, all shocked and grief-stricken at Lawrie's death.

Sally received all of them with quiet dignity, showing nothing of her own bitter grief to the councillors, businessmen, churchmen and people Lawrie had helped, together with numerous friends and neighbours. It was only when a ragged woman came bringing a bunch of anemones which Sally knew she could ill afford, that Sally broke down and wept with her.

'What'll we do without him?' the woman cried. 'He's kept us afloat. Not just what he give us, but he was always that cheerful and kind. No one knows —' She sobbed, and Sally sobbed with her.

In addition to his other duties connected with Lawrie's death, Greg had undertaken to tell Mary and Sam the sad news. He sent a cable to Sam's office, so that he could break the news to Mary, and followed it with a letter. The letter was brief as Greg was too busy and too grieved at Lawrie's death to give many details, but he said that Lawrie's end had been peaceful, with his family around him, and that Sally was bearing her loss well and being comforted by family and friends.

Sam cabled immediately with condolences and said that a letter would follow. He must also have contacted a florist as a huge cross made of red and white flowers was delivered on the morning of the funeral.

The fact that Sally and Lawrie, although they lived by Christian principles, never attended church had never been a problem. Open-minded and tolerant, they had always respected the beliefs of other people, and when Cathy was a child had allowed her to help their old neighbour, Mrs Malloy, to the Roman Catholic church and to stay for the Mass with her.

Later, when Greg wished to become a Roman Catholic after the War and Cathy decided to join him, there had been no opposition from her parents, but now Sally felt that there was a problem.

'You know Dad always held back from churchgoing because of all the trouble about religion in this city, and said a lot of wars were fought about religion, but he was a Christian and I don't know what to do about a service.'

'What about the church where you were married?' Greg suggested. 'I'll see if I can arrange it.'

The funeral service was duly arranged. The church was full, and dozens of people stood outside and followed the coffin to the cemetery in spite of the intense cold. Sally spoke quietly to the young minister before they moved to the graveside. 'Will you make it very short?' she said. 'Some of these people haven't got the clothes for this weather, and it would have worried him to see them freezing here.'

'I know,' the minister said. He turned away, wiped his eyes and blew his nose to hide his emotion, and did as Sally asked. Even the wealthy men in good Melton cloth over-coats shivered in the icy wind, and the poorer people in their inadequate clothes looked chilled to the bone in spite of the brevity of the service at the graveside.

'I don't care. I had to be here,' a poorly dressed man said to Greg. 'He was gold, pure gold, Lawrie Ward. If he's not in heaven now, there's no God.'

Sally had given a general invitation to anyone who wished to return to the house, and Peggy Burns and Josie Meadows had worked hard to prepare food and drink in large quantities.

Josh had offered the use of his parlour and Sarah thought it strange how the more prosperous people seemed to gravitate there, the others to the kitchen. Peggy was serving the food in the parlour at first, but then she asked Josie to change places with her.

'All the posh ones seem to be going in the parlour,' she

said, 'and you're more used to those sort of people with your job.'

Sarah was shocked at first at the hilarity in the kitchen as people told anecdotes of Lawrie and quoted some of his jokes, but gradually she began to feel comforted by it. She was sorry that John had not returned to the house as she felt that he too would have enjoyed hearing these tales about his grandfather, and seeing how much he was loved by all who knew him.

John had turned away after the burial, and walked rapidly away from the graveside, his hands thrust in his pockets and his head bowed against the bitter wind. On and on he strode for hours, over broken slates and bricks, then as he reached the outskirts of the city, over twigs and leaves torn from trees by the gale, oblivious to all of them.

His heart was full of bitter anger. Why? Why? beat in his head like a refrain. Why Lawrie when so many survived who would be missed by nobody? Far from comforting him, the number of mourners and their grief only made him more bitter as he thought how much Lawrie would be missed by everyone.

It was very late when he returned home and his father was angry. 'Mum's been very worried about you,' he told his son. 'You might have shown her more consideration on a day like this.'

'What do you know about it?' John said sullenly. 'There were plenty of people here anyway.'

'*You* weren't here, that's the point,' Greg said. John made no reply, and sprang upstairs two at a time to his bedroom.

Cathy came out of the kitchen. 'Was that our John? Where is he?'

'Gone up to bed,' Greg said briefly. His face was white and a tic in his cheek showed the effort he was making to keep his temper, but Cathy was only concerned about John.

'Has he had anything to eat? He must be starving and frozen.'

'If he needs anything, he knows where the food is,' Greg said, but Cathy pushed past him and went upstairs.

'John,' she called, tapping at the bedroom door. He opened it. Mick was sound asleep, but before speaking John looked down into the lobby. His father had gone into the kitchen, and John stepped back to let his mother into the bedroom.

'Where have you been, son?' she asked.

'Just walking,' he said gruffly.

'Have you had anything to eat or drink?'

'I'm not hungry,' he said.

She looked at his pale, strained face and said gently, 'All right, love. Get into bed.'

Cathy went downstairs and through to the back kitchen where she made a mug of cocoa and a cheese sandwich. Greg's lips tightened as she carried them through the kitchen but he said nothing as she took them up to John.

'Have these, son,' she said. 'Then try to sleep. We'll all be glad to put this day behind us.' She kissed him and went downstairs.

She could see that Greg was burning to comment and said quickly, 'Let's go to bed, Greg.'

Cathy had been longing to go to bed to shed the tears she felt she had been holding back all day, but she had been too worried about John to retire while he was still out.

Now that she knew that he was safe, she went to bed expecting to lie awake, grieving for her father, but she fell almost immediately into an exhausted sleep.

Greg lay awake for some time, burning with anger against John. He was furious that worry about John had been added to Cathy's and Sally's grief.

He's selfish and irresponsible, he thought, and if I say anything to him I'll be considered a monster, but I've had enough. He'll toe the line and have some thought for others in this house, or he can get out.

Sally was also lying awake in the bed which she had shared with Lawrie for so long. Greg and Mick had moved the furniture back to the bedroom immediately after the funeral and lit a fire in the bedroom grate.

Cathy and Greg had suggested that either Cathy or Sarah should sleep with Sally in the double bed, but she said quietly, 'No thanks, loves. I might as well begin as I mean to go on,' and they had not persisted. They only asked her to let Sarah sleep in the bed in the small bedroom in case her grandmother needed her company during the night and Sally agreed.

It was a relief to Sally to be alone and to let her tears flow unchecked as she lay thinking of Lawrie and trying to face the fact that he had gone for ever.

Her mind turned away from the future, unable to face the bleak years without him. She thought instead of the past, and of the love and grief for him that had been shown by so many people in the days since his death. Then her mind went further back over their life together. The hard times when her father lay in the parlour, a helpless and difficult invalid, and Lawrie was out of work, and how their love for each other had helped them to face the hardships and worries.

The kindness of other people too. Old Sally who had made the difficult task of selling their possessions easy, and with tact and kindness had helped her to keep face before the neighbours.

Mrs Malloy, her staunch friend and neighbour in whose house Lawrie had lodged, and who had helped and supported them in good times and bad. Was Lawrie with her now, Sally wondered, and with his family who had gone before him? Cathy and Greg believed he was, she knew.

Sally thought of the happy time of her courtship and of the day soon after she met Lawrie that they had spent at Eastham. The memory of that day had been like a jewel throughout her life, often taken out and examined, and she thought of it now, lovingly.

How proud she had felt when she boarded the ferry boat with Lawrie. The sun had shone and the musicians played as they sailed through the river crowded with shipping towards Eastham.

When they alighted they had walked through the quiet woods and stopped at a cottage for a cream tea. She had felt nervous at first among the confident young people there, but Lawrie told her that she was the prettiest girl in the room and he was proud of her, and her nervousness vanished.

Sally smiled tenderly as she remembered lying in his arms on the boat home, the tranquillity as twilight fell, and the soft young voices singing, 'Beautiful Dreamer'.

She fell asleep with the smile on her face as the grey dawn appeared round the window blind, and was still asleep when Sarah peeped into the bedroom. The girl quietly put coal on the fire which was nearly out, then she went down and stirred the kitchen fire, before creeping out of the house and across to her own home.

Her mother was serving porridge for the family who sat round the table, and thick slices of bread were frying in a pan on the fire.

'Grandma's asleep, Mum,' Sarah said. 'I just put more coal on the bedroom fire and she didn't wake up.'

'She'll be tired out,' Cathy said. 'You weren't up at all during the night?' And when Sarah shook her head, she said, 'Sit down and have your breakfast, love. I'll go over as soon as I've got you all off.'

'I stirred the kitchen fire up and put another lump of coal on so the kitchen should be warm,' Sarah said. Cathy pressed her shoulder as she put a bowl of porridge before her.

'You're a good girl,' she said. Her father smiled at Sarah, but John kept his head bent over his plate.

A few days later the nation was saddened by the death of King George V on January the twentieth but it meant little to Lawrie's family, still overwhelmed by grief at his death. For John it was another cause of bitterness as tributes to the dead King poured in from all parts of the world, and arrangements were made for the elaborate funeral.

'He wasn't half the man Grandad was,' John said bitterly to Cathy. 'This fuss disgusts me.'

'No, and he won't be mourned by his family and friends the way we've grieved for Grandad,' Cathy said. 'But he was a good man and did his best in the job he was born to. The fuss is something he's had to put up with all his life, and maybe his family might like a quieter funeral but they can't have it.'

John shrugged. 'It just annoys me,' he said. 'What recognition did Grandad get for all he did?'

'Try not to be so bitter, John,' Cathy said gently. 'Grandad was never bitter.'

'Perhaps he should have been,' John muttered. 'I'm going out.' Cathy was glad to see him go. She was always afraid that he would air his views to his father, and provoke more trouble between them.

She knew that Greg was becoming more and more

annoyed by John's attitude, but had pleaded with him to make allowances for their son's grief.

'He's not the only one who's grieving. We all miss Dad, and particularly you and your mam, so I don't see why he should be allowed this behaviour,' Greg said.

'Yes, but we're older. Young people take things harder and there was a special bond between Dad and John,' Cathy said.

'There was indeed,' Greg said grimly, but she changed the subject determinedly.

Sarah was the one who paid most attention to the death of the King. Mabel Burroughs was an ardent Royalist and she came to the shop with red eyes on the day after King George V died.

'I've cried all night,' she told Sarah. 'I thought it was lovely the way the man on the wireless said: "The King's life is drawing peacefully to its close," but so sad. I loved my King.'

Sarah tried to sympathize with Mabel. The people in the shop had been very kind to Sarah after her grandfather's death, and she wanted to show that she appreciated it.

Mabel and Anne, and Mr and Mrs Dyson and the bakehouse staff, had put together and sent a wreath, and Dennis, the boy from the bank, had organized a collection among the customers for flowers for the funeral.

Sarah might have felt better if Michael had been the one to organize the collection, but he seemed embarrassed by her grief and only mumbled condolences when she served him in the shop.

He had muttered a few days later, 'I don't suppose you want to come to the pictures?'

'Of course not,' she exclaimed. He said nothing about meeting her for any other reason. Sarah knew that he must have gone to the pictures anyway because he joined in a discussion about the Pathé News shown at the cinema.

The funeral of King George had been the main item on the news, and everyone in the shop was talking of the incident when the cross fell from the State Crown as the gun carriage carrying the coffin went over tramlines. A quick thinking guardsman in the Guard of Honour swiftly picked up the cross and put it in his pocket, and people in the shop praised him for his action.

'What a thing to happen though,' one woman said. 'Right in front of the Prince of Wales, too.'

'He's not the Prince of Wales now,' someone else said. 'He's Edward VIII.'

'They'll need to look after him,' one woman sighed. 'It'd be terrible if he died before he was crowned. Remember Gypsy Rose Lee said he would come to the throne but never be crowned.'

'God forbid,' Mabel said. 'He'll make a good king. Remember when he was in the mining villages and saw the poverty. He said something must be done, and he'll get it done, I'm sure.'

Sarah let the talk wash back and forth over her, taking no part in it, only conscious that Michael at the back of the queue was discussing the news shown at the cinema. Anne was serving fruit cake and Sarah went to her. 'Will you let me do that and you serve the pies?' she asked. 'I don't want to speak to him.'

Anne agreed and Cathy weighed the cake and wrapped it, determined not to look at Michael. I'll just see if he bothers to come over to speak to me, she told herself, but he only murmured, 'Hello, Sarah,' as he pushed his way out of the crowded shop.

'I don't know why you bother with him,' Anne said. 'You could do better for yourself, Sarah.'

But Mabel sighed romantically. 'He's such a lovely-looking lad though, Sarah. "If I had nothing to eat I'd want something to look at," my old mother always used to say.'

'That's all very well, Mabel, but I think character counts for more than looks in a husband,' Anne said. Sarah said nothing, and the talk turned to the subject of the weather.

February was even colder than January and tugs had to break the ice on the Leeds and Liverpool canal to allow the barges through. Even the sea froze at Southport.

Sarah often spent the evening with her grandmother. Josh had slipped into the habit of sitting on in Sally's kitchen after their evening meal, until he left for his nightly visit to Maybury's public house at nine o'clock, but Sarah stayed on after Josh left and talked to her grandmother.

Mabel had told her that she should talk about her

grandfather to her mother and grandmother.

'It upset me when Willie died that no one would ever talk to me about him. One woman actually said she didn't want to remind me – as though he was ever out of my mind. People used to cross the street to avoid me, so they wouldn't have to talk about him.'

'I suppose they feel embarrassed,' Anne said. 'They don't know what to say.'

'Don't you make that mistake, Sarah,' Mabel said. 'It'll be a comfort to your gran especially, to talk about him.'

'I agree with that,' Anne said. 'You know I'm the youngest in our family, but before I was born my elder brother died. Our Maureen was three and Patrick was six when he died. He was only ill for twenty-four hours but our Maureen was sent to my gran's when he took ill. She screamed and carried on because she didn't want to go, and when she came back Patrick had disappeared. All his clothes and his toys as well. Nobody ever mentioned him to her and she was afraid to ask because she thought he'd gone because she'd been naughty about going to Gran's. She fretted about it for years before she found out the truth.'

Sarah found it easy to talk about her grandfather because it seemed that Lawrie was still with them as she sat with her grandmother. Greg had packed cracks round the window frame and put felt round the doors but even so the bitter cold seemed to penetrate the kitchen, in spite of a good fire. Sally and Sarah both wore crocheted squares like shawls around their shoulders.

'Grandad would have been worried about poor people in this, wouldn't he?' Sarah said.

'He would, love. People who couldn't afford extra coal or warm clothes. It would've upset him not to be able to do enough to help them.' Sally sighed. 'He's spared that anyhow, love.'

Usually when they talked it was on happier themes, and Sally told Sarah of the days of her youth, and about when she and Lawrie were young parents. Mrs Malloy often came into the conversation and Sarah said one night, 'Mam was talking about her the other day. She said she knew the poet Gerard Manley Hopkins.'

'Yes, he was a priest at Saint Francis Xavier's round about

1880,' Sally said. 'That's how Mrs Mal knew him.'

'Mum said Mrs Malloy didn't think he was a good preacher, or at least she couldn't understand him very well, but his poetry's lovely, Gran.'

'Grandad liked it, I know,' Sally said, smiling at her.

'Yes, he said it was more difficult to understand than Wordsworth or Tennyson, but it was worth making the effort for.'

'Does Michael like poetry?' Sally asked.

'I don't know,' Sarah said stiffly, and Sally suggested a cup of tea.

Cathy also spoke about Michael, to ask if he had invited Sarah out.

'No, Mum. He knows I can't go to the pictures while we're in mourning,' Sarah said, blushing, and Cathy said no more.

She grieved for her young daughter though, knowing that she was suffering disillusionment in her first love to add to her grief about her grandfather.

Sarah saw no connection with this conversation when, a few days later, her grandmother told her she wished her to have her grandfather's books of poetry as she would appreciate them, but the gift soothed her sore heart and gave her many hours of pleasure.

Chapter Twenty-Three

Cathy was careful not to criticize Michael to Sarah, partly because she feared to hurt her and partly for another reason. The family had been amazed by the number of letters of sympathy they had received, many of them from people with whom they had lost touch but who had heard of Lawrie's death.

One of the letters Cathy received was from an old friend, Norah Benson, who had married Greg's friend Jack Carmody. Jack was a Catholic and Norah a Protestant, and both their families had opposed their marriage on religious grounds.

Cathy had sometimes wondered if this opposition had driven Norah and Jack together, and if they were really suited. They had married during the war when Jack had been wounded and Norah had gone to the hospital in London where he had been taken. Later they had made their home there.

Cathy had lost touch with them, and was sorry to learn that the marriage was now over.

'We had no children so they needn't have all been carrying on about how they'd be brought up. When it came to living down here with only ourselves to rely on, no old friends or relations near, we realized that we were totally different from each other and not suited at all. Jack is now working in Ireland and I have a live-in job in this boys' school. I often think of our happy days with the Mersey Wheelers, Cath,' Norah wrote.

She also said that she shed tears when she heard of Lawrie's death, as he was her ideal of what a man and a father should be. 'I envied you for many things, Cath,' she wrote, 'but most of all for your happy home and loving parents. Tell your mam I will pray that God will comfort her in her great sorrow.'

Cathy cried when she read Norah's letter. After Greg had read it, she said to him, 'We won't have to make that mistake with Sarah, Greg. If we don't like anyone she goes out with, we'll have to be very careful not to be so much against him that it drives them together, like Norah and Jack.'

Greg agreed but said that he had always felt that Jack and Norah were not suited. 'They were both great characters individually, but together they didn't seem right.'

'Norah said once that if they had gone out a few times, they might have carried on courting or might not, but with the way the families carried on they had to make up their minds whether they wanted to get married before they really knew each other,' Cathy said. 'We'll have to be very careful with Sarah.'

She said nothing more about Michael to her daughter and Sarah seemed glad to avoid the subject. The family clung together, helping each other come to terms with their loss.

Only John drew no comfort from the family. He went out as soon as he had eaten his meals. Cathy and Greg were laying careful plans for their treatment of Sarah, but neither realized that Greg's opposition to John's friends was driving him closer to them and making him even wilder and more reckless.

He had moved from associating with the younger group at the club to the older and more experienced men, and they found him a willing listener to their stories of clashes with the police and impatience with the established order. He said nothing of this at home and his mother, immersed in her own grief and worries, was unsuspecting.

It seemed to Cathy that every time she went into her mother's house she found Peggy Burns there with her, sipping the inevitable cup of tea as they talked in low voices, or simply sitting together in quiet companionship.

'I can understand how your mam feels,' Peggy said to Cathy when they met in the street. 'No one understands how a widow feels except another widow.'

Cathy made some reply, and escaped into her own house. She was upset to be told that Peggy could share her mother's grief better than the family who loved her, and were themselves grieving for Lawrie.

She resented too the loss of her father being classed with the loss of Jimmie Burns, and when Greg came in told him of the conversation.

'I think Peggy Burns had a cheek to say that,' she said indignantly.

'I don't know, Cath, she may be right,' he said thoughtfully. 'We try to understand how Mam feels but I suppose no one can *really* understand, except another woman who's lost her husband after years of marriage.'

'It's *our* loss though,' Cathy insisted.

'I know, love, and Mam needs us, but perhaps she needs Peggy too,' he said. 'Anything that can help her – I think we should welcome it.'

'I suppose so,' Cathy conceded. 'But I still think it's a cheek to compare losing Dad with losing Jimmie Burns. He was a different sort of man altogether, and it was a different marriage too.'

'I agree, Cath, but I don't suppose Peggy sees it like that,' said Greg. 'And after all, they'd been married a long time.' Cathy still felt hurt and confused but he put his arms around her and kissed her.

'No one can come between you and your mam, love,' he said gently. 'It's just a bit of extra help for her, that's all.'

Cathy clung to him. If I lost Greg . . . she thought. *No*, I can't bear even to think about it. She lifted her head and kissed him passionately.

The next day she was alone with her mother, both pottering about the kitchen, when Cathy opened a cupboard and saw a cap belonging to her father on the shelf. She snatched it up and pressed it against her cheek, then burst into tears. Sally came up beside her and they clung to each other, weeping bitterly.

Memories of Lawrie wearing the cap were in both their minds. They remembered him, the cap at a jaunty angle on his curly hair, striding down the street, whistling cheerfully, and the thought that they would never see him again nearly broke their hearts.

'Oh, Mam, Mam, how can we bear it?' Cathy sobbed as their arms tightened about each other and tears poured from their eyes.

Sally murmured brokenheartedly, 'Lol, Lol.'

When the first violence of their weeping subsided, Sally patted Cathy's back and said, 'There, there, love,' as she had done when Cathy was a baby.

Cathy kissed her impulsively. 'Oh, Mam, I should be comforting you,' she said, her voice rough with tears.

'We'll have to help each other,' Sally said. 'But, Cathy love, what will we do without him?' They sobbed again, but again Sally was the first to recover. She dried her eyes and straightened her shoulders, and Cathy wiped away her tears, fortified by her mother's quiet courage.

Gently she laid the cap back in the cupboard. 'We'll have to do something about his clothes,' Sally said. 'But not yet.' They went to sit by the fire, each drawing strength and comfort from the other.

'How's Mick?' Sally said presently.

'A lot better. I've kept him in bed and given him aspirins and a blackcurrant drink,' said Cathy. 'It's this awful weather. Sarah's full of cold too.'

'I haven't seen John,' Sally said. She hesitated. 'Is he all right, love?'

Cathy pressed her hand. 'I think so. We hardly see him ourselves. He just bolts down his tea, hardly says a word, and then he's up in his room or out. With Mick in bed now, he usually goes out somewhere.'

'Is he still seeing that Hanson lad?'

'I don't know, Mam. Greg asked him and John snarled at him. There's no other word for it. Greg was livid. He let it pass but said afterwards he felt like knocking John down. Still, we've got to make allowances just now.'

'Poor lad, he's brokenhearted,' Sally said with a sigh. 'Nobody knows what John meant to Dad, Cathy. From when he was a baby in this house, he brought that much happiness.'

'Yes, they were always close,' Cathy said. 'And John loved his grandad more than anyone.'

When the evening meal was over at Cathy's house that night, John rose from the table and went into the lobby. Cathy followed him. She laid her hand on his arm as he started to walk upstairs. 'Grandma was asking about you, son. Try to go and see her, John.'

'Is she all right?' he asked gruffly.

Cathy sighed. 'You know Grandma. She doesn't say much, but she needs us, love.'

'I know, Mum. I'll go over a bit later on.'

Cathy went back to the kitchen where Sarah was clearing the table and they took the dishes into the back kitchen and began to wash up.

'I'll go over to Grandma's when these are done,' Sarah said. 'I've got some sweets for her.'

Cathy turned from the sink. 'Will you leave it for a bit, love? John's going over. He hasn't been for a while and Grandma was asking about him.'

She expected some protest from Sarah, but her daughter only said quietly, 'I don't think John can bear to go in the house, Mum, without—' Their eyes met in the shaving mirror above the sink and suddenly Sarah's filled with tears and she turned into her mother's arms. Cathy held her and stroked her hair.

'It'll get better, love,' she said gently. 'It'll be easier to bear in time.'

'But I don't want it to, Mum,' cried Sarah. 'I don't want to forget Grandad.'

'I understand, love,' Cathy said. 'I remember when I was a bit younger than you and Mrs Malloy died. I thought I was being disloyal if I wasn't miserable all the time, but Grandad took me for a walk and talked to me. He said Mrs Mal would have given me a right telling off, what she called the rounds of the kitchen, if she knew I was moping about because of her. And it was the truth, Sar. Grandad would feel the same.'

'I know,' she said. 'He told me one day – we were talking about Rupert Brooke – and Grandad said if no one ever died, there'd be no room for others to be born. The earth would be full and we'd all be slipping off the edge.'

Cathy smiled fondly. 'That was Grandad,' she said. 'A joke about everything. That's what we should remember, love, the happy times, and there were plenty of those with him, weren't there?'

'Yes, and the things he said like: "To everything there is a season. A time to be born and a time to die." ' Sarah's voice wobbled slightly as she said the last word, but John came to the door of the back kitchen and she smiled at him.

'I'm going over to Grandma's, Mum,' he said. Cathy took a clean apron that was folded on the sideboard.

'Take this, will you, son? I forgot it when I took the ironing.' John took it, and when he had gone Sarah looked at her mother in surprise.

'That was your pinny, wasn't it, Mum?'

'Yes, but it'll give him something to say when he first goes in,' Cathy said. 'Grandma won't let on it's mine.'

When John went in to Sally's kitchen she was sitting in her usual chair by the fire and Josh had turned his chair away from the table and was sitting smoking. He stood up immediately and greeted John, then said that he would go and have a look at his newspaper.

John held out the apron to Sally. 'Mam sent this, Grandma.'

Sally said calmly, 'Thanks, love. Just put it on the dresser.' As he turned back from the dresser she stood up and pushed Lawrie's chair nearer the fire. 'Sit close, lad. Did you ever know such weather?'

Her calm assumption that John would sit in his grandfather's chair removed any awkwardness he might have felt, and she went on talking about the weather as he sat down.

'Peggy put some sheets to soak in the dolly tub last night, she told me, and she had to break ice on the top of the water this morning, and the tub was in the back kitchen overnight.'

'The worst weather for thirty-five years, someone in the office was saying.'

'Mick's chosen the right time to be sick,' Sally said. 'Trust him.'

John smiled. 'You should see him. He's got a jersey on over his pyjamas, and mitts and a woolly hat. You know, Grandma, the kind you see on foreign sportsmen skating or skiing. I don't know where he got it from, but he's a nasty sight when I wake up in the morning.'

Sally stood up to make cocoa and John watched her covertly, looking for signs of change in her, but he could see none. Her spare figure was dressed in a black dress and her hair was in the usual neat bun on the nape of her neck. Her face was pale but as calm as ever, and only a slight tremor in her hands betrayed how much she had suffered. They spoke of trivial matters, storm damage and events in the street, and it was not until John was about to leave that they spoke of Lawrie and then only indirectly.

John put his arms about his grandmother and kissed her and she held him close. 'Don't stay away, lad. I love you too, you know, and – he'd have wanted it.'

John found his eyes full of tears and swallowed rapidly. 'I know, Gran,' he said. 'I'll see you tomorrow.' He kissed her again and hurried away down the lobby, then walked around for a while before going back into his own house.

Sarah had been watching from the parlour window and had seen him come out. She went over to see her grandmother and take her the sweets. She helped Sally to fill two hot water bottles and put them up in her and Josh's beds, then took coal up for the fires which Cathy had lit in both bedrooms.

'I didn't ask John to take the coal up, love,' Sally said. 'I thought it was a bit too soon for him to face going in the bedroom, but you've been up there often.'

'D'you know, our parlour window is thick with ice on the inside because we've had no fire there,' Sarah said. 'Just shows what the bedrooms would be like without the fires.'

'Aye, I always say money for coal is money well spent,' Sally said. 'Especially in weather like this.' As they worked, they spoke without constraint about Lawrie.

Sarah felt that she could talk about Michael, too, to her grandmother. Sally said nothing, and kept her eyes on her knitting as Sarah spoke about her disappointment in him. 'He mumbled a few words the first time I saw him after – then he said nothing more. *Then* he asked me to go to the pictures! He just doesn't care about how I feel, Grandma.'

'Don't be too hasty, love. He's only young and some people can rise to the occasion better than others,' Sally said. 'Don't fall out with him. Just let things take their course.'

'Mabel says he's just shy, but Anne says he's as limp as a wet Echo and I can do better for myself.'

'You're the one who knows how you feel, love, not Mabel or Anne, although I suppose they mean well. Just wait and see. You've got plenty of other things to interest you.'

Sarah smiled gratefully at her grandmother and touched

her hand briefly. Both reserved and undemonstrative, they understood each other perfectly, and drew even closer in the weeks after Lawrie's death.

Cathy was frequently employed by the catering firm during these weeks, and welcomed the arrival of the 'Please be at's'. Her spirits were lifted by working in lively company and the women she worked with, most of whom had known bereavement, were kind and considerate towards her.

The first time she worked after her father's death, Cissie gripped her arm. 'You've lost your da, girl, haven't you?' she said. 'He done a lot of good in his life but his time had come. Better to go like that than lay for years, a trouble to himself and everyone else.'

'Cissie's right,' another woman said, 'be thankful he didn't suffer much, Cathy. Not like that poor man in our street. They've give him so much morphia that it doesn't have no effect now, and the screams out of him are terrible.'

Even Mrs Nuttall, perpetually busy, took time to say to Cathy, 'I'm sorry about your dad, girl. You'll miss him, but hard work's the best cure, I found. I'll see you get plenty of jobs.'

She was true to her word and the postcards arrived for Cathy three or four times a week. This meant she worked sometimes with different women, but she liked all she worked with and was confident now about her own skill.

The extra money was very welcome and Cathy found that she was able to put a few shillings in a Post Office account nearly every week. Her pride in being able to save without having to rely on her mother to help her made her feel more mature and helped to deaden the pain of her loss, although her father was never far from her thoughts.

She liked best the jobs where Josie and Freda were also called for, and this happened quite frequently because they were young and strong, in addition to being willing workers. Cissie was also on most of the jobs, in spite of her free and easy comments.

Cathy's first job after her father's death was a Masonic dinner, and she was moving down the room serving vegetables when suddenly she thought of Lawrie and she stood still, her eyes filling with tears.

A red-faced man rapped on the table. 'Come along,

waitress, come along,' he ordered.

Cissie was serving nearby and immediately said loudly, 'Are you all right, girl? He just can't wait to paddle.'

Mrs Nuttall, ever vigilant, swooped down on them. 'Give me that dish, Cathy. Go and get a drink of water.' To Cissie she hissed, 'More roast potatoes on the other table.'

The man was now purple in the face. 'What did she mean? What did that woman mean? I won't have impertinence.'

'She thinks the other girl needs a holiday,' Mrs Nuttall said glibly. 'A little more cauliflower, sir?' Cathy and Cissie had moved away, and the man nodded grumpily.

'I'm not satisfied with the service, not satisfied at all,' he said, but Mrs Nuttall had moved on to serve his neighbour.

Cathy drank some water and composed herself then took a full dish of vegetables and went back, murmuring 'Sorry' as she passed Mrs Nuttall with the empty dish.

There was no time for further speech as the rest of the dinner was served, but later Cathy said to Cissie, 'I didn't get that, Cissie, about paddling.'

Cissie cackled. 'He did though, didn't he? That's why he got such a cob on.'

'You'll go too far one of these days,' Mrs Nuttall said. 'It took me all my time to calm him down.'

'Agh, they make me sick,' Cissie said. 'I seen that same fellow strutting round town one day and I thought to meself, "I know what you get up to, lad." '

'Don't forget they pay your wages though,' Mrs Nuttall said. 'You could get us all into trouble.'

She went out and Cathy asked Cissie again: 'What did you mean, Cis, about the paddling?'

'He's a Mason, isn't he? I seen them one night, and if you'd have seen the cut of them! Their chests showing and their trouser legs rolled up. That's why I said that about the paddling when I heard him barging at you because you'd stopped for a minute. Bloody bully. Thought I'd let him know I knew what he gets up to.'

'But how did you see that?' one of the women asked. 'They always lock the doors.'

'Aye, but there was a little one in the corner that they never seen because it was behind a curtain. I only went in it because I thought it might be a short cut, but then I seen them. I dodged out quick in case they noticed me, but I got an eyeful first, and I recognized a couple of them. I've had many a laugh at them an'all that they don't know about.'

Mrs Nuttall came beside them. 'Your tongue'll get you hung, Cissie. You'd better keep your mouth shut about what you seen that night or you might get into a lot of trouble.'

Cissie was unabashed. 'They had little aprons on them too. Laugh!' she said quietly to Cathy. 'And they try to tell the likes of us what to do.'

Cathy laughed as she told Greg about it when she reached home, and he laughed too but seemed to agree with Mrs Nuttall.

'Cissie should be careful, Cath,' he said. 'Those men are very influential, you know.'

'I wonder if it was true – what she said she saw?'

'I think it probably was, but she'd be wiser to say nothing about it.'

Cathy told Cissie about Greg's advice, but she only said airily, 'No good worrying, girl. I never worry now 'cos the things I've worried about never happened, but something else what I'd never thought about comes up and hits me in the gob.'

Cathy said no more, feeling that she had plenty of other things to think about at this time. Several letters had arrived from Sam since the funeral. He wrote that Mary was heart-broken about her father, and he was taking her for a short winter holiday to take her mind off her sorrow. Later he wrote that they had returned from their holiday and their friends had arranged parties for Mary to console her, but she was still too upset to write to her mother.

Eventually a letter came in which she said that she had been prostrated by news of her father's death. 'The worst part was the fact that I was not with him as he would have wished. You know he always idolized me,' she wrote. 'Thank goodness he had the joy of seeing us last year, which must have helped him in his last hours.'

Sally handed the letter to Cathy without comment, and she read it and handed it back, saying, 'Artistically tear-stained, I see.' She felt that she was being catty but Sally nodded her agreement, and they looked quizzically at each other.

Chapter Twenty-Four

As the months passed and spring came all the family found that the first sharpness of their grief passed too. Sally had told Sarah that she must feel free to go out and enjoy herself.

'Your grandad didn't believe in people mourning, you know, love. Not public mourning anyhow. And he didn't think that insurance money should go on black clothes in case the neighbours talked, either.'

Sarah glanced down at her black dress. 'I wanted a black dress though, Grandma. I thought it showed respect.'

'Then it was right for you to have it, love, and *I* wouldn't feel right in anything else but black. What Grandad was talking about was women rigging out the whole family in deep black out of the insurance money, when they would need it to pay a debt or to feed their family with the bread-winner gone.'

'I suppose so,' Sarah said doubtfully. 'But when Mr Mullen died, Mary said it was the only time they ever had new clothes.'

Sally smiled at her. 'Like I always say, love, there's always two sides to everything. What I mean is, if you want to go to the pictures, love, you should go. It might help you, and it wouldn't mean that you didn't love Grandad or grieve for him. Plenty of time for that while you're on your own, but he wouldn't want you to be sad on his account, Sar.'

'I wouldn't go with Michael,' Sarah said. 'He won't ask me anyway now.'

'But you're still friends,' Sally said.

'Yes, we say a few words when he buys his pie, but nothing personal.'

Cathy was pleased when Sarah told her what Sally had said. 'I'm glad Grandma's mentioned it to you,' she said.

'I've been thinking you should get out more, but I wasn't sure how she felt about it.'

'She said Grandad didn't believe in mourning. Well, only in just the way you were bound to feel yourself, but not for other people to see or for any set time.'

She found that she could speak quite naturally about her grandfather now. Her mother only sighed and said, 'Aye, Dad had his own view of everything, and the right one, that other people came round to in time.'

'I might ask Anne to go to the pictures,' Sarah said.

'Yes do, love,' Cathy encouraged her. 'You know, Sar, it helped me a lot going out on the jobs, and I enjoy them as much as the pictures. It's no different just because I get paid for them.'

Mick had been upset at the funeral, but since then had not said much about the loss of his grandfather. Cathy was surprised and touched when she was told that he had been set an essay on Great Men and had written about his grandfather.

Greg met one of the masters from the College at church and he told him about it.

'An excellent essay. Your father must have been a remarkable man.'

'My wife's father, actually,' Greg said. 'But I agree with Mick – er – Michael. Lawrie was a great man, and he's greatly missed.'

The master smiled. 'I told Michael that I expected him to write about Cardinal Newman, William Wilberforce or someone of that stature, but he told me, politely but firmly, that they were famous men but his grandfather was the greatest man he had ever known. He's a young man who knows his own mind and is not afraid to speak it.'

'Perhaps he inherited that trait from his grandfather,' Greg said with a smile.

He repeated all that the master had said to Cathy, and she in turn repeated it to her mother. They both wept a little, but they were tears of pride rather than of sorrow.

John was the only one unable to come to terms with his grandfather's death. He was still filled with anger and bitterness when he thought of Lawrie's lifelong fight to improve conditions for the poor, and the little he had been able to achieve. He spent most of his time either at the Club, where he met members he thought of as men of action, or at open air meetings.

He saw little of Gerry but became friendly with a man of his own age who had been unemployed since leaving school, and was as bitter as John. They were proud to meet Leo M'Gree, who had led the Birkenhead Unemployed Demonstration against the Means Test and had been sentenced to twenty months' hard labour as a result.

'That's the way to do it!' John exclaimed to his friend Bill. 'Action. It showed the bosses were scared when Leo M'Gree got that sentence, and it made a lot of people aware of what's going on today. My grandad spent his life battering his head against a brick wall, with hardly anything to show for it.'

'He did a lot of good, though, John,' said Bill. 'He was very well thought of among the people I know.'

'I know he was, and I'm not belittling what he did,' John exclaimed. 'I'm just mad to think that he worked so hard, and made sacrifices, and because he tried to do things constitutionally he got virtually nowhere. Mind you, he said to me once he'd given hostages to fortune by having a wife and children to consider. That's one mistake I won't make.'

'Neither will I,' said Bill, adding bitterly, 'how could I keep them anyway?'

They were in this mood on a fine June evening when there was a meeting of unemployed men on some waste ground in Everton, and John and Bill went to listen to the speakers.

One of the speakers was insisting that the men's patriotism was not in doubt, and they were loyal Englishmen who only objected to the way they were being treated by the men now in power.

'I love my country,' the speaker said, and suddenly John's bitterness overflowed. He jumped up on to the platform and snatched the loud hailer from the speaker's hand.

'So you love your country,' he shouted. 'Does your country love you? "What did you do in the war, Daddy?" That was the slogan they had the cheek to use to get you in the Army. What *did* you do? You men who had never known anything but hunger and misery. Waiting at the

Dock Gates from four o'clock in the morning, ragged and hungry, on the chance of half a day's work – and more often than not sent away, not wanted.

'But you were wanted when the war came, weren't you, and you went off like sheep to fight for the rich who stayed at home. You fought and died to keep their comforts intact. That's what you died in your thousands for, not for yourselves or your families. You had nothing when you went and you got nothing when you came back – those who did come back.'

The men on the platform had been trying to wrest the loud hailer from John, and there had been growls of disapproval from the crowd, but suddenly a man shouted: 'He's right, the lad's right. We were bloody fools,' and John dragged back the loud hailer and shouted again.

'Homes fit for heroes you were promised. Did you get them?'

And the crowd roared, 'No.'

'Will you fight for them if there's another war?' John yelled again, and again the crowd roared, 'No.'

There were concerted angry shouts and John was suddenly aware of a ring of policemen with drawn batons surrounding the crowd. A man on the platform shouted frantically, 'Clear off. Clear off, men,' but at the same moment John felt a blow on his head and a policeman's hand clutched his collar.

'Clear off, men. Vamoose,' the speaker on the platform was still yelling. 'Don't give them an excuse for a baton charge.' But the charge had already begun.

John was dragged away and bundled into a police van, and a short time later he was in a cell at the Main Bridewell. His shirt was torn and he had lost a shoe, and in addition he had a black eye and two broken fingers, but none of this mattered to him.

He was still in a state of euphoria after his first experience of carrying a crowd with him, and told himself that he didn't care what they did to him now. He had made his protest and he knew now that he could speak in public as his grandfather had dreamed he would do.

After an uneasy night spent lying on the sloping plank bed he felt less cheerful but still felt proud of the part he had played. He was brought before the magistrates with about twenty other men who had been present at the meeting. He held his head high, quite prepared to give another speech if he had the opportunity.

On the previous evening Cathy and Greg had gone to the dance at the Grafton Rooms with Josie and Walter, for the first time since Lawrie's death. They had enjoyed the dance and their stroll home through the balmy evening, but when they reached home they found Sally sitting with Sarah.

'Mam, what's happened?' Cathy exclaimed. 'Is it Kate – Mick?'

'No, they're all right,' Sally said. 'John's in a bit of trouble, that's all, so I came to sit with Sarah.'

'What sort of trouble?' Greg asked.

'Something and nothing, probably,' Sally said calmly. 'There was a message that he had been arrested at a meeting, you know how the police just gather anyone up, but he's been taken to the Main Bridewell.'

Cathy's hand flew to her mouth. 'Oh, Greg,' she said faintly. He gave her a reassuring hug.

'Don't worry, I'll go down there and sort things out. I may be some time, so I hope you'll all go to bed.'

'I couldn't,' Cathy exclaimed. 'Not till I know he's all right.'

A look passed between Sally and Greg, and Sally said firmly, 'No sense in us all being up, Cathy. It could take hours. You know the red tape in those places, so I'm going to bed and I think you should too.'

Cathy agreed to go to bed after she had seen her mother home safely, and Greg went to the Bridewell. Cathy was still awake when he returned alone and told her that John would be detained overnight and would face the magistrate on the following morning.

He went downstairs again and it seemed to Cathy that he was gone for hours. She had fallen asleep by the time he came up to bed.

The men who had been arrested were in a group waiting to go into court when a clerk came up to the policemen who were guarding them. He was holding a sheet of paper, and said: 'Redmond. Which is Redmond?'

'I'm here,' John said eagerly.

The man ignored him. 'Put him up last,' he said to the policemen, then disappeared. John held his head high, smiling proudly. That's because I made the speech, he thought exultantly.

The men were ushered into the court and quickly dealt with. Most of them were sentenced to two weeks in gaol or a fine of two pounds, but two men received sentences of six weeks with no option of a fine and were warned by the magistrates about their future behaviour. Most of those with the option elected to serve the fourteen days, as they were unable or unwilling to pay the fine.

I wonder what they'll do to me, John thought with dismay mixed with pride as the order was given: 'Put up Redmond.' But he had to stand in the dock, ignored, as a letter was passed round the magistrates. They conferred for a few moments, with the youngest magistrate seemingly persuading the others, a white-haired man and a woman.

The charge was read out, then the clerk of the court called, 'Gregory Redmond', and John was astounded to see his father. Greg wore the dark suit and white shirt he wore for special occasions, and answered confidently in his deep pleasant voice the questions asked by the magistrates about the letter which he had evidently written.

John listened as though in a dream, then sudden anger seemed to make a red mist before his eyes. He tried to speak, to shout angrily at his father to leave him alone. He started forward but his arm was gripped more firmly and a policeman muttered ferociously, 'Button your lip.'

The grip on his arms was tightened agonizingly as his father returned to his seat, and for the first time, it seemed, the magistrates looked at John.

'In some ways your behaviour has been more reprehensible than that of the other men because you have had the advantage of a good home, and a good father to guide you. You have chosen to flout his authority and mix with bad companions who've played on your vanity and idealism to lead you astray,' the youngest magistrate said, severely. 'Nevertheless, your father has come here today to ask for clemency for you and to promise that this behaviour will not be repeated. For his sake we are prepared to give you another chance. You will be fined five pounds. Consider yourself a very fortunate young man. It will be hard labour the next time.'

John was hustled out of the court before he could speak, and was furious to be told that his father had paid the fine.

'Don't I have the option of gaol?' he demanded.

'Shut your gob and get out while the going's good,' the sergeant advised him. 'And don't come back. You won't get off so light the next time.'

The next moment he found himself outside the court, walking along beside his father. 'I didn't want you here,' he said angrily. 'You made a fool of me before my friends, as though I was a child. Led astray, for Godsake.' He banged his hand on a wall as they passed it, almost speechless with fury as he hobbled along wearing only one shoe.

'Do you think I enjoyed going there?' Greg demanded. 'Admitting that my son was in the dock. Humiliating myself to plead for you.'

'Then why did you?' John demanded. 'I'd rather have gone to gaol with the others. I don't want any favours. You seem to forget I'm twenty years old. I'm not a child.'

'Then stop behaving like one,' Greg snapped. 'Why did I go? Not for your sake, believe me. A gaol sentence might have cured you of these heroics, but what about your mother and grandmother? What do you think it would do to them? Try thinking of others instead of yourself, for once.'

His mother! For the first time John thought of her and how she would feel about his arrest. He was silent until they reached Egremont Street.

'I'd better go through the jigger,' he muttered to his father, turning into the back entry behind the houses.

'I'll come that way too,' his father said. 'We'd better go in together.'

Cathy exclaimed in horror at her son's appearance. 'John, your eye, your face – and where's your shoe?' She looked anxiously at Greg. 'What happened this morning?'

'A fine of five pounds and a warning,' he said briefly, then as Cathy went for a bowl of water to bathe John's eye, he said, 'Five pounds and five shillings costs, a new pair of shoes and a new shirt needed, a half day's pay lost by me, and possibly your job lost. A high price for your dramatics. I hope you're satisfied.'

He walked into the back kitchen to wash his hands as Cathy came through with the bowl, and a moment later he reappeared. 'I'll go right away,' he said to Cathy.

'Wait for a cup of tea at least, Greg,' she said. 'You've had nothing.'

'I don't want anything, thanks,' he said, then kissed her and went without a glance at John.

Cathy gently bathed his eye. 'What happened, son?' she asked. 'Did you get caught up in the crowd?'

'No. I got on the platform and spoke,' he said, unconsciously lifting his head proudly. 'I think that's why the police charged us.'

'Why? What did you say?' Cathy said in alarm.

'I told them they'd be fools to fight for a country that treated them so badly.'

'But that's treason!' she exclaimed. 'No wonder the fine was five pounds. It's a wonder they didn't send you to gaol.' She had finished bathing his eye. Now she stood up and picked up the bowl.

'It makes me mad,' John burst out, 'to know the way these men have been treated, and see them licking the boots of the people who tread on them . . .'

'That's wild talk,' she said. 'I suppose that's what you hear in that Club.' John looked startled and she said angrily, 'Oh, I know you still go there. I tell you straight, John, Grandad didn't approve of that crowd and it seems he was right. That kind of wild talk doesn't help anyone.'

'You don't understand,' he said. He stood up and went upstairs.

Cathy was bitterly hurt by John's remark that she wouldn't understand. Hadn't she always listened to his views and sympathized with him? Come to that, they were her views too; she had worried about destitute people and tried to get things changed long before John was born, and her dad had worked all his life to improve things. Greg's right, she thought. John's getting too big for his boots, thinking he's the smart guy who can change things overnight. He didn't deny that he goes to that Club either, she thought.

Cathy was worried too about the amount of the fine. Five pounds! Could it be paid by instalments? she wondered. She decided to ask John when he came downstairs, but when he appeared, wearing a clean shirt and an old pair of patched shoes, and supporting his left hand with his right, she forgot everything else at the sight of the pain on his damaged face.

She started forward in alarm. 'John, your hand? What happened to it?'

'Two fingers broken, I think,' he said. 'They were aching all night and I've just knocked them, changing my shirt.'

'You'll have to go to the hospital,' Cathy said, looking in horror at his swollen and misshapen hand.

'I'll have to go to the office first,' he said. 'Find out if I've got the sack.'

'But you can't!' she exclaimed. 'Not with your face like that. And you'll have to go to the hospital right away with those fingers.'

'They'll have to wait,' John said. 'And I can't stay off until my face is all right or I certainly will get the sack.'

'Wait, until tomorrow at least,' Cathy begged him.

'No, I'd rather go in now and see where I stand,' John said stubbornly. 'If I get the sack I'll go straight to the hospital, and if I don't I'll go on my way home.'

Cathy insisted that he had a cup of tea and a cheese sandwich before he left, and as soon as he went hurried over to see her mother.

'Greg called in,' her mother said as soon as she appeared. 'Thank God the lad was able to come home, anyway. I was afraid they'd send him to gaol.'

'John's gone into work. I didn't think he should. He's got a black eye and his fingers are broken, but he's worried about his job.'

'He'll have to go to the hospital, surely,' Sally exclaimed.

'That's what I said, but he said he'll go to the office first to find out where he stands.'

'Greg didn't say John was hurt. He just said he was home and it was only a fine. Fancy that magistrate being at school with Greg.'

'He didn't tell me that,' Cathy said. 'He hardly spoke before he rushed off to work.'

'Poor Greg, he must have felt small, but it probably helped with John. Peggy said all the others have gone to gaol.'

'How does she know?'

Sally shrugged. 'How does Peggy know about anything? She's got a talent for finding someone who knows someone else.' She smiled but Cathy still looked serious.

'John's lost one of his good shoes,' she said. 'He had to go to work in a patched pair.'

'If that's the worst he's got to worry about, he'll be lucky,' Sally said dryly, then her face softened. 'Poor lad. He doesn't know what to be at. He can't get over losing his grandad.'

'I know,' Cathy agreed. 'He seems to have gone off the rails lately. He's always out and he never says where he's been. I think he's with that wild crowd from that Club, but if I ask him he snaps my head off.'

'Never mind, love. This might bring him to his senses,' Sally comforted her.

'I'm afraid it'll mean more trouble between him and Greg,' Cathy said. 'I went to get water to bathe John's face and I heard Greg ranting at him before he dashed off.' She stood up. 'I'd better get back in case he got the sack and comes home before he goes to the hospital.'

'He must be in pain if his fingers are broken,' Sally said.

'He was. His hand looked terrible, all swollen and twisted. If it was anyone else, Greg would have been doing his First Aid stuff, but with John he didn't bother at all.'

Sally walked down the lobby with her and detained her by the door. 'You can't blame Greg for being vexed with John, Cathy,' she said. 'He's got every right to be. Most fathers would have given the lad a good hiding instead of going to court to speak up for him.'

'I suppose so, Mam,' Cathy said, smiling briefly and turning away.

Mam's always on Greg's side, she thought resentfully. Anyone would think he was her son instead of her son-in-law, and they both seem to forget that John's a man now. Part of her resentment was due to the fact that Greg had told her mother more than he had told his wife, but she was unwilling to admit this, even to herself.

Chapter Twenty-Five

Cathy busied herself about the house, expecting John to arrive at any moment and tell her that he had lost his job, but Greg and Sarah arrived home before John appeared.

Cathy greeted Greg coolly. She was still angry that he had not given her more information before dashing off to work, and determined not to ask for any details before he volunteered them. Greg seemed equally determined not to ask about his son after a quick glance at his empty place, even when he saw Cathy putting John's dinner between two plates.

Fortunately Sarah and Mick asked questions about what had happened at the court and why John was not at home now.

'He's probably at the hospital,' Cathy said. 'As well as the damage to his face, he had two broken fingers. His hand was in a dreadful state, all swollen, and he was in a lot of pain.' She darted a reproachful glance at Greg as she spoke, but he continued to eat his meal without making any comment. A little later John arrived home. His fingers had been heavily bandaged and supported in a sling, and the bruising round his eye was even more noticeable.

By this time Mick and Sarah had both gone out and Cathy and Greg were alone in the kitchen. John ignored his father, went to his mother and kissed her.

'Sorry I'm late, Mum,' he said. 'I went to look for my shoe after I'd been to the hospital but I couldn't find it.'

'What happened at the office?' Cathy asked anxiously.

'I had to go to see old Meredith,' John said. 'He read me a lecture a mile long but he was all right really. Just a reprimand. Lucky it's my left hand so I can still write. The fellows pulled my leg about this black eye.'

Greg had been sharpening a pencil on to a newspaper

resting on his knee. He stood up and shook the shavings into the fire, then walked into the parlour without a word. Cathy cut up the meat on John's plate so that he was able to eat his meal, and suggested that they should go to see his grandmother when he was finished.

She hesitated in the lobby and then looked into the parlour where Greg was sitting listening to a record on the gramophone.

'Just going over to Mam's to tell her what's happened,' she said shortly.

'Right. Will you tell her the wood'll be delivered tomorrow, please?' Greg said. Cathy nodded and followed John over to her mother's house. At least John could be sure of sympathy there, she thought as she walked down the lobby and heard Sally and Josh exclaiming in horror at the sight of his hand and eye.

When Cathy and John returned, Greg was sitting in the kitchen reading, and John went straight upstairs to bed.

'Did you remember about the wood?' Greg asked.

'Yes. Mam said she'll be glad of a new drainboard. She doesn't fancy using that one now it's split,' Cathy said. For both of them the wood served as an uncontroversial subject that enabled them to speak to each other without mentioning John.

For a while they sat in silence, Cathy knitting and Greg reading, then he closed his book.

'I'm going to insist on changes here, Cathy,' he said quietly. 'In future I'll want to know where John is and who he's with. I'm not having any repetition of what happened today.'

'You can't treat him like a prisoner,' she said angrily. 'Just because he was unlucky enough to be caught up in that trouble last night. He was only standing up for what he believes in.'

'He wasn't "caught up" in anything. He was a ringleader, shouting through a loud hailer to try to incite trouble. I saw some of his so-called friends today, and I'll see he keeps away from fellows like that in future.'

'Unemployed, were they?' Cathy taunted him. 'You might have been one of them yourself if you hadn't been lucky enough to have Josh speak for you for a job.'

Greg face grew red with anger. 'I don't know why it is that any time I speak about John you turn on me like a tigress. You just can't bear to hear him criticized.'

'I should be well used to you criticizing him,' she flared, 'you've done it all his life. He just can't do anything right as far as you're concerned.'

'And he can't do wrong in your eyes,' Greg said furiously. 'But I've had enough. He'll toe the line and behave himself, or get out.'

'You'd like that, wouldn't you?' Cathy said. 'The further away the better, as far as you're concerned. Just because *he's* got the courage to stand up for what he believes in.'

'It's a waste of time trying to talk reasonably to you about him,' Greg exclaimed angrily. 'But I mean what I say. He'll either behave himself or get out of this house, and I intend to tell him so.'

'You do – you drive him out, Greg Redmond – and we're finished. I'll never speak to you again.'

They were shouting by this time and suddenly the kitchen door was flung open and John appeared, wearing pyjamas.

'Stop it!' he yelled.

'Clear off and mind your own business,' Greg shouted, but John turned on him.

'It *is* my business. You're talking about me. I'm not having you bullying Mam on my account.'

Greg's face was purple with rage. 'Don't you speak to me like that, you impudent swine! Defending your mother from *me*. You've shown a lot of concern for her, haven't you?'

Mick came walking down the lobby as John and his father were both on their feet yelling, and his mother was also shouting 'John, John,' and trying to push him towards the door.

'Is this a private fight or can anyone join in?' Mick asked cheerfully. He was astounded when his father swung round and gave him a box on the ear.

'Don't you start!' Greg yelled. 'I'm having no impudence from you, either.'

Mick looked at him in amazement, his hand to his ear, and John snarled, 'That's right. Pick on him. Why don't you hit someone your own size. Hit me.'

He squared up to his father who raised his fist, but Cathy stepped between them, gripping Greg's arm.

She turned her head to shout at John as Sarah came down the lobby and stopped, horrified at the tableau.

'What's up? What's happening?' she exclaimed.

'Don't ask,' Mick advised her. 'I tried to cool them down and got a clout on the ear for my trouble.'

Sarah dived into the group, pushing her father and John apart with a hand on each, then flinging her arms round her mother. Cathy burst into tears and Sarah said furiously, 'What are you doing to Mum?'

The angry colour left Greg's face. He grew pale, and sat down heavily in his chair.

'Go to bed,' Sarah ordered John as she helped her mother to her chair and knelt down beside her. He turned and went meekly out of the room, and Sarah ordered Mick to put the kettle on for tea.

'Don't cry, Mum,' she said, kneeling with her arms round her mother and shooting angry glances at her father. Greg sat with his head bent, looking at the floor, his hands clasped between his knees.

Sarah took a bottle of aspirins from a cupboard in the back kitchen, and gave two and a mug of tea to Mick. 'Take those up to our John, but don't talk about all this,' she instructed him. 'Just ask him if he's going to work tomorrow.'

She poured four cups of tea and took the tray into the kitchen. Her parents both accepted the tea with a murmured thanks, and Mick came down and picked up his cup. 'Can I take a piece of fruit cake, Mum?'

'Yes, and you take some too, Sarah,' Cathy said quietly.

'I don't want any, thanks,' Sarah said. 'I had some supper in Edie's.' She drank her tea quickly and made a sign to Mick, and they both said goodnight to their parents and went to bed.

After they had gone, Cathy leaned back in her chair with her eyes closed while Greg stood up and wound the clock on the mantelpiece. His face was pale and he looked unutterably weary, but he bent and laid his hand on Cathy's.

'I'm sorry, Cath,' he said. 'Come to bed, love.'

She stood up without a word and closed the damper in the

fire while Greg locked the door, and they both went wearily upstairs. They undressed in silence, but when they were in bed he said suddenly, 'I regret striking Mick. He was only trying to help.'

'I know,' Cathy said. She seemed too tired to say more and after murmured goodnights they both fell into an exhausted sleep.

Greg was awakened by Sarah's hand on his shoulder. She put her finger to her lips and indicated her mother who was still soundly asleep, then held up Greg's pocket watch to him. He looked in dismay at the time. Sarah crept from the room while he jumped up and dressed, taking care not to waken Cathy.

When he went downstairs Sarah had made tea, and wrapped sandwiches and cake for his lunch. Neither of them mentioned John but a used cup and plate on the table showed that he had had his breakfast and gone to work.

Sarah started work later than Greg and she said that she would waken Mick before she left so that he could look after Kate if Cathy still slept.

Cathy woke and came to the head of the stairs in her nightdress as Sarah was in the lobby putting on her hat.

'Have they gone, love? Dad and John,' she said anxiously.

'Yes, Mum. I did tea and toast for them and Dad's sandwiches,' Sarah said. 'I'll have to go or I'll be late.' She ran upstairs and impulsively kissed Cathy. 'Don't worry, Mam,' she said, hugging her mother.

'You're a good girl,' Cathy said, her eyes filling with tears.

Sarah walked rapidly along the street, feeling a black cloud of depression settling on her. Why was everything so horrible? she thought miserably. Grandad gone, and everybody quarrelling and snarling at each other, and Michael not bothering even to speak to her now. No matter how much she told herself she didn't give tuppence for him, she knew she had only to see him and she was filled with love for him.

And Mabel with her daily announcements of people who had died in the neighbourhood! Anne said Mabel was only trying to make her feel better because she wasn't the only one who had been bereaved, but Sarah felt that if Mabel announced another death today, she would scream at the top of her voice.

Fortunately only Anne was in the shop. She said Mabel had gone to the Dispensary to have a boil on her neck lanced.

'Thank God,' Sarah said. 'I hope they keep her a long time. I just couldn't stand her going on about deaths today.'

'As bad as that, is it?' Anne said sympathetically.

'Worse,' Sarah said. 'Our house is upside down and everyone at each other's throats because of these barmy ideas of our John's. You should see his face, and his hand was in a sling this morning. He said he's broken two fingers.'

'It's a pity he doesn't start courting, keep his mind off politics,' Anne said. 'But he doesn't seem interested in girls, does he?' Her face coloured as she spoke and Sarah glanced at her. Don't tell me Anne's going to fall for our John, she thought. That would be the last straw, if I had to worry about her as well.

Aloud she said carelessly, 'No. He's just wrapped up in this business.'

She was slightly cheered later when Michael came in for his pie. The girls had new green overalls, and as Sarah handed the paper bag to Michael, he said quietly, 'That colour suits you.' There was no time for further speech as she and Anne were frantically busy without Mabel's help, but Sarah thought constantly about his words and his smile as she dashed about the shop, and went home in a happier frame of mind.

She had been kept late at the shop and when she reached home found that John and her father had both had their meal and gone out. 'Dad's gone to the St Johns Ambulance,' her mother told her. 'I don't know where John's gone.'

John had gone defiantly to the Club. He wondered what his reception would be as he was free when so many others were in gaol, but found he was regarded as a hero by the younger men. He was still bitter towards his father and told his friends that he intended to leave home, and asked if any of them knew of a room to let.

Later he was called into an inner room with some of the older more experienced men and asked to tell all that had happened. He enjoyed telling them about his speech at the meeting and what had followed, telling them how angry he was that his father had interfered and paid his fine.

He also told them that he had quarrelled with his father and intended to leave home as soon as possible, but was surprised to be told that he should continue to live at home. 'You'll be a marked man for a while,' one of the men told him. 'Stay at home, keep your head down, and don't have any more rows.'

John protested and was asked if he had read about what was happening in Spain. The legally elected government of the Popular Front was being opposed by General Franco, who had called upon the caretaker Prime Minister to declare a state of war to prevent the Popular Front taking power. He had been exiled to the Canary Isles, but John was told that might not be the end of it. Workers of the world might need to unite to help their comrades.

'But what's that got to do with me?' he asked, bemused.

'You'd want to help, wouldn't you?' a man said. 'So keep your nose clean and your head down until you're called for.'

John walked home feeling as though he was treading on air: to be accepted by these men as one of them, men who had experienced hard labour and trouble in other parts of the world, and who talked of international affairs as knowledgeably as about matters in England.

He thought with contempt about Liverpool, where religious differences frustrated the efforts of people like his grandfather to improve life for the poor. He had been singled out by these men as fit for a wider field.

The only drawback was having to eat humble pie and stay at home.

He had been warned not to repeat the conversation in the back room to anyone, and advised to tell his friends that he had decided to stay at home because of his mother. John felt uncomfortable about using her as an excuse, but when he reached home everything was made easy for him.

Greg said nothing about his leaving home even though he had reached home before John and must have known that he had defied him to go to the Club. He said goodnight curtly when John prepared to go to bed, and John hesitated then said gruffly, 'Sorry about what happened, Dad.'

'That's all right, we'll forget it,' Greg said, and Cathy

smiled at John with such delight that he felt ashamed of himself. It's all for the Cause, he told himself, stifling his qualms.

For the following weeks John stayed at home most nights, reading or listening to the wireless, or sometimes going over to sit and talk to his grandmother. The bruises on his face soon faded and his fingers healed, so that Cathy was able to believe that the whole episode was over and John had learned a lesson from it.

Greg had told Mick that he regretted striking him as he realized he had been trying to help on the night of the row, so harmony reigned in the family.

In July everyone was sorry to hear of the untimely death of Wilf Hamer, the Band Leader at the Grafton Rooms. They were impressed by the courage of his wife who immediately took over leadership of the band.

Greg and Cathy went with Walter and Josie to the Thursday night dance at the Rooms, and on the Friday Cathy and Josie were called by the catering firm for a job. The conversation between the women was of Wilf Hamer, and another man who had died of pneumonia at the age of thirty-five, leaving three young children.

There were several widows among the women, including Freda, and one of them said thoughtfully, 'Nobody'd want to be a widow but there *are* compensations. Men are selfish beggars, even the best of them.'

To Cathy's amazement, Freda agreed with her. 'I know,' she said. 'I was heartbroken when Les died, but my life is a lot easier living with our Margie. I don't have to account for how I spend my money, and she'll always help with the kids. Les would if I was ill, but if I only had a headache I had to get on with it, and if there was nothing wrong with me he wouldn't dream of helping.'

'I'm on my own,' a woman called Jane said, 'and it suits me that way. I can please myself what I do and where I go, and I can go to bed and sleep at night without any moans and carrying on because I don't want – you know.'

'You don't miss the other then?' another woman said.

'Indeed I don't,' Jane retorted. 'I always thought it very overrated anyway, and very undignified.'

Cathy and Josie exchanged smiles and then Cathy was

startled to hear Freda say: 'Another thing is, I can bring up the kids my own way. Les and I were always falling out about them, especially about my eldest lad.'

If Greg wasn't there, Cathy thought, I could guide John gently. He'd behave for me if his father wasn't there, ranting at him and making him more obstinate and wild. Suddenly she pulled her thoughts up short, horrified at what she had been thinking. Wishing Greg dead. She felt cold at the thought.

The conversation went on round her but she heard none of it. Her mind was filled with horror at the thoughts which had sprung into her mind at Freda's words. The situation between Greg and John must have upset her more than she realized, she decided, if her subconscious could bring up thoughts like that, even for a moment.

She was quiet and subdued all evening and for the following days watched Greg nervously, with a superstitious fear that she had been tempting fate by allowing herself even to think of his death. He, fortunately unaware of the reason for her concern, responded by making love to her passionately.

Cathy was able to respond as passionately to him, because the resentment she had felt since the day of the court case had at last disappeared. She had been angry that Greg had told her mother that the magistrate was a school friend of his but had not told her, and when he subsequently made a casual reference to the man, said stiffly, 'Mam told me you knew the magistrate.'

Greg looked at her in surprise. 'But you knew, didn't you, that I was at school with him?'

'*You* didn't tell me,' Cathy said. 'I went to tell Mam that John was home from the court, and she said you'd been in and told her about that fellow.'

He thought for a moment. 'That's right, I remember. I didn't want to say anything in front of John that lunchtime, but surely we've mentioned it since.'

'Not until now,' she said. 'What happened?'

'Nothing really. We recognized each other and nodded when I was waiting for John's case, but we didn't speak to each other, of course. It may not have influenced him at all. I think the other magistrates wanted to be harder on John but he did seem to be persuading them to be more lenient, possibly because of the letter I'd written. He was a smug little creep at school and still seemed a pompous ass,' said Greg. 'Satisfied?'

Cathy nodded and smiled but said, 'And that five pound fine. How did you manage that?'

'Stan Johnson lent it to me when I asked him for time off to go to court. Just pulled it out of his pocket and told me to have it on me in case. He's a good fellow.'

'He is,' Cathy agreed. 'Very thoughtful.'

'I'm paying it back at five shillings a week,' Greg said. He grinned ruefully. 'Now I know that's something I haven't told you, Cathy, but I thought it was better not to – as things were.'

She bent her head over her knitting and picked up a dropped stitch, thinking that it was a pity that she had not spoken sooner about her grievances.

Chapter Twenty-Six

Although grief for her father was still with Cathy, like a sore spot in her mind, and she missed him every day, she was happier about the situation within her own family.

John seemed to have settled down and rarely went out at night. He went swimming or cycling at weekends with friends from the office, and never mentioned politics at home now.

Mick was doing well at school, passing examinations with ease, and had been Victor Ludorum at the College Sports. Everyone predicted a brilliant future for him but he went happily on his way, doing whatever occurred to him without bothering about anyone's opinion.

His latest idea was to join the dancing school where Kate was a star pupil, and learn step dancing. He paid for the lessons himself from the money he earned helping a milkman in the early mornings, and no amount of ridicule put him off.

'People might think you're a pansy,' John told him, but Mick only shrugged.

'They don't say that about Fred Astaire, do they?'

'And you think you're like Fred Astaire,' John jeered.

'Not yet,' Mick said coolly, and went on with the lessons.

Kate was annoyed when Mick seemed to overshadow her, but was speedily consoled when she was chosen as one of the children to appear in crowd scenes in the Empire Theatre production.

It was only a brief appearance but Kate behaved as though she was the star of the show, and all the family were tremendously proud of her, especially Josh. Parents were allowed back stage after the show and Cathy and Greg took Sally and Josh with them.

Greg introduced Josh to various people as the man who

had paid for Kate's dancing lessons. One man shook hands with him when he was introduced. 'Pretty little girl, sir,' he said. 'Should go far.' Josh beamed at him and the man embraced him before saying, 'Must go, dear, body's wanted.'

Cathy looked nervously at Josh, but he said with a blasé air, 'Different from us, Cathy, these theatre chaps. Did you hear what he said. Kate should go far. I think he was the producer feller.'

Cathy doubted if this was so, or even whether the man knew who Kate was, but she was pleased to see the good old man so happy and proud.

She was happier about Sarah too. She had lost her timidity since working in the shop, but had seemed sad and subdued since her grandfather's death, partly, Cathy suspected, because she was disappointed in Michael.

Lately though she had seemed much happier. She spent a lot of time with Anne Fitzgerald from the shop. Cathy liked Anne and thought her a much more suitable friend for Sarah than the boisterous Edie Meadows.

Anne was one of seven children, all cheerful and extrovert, and Sarah had been drawn into many of their activities. They seemed to go about in a group, and Sarah went with them to dances or cycling on the Wirral, girls and boys wearing shorts and open-neck shirts and coming home, sunburned and happy, full of fresh air and high spirits.

Cathy felt that all the family discord was behind them now when she saw John and Greg chatting together, and looked forward happily to the future, unaware of happenings far away which would change their lives.

In late July Greg looked up from the newspaper he was reading. 'I think the world's going mad,' he said. 'The King had a loaded revolver thrown in front of him after he'd presented new colours to the Guards, and in Spain the Generals have revolted against the Republican Government. It'll mean Civil War, I'm afraid.'

'Was the King hurt?' Cathy asked.

'No, and they've got the man who did it, but it should never have happened. What were the police thinking of?'

'You'd think they'd be extra careful after that Gypsy Rose Lee saying he would become King but he would never be crowned,' Cathy said. 'People think it means he might fall ill and die, but he could be killed, couldn't he?'

John listened to them with mounting impatience. Going on about some stupid incident in London, he thought, instead of saying more about what was happening in Spain. He longed to ask for more details but on his last hurried visit to the Club had been warned again about keeping his head down. 'You've got a conviction against you, remember,' he was told. 'Let your parents and everyone think you've changed.'

He jumped to his feet, unable to keep quiet any longer. 'I think I'll go and see Tom,' he said. 'Ta ra, Mam.'

'Ta ra, son,' she said absently, still looking over Greg's shoulder at the newspaper.

John walked briskly down into the town and slipped into the Club. Bill was in the outer room and greeted him in half in fun, half in earnest: 'Hello, stranger.'

John forced himself to stand and chat for a while until others joined their group and he was able to slip away and into the back room.

He found the men there looking serious and yet excited. 'They'll bring Franco back,' one man told him. 'It's all part of the plot. They've been scheming for a long time.'

'Aye, and we've been planning, too, as they'll find out,' another man said.

'But what can we do?' John asked. The man's hand fell heavily on his arm. 'We can stand shoulder to shoulder with our brothers, lad. We'll show them what we can do when the workers stand together.' Other men, equally excited, joined in, but John saw the man he'd always thought of as being like his grandfather on the opposite side of the room, and made his way over to him.

He greeted John quietly, and John asked if he knew what was happening in Spain. The older man nodded.

'Yes, we're in touch with the Spanish UGT, that's the same as our Trades Union Council. We'll get the truth from them.'

John asked again as he had asked the other men, 'What can we do?'

'Nothing yet,' he was told. 'Don't worry. We'll give practical help to our comrades, stand with them, but not yet. It'll all have to be organized.'

John looked unconvinced and the man told him he would be kept informed and meanwhile must go on as he had been doing.

He found it difficult to hide his impatience as the months passed, and to keep quiet when his father read aloud about events in Spain from his newspaper. It was rare for Greg to comment on Spain though, as he was far more interested in Herr Hitler's doings since he had invaded the Rhineland in March, and the behaviour of Mussolini in Abyssinia.

Addis Ababa had fallen to the Italians on May the fifth and since then there had been reports that poison gas had been used by Mussolini's troops.

'God forgive them if it's true,' Cathy said. 'God forgive them anyway taking another country, and that Hitler fellow too. Why can't they stay in their own countries and mind their own business?'

The *Liverpool Echo* was a local paper and it was usually local news that Greg read aloud, but everything irritated John. 'Why the hell can't he just read the paper like anyone else?' he said to Sarah one night. 'Everybody else has to listen to a running commentary.'

Sarah laughed. 'I know. It gets on my nerves sometimes, but Mum said for years Dad couldn't afford a paper so I suppose he's enjoying it now.'

'She always makes excuses for him,' John exclaimed, and Sarah looked quizzically at him.

'She does for you too, for any of us, in fact, but you don't moan about that.'

John grinned at her. Sometimes he was tempted to talk to Sarah about his visits to the Club, but he drew back because she was so close to her mother and grandmother. He felt that she might innocently say something which would lead to more questions and more rows.

Many people confided in Sarah, and her mother and her grandmother spoke freely to her. Her gentle manner and air of integrity made it seem easy and safe to talk to her, and she never repeated anything except occasionally to discuss something with her grandmother.

They were talking one day about Sarah's friend, Lucy Ashcroft, who was expecting a baby. A hurried marriage had been arranged by Lucy's family between her and the father of her child, and Sarah said to her grandmother, 'I wish Lucy didn't have to get married. I don't like Des much anyway, and Lucy doesn't really want to get married like this. She says Des will throw it up to her every time they have a row, that he was forced into it.'

'Not much chance for the marriage if she thinks that before they start,' Sally said with a sigh. 'Poor girl. It's a pity the family are insisting on it.'

'But Lucy wants to keep the baby, Grandma, so what else can she do?' Sarah said. 'She's had to leave the factory too. They said it wasn't fair to the other girls to keep her on.'

'Hypocrites!' Sally exclaimed. 'How could she affect the other girls?'

'I know. I said to Lucy, Our Lord said, "Let he who is without sin among you cast the first stone," and no one could. Lucy said the woman in the sweet shop by the works told her she was just being punished for being found out. She knew how the other girls behaved with their boyfriends from the way they talked in the shop, but they were too crafty to get caught.'

'It's true what they say, love, it's the good girls who have the babies,' Sally said. They put the last of the dishes away and went into the kitchen.

'D'you know what else Lucy said, Grandma? She said Des was always pestering her, and she gave in because she didn't like to hurt his feelings.'

'I can believe it,' Sally said. 'I worried about your mum for that reason.'

'About Mum?' Sarah exclaimed.

'Yes, because she was so soft-hearted. Anyway, she was only fifteen when she met your dad so I needn't have worried.'

'Fifteen? So she was younger than me when she was courting properly,' Sarah said.

'Yes. Grandad tried to stop it. He thought she was too young, but I was glad because I knew she was safe with your dad.'

'I remember now. Didn't he say something about King Canute? Someone told me about it years ago.'

'No, it was Peggy mentioned King Canute. She told me

to ask Grandad had he ever heard of King Canute when he was trying to stop them courting. She said Grandad had about as much chance.'

They both laughed, but Sarah said, 'Fancy, Mrs Burns! I didn't think she'd know about King Canute. She never reads, does she?'

'She remembered a picture in her school book of King Canute sitting by the shore on his throne, with his crown on and the waves coming in to his feet. But Peggy's no fool,' Sally said with a shade of reproof in her voice.

'I know, Grandma,' Sarah said hastily. 'But I know she doesn't read.'

'She didn't have much chance. She only had a few years of schooling because she had to stay at home and help her mother, and they weren't so strict in those days. Your generation are lucky, the chances you have.'

'Did you worry about Auntie Mary?' Sarah asked.

'I did, but not for the same reason,' Sally said rather grimly. 'Mary always knew how many beans made five.'

Sarah appreciated her grandmother even more now, because she had met Anne's grandmother who lived with them. The family were Catholics although in a different parish to the Redmonds, and the old lady was fanatically religious. Anne and Sarah were in the parlour one night with several of Anne's brothers and sisters, when Anne said to her brother Terry, 'Sarah's grandmother is marvellous. Sarah can say anything to her, can't you, Sar?'

'Such as?' Terry asked.

'Well, unmarried mothers,' Anne said. 'Sarah's grandmother said it was the good girls who have babies. The others are too crafty. That's right, isn't it, Sar?'

Sarah nodded, blushing. She was amazed to hear Anne say such things to her brother, but he only laughed and said, 'She *is* unusual. Imagine Grandma . . .'

They all laughed, including Sarah, and Terry went on, 'She'd be sprinkling the poor girl with holy water and telling her the devil had her in his clutches.'

Sarah had told Anne of her grandmother's remarks without mentioning Lucy. She looked uneasily at her friend, wondering if she had guessed who they had been talking about, but Anne said gaily, 'You should see Gran's room, Sarah. It's like an extension on the Cenacle Convent. Statues and holy pictures everywhere. A life-sized statue of our Lady just inside the door. It gave me a nasty turn when I took her a cup of tea one morning.'

'She goes to bed at eight o'clock at night to get her night prayers finished by ten,' Terry said.

Another brother, Stephen, said teasingly, 'Our Maureen's understudying her. She falls asleep on her knees saying her prayers.'

'Once,' Maureen cried indignantly. 'That's you, Anne, telling tales.' She turned to Sarah. 'I wanted to finish a novena but I was very tired. I knelt by my bed and fell asleep, that's all that happened.'

'She gained Grace with her Novena,' Anne laughed, 'and made me commit a sin. I said some bad words, believe me, when I had to get out of my warm bed and wake her up.'

Maureen smiled then said thoughtfully, 'I'm not criticizing your gran's view, Sarah, but surely you can't divide girls into those who have babies because they're innocent, and those who are crafty enough to know how to prevent them. What about all the girls like us where the question doesn't arise?'

'We were talking about a specific case we'd heard of,' Sarah said, her face pink. 'This girl works in a clothing factory and she'd been sacked in case she – she sort of contaminated the other girls. That's what it seemed like anyway, and someone said the other girls were immoral but too crafty to have babies.'

'The ones who were being protected from the first girl?' Terry said. 'That's a damn' disgrace, all the same. Hypocritical.'

'That's what Grandma said,' Sarah said eagerly. 'She meant that the girl I know is a good girl really.'

'Yes, I know anyone can make a mistake,' Maureen said. 'But my point is, just because you don't have a child before marriage, it doesn't mean you're just crafty. Most girls I know – well, I can't speak for other people, but *I* wouldn't allow anything to happen before I was married, and I think that goes for many others too.'

'It's a question of self-respect. I'd feel cheap if I did,' said Anne.

'The same goes for a fellow,' Terry said. 'You want to respect the girl you marry.'

Eileen Fitzgerald was lying on the rug reading. Now she lifted her head. 'It's a sin anyway, and you'd have to tell it in Confession. That's enough to put you off.'

They all laughed but Sarah said quietly, 'I think respect is what matters. I wouldn't respect a fellow who suggested it, knowing the risk to the girl.'

'He couldn't really love her,' said Anne.

The eldest brother lay in an armchair with his long legs stretched out and his eyes closed. Now he opened them and said, 'I agree with you about respect. I wouldn't respect a girl who gave in to me if I *did* ask her, and certainly I wouldn't want to marry her. The point is, if a girl gave in to me, she'd probably done the same with other fellows she'd been out with.'

Mrs Fitzgerald looked into the room. 'There's a tray ready if any of you drones would like to get it,' she said cheerfully.

'OK, Ma,' said Anne, jumping to her feet, and the talk turned to other matters during supper.

Later when Sarah went home, with Anne walking part of the way with her, she said dreamily, 'I think I'll have six or seven children when I'm married. I think big families are fun.'

'But you've got brothers and a sister,' Anne said.

'I know, but we're more spaced out. I love the discussions in your house. We all get on well, but we don't have talks like you do, Anne. Kate's too young and the boys are too single-minded.'

'John with his politics, you mean.'

'Yes, and Mick with his aviation. He thinks of nothing else now. Always hanging round Speke Aerodrome and talking to the Dutch pilots, and his side of the bedroom has the wall covered with pictures of aeroplanes and Jim Mollison and Colonel Lindbergh.'

'Is he still step dancing?' Anne asked.

'Oh, yes, and playing cricket and running. I don't know how he finds time to study.'

'I bet that'll be my claim to fame in years to come, that I knew your Mick,' Anne said with a laugh. 'I'm sure he'll be really famous one day. He's so clever.'

'He's always top of the class,' Sarah said, 'and good at sport too, and the annoying thing is it's all so easy for him. He never worries about a thing and yet everything turns out right for him.'

'Don't sound as though you want him to come a cropper,' Anne teased her.

They parted at the corner and Sarah walked on, thinking how glad she was to have Anne as her friend. They agreed about almost everything. The fact that Anne loved books and poetry as much as she herself did had attracted Sarah at first, but the more she knew of Anne the more she appreciated her goodness and generosity of spirit, and her sense of humour.

She liked all the Fitzgerald family. She loved the discussions they often had, sometimes serious like tonight, sometimes on films or books, but always lively, everyone with an opinion and determined to express it. Anne told her that they often quarrelled but always made up quickly, and she could believe it.

I hope Anne's not going to fall for our John, Sarah thought. I'm sure he's up to something, although he seems so meek and mild now.

John would be twenty-one years old in September and Cathy had suggested a party to celebrate, but he turned down the idea. 'But you're only twenty-one once, son,' she said. 'Why don't you want to celebrate?'

'I don't know, Mum,' John mumbled. 'I'd just rather not have a party.'

The truth was that John was deceiving his parents about how he spent his evenings, and knew that he must deceive them even more and cause them much pain when he was able to carry out his plans. In spite of that he was determined to go to Spain, but felt unable to let his mother arrange a party for him while he was planning to leave home.

Cathy thought that he would find a party unbearable without his grandfather present, so she said no more about it. John realized the mistake she was making and felt mean, but told himself that the Cause was all that mattered now.

He had copied out and hung on his wall the words written by Emiliano Zapata and quoted by Dolores Ibarruri, known as La Passionaria. "It is better to die on your feet than to live on your knees." He said them over to himself every night before he slept.

At the end of October he told his mother that he was going to spend a weekend in Paris very soon. His father was out at the St Johns Ambulance Headquarters at the time, but Cathy was pleased to hear her son's plans.

'It'll do you good,' she said. 'You need a break, but I hope the weather won't turn nasty before you go.'

'I'm going next weekend for that reason, Mum,' he said glibly.

'Next weekend! I'll have to look through your clothes, get your shirts ready,' she exclaimed.

'Don't worry. I'll only be taking a rucksack,' John said. He made an excuse and escaped before he was asked any more questions.

Greg returned some time before John, and Cathy told him excitedly about the weekend in Paris.

'I'm glad he's having a break, Greg,' she said. 'I was thinking – we had money put aside for his twenty-first party, but since he wouldn't have it, how about giving him that now, to help with his holiday expenses?'

'Just as you like,' Greg said. He questioned Cathy closely about who John would be with and where he would be staying.

She said impatiently, 'We didn't have time to go into all that. He had to meet someone, but I suppose he'll be going with those lads from the office, the ones who go hiking in Germany. He said he was only taking a rucksack.'

She had been on a catering job in the afternoon, a children's party which had been very tiring, and now she went to bed. Greg stayed downstairs. When John arrived home, it was his father who greeted him.

'I believe you plan a weekend in Paris?'

'That's right,' John said. 'I'll go up, I think, I'm very tired.'

Greg barred his way. 'Tell me more about this weekend, John.'

He shrugged. 'Not much to tell,' he said. 'It's just a short holiday.'

'Is it?' Greg said. 'I think it's more than that. If it is, John,

I want you to tell your mother the truth.'

'I don't know what you mean!' John exclaimed, flushing.

'I think you do. I know about the recruiting office in the Old Haymarket, and the weekend trips to Paris, often by men who've been unemployed for years and are almost in rags.'

'If you know all that, you'll know we're really making for Spain,' John said. His face was flushed and his eyes bright, and he gripped the back of a chair as he spoke. 'I'm not ashamed – I'm proud to be going to fight alongside my comrades. It's what Grandad always dreamed of, working men of every country standing shoulder to shoulder.'

'Yes, I realize you're making for Spain,' Greg said. 'And I wouldn't stop you if I could, if it's what you believe in, but you must be honest with your mother.'

'I don't want to upset her,' John said, looking down at his hands.

'She'll be upset if you deceive her, John,' said Greg. 'Mum's very strong, you know. Obviously she won't want you to go into danger, and neither do I, son, but we know you'll be doing what you believe in.'

'You don't seem surprised Dad.'

Greg smiled sadly. 'I've expected something like this for a long time. I knew a man years ago whose family had originally come from Ireland. They were always talking about Ireland's wrongs and singing sad songs about emigration, and when the troubles started in Ireland he went there to fight and was badly wounded. He said to me, "My father dreamed the dreams, but my flesh found the reality." '

John looked puzzled. 'I don't understand.'

'Never mind,' said Greg wearily. 'All your plans are made, I take it? Can you tell me about them?'

'Yes, but it must be confidential, Dad. We'll go to Paris, and there'll be Frenchmen there who'll take us on to the next stage.'

'You'll be with friends, I suppose?'

'We're all brothers,' John said grandly. 'It's not just men of all nationalities who'll fight together, but men of every class too. Public school men and Varsity men and intellectuals who belong to the Left Book Club have joined working men because they see the justice of the Cause.'

'Yes, and among all these presumably there are men you know personally?' Greg said dryly, but John was too excited to notice his tone.

'Yes, Liverpool men. Henry Vaughan's there already. He made his own way there, though.'

'We'd better get to bed. Don't forget, your mother must be told the truth,' said Greg.

As soon as John arrived home from work the following evening, he told Cathy the real reason for his trip to Paris. He explained that it must be done this way otherwise he might be prosecuted under the Foreign Enlistment Act, and that he would be travelling with friends.

His eyes sparkled as he spoke about the arrangements although he also said that he was sorry to upset his mother. Cathy shed a few tears and held him close, then she said firmly, 'You must do what you believe is right, John.' As Greg had said, she could be strong when it was necessary, and she began to plan comforts that he could take with him.

John urged the necessity of caution until he was safely away, and she said calmly, 'I'll tell Grandma the truth. I've already told her about you going to Paris for the weekend, and I know she thought it was odd.'

Later John went with his mother to see his grandmother. She sat as usual with her right thumb under her chin and her forefinger across her lips as she listened.

'Well, I hope you know what you're doing, lad,' she said when he finished. 'You haven't been right all year, I know. Maybe this will get it out of your system, but don't take any chances, will you?'

'I won't, Grandma,' he promised, thinking that she always knew how to cut him down to size. Get it out of his system!

Dad surprised me, John thought. I felt closer to him last night, somehow, than I've ever felt before. He seemed almost like Grandad.

Chapter Twenty-Seven

It seemed to Cathy that before she had time to realize what was happening, the day of John's departure to France had arrived. He was to meet up at the London Coach Terminal in St John's Lane where he would be given a ticket for the coach, then he and the others would be met in London and arrangements made for them to buy a ticket on the boat train to Paris.

He took only a change of clothes in a rucksack. Cathy packed sandwiches, some chocolate and a packet of raisins for him, and also an aluminium flask of home-made lemonade. Greg and Sally both gave him money.

'I'm all right, honestly, Grandma,' he said. 'Tickets and everything are organized for us.'

'You never know. Keep it in case, lad.'

John also protested about taking money from his father, but Greg said firmly, 'Put it somewhere safe. If you find you've made a mistake, John, use it for your fare back – and don't be too proud to admit it and come home. There'll be no reproaches from us.'

Cathy wept and clung to John for a moment when he was ready to leave, but she dried her eyes and tried to look cheerful as they waved him off. Sally had joined them to say goodbye as John said that he wanted the farewells at home and to go alone to the coach station. When he had turned the corner of Egremont Street, Cathy and her mother wept without restraint.

'Now how about a cup of tea?' Greg said cheerfully. 'And then the pictures for all of us. There's a Laurel and Hardy we haven't seen.'

At first they demurred, but, first Cathy because she thought it might cheer up her mother, and then Sally because she thought it would help Cathy, both agreed.

Sarah was staying in to wash her hair, so it was arranged that she would put Kate to bed while Mick went with his parents and grandmother to the cinema.

He began to laugh as soon as the film started, and laughed louder and louder as it progressed until he was almost falling from his seat in paroxysms.

Cathy, Sally and Greg laughed too, as much at Mick as at the film, and people sitting nearby turned to laugh with him. 'He's like the Laughing Policeman outside the fun fair at Blackpool,' Greg whispered to Cathy.

She nodded. Thank God for Mick, she thought. She would never have to worry about him going off to fight. He was too busy enjoying life to care about Causes.

When they reached home, Mick was still laughing about the film and told Sarah about it.

'I'm glad I wasn't with you,' she exclaimed. 'I remember going to see a Charlie Chaplin film with you and you made a show of me. Everyone in the pictures was turning round to look at you.'

But Mick disregarded her. 'Remember that last bit?' he said to his father. 'Where Hardy got squashed little and fat in the press in the dungeons and Stan Laurel was stretched out long and thin on the rack?' He went up to bed still laughing and they soon followed him.

Greg thought that the cinema visit had taken Cathy's mind from her worry about John, but as he kissed her goodnight he found her cheeks were wet with tears, and put his arms around her and held her close.

'Oh, Greg, he looked so young and so happy,' she sobbed. 'What if something happens to him?'

'It won't,' he said confidently. 'I don't think this will last long, it might even be over before he arrives in Spain, or where the fighting is, anyway.'

'They'll win, you mean? His side,' Cathy said.

'I don't know about that,' Greg said. 'I've heard that Hitler and Mussolini are helping General Franco, and the peasants who are fighting for the government are poorly equipped.'

'I don't understand it at all,' Cathy said with a sigh. 'Mussolini is a bad man – he did awful things in Abyssinia – and Herr Hitler doesn't seem much better, does he? So why are they helping General Franco?'

'Because the three of them are birds of a feather,' Greg said. 'They're all tarred with the same brush – dictators.'

'But the church is on Franco's side,' Cathy said. 'He was prayed for in church last week.'

'That's because the Spanish Government is anti-clerical.'

'I don't understand and don't care which one's right, as long as John comes home safely,' said Cathy.

Greg kissed her. 'Don't worry, John can take care of himself. He's a big strong lad, remember?'

Cathy fell asleep, comforted by his words.

She tried to avoid Josie for a few days as John had warned them to give no details of his destination to anyone until he was safely away.

The weekend was easy as they were busy with their families and Monday was washing day for both of them, but on Tuesday morning Josie called in to see Cathy.

A card had come for a catering job, and also a plain postcard from John, saying that he was well and happy and enjoying sightseeing in Paris. He sent love to all the family.

'Did you get a card for a job tomorrow?' Josie asked. The card was on the sideboard with the card from John, and Josie glanced at them. 'I see you did, and you've had a card from your John too. Is he home?'

'Not yet,' Cathy said evasively. 'It's a reunion dinner tomorrow, isn't it?'

'Yes, at Mount Hall. It's a good place, kitchens handy for the dining room,' Josie said. 'Your John isn't home then? I thought he only went for the weekend.'

'No, he's staying on for a while,' Cathy said, but she knew that she was blushing.

'He doesn't get holidays with pay, does he?'

'No, only the people who've worked there for a long time, twenty years I think it is, get a week's paid holiday.'

She looked at Josie who was obviously about to ask more questions and thought suddenly, it's no use. I'm no good at telling lies. I'll have to tell her, and he's in Paris now, anyway.

'Our John won't be back for a while, Josie,' she said. 'He's going on to fight in Spain.'

'Good God, what put that in his head?' Josie exclaimed.

'He's been thinking about it for a while,' Cathy said. 'A

317

lot of Liverpool lads are going, he says.'

'But what about his job?'

Cathy shrugged. 'I don't know what'll happen about it. It all seemed to happen so quickly. I didn't have time to ask him many questions.'

'You'll miss his wages,' Josie said. 'And I don't suppose he'll be sure of his job when he comes back, will he?'

'I don't know,' Cathy said, mentally adding fearfully, 'If he comes back.'

Josie was still thinking about John's wages. 'Still, I suppose at his age he could have been getting married and you'd still have been at the loss of his wages, wouldn't you?'

'Marriage is the last thing on our John's mind.'

'The years you've got to keep them,' Josie went on, 'then they're earning for a few years, and the next thing you know they're off, married or something.'

'You can't stop young people getting married,' Cathy said, pleased to turn the conversation away from John.

'Our Edie's fallen out with Harry again,' Josie said. 'They were talking about getting engaged, she told me, and the next thing they were having a row.'

'They always make it up though, don't they?'

'I hope they do. She'll never find anyone else who can turn those sort of wages up to her,' Josie said. 'Five pounds a week. No wonder they say you need a letter from the Holy Ghost to get a job as a printer.'

'I'm sure they'll soon make it up,' Cathy consoled her. 'He's a nice lad, isn't he?'

'Yes, but I don't want them to get married too soon. The expense of a wedding, and then losing her wages before we're properly on our feet.'

'It's a pity girls can't stay on at work,' Cathy said, but Josie looked offended.

'Crawford's don't employ married women,' she said. 'Anyway, Harry wouldn't let her. He'll be able to keep her.'

When Greg came home, Cathy told him that she had told Josie about John's plans. 'She saw the card and started asking questions, and I had to tell her. He's safely away and she was more interested in how I'd manage without his wages anyway.'

'I'd warn her not to talk about it when you're at that job tomorrow,' Greg said.

'I never thought of that,' Cathy admitted. 'Snowy White asked Mam about John, you know.'

'Snowy White did?' Greg exclaimed.

'Yes. He might just have been trying to be polite,' Cathy said. 'You know the little boy who got knocked down – Mam was with his mother, and Snowy White was there and asked her how her grandson was doing, but I don't suppose it means anything. He's only the copper on the beat, after all.'

Greg looked thoughtful. 'What did he say exactly?'

'He asked how he was, and Mam just said, "He's fine," and Snowy said lads have these wild spells and get over them.'

Greg looked relieved.

The following morning Cathy went to see Josie's mother who had become more and more infirm, and was now confined to bed. She took a baked custard which Mrs Mellor said she would enjoy. 'I always relished me food, Cathy,' she sighed. 'But now I can't fancy nothing, hardly. I think I'm done for, girl.'

'Don't say that, Mrs Mellor,' Cathy replied. 'You've got to see your granddaughters married, Edie and Bella's girl.'

'You're a good girl, Cathy,' the old lady said. 'Like your da. I miss your da, you know. I always felt safe while he was here to sort things out.'

Josie had come into the room, and Cathy helped her to change the sheets on the bed and make her mother more comfortable and Mrs Mellor drifted off to sleep.

Josie and Cathy went downstairs and Josie said with a smile, 'You were always a favourite with Mam, Cath, and she thought the world of your dad. She broke her heart crying when he died. She said he was the only man she ever knew who was good through and through.'

Tears filled Cathy's eyes and Josie wept with her for a moment. 'Your mam has always made me welcome here,' Cathy said. 'There's been some good "do's" here, haven't there?'

'Yes,' Josie said, and laughed. 'She always hated your Mary though. Mam reckoned she was the favourite with your dad.'

'Dad didn't make favourites,' Cathy said indignantly. 'He was very proud of Mary, but he never made any distinction between us.'

'I know. Makes me laugh when I think the way Mam makes a favourite of *our* Mary, who never does nothing, and never says a good word about me who does everything for her.'

'I'm sure she appreciates you really,' Cathy said. 'Listen, Josie, I wanted to ask you – will you keep it quiet about our John going to Spain? He might get into trouble about it.'

'Yes, sure,' Josie said. 'I've kept our Dolly off to look after me mam. She's gone for the messages now. She's only got another couple of months before she leaves school, anyway, and I'll be glad to get out for the job, to be honest.'

Cathy thought that she too would be glad to go out and forget her worries for a while, but she knew if she said that to Josie it would lead to too many questions so she said nothing.

For years, although she always seemed cheerful and happy, the worry about the conflict between Greg and John had been constantly in her mind, sometimes lying dormant when things went well between them, but always recurring at the first sign of friction.

Since John had appeared in court, the tension had eased between him and his father and there had been no arguments between them. Cathy had lost the sensation of living on a volcano which might erupt at any moment, and this had been a reason for happiness to offset her sadness at her father's death.

It seemed hard that now there was a fresh cause for worry, about John's safety, just when things had been going so well. She lay awake for hours at night, wondering where he was and what was happening to him, and praying for the night to end though she was worried during the day too.

Particularly when she was ironing, Cathy's mind seemed free to range over dreadful possibilities, and she pictured John blinded, or with limbs missing, or taken prisoner, and sometimes the most dreadful possibility of all – his death in action.

It was a relief for her to meet Josie, and take the tramcar to Mount Hall where she was pleased to see Cissie too. She was such a good worker that she made the job lighter for everyone else, and could always be relied on to provide amusement, whether intentionally or not.

The occasion for the dinner was a reunion of middle-aged men who seemed very pleasant, and the menu was simple so the work was easy. Cathy was following Cissie, serving vegetables. She was delayed for a moment. When she caught up with Cissie, she was bending over a man who had turned to look up at her.

'Don't you worry, lad,' she was saying. 'My girl had my heart scalded, but she's settled down now as good as gold. They turn out all right in the long run.'

She moved on and Cathy was relieved to see that the man was smiling and his next-door neighbour was saying, 'There you are, Jim. The next time you write, tell Nigel he has your heart scalded, but don't waste time battering him.'

Later, when the rush was over, Mrs Nuttall said to Cissie, 'What was all that in aid of with that fellow?'

'Ah, poor bugger. He was telling the other feller he was worried about his lad, so I told him: "Girls is worse. I battered our Daisy but it never done no good."' She sighed theatrically. 'We all has our troubles, don't we?'

'Yes, and you're mine,' Mrs Nuttall said. 'You'll get me hung before you're finished.' Cissie went on to tell them that she had been ironing when she saw a cockroach run along by the skirting board in the kitchen. She threw the flatiron at it just as Bert came in the door and he had run out again into the entry. 'He kept shouting up the yard, "What was that for? I never done nothing." Laugh! I nearly wet meself,' Cissie said.

Cathy came home in a much more cheerful frame of mind, deciding that she would look on the bright side and refuse to let her imagination conjure up any more horrors about John.

'I'm glad of the four shillings,' she told Josie, 'but I'd do the jobs for nothing as long as Cissie was there.'

Sarah missed John and worried about him, but she had too many other interests to brood about him very much. The unsatisfactory affair with Michael still dragged on. He asked her out about once a fortnight, always to see a film, and always when he took her home simply said goodnight and walked away.

'I don't know why he bothers. He obviously doesn't care about me,' she said to Anne.

'It's the queerest courtship I've ever heard of,' Anne agreed.

Often Sarah told herself that she would refuse to go out with him, but always she agreed, hoping that this time it would be different. She felt that she knew as little about him as when he first came in the shop, although Anne was able to tell her that he attended her church, and her sister Maureen saw him sometimes at Benediction.

'Maureen says he looks as though he should have a laurel wreath round his head, and I agree,' Anne said. 'He looks like "the noblest Roman of them all", doesn't he?'

Sarah nodded. She felt that she had only to close her eyes and she could instantly recall every detail of Michael's appearance. His dark blue eyes fringed with dark lashes, his straight nose and firm chin, and his dark hair in close curls over his head. It was true that his profile was that of a coin, and he was tall and muscular too.

No wonder I love him, she thought, but evidently he doesn't love me. Then a doubt entered her mind. Do I love him really, or do I just love his looks? I don't know, but I'm going to try to forget him.

Her visits to Anne's home and outings with her family helped to ease her heartache, and then she and Anne discovered another interest. They joined an Irish dancing class being held in a parish hall. Both slim and light-footed, they soon learned the steps and became excellent dancers. They began to spend most of their evenings at ceilidhes held at various church halls and clubs.

Anne with dark hair and brown eyes, and Sarah with blue eyes and light chestnut hair were a contrast in colour, but both usually looked quiet and serious. At the dances, excitement made their eyes sparkle and gave colour to their cheeks, and young men rushed to claim them as partners as soon as the music started. They were usually escorted home and asked for dates.

'I'm going out with Joe Hammond on Wednesday, and to the pictures with Ronnie Riley on Friday,' Sarah said to Anne, 'but I'm not going to get serious with anyone.'

'Neither am I,' declared Anne. 'Matt Doyle said I was a two-timer, but I told him there's nothing wrong in going out with two fellows at once if they know about each other. If he doesn't like it, he knows what to do.'

Eventually the day came when Michael asked to take Sarah to the cinema and she was able to tell him that she already had a date for that evening. She hoped to provoke him but he only said calmly, 'Another time then,' and smiled at her before moving away.

Sarah escaped to a small store room and shed a few tears, but then she became angry. That's that, she told herself. Now I'm *really* going to forget him. I won't go out with him again.

On December the second the Bishop of Bradford made a reference to King Edward VIII in a sermon, which gave the newspapers an excuse to open the floodgates of speculation about the King and Mrs Simpson.

People were bitterly divided, some condemning the King for consorting with a divorced woman, others saying that he had the same right as other men to fall in love, but all were united in detesting Mrs Simpson. Even children sang, 'hark the herald angels sing, Mrs Simpson's pinched our King'.

Edie Meadows was in tears about it and told Sarah that all the girls she worked with loved the King.

'These old men who are against him don't know what they're talking about,' she wept. 'He's a lovely man.'

Sarah agreed with Edie in supporting Edward VIII.

'He'd be a good King,' she said that evening at home. 'Look at the interest he took in the miners. He said something must be done about their conditions.'

'He also said he was going to cut away a lot of dead wood in the Royal Household and make various other reforms,' Greg said. 'I'm afraid he's stirred up too many hornets' nests, and they'll get him out on one pretext or another.'

'What do you think of Mrs Simpson, Dad?'

'I think she's a determined woman, but she's under-estimated the strength of the opposition.'

Sarah laughed. 'Sometimes you sound like Grandad,' she exclaimed. 'The way he always had a different slant on things.'

Events were moving swiftly and on December the eleventh the King abdicated after a moving speech on the wireless. Mabel Burroughs was in a state of constant distress about it, and bitter in her condemnation of Mrs Simpson, and her dislike of the new King and Queen.

'I believe she's a Tartar,' she told Sarah and Anne. 'Goes round the house with white gloves on, looking for dust, and him with a stammer like that! What sort of a King will he be?'

'That's unkind, Mabel,' Anne protested. 'I'm sure he didn't want to be King, but was pushed into it.'

'No, but *she* wanted to be Queen, the Duchess of York,' Mabel said. 'I shouldn't have said that about his stammer. I think he's a good man and he'll do his best, but it should never have happened.'

Sarah soon lost interest in the affairs of Royalty. She could only think that Christmas was approaching, and compare it with the happy holiday of the previous year when her grandfather was still with them and John was at home, and when she had been so happy and hopeful because she had been out with Michael and he had given her the topaz brooch.

A week before Christmas he came into the shop and waited until most of the pie queue had been served before approaching Sarah and asking if he could see her that evening. She was about to refuse when he said quietly, 'I want to talk to you, Sarah. Explain something. I thought we might go to a café and talk.'

She agreed and arranged to meet him, puzzled by his serious manner and wondering what he needed to explain.

They found a table in a secluded corner of the café and Michael waited until they had ordered and eaten a simple meal, then leaned over the table and took her hand.

'I think what I'm going to say will be a shock to you, Sarah, and I think perhaps I haven't been fair in not mentioning it to you before this,' he said. 'I'm hoping to become a priest.'

'A – a priest!' she stammered.

'Yes. I've thought for a long time that that was what I wanted. That I had a vocation. I'd almost decided to apply last year when I met you and was attracted to you, Sarah.

It raised doubts in my mind and I thought this might be God's way of showing me that I hadn't a true vocation.'

'But I don't understand,' she said. 'You've been asking me out all year.'

'I know. I've been wrestling with the problem all this time. I felt so drawn to you, I thought I was falling in love with you, yet something seemed to hold me back. I kept hoping for some sign to show me the way, then when you told me that you were going out with someone else, that was it.'

Sarah shook her head. 'I *still* don't understand. How could that — ?'

'It showed me that I wasn't being fair to you, for one thing, and for another — ' He hesitated and said gently, 'Don't misunderstand me when I say this, Sarah. I knew that I should have felt distress and jealousy when I thought of you with someone else, but I didn't. Don't be hurt. The lack was in me.'

'I'm not hurt,' she said slowly. 'I'm glad you've told me. It explains such a lot. You know, Michael, I always felt that there was something wrong. I thought at first it was that we were both shy, but then I realized it wasn't that, but couldn't work out what it was.'

'I'm very sorry,' he said.

'Don't be. I'm relieved. I'd begun to think that there was something wrong with me.' She smiled.

'I'm glad I haven't upset you, Sarah,' he said. 'I'll always value your friendship.'

The café was almost empty. They left and walked slowly back to Egremont Street.

Michael told her that he had talked with his parish priest and the first steps had already been taken for his entrance to a seminary to be trained for the priesthood.

'Will you pray for me?' he asked. 'A late vocation isn't easy.'

'I will, and I'm sure you're doing the right thing,' she said. 'I mean, I'm sure you truly have a vocation, Michael.'

He smiled. 'Time will tell,' he said. 'I've a long way to go yet.' And he bent his head and gently kissed her goodbye.

It was a brotherly kiss, and as Sarah left him and went indoors she thought ruefully, I waited a long time for that kiss, and it could have come from John or Mick!

Chapter Twenty-Eight

At the beginning of December another letter had come from John, this time from Lyons. 'That's about three hundred miles from Paris,' Greg said. 'He's getting nearer to the Spanish border.'

John wrote that he was with a small group, all from very different backgrounds but all united. 'It's a wonderful experience to meet these fellows, all different types and from such different backgrounds yet all wanting to fight for a world where all men are equal, and people have an equal chance in life.'

'Well, he seems happy enough,' Cathy said. 'And still thinking the same way. I was afraid he would get there and find he'd made a mistake.'

'If that was the case, he'd be able to pay for his journey home, anyway,' Greg comforted her.

Just before Christmas two more letters arrived from John, one written from a town twenty miles from the Spanish border, and the second from the Spanish town of Figueras. In the first letter he said that so far they had been travelling by train and sightseeing, but now the real part of the journey would start.

In the second letter he wrote exultantly:

We've made it! We came over the Pyrenees, first with French guides then with Spanish, and now we're enrolled in the International Brigade. I've met some marvellous fellows, from all parts of Britain and some other nationalities. Many Americans, but I believe they'll go to a different camp to us. Some great chaps from Liverpool, Bootle and Birkenhead. I hope you're not worried about me. I'm really happy. My only regret is that I can't tell Grandad about all this.

I'm sorry I can't send any Christmas presents, only my love to you both, Mum and Dad, and to Sarah, Mick and Kate. Remember me to my friends if you see them. I've written separately to Grandma. I think of you all very often.

> Your loving son,
> John

Cathy read and re-read the second letter and knew that Greg did too. She felt that in the loving, warmhearted letter Greg was seeing John for the first time as the son she had always known.

On the Sunday before Christmas, when all the family were at Sally's house for tea, she said she hoped they were all determined to make it a good Christmas. 'It's what Grandad would have wanted for one thing,' she said. 'And then we don't know what's going to happen in the future, good or bad. Kate might go to Hollywood or Mick might stow away on an aeroplane, so we'll have a good time while we're all here and have something to remember next year, eh?'

Kate and Mick were delighted with her guesses about their future, and there was much laughter and joking, but in later years Cathy often wondered if her mother had second sight.

Cathy and Greg were anxious to make it a happy time for Kate particularly. She had been disappointed at not being chosen to appear in the 'Puss in Boots' pantomime, but with everyone fussing over her, buying her presents and praising her appearance in new outfits, she was perfectly happy.

On Christmas Eve a parcel arrived from America with gifts chosen by Mary and Sam. There was a tiny watch for Sarah and a bangle for Kate, a book on aviation for Mick with a twenty dollar bill as a bookmark in it. Sam wrote that they had no address for John but he hoped that they would either send him the enclosed fifty dollars or buy something for him with it.

For Greg there was an expensive fountain pen and for Cathy a pair of diamanté clips which transformed the plain black silk dress she still wore for best.

During the year letters had arrived more frequently from both Mary and Sam, and the letter in the parcel was quite bulky.

Mary told them about a holiday she and Sam had had with some friends, but said she was quite pleased to get home to California.

> Coming here was the best thing we ever did. Sam says out of evil cometh good, and it's true we would never have left New York if that crash hadn't happened.
>
> I'm having a marvellous life here. Wonderful weather and a beautiful house and so many friends. We are at beach parties or cocktail parties or dinners nearly every evening, and everyone makes such a fuss of me. Sam is so proud of me!!!
>
> We have a couple to look after the house and Mamie the maid says she has never worked for such a beautiful lady, and believe me in this part of the world that's really saying something.
>
> P.S. I feel sad at times, thinking of Dada. Mam seems all right now visiting the picturedromes so often with Peggy.

A parcel had also gone to Sally's house, containing a book with pictures of film stars' homes and details of their lives, and a long, broad scarf in very fine pink wool.

'We used to call these fascinators when I was young,' Sally told Sarah. 'Not that I ever had one.' She flung it around her head and crossed it loosely around her neck.

'It's lovely and warm,' she said. 'They've put a lot of thought into these gifts, Sarah.'

She nodded. She felt that she could never really like her Aunt Mary, but she acknowledged that she was kind and generous at times. She felt sorry for her too, since her grandmother had dropped a hint that Mary had been disappointed that her father had preferred her mother from the beginning.

Sally read Mary's letter to Cathy and afterwards pursed her lips. 'I love me, who do you love?' she quoted ironically. 'I think she'd had a few of those cocktails before she wrote that letter.'

'She certainly let herself go,' Cathy laughed. 'But she seems to be having a good life, Mam. A maid too. Sam must be doing well.'

'He deserves to,' Sally said, 'he's a good lad.'

After Lawrie's death she found that her allowance from Sam was increased, and had written to him to protest. He had replied that it was in the terms of the original arrangement that he had made with the company who administered the annuity, and could not be changed.

'Use the money for little treats,' Sam wrote. 'Take Cathy and Greg out to dinner in Southport, or use it for your outings with your friend Mrs Burns. I'm sure you'll think of something.'

Sally read the letter aloud to Peggy and insisted that Sam's money must pay for their twice-weekly visits to the Palladium or Olympia cinemas in West Derby Road, and for their ice creams in the interval.

On Peggy's birthday Cathy went with them and they went to the luxurious Forum Cinema in Lime Street. There was a café there, and emboldened by having Cathy with them, they went for a meal before the performance. Sally had bought the best seats and Peggy settled back with a sigh of bliss. 'This is the life, Sally,' she murmured.

When the organ rose from under the stage at the interval, with Reginald Foort playing it, Peggy was speechless with delight.

'That's the best birthday I've ever had,' she declared as they left the cinema.

'You should go there sometimes as a change from the Olympia,' Cathy said. 'Go to the café again, now you know they're only people like yourselves there.'

'I think we will,' Sally declared. She giggled like a young girl. 'We're getting hardfaced in our old age, Peg,' she said. Cathy looked at them with deep affection. What hard lives they had both had, and how little it took to make them happy, she thought.

Sally planned more treats with Peggy after the holiday but Christmas was for the family, they both felt.

Kate had lost her faith in Father Christmas, thanks to an older girl at the dancing class, so on Christmas Eve she slept with her grandmother while the rest of the family went to Midnight Mass. They felt soothed and uplifted as they knelt in the crowded church.

Cathy felt close to her son as she prayed for John's safety

and happiness, and Sarah prayed that Michael would find happiness in a true vocation to the priesthood. She realized thankfully that she could make this prayer without any regret for what might have been, and feel only a friendly interest in him.

Greg too prayed for John's safety, and thanked God for his wife and children as he glanced at the intent faces of Cathy and Sarah. When the Mass was over they exchanged Christmas greetings with friends, then they walked home through the starry night, linking arms and softly singing "Silent Night".

The anniversary of Lawrie's death revived all their feelings of loss and sadness, but Sally met the occasion with her usual fortitude. The family had gathered in her kitchen after work and school, and she said quietly, 'I know none of us will ever forget Grandad, but we must remember, he did a lot of good in his lifetime and he had a peaceful death with his family round him and wouldn't have wished for more. We'll just be thankful we had him with us for so long.'

Greg stood up and put his arm around her. 'You're a brave woman, Mam,' he said. 'It was your care that meant we had him with us for so long.'

'That's true,' Cathy said. 'We should all try to be as brave as you, Mam.'

'A drop of something to warm us?' Josh suggested.

'Good idea,' Greg agreed, but Sally said quickly, 'You and Greg have a drop of rum, Josh, but me and Cathy'll stick to tea, and so will Sarah, won't you, love?'

'Yes please, Grandma,' she said.

Mick stuck his thumbs under his shirt collar. 'I'll have a drop of rum, Dad,' he said with a lordly air, and Kate echoed, 'I'll have a drop of rum.'

'That's what *you* think,' Greg said. 'Ginger beer or tea, which is it?'

'You wouldn't be able to dance if you drank rum, Katie,' Josh said fondly. 'Why don't you do your new dance for us?'

She readily obliged, and followed it by several other dances and a song she was to sing in the next show.

Later, when they were at home and Kate was in bed, Cathy said to Greg, 'No one could accuse Kate of being shy or backward in coming forward, could they? Wouldn't you wonder at the difference in our children?'

'She might be a throwback to my grandmother,' Greg said. 'My mother told me once that her mother had been an actress and had a sweet singing voice. Her father didn't like it talked about because he was a solicitor in a small country town, and was ashamed of marrying an actress.'

'But she didn't carry on after they were married, did she?'

'No, I don't think so,' he said. 'Mother only spoke about it once. She was complaining about her unhappy childhood, and said her mother thought she was Sarah Siddons. She used to throw out her arms dramatically and say, "I could have been anything, *anything* if I hadn't married that awful man." She hated her husband apparently, and I think Mother hated *her*.'

'Oh, Greg, how awful!' Cathy exclaimed.

He shrugged. 'Mother may have been exaggerating, but I know she was bitter about an unhappy childhood although I don't know all the details. Her mother was selfish, I think.'

'Your mother was quite dramatic herself, wasn't she?' Cathy said. 'Quite a good actress.'

Greg nodded but said no more, and neither did she. Later, in bed, she lay thinking of their conversation. So Greg thought Kate might be a throwback to his grandmother? Or even worse, in Cathy's estimation, to his mother.

How she had detested that selfish old woman, who had hastened her husband's death by her demand for luxuries, and had pretended heart attacks to try to prevent Greg leaving her for even a few hours. I hope he's wrong, Cathy thought.

Mrs Mellor always said that Kate was like Mary and Cathy had hoped she was wrong, but better a thousand times that Kate should be like her aunt than like that old harpy Mrs Redmond. It's a good thing she has the dancing, Cathy reflected. She's not good at anything else.

There had been no suggestion that Kate might go in the scholarship class, and only Greg's careful coaching saved her from being relegated to the B stream in school. She showed no interest in reading, her only passions were her appearance and her dancing, but she seemed happy enough, and Cathy decided not to worry about her.

Thinking of Mrs Mellor reminded Cathy that she had not called in to see how she was that evening. The old lady was sinking fast. She was now very confused and doubly incontinent, and Cathy and her mother had been helping Josie with the nursing during the day.

Sally had offered to help in the evening too but Josie had refused. 'No, I'm not putting on good nature,' she said. 'Our Edie's a big strong girl and she can help me.'

'But is it suitable for a young girl? I don't mind coming over,' Sally said. But Josie said firmly that Edie must learn.

'I don't want any of our Mary's capers out of her,' she said.

Her sister Mary had said that she couldn't stand sickrooms, and anyway it was heavy work and why couldn't *he* do it? 'I knew she'd have to get a dig in at Walter somehow,' Josie said. 'I told her she'll finish up in a lunatic asylum the way she goes on about men.'

'She did have a terrible experience with her husband though, didn't she?'

'Yes, but she was lucky. He got killed in the war. Other women have to put up with that all their lives,' Josie retorted.

Cathy went in to see Mrs Mellor the following morning and found her much worse. She moaned constantly as though in pain, and from time to time she muttered, 'What have I got to do? Oh God, what have I got to do?'

Josie wept as they changed the bed and gave her mother the powders the doctor had left for her. 'If only she wasn't so worried,' Josie said. 'And in such pain.'

'The powders might ease her, and you're doing all you can,' Cathy comforted her.

'I wish I hadn't had so many rows with her,' Josie said.

In the late afternoon Sally was with Josie when Mrs Mellor gave a convulsive jerk, then lay making a rattling noise in her throat. Sally bent over her and took her wrist, then after a moment she said quietly to Josie, 'That's it, love. It's a happy release for her, poor soul.' She drew the sheet over Mrs Mellor's face, and took Josie downstairs to make her a cup of tea.

Sally sent a child in the street for Cathy, and when she came Josie said in a bewildered way, 'I don't know what you're supposed to do.'

'Me and Cathy'll see to the laying out,' Sally said.

'And Greg will help Walter to make arrangements,' Cathy offered.

'Will he? That's good,' Josie said gratefully. 'There's no men in our family now, only Walter, with the lads all being killed in the war.'

'Your poor mam had a lot of trouble and sorrow, didn't she?' Sally said. 'Losing her four lads one after the other, and then your dad so soon after the war.'

'It finished me dad, losing the lads,' Josie said. 'And it's funny, he was so quiet but we didn't half miss him when he went.'

Cathy felt more sad at Mrs Mellor's death than she expected. She had been a link with Cathy's carefree youth and had always treated her kindly, although she was regarded as a Tartar by most people.

Cathy remembered that when her father died, Mrs Mellor had heaved herself up from her armchair, which she rarely left, and waddled over to pay her respects to Lawrie and say how much she had valued him as a good neighbour. That had meant a lot to her mother, Cathy knew.

Greg helped Walter with the arrangements for the funeral, and looking round the church, Cathy thought how sad it was to see the pews filled with the widowed daughters-in-law and their children, with Walter and two adolescent grandsons as the only male members of the family.

Thinking of the men who had been killed in the war revived Cathy's fears for John's safety. More letters had come from him. In the first he said that they had made a long journey by train to Albacete, the headquarters of the International Brigade, and there he had met other men from Liverpool.

> They gave me a lot to think about. I feel sometimes like a boy among men. Although some of them are no older than me, they have been on hunger marches and really suffered hardship. The Spanish people welcomed us and gave us oranges when the train stopped anywhere. Strange to see oranges growing on twigs with leaves.

The next letter was brief and said that he was training at Madrigueras, and hoped soon to be ready to be drafted to the fighting area. The days were very hot, he wrote, but the nights freezing cold.

It was only when Cathy re-read the letter and folded it up again, that she realized that there were a few more words written on the back of the paper.

Dear Mum and Dad,
This is it. The trucks are here and we'll soon be moving off. We are to defend the road to Madrid. I'm looking forward to it. Pray for me. Love to all.

John, Feb. 1st

'February the first,' she exclaimed. 'But that was weeks ago.'

It was a Saturday and Greg was home at one o'clock. He examined the letter and the outer envelope in which it had been enclosed. 'This is postmarked Liverpool,' he said. 'That means someone has brought it home and posted it, so John must be all right.'

'I don't see how it means that John's all right,' Cathy said doubtfully.

Neither did Greg, but he said cheerfully, 'Yes, I'm sure it's a good sign, Cath,' and she stifled her doubts.

Later he went out ostensibly for screws, but walked down to the Old Haymarket to see the Spanish Aid representative. They told him that John's battalion was fighting in the Jarama Valley, to prevent Franco's troops cutting the road to Madrid. His name was not among the casualties as far as they knew, but Greg must understand that things were rather chaotic out there.

Greg gave Cathy and Sally a carefully edited version of this news, and a few days later another letter came from John. He wrote that he had been wounded in the foot and was now in a field dressing station but all right. The second part of the letter was from hospital and said that his wound had been treated although medical supplies were limited. He had been given an anti-tetanus injection.

'He's out of the fighting, anyhow, Mum,' Sarah said.

Cathy was convinced that he would soon be home and made preparations for his return. Mick's possessions had gradually flowed over John's part of the bedroom, but she made him clear them away and put fresh sheets on John's bed in readiness.

The weeks dragged on but no more letters came from John and Greg could get no information about him. The date set for the Coronation of Edward VIII was used for the Coronation of George VI as plans were so far ahead at the time of the Abdication, and Liverpool streets were decorated and street parties planned as there had been for the Jubilee of George V and Queen Mary.

None of the Redmonds except Kate could feel any enthusiasm for the event. Worry about John clouded all their days, although they told each other that no news was good news. Sarah had been involved in several arguments with people at the ceilidhes when she said her brother was with the International Brigade in Spain. They told her that John should be fighting on the side of Franco who was fighting to defend Christianity, but Sarah and Anne argued that he was doing what he believed to be right.

Eventually another letter came from John in hospital. In it he said that he hoped when his foot was fully healed he could go back to the Front, and told them a little about the battle at Jarama.

We held the line and prevented the Fascists breaking through although they had so much more than us in the way of equipment, a lot of it supplied by Italy and Germany. Ten thousand men with air and artillery supplies, I heard, but our fellows fought like tigers. Our Chief of Staff, Major Nathan, was up and down the hillsides on a motor bike encouraging us, driven, I'm proud to say, by a Liverpool man, Alan Galloway.

By the way, if anyone tells you this is a Holy War by Franco, tell them that Spanish Moroccan Muslims were among the troops fighting for him, and villages have been bombed from the air and innocent people and children killed by them.

I've met several Liverpool lads here, and two brothers named Bibby from Birkenhead. I'm giving this letter to a chap who is being invalided home as he has lost four fingers of his right hand.

Fond love to all. I thought of everyone and particularly of Grandma on Grandad's anniversary. I feel very close to him here with men who believe in what he did, and suffered as he did, which I've never done. I've found a lot to think about here, believe me, and I look forward to a talk with Dad.

Your loving son,
John

'So some men are being invalided home,' Cathy exclaimed. 'Why not John?'

'It can't be a very bad wound,' Greg said.

'I wish it was,' said Cathy, then put her hand to her mouth. 'Oh, Greg, it's like the war when we hoped our men would be wounded badly enough to be out of it.'

'A blighty one,' he said. 'But it had to be bad for that, Cathy, very bad. We don't want anything like that for John.'

Chapter Twenty-Nine

Sarah was pleased to have the details about the Moors in Franco's Army to use in any argument about John, although her spirited defence of him had made people wary of challenging her.

'I didn't know you were such a firebrand,' one of the boys she went out with remarked. 'I can see I'll have to watch my step.'

Sarah and Anne were still making dates with various boys after the dances, without becoming serious about any of them. As the summer approached they went out nearly every Sunday to North Wales, on the pillions of motor cycles owned by two brothers from Allerton. They usually went fairly early and arrived back in time to get ready for the dance, but Cathy was nervous about Sarah riding on a motor cycle.

'Hold on tight to him,' she begged Sarah one Sunday when Jimmie had called for her and she was sitting on the pillion with her arms round his waist.

'I will, Mum,' Sarah said, laughing and winking at her. Josie was at her door and laughed heartily.

'Your Sarah hasn't half come out of her shell these last few years,' she said as the motor bike roared away.

On the day of the Corpus Christi Procession in June, Kate had been chosen for a special part in the Procession. She wore a red dress and carried a sheaf of wheat and a bunch of grapes to signify the bread and wine of the Eucharist, and walked beneath an arch held by two other girls.

Greg had tried to impress on Kate the religious significance of the event, but she could only see it as an occasion when she would be in the public eye.

Anne came to the Procession and afterwards to tea with Sarah. Later they went for a walk until it was time to prepare for the dance being held afterwards, and they strolled along arm in arm, deep in conversation. There was a narrow alleyway beside a warehouse and they walked through it as a short cut to the main road.

They heard loud laughter and saw a group of boys there but, deep in conversation, paid no attention to them until, as they drew nearer, they saw that the boys were surrounding a girl who was pinned against the warehouse wall by them.

Two of the biggest boys seemed to be fighting over her, each holding one of her arms and trying to pull her towards him.

'Meg!' Sarah suddenly screamed, and plunged into the group. Anne followed her, laying about her with her handbag, but the boys scattered and ran away, even the two louts who had been pulling at Meg's arms.

Meg stood looking from Sarah to Anne and smiling uncertainly, and Sarah saw with horror that her knickers were around her ankles.

'Meg, are you all right, love?' Sarah said breathlessly. She nodded. 'It was a game,' she said tremulously. 'They were going to show me a new game.'

'Oh, poor kid,' Anne said, putting her arm around the girl.

Sarah said firmly, 'Pull your knickers up, Meg.' As Meg bent obediently, Sarah whispered over her bent head, 'Don't fuss her, Anne.'

Meg stood up and Sarah stood in front of her. 'Did those boys do anything to you?' she asked.

Meg shook her head. 'They pulled my knickers down,' she said. 'It was going to be a new game. Was I naughty, Sarah?'

Anne was about to speak but Sarah said firmly, 'Yes you were, Meg. You know your grandma has told you not to play with big boys. Come on now, we'll go home.'

Meg hung her head and Anne scrabbled in her handbag. 'I'll get her an ice cream,' she whispered to Sarah.

Sarah said, 'Don't, Anne, please.' Her friend looked indignant but walked along in silence.

'Do you mind going in our house, Anne, and I'll take Meg home?' Sarah said.

But Anne said shortly, 'I think I'll go home and get ready.

I'll see you at the dance.' She kissed Meg and walked away, and Sarah went with the girl into the Burns' house.

'There you are!' Peggy exclaimed with relief. 'I've been out of my mind worrying about you. Uncle Michael's out looking for you.' She glanced from Meg's downcast face to Sarah. 'What did she do?' she said fearfully.

'Nothing, Mrs Burns,' Sarah hastened to say. 'She's all right.'

'Go and get a cup of water in the back kitchen and close the door,' Peggy said to Meg.

When she had gone, Sarah said quickly, 'There was a gang of lads round her in an entry but they hadn't done anything, only got her to pull her knickers down.'

Peggy collapsed into a chair and put her hand to her mouth. 'I knew it, I knew,' she gasped. 'I was frantic when she went missing.'

'She's all right, honestly,' Sarah assured her. 'The lads ran away when they saw us. They'd told Meg they'd show her a new game, but nothing happened so don't worry, Mrs Burns.'

'Thank God you were there,' Peggy said.

Her face was white and Sarah said gently, 'Do you want Grandma?'

'No, it's all right, love. I'll go in to her after,' said Peggy.

'Meg was frightened, I think, and Anne wanted to buy her an ice cream but I wouldn't let her,' Sarah said. 'Meg asked if she'd been naughty and I said yes, because you'd told her not to play with big boys.'

'You did right, girl,' Peggy said. They could hear Meg blundering about in the back kitchen and she opened the door.

'I'll go,' Sarah said. 'Ta, ra, Meg. Ta, ra, Mrs Burns.' She went down the lobby and only as she let herself out of the front door did she realize that she was trembling.

'Where's Anne?' her mother asked when she went home.

'She's gone home. We saw a gang of lads round Meg Burns and chased them. Meg was a bit frightened and I think Anne was a bit huffy because I wouldn't let her buy an ice cream for Meg.'

'Worst thing she could have done,' said Cathy. 'Was Meg all right?

'Yes. They'd told her to pull her knickers down but nothing had happened to her.'

'Poor Peggy. She's out of her mind trying to keep that poor child safe,' Cathy sighed.

'That's the trouble though, Mum, isn't it?' Sarah said. 'Meg's not a child now, except in her mind. Those damn lads – they must have known she was backward.'

'God forgive them,' Cathy said. 'Thank God you and Anne walked up there.'

'I think Anne thought I was hard. She was annoyed with me,' Sarah said.

'You'll have to explain to her. Tell her Meg would do it again if she got ice cream and you fussed over her. It's the only way she knows right from wrong if people are cross with her over something like this. Are you going to the dance?'

'Yes, I'm calling for her,' Sarah said, but her face was still troubled. 'Do you think I should have told Peggy, Mum? I didn't want to worry her but I thought she should know, but she seemed so upset.'

'She'd have been more upset if she got half the story from Meg. You did right to tell her, love. Now Peggy can talk to Meg and try to warn her, and she knows exactly what happened so she's not imagining all sorts of things.'

Sarah gave a sigh of relief. 'I'm glad you think that, Mum. Can I take this hot water for a wash?'

'Yes, but don't forget to bring the kettle down again,' Cathy said. She shook her head at Sarah and called after her, 'And don't be such a worrier.' Sarah laughed and ran upstairs.

When Sarah reached Anne's house, Maureen opened the door and ushered her into the hall. Anne came running downstairs, smiling. 'Hello, Sar,' she said. 'How's Meg?'

'She's OK,' Sarah said rather stiffly.

'That's good. I was wrong to want to buy her ice cream,' Anne said. 'I told our Maureen and she told me off, didn't you, Mo?'

'I said you were foolish,' Maureen said. 'The girl herself felt that she was wrong and wanted some guidance when she asked if she'd been naughty. You'd have upset the apple cart if you gave her ice cream. She'd think it as a reward for doing something good.'

The parlour door was open and Terry called, 'Here endeth the first lesson by Professor Jung.'

Maureen blushed and Anne shouted, 'Shut up, Terry, and mind your own business.'

She took her coat from the hallstand. 'We won't bother going in to that lot,' she said. 'Mum and Dad are at church. Should we try a different place tonight?'

'Yes, I'd rather dodge Jimmie and Dan,' Sarah said. 'Jimmie was quite narky because I wouldn't go out on the bike today.'

'So was Dan. We'll have to nip that in the bud. We could try West Derby or Green Lane – there's a few dances on there tonight.'

Eventually they decided to take the tram to West Derby, but as soon as they walked in the Hall they found several people whom they knew there.

'So much for a change of scene,' Anne whispered to Sarah, but as usual they were asked for every dance.

They were escorted home by two of the young men who had partnered them in the dance, and arranged to see them later in the week.

Mabel was disapproving when Anne and Sarah talked about their various young men, but a new girl who had been engaged to help in the shop listened to them with shining eyes.

'Look at her. It's like a serial story to her,' Mabel exclaimed. 'Don't you be modelling yourself on them now, Rosie. They'll be getting a bad name the number of lads they go out with.'

'You know that's not true, Mabel,' Sarah protested. 'The lads we go out with are as harmless as us. I've never come across a bad lot yet.'

'It's all like one big family anyway,' Anne said. 'The fellow I came home with last night was Johnny Carroll's cousin.'

'And mine – his father used to work with Dad,' Sarah laughed.

Cathy felt no worry about Sarah, only pleasure that she was enjoying life and not fretting about Michael. Time enough for her to settle down, she thought, when she met the man she really loved.

She was less confident about Kate. Although she was only eleven years old, Kate's figure was beginning to mature, and she cast flirtatious glances at every man in sight. An uneasy memory stirred in Cathy of her sister Mary's behaviour but she told herself that Kate was only a little precocious because of her stage appearances.

No more letters had arrived from John and Cathy was getting steadily more and more worried about him. Greg had been again to the Old Haymarket office but this time he had been treated with suspicion and given no information. 'I believe there have been men going there who they think were detectives or spies. It's illegal to volunteer for the International Brigade because of the Non-Intervention Pact, you see.'

'What's that?' Cathy asked.

'Countries have agreed not to send aid to either side,' Greg explained.

'But John said Germany and Italy are sending troops and guns to Franco.'

'It's like all these pacts,' he said. 'Honoured more in the breach than in the observance. The net result is that I can't get any information about John. But don't worry, love, I'm sure he's all right.'

If only John could come home, Cathy felt that she could be happy and without any worries. For the first time for many years she had no money worries at all.

Stan Johnson, owner of the woodyard where Greg worked, had become more and more prosperous, extending the yard to twice the original size, and also buying property and a share in a car repair business. He was negotiating to buy a small engineering business too but paying a price for his success. He had developed a stomach ulcer and been told by his doctor that he must take life more easily. He realized that he had been overworking for years.

Keeping the books for all these interests had meant a lot of hard work for Greg, although he now had two assistants, but Stan had been generous with wage rises and bonus payments to him. 'An honest man is worth his weight in gold to any business,' Stan told Greg. 'You're worth every penny I pay you.'

As usual, as soon as Stan realized the position with his health he acted swiftly. He booked a lengthy cruise for himself and his wife, and appointed a manager for the woodyard and another man to collect rents and arrange repairs to his property. He withdrew from the negotiations for the engineering works, but still kept his half share in the car repair works and made Greg General Manager in charge of all his business affairs.

All decisions on expenditure had to be passed by Greg, but Stan told him that it was only for three months.

'By then I'll come back a new man,' he said. 'I know it's going to mean a hell of a lot of work for you. Don't think I'm trying to save my own life by killing you. I'll be back in three months to take the weight off you.'

'I'm glad you've seen sense,' Greg said frankly. 'You've been doing three men's work for years, but the cruise won't cure you unless you forget all this while you're away. I'll look after things as well as I'm able, I promise you.'

'I know you will,' Stan said. 'And I appreciate it. A step up like this would mean a rise usually, but as this is only temporary I think a bonus would fit the bill better. We'll sort that out when I get back.'

Cathy was excited when Greg told her that evening, but a little apprehensive. 'If so much hard work has given him an ulcer, I think you should be careful, Greg. And you're bound to worry more than him because it's not your own money.'

'Yes, but the point is, Cathy, it's only temporary. Only for three months. That's why he won't give me a rise but will arrange a bonus when he comes home.'

'You'd think he'd give it to you while you were doing the job,' she said. 'It seems to me he doesn't trust you.'

'He does,' said Greg. 'But he's a businessman. He'll want to see what's been happening before he decides what to give me, I suppose. He hasn't got on as much as he has by being soft, although he's been very good to us, Cath.'

Greg was now working until very late every evening and most of the weekend, and was rarely able to spend any time on the allotment. Michael Burns had been helping him for some time, as Mick showed no aptitude for gardening or interest in it, and Sarah, though she had always loved working on the allotment, had too little spare time for it now.

Michael suggested that his nephew, son of his brother Ben, should help him and the boy proved to have 'green fingers' just as Lawrie had. Sally and Peggy sometimes went to the allotment on Saturday afternoons, taking Meg who always wanted to help the boys but annoyed them by pulling up freshly planted seedlings, thinking that they were weeds.

A widower who worked the next allotment was endlessly patient with her, giving her simple jobs to do and showing her how to plant cuttings. He even gave her a small plot of ground and let her plant seeds there, and patiently explained that she must not dig them up to see if they were growing.

'My girl would have been about her age,' he told Sally and Peggy. 'Her and me wife died when she was born.'

'He must have been married young,' Sally said when he moved away. 'He's still only a young man, but grief like that has made him more patient than most.'

It was a relief to Peggy to have Meg happily occupied where she could see her. She had watched Meg even more closely since the incident with the boys, but as she told Sally it was hard to watch her grandchild constantly and keep her happily occupied.

Sally knew that Peggy's greatest worry was about what would happen to Meg when she was no longer there to look after her. 'The girls say they won't let her go in a Home but they've got husbands and families to think about, and the husbands might get fed up with them spending so much time looking after her.'

'Don't worry, Peg,' Sally said. 'She's a very lovable girl, and so affectionate. I'm sure she'd fit in with any family and all the children love her, don't they? And you've trained her well, so even if she stayed here with Michael she could do some cooking and cleaning and look after her own clothes.'

'I've done my best,' Peggy said, but she still worried. Sarah and Anne took an interest in Meg after the incident and often took her with them for a ride on the ferry or a walk when they would buy her ice cream as a treat.

Anne was very excited at this time because one of her brothers was coming home from sea after a long voyage.

346

'What's he like?' Sarah asked. 'Is he like you?'

'More like our Maureen although we're all fairly alike, aren't we?' Anne said. She laughed. 'I don't think he's as devout as our Maureen but he's quiet like her. That's if he hasn't changed, but he's been away for two years, don't forget.'

'I wish our John was coming home,' Sarah said, and Anne looked abashed.

'I shouldn't be going on like this when you don't know about your brother,' she said, but Sarah told her not to be daft.

'I'm just glad that Joe's coming home safely. I'm made up for your mother.'

Sarah had been to tea at Anne's house and found all the family excited about Joe's homecoming. 'You wouldn't think one would be missed out of all this crowd, would you?' Terry said to her, laughing. 'But he is.'

Anne and Sarah had parted from the brothers who owned motor bikes as they felt that they were becoming too possessive, and had resumed their cycling excursions with Anne's brothers and sisters. Occasionally Maureen and Terry and Tony came to the dances, and Helen, Tony's girlfriend.

'We'll have to get a bike for Joe,' Tony announced, but Anne and Maureen told him to let Joe decide what he wanted to do.

'I'll bet you don't argue like this in your house, Sarah,' Tony said.

'There aren't as many of us, but we still argue. My grandma said our John would argue with a lamppost if there was nothing else handy.'

Sarah thought of this conversation as she lay in bed. Would John still be the same? Would he still be so ready to argue with their father? I think he'd begun to change anyway since Grandad died, she thought, and he might be quite different when he comes home. She shivered as the thought came, *If* he comes home.

The family were dashing about as usual the following morning, getting ready for school or work, when three letters arrived from John. Greg went through them quickly and dropped two on the table.

'This is the last one, Cath,' he cried, and they stood reading it together.

'He's coming home,' Cathy shouted. 'Oh, Greg, thank God, thank God.' She burst into tears and he put his arm around her and held her close.

'What does it say? Is he all right?' Sarah exclaimed, and her father passed the letter for her and Mick to read while he and Cathy read the others.

Kate stamped her foot with impatience. 'Tell me. Tell me,' she demanded.

Stan Johnson had given Greg a wrist watch before he left. He glanced at it now. 'I'll have to go,' he said, 'but listen – we must celebrate. What about the Forum for all of us, and a meal at the café? Will you book, Cath? I promise I'll be home. Ask Mam to come too.'

He dashed away and the letters were passed around, then Cathy ran over to her mother's house, waving them as she rushed in.

'John's safe. He's coming home,' she cried, and Sally put her hand to her heart.

'Thank God! Oh, thank God,' she said.

Sarah hurried to the shop, anxious to tell Anne and Mabel her good news, and they were both delighted.

'Now I feel I can *really* look forward to our Joe coming home,' Anne declared. 'I'd have felt terrible if he was still away when Joe came.'

'He's being invalided home because his ankle won't heal,' Sarah explained. 'But Dad says they probably haven't got the right medical supplies and he'll be all right when he gets here.'

'I'm sure he will,' Mabel said. 'I'll bet your grandma's got something that will cure it. Her cough mixture can do wonders.'

'Not as much as her jollop for female complaints,' Anne said, and the two girls fell about, screaming with laughter.

'You two are over-excited,' Mabel said. 'What's the joke?'

'If I tell you, Mabel, you won't tell anyone else, will you?' Sarah said, still laughing. 'Mum told me one night when we were up late talking, but I think it was only to cheer me up after Michael so don't repeat it.'

'I won't,' Mabel promised.

'Grandma started making this stuff for women who had internal troubles and a lot of pain after having a baby, or for women who had a growth, to ease them. Mum said she put all sorts of things in it but the basis was her own rhubarb wine that was very potent. It did ease the women, but the husbands started taking it too.'

'That's disgraceful,' Mabel said. 'I mean, if men are working they're on the panel and can go to a doctor free, but women won't go because they've got to pay.'

'I know,' Sarah said. 'Mum said Grandma was furious but she didn't say anything when she found out. She just told everyone that it was good for female complaints but it would make men impotent.'

Mabel gave a shout of laughter. 'Typical,' she said, 'Typical of your grandma, Sarah. She could buy and sell any of them before they got up in the morning.'

From time to time as Sarah and Anne passed each other behind the counter, they would murmur to each other, 'Female complaints,' and instantly collapse in giggles.

'You're all very happy today,' one of the customers commented.

Mabel said, 'Yes. Their brothers are coming home from abroad and I can't get any good of them today.' But she was smiling too.

Chapter Thirty

Cathy had corresponded with her old friend Norah since she had sent condolences when Lawrie died. In the spring Norah had written that she and a friend were starting a guest house at Morecambe, inviting Cathy to visit her at any time. She had often repeated the invitation.

Now Cathy decided to take Kate there for a day out. 'I couldn't settle to anything until I heard from John,' she said, 'but I'll take Kate for a day before she goes back to school.'

Norah insisted that they must stay at least one night, and a few days later Cathy and Kate set off. Kate was wildly excited and Norah made them very welcome.

She introduced them to the friend who shared the ownership of the guest house with her. 'I'm a Lancashire lass,' Minnie said, 'from near Bolton. I often came to Morecambe on charabanc trips, and Norah had been, so we settled on it for our guest house.'

'You've picked a lovely place,' Cathy said. Later Norah told Cathy that when she and Jack had parted she had very little money and a big house so she took in lodgers. Minnie had helped her with the cooking in any free time she had from caring for her elderly mother, but they both hankered to come back North. When Minnie's mother died they sold their houses and looked for a guest house to share.

'Are you doing all right?' asked Cathy, feeling that the guest house was a safer topic than Norah's husband.

'Yes, we're always full,' Norah said. 'Minnie's a very good cook and word gets around.' Later they walked along the sea front and stopped to look at a Pierrot show. Children were invited on to the stage and Kate went up immediately. She sang 'Bye Bye, Blackbird' and did some tap dancing, and was loudly applauded.

'She's never backward in coming forward,' Cathy said. 'No one could say she was shy.'

'Your Mary never was, was she?' Norah said, laughing. 'Strange to see things coming out in the next generation, isn't it?'

'It is,' Cathy agreed uneasily.

'Is Sarah courting?'

'No. She's always making dates with fellows from the dances but she never gets serious with any of them.'

'Just as well. She's got plenty of time before she thinks of settling down,' Norah said. When they were walking on again, and Kate had run ahead, Norah said quietly, 'Be careful with your girls, Cath. See that they're really sure when they come to get married.'

They spoke of old times, and Cathy talked of her family and gave Norah news of old friends like the Mellors and the Burnses. Cathy was sorry to leave the following day but anxious to return to her family and hoping to hear more news of John's return.

Joe Fitzgerald arrived home before they heard from John again, and on the Saturday night the Fitzgeralds gave a party to celebrate his homecoming and the engagement of Tony and Helen.

Cathy and Greg were invited to the party as well as Sarah, and they liked all the Fitzgerald family.

'I'm glad Anne and Sarah are friends,' Mrs Fitzgerald said. 'I think it's important for girls to have nice friends.'

'They certainly enjoy life, don't they?' Cathy laughed.

'Yes, and why not? Youth's the time for that,' said Mrs Fitzgerald. As usual at these family parties the older people were sitting in the Fitzgeralds' roomy kitchen while the younger generation gathered in the parlour.

Sarah had been introduced to Joe, but he had immediately been whisked away to be introduced to someone else. Anne came up beside her friend. 'What do you think of our Joe? He's nice, isn't he?'

Sarah agreed. Joe was dark-haired and brown-eyed like all the Fitzgeralds, and as tall as his brothers, but except when he was laughing his expression was serious.

'I think he's like your Maureen. He looks serious like her,' Sarah said.

'He's quiet but he's good company. We've had some good laughs,' Anne said. 'I wish he could get a job ashore. He doesn't really like the sea, but it's better than being unemployed.'

Later Sarah found herself beside Joe. She said shyly, 'You've been on a long voyage, haven't you?'

'Yes. To China,' he said.

'You must be glad to be home.' He'll think me a brilliant conversationalist, she thought wryly, but Joe seemed as shy as she was.

'I am. I miss the family,' he said.

Terry came up beside Sarah, and put his arm round her. 'Ah, you've met the Queen of the Ceilidhes,' he said to Joe. 'Sarah and Anne have been out with half the lads in Liverpool between them.'

'You're only jealous because you can't get a girl,' Anne called over to them.

'Not so,' Terry declared. 'I just can't choose. The girls all fall flat before me, you see, and I can't see their faces.'

'As modest as ever, I see,' Joe observed.

Stephen and Eileen had been handing round glasses of punch, and there was a commotion near the door as the older people began to crowd into the parlour, among them Mr and Mrs Fitzgerald.

'Welcome, everyone,' Mr Fitzgerald said loudly. ' This party is for two reasons. One is to welcome home our Joe. Step forward, Joe.'

He did so and Sarah felt sorry for him when she saw how red and embarrassed he looked.

'Welcome home, lad,' said Mr Fitzgerald. 'Good health.' Everyone echoed 'Good health', and sipped their drinks.

'The other joyful reason we're here,' Mr Fitzgerald announced as Joe thankfully slipped back into the crowd, 'is to announce the engagement of Helen and Tony, and to welcome Helen into our family.'

Helen and Tony stood up together, Helen scarcely reaching Tony's shoulder, and a burly man called, 'Why didn't you pick someone your own size, Tony?'

'Trust Uncle Fred,' Anne groaned.

Tony only said cheerfully, 'Good stuff in small parcels, Uncle Fred.'

'Now then, Fred,' Mr Fitzgerald said, 'that's for fighting and Helen and Tony won't be doing that.'

'Wanna bet?' Fred guffawed, but there were cries of 'Gangway' and Maureen wheeled in a tea trolley with a large iced cake on it.

'It's too nice to cut,' Helen said.

But the irrepressible Fred shouted, 'Come on, girl. The sooner it's cut the sooner we can eat it,' and Tony and Helen made a cut in the cake.

'Raise your glasses,' Mr Fitzgerald said. 'Long life and happiness to Helen and Tony.'

'If I ever get married, I'll make sure Uncle Fred's out of the country,' Anne said.

But Terry said easily, 'He's harmless.'

Maureen, who had joined them, said, 'He's very kind to Grandma, and we know it's not easy living with her.' To Sarah Maureen said, 'Grandma lived with Uncle Fred for ten years, then she decided to come here. She was only with us for two years but nearly drove us mad, and now she's gone back to Uncle Fred and Aunt Carrie. They knew what she was like but they welcomed her back and are very good to her.'

Joe put his hand on her shoulder and said quietly, 'Still seeing the good in everyone, Mo?'

During the following weeks the Fitzgeralds went out often as a family party with Sarah included. They went to the ceilidhes, where Sarah danced most of the dances with Terry as her partner, and to the theatre or cinema, but Sarah had little chance to talk to Joe.

Joe was still at home when John arrived two weeks later. All the family were on Lime Street Station to meet him, except his grandmother, and they saw other families waiting and officials who had organized the recruiting for the International Brigade.

Eight wounded men arrived but John's family were too intent on him to notice any of the others. John was walking on crutches and looked gaunt and tired. His foot was swathed in bandages, the outer layer dirty, but his face lit up when he saw the family. 'Mum!' he exclaimed, then hugged each of them in turn.

As they left the station, several men came up to John and

shook his hand. Cathy heard him say to one man with an authoritative manner, 'Yes, I will. Tomorrow.'

'What are you planning to do tomorrow?' she demanded.

'To make a report, Mum,' he said.

She declared, 'You won't put that foot to the ground tomorrow. I'll see to that.'

Greg glanced warningly at her. 'Is the foot very painful, John?' he asked.

'Not too bad,' he said. 'Worse some times than others.' Greg hailed a taxi and helped John into it, then Cathy and Sarah followed, and Greg and Kate. Mick had volunteered to walk, but Kate was delighted to ride in the taxicab.

'I'm glad you've come home, John,' she announced. 'I've never been in a taxi before.' She bounced up and down on the seat. 'I'm going to ride in taxis all the time when I'm grown up,' she said. 'Or have my own motor car.'

'My God, I seem to have heard that before, or something very like it!' Cathy exclaimed.

'I've never said it before. I've never been in a taxi before,' Kate said.

'Not you. I was thinking of your Auntie Mary.'

'How is she – and Sam?' John said. 'I couldn't write to thank them for that money.'

'They seem very well,' Cathy said. 'Sam seems to be prospering and Mary's playing the grand lady.'

'I met an American who'd heard of Sam's business although he didn't know him,' John said.

The taxi had reached Egremont Street and Sally opened the door of the Redmonds' house and came down the steps to kiss John. 'Welcome home, lad,' she said. 'Thank God you're safe.'

Cathy had put pillows on the sofa before she left for the station and John sank down on it thankfully and propped up his leg. The table was laid with a big spread of food and Sally had made tea which she began to pour immediately.

'A cup of tea,' John said. 'I've been dying for a cup of your tea, Grandma.'

'What do you fancy to eat, John?' Cathy said. 'Anything on here or would you rather have egg and bacon?'

'Anything at all, Mum,' he said. 'Except beans. We've lived on them, and I never want to see another bean.' He looked round all the faces smiling at him, then swallowed and fumbled for his handkerchief. Without a word Cathy took a clean one from the dresser drawer and handed it to him. He blew his nose noisily, then took a gulp of tea.

'Thanks, Mum,' he said. 'You don't know how good it is to be home.'

'We're just as happy to have you home,' Cathy said.

She turned to Kate who was looking over the table and saying, 'Can I have a pasty? Can I have a madeleine?'

'Can I have? Can I? Have, that's all you ever say,' Cathy snapped.

She had already shouted at Mick for being clumsy, and now thought, What's wrong with me? Why am I so irritable when I'm so happy to have John home? It must be because I couldn't really believe it until I saw him get off the train.

She spoke of her bad temper to Greg later when he and Mick had helped John to bed, and Greg had dressed John's foot and rigged up a cage with a small fireguard to keep the bedclothes off it.

'I should be so happy to have him home,' she said. 'I *am* happy, Greg, but I can't stop myself from snapping at everyone.'

'Just nerves,' he said. 'You've been very worried, and now you can stop worrying so your mind's confused. You'll be all right tomorrow.'

She smiled. 'Mum's made up. I didn't realize how worried she was about John until I saw how happy she was tonight.'

'John's very dear to her,' Greg said, then as Cathy glanced at him he added hastily, 'All our children are. She's not like Peggy with dozens of grandchildren.'

'It doesn't look as though Mary will supply any,' Cathy said. 'Poor Sam. What did you think of Kate in the taxi? Didn't she sound like our Mary?'

'She often does,' said Greg, laughing.

John slept until noon the following day and Cathy firmly vetoed the idea of him going out. 'Dad left this paper and pencil for you,' she told him. 'He said if you write out a report, he'll take it to the Old Haymarket after work.'

'I'll be glad to do that,' John admitted. 'My foot's less painful but I feel weary.'

'You're very thin, son.'

'I had a sort of dysentery,' he said. 'The Spanish people were very good. They had so little yet they'd want to share it with you, and try to help you. They gave me leaves to chew for the dysentery and it stopped it for a while but it came back again.'

'I'm glad to know there's another reason for you being thin,' Cathy said. 'I was afraid it was because the wound was so bad.'

'No. Just diarrhoea, I'm afraid. Not a very heroic figure am I, Mum – for all my big ideas,' he said ruefully.

'Don't talk daft,' Cathy said. 'Don't worry, son. We'll soon have you right. Between Dad with his St John's training and Grandma's remedies, you're in the right family.'

'Fallen on my feet, in fact,' he said with a grin.

He wrote out the report and Greg took it to the office in the Old Haymarket. His reception was more friendly this time and he chatted to several of the men there and heard their views. When he came home he told Cathy that he had been impressed.

'I thought John had fallen in with bad company with these men really, Cath, although I didn't say so to him. I thought he should find it out for himself. But now I think they are idealists, and sincere. Misguided, in my view, but still sincere.'

Greg went up to see John and to tell him that he had handed in the report. 'They were satisfied to have a written report, and sent their regards,' he said.

'What did you think of them, Dad?'

'I thought they were sincere,' said Greg.

He said no more and they sat in silence for a few minutes, then John said suddenly, 'I feel an imposter, Dad.'

'Why? In what way?'

'I've always had such an easy life. It was all a sort of dream of getting things done and righting wrongs. I can still feel indignant about the inequalities and injustices of the system, but I don't feel that I can do anything about them any more. I feel useless.'

'I would have thought your experiences in Spain made you more qualified rather than less,' Greg said quietly.

'It's made me see myself as I am,' John said bitterly. 'Some of the men I was with had known hunger and poverty all their lives. They'd been unemployed except for a few days' casual work on the docks, and their fathers had been the same. When they talked, I felt ashamed.'

'But you did what you could to change things,' Greg said.

'I talked a lot, Dad. These men fought. They were intelligent men but they fought in the only way they could, with hunger marches and demonstration, risking gaol, going to gaol very often. I felt the only thing that gave me any credibility in their eyes was that I was Lawrie Ward's grandson and they respected him.' Greg sat listening to him in silence, knowing that John needed to talk.

'I wasn't the only one who'd had a soft life,' John continued. 'I met up with a chap from Cambridge University who'd belonged to the Left Book Club, and he said he was glad to be able to come to Spain, to do something constructive, because so far he had only been debating and writing pamphlets to try to change the system. He said they had clashes with Mosley's crowd at meetings and tried to help the hunger marchers but they couldn't do anything constructive.'

'I suppose there were many men like that, son,' Greg said. 'I read somewhere that there were about sixty thousand members of the Left Book Club.'

'But you see what I mean, Dad? The intellectuals – they were doing well out of the system but they were willing to change it. They used the way they knew best – words. The chaps I knew from Liverpool who'd never had a decent pair of shoes or enough food, didn't let themselves be cowed down by the Board of Guardians and people like that who treated them with contempt – they fought back with hunger marches and demonstrations.'

John's face was flushed and his voice was rising. Greg put his hand on John's arm. 'Don't get worked up about it, son,' he said.

John drank some water and said more calmly, 'What I'm saying, Dad, is that I fell between two stools. I was neither fish, fowl nor good red herring as Grandma would say, and I let Grandad down. His plan was for me to get elected to the city Council then go on to become an MP and speak up about injustice when I got into Parliament.'

'You can still do that,' Greg said, but John shook his head.

'No. I think I've blotted my copybook,' he said. 'I knew what Grandad planned but I wasn't prepared to work steadily towards an objective. I was the big fellow who could take a short cut. I tell you, Dad, I saw myself very clearly when I was lying out on a hillside in Spain, and I didn't like what I saw.'

'I think you're far too hard on yourself,' Greg said calmly. 'You didn't let Grandad down. He was very proud of you, and he died a happy man believing that you would carry on fighting for what he believed in.'

'But I didn't, not in his way anyway. I don't regret going to Spain. I saw it there for a while, what we are aiming for – a classless society. You know, I got separated from the Brigade. Spanish peasants looked after me and I fell in with the Spanish Militia for a while. I saw it there, no distinction between officers and men, everyone on a level, and all respecting each other and sharing whatever they had with each other, and with a stranger like me. If only we could have that here. But I don't know what I could do to bring it about.'

'What you must do is stop tormenting yourself,' Greg said firmly. 'You must put everything that's happened to the back of your mind and stop worrying about the future. Just think about getting better.'

'Easier said than done.'

'Yes, but you must do it. For one thing you can't make a balanced judgement because you're too close to what has happened, and for another you're not well enough,' Greg said. 'I think Mum's bringing your supper up now.'

Greg went downstairs and a few minutes later Cathy came up with John's supper. She sat and talked to him for a while, telling him family news and making him laugh with stories of the jobs she had been on and Cissie's exploits.

When she had gone his father came back with three books, an electric torch and a small glass of dark liquid.

'Drink this,' he said. 'It's a concoction of Grandma's. She says it'll help you to sleep. If you wake in the night, John, don't lie there thinking – read one of these.'

John picked up the books. 'W. W. Jacobs,' he read. 'Arnold Bennett and *Just William* by Richmal Crompton. Quite a mixed bag, Dad.'

'Yes, but all easy to read. There's a short story in the W. W. Jacobs selection that frightened me more than anything I've ever read, so perhaps you'd better not read that: "The Monkey's Paw".'

'I can always wake Mick if I'm frightened,' John said with a grin. He lay down and Greg settled his leg comfortably before saying goodnight and going downstairs.

John lay for a while thinking of their earlier conversation. I'd never have believed it, he thought, that I could talk like that to Dad. He remembered what Greg had said about his grandfather, and felt a glow of pride and comfort. Why did I always almost hate Dad and think he picked on me? I must have been barmy, he thought as he drifted off to sleep.

He slept heavily until he was awakened by Mick getting ready for school. Mick brought him a cup of tea and later, when Cathy brought up his breakfast, she asked if he felt well enough to come downstairs.

'Dad thinks you'd be better down there today as long as you keep your leg up on the sofa,' she said. 'What do you think?'

'Yes, I feel fine, Mum. I've had a real good sleep,' he said. He thought that his father had worried about his mother having to go up and downstairs to him, but realized later that Greg had suggested it for a different reason.

His grandmother came over and John said, 'That was good stuff you sent me last night, Grandma. What was in it? I went out like a light.'

'Just herbs, lad,' she said. 'Sleep's the best medicine for you at present.'

A little later Kate came home from school for her lunch, and she told John all about her part in the theatre and her singing and dancing. Sally was still there and said sharply, 'We don't want a performance. John's not well enough.'

Kate pouted and Cathy said hastily, 'Run along to Mrs Meadows with this dress, Kate.' When she had gone Cathy said to her mother, 'I've been putting a patch in Josie's dress for work. She burst the stitches in the armhole when we were on that job in Litherland.'

'She's putting on flesh,' Sally commented. 'She'll go like her mother if she's not careful.'

'She's got a long way to go yet, Mum,' Cathy laughed.

A little later Josie came to thank Cathy and to bring some coconut ice and some cigarettes for John.

'I made some for the kids and I thought you might like some.'

'The cigarettes, you mean?' John said innocently, and she laughed and struck his arm playfully. She left and Peggy Burns arrived with Meg.

They brought him a gingerbread cake and Meg said proudly, 'I helped Gran to make that.'

'Then I'll enjoy it twice as much,' John said.

They accepted cups of tea, and when they had gone Cathy said mischievously, 'I don't know about Josie putting on weight – you'll be like the side of a house if this goes on. What did you think of Meg?'

'She seems much quieter,' he said. 'I suppose she can't work.'

'No, even if she could get a job, but her Gran's done wonders with her. Training her to cook and clean, and even some simple shopping. She worries about what'll happen to her after she's gone.'

'It's a shame Meg's like that, isn't it?' he said. 'She's such a pretty kid too.'

He was amazed when Kate returned again from school, followed a little later by Mick.

'I'd no idea that was the time,' he said. 'What time will Dad get in?'

'Not till late tonight,' Cathy said. 'He took last night and the day before off, but he's mad busy looking after everything while Stan Johnson's away.'

John was surprised at the sharp stab of disappointment he felt at the news, and to realize how much he had been looking forward to another talk with his father. He had realized why Greg had suggested that he spend the day downstairs, too. There had been no chance for him to brood as the constant stream of visitors passed through the kitchen throughout the day, and John was grateful for his father's consideration for him.

Chapter Thirty-One

Sarah knew that the Fitzgeralds hoped that Joe would be able to get a job ashore, but Anne came into the shop one day looking downcast. 'Our Joe's signed on again,' she said. 'It's for a nine months' trip and he thinks jobs might be easier by the time he gets back. The other lads will keep looking out for one for him.'

'Nine months will soon pass,' Sarah consoled her.

'He doesn't go aboard until Tuesday,' Anne said. 'If it's fine on Sunday, we thought we'd go for a run to Thurstaton and Joe can borrow Tony's bike.'

Sunday was a hot sunny day and it was arranged that the Fitzgeralds would call for Sarah on their way to the Pier Head. They arrived just as she discovered a puncture in the front tyre of her bicycle, and Mick started to mend it.

Cathy invited them in for lemonade while they waited for Sarah. Tony and Maureen were not with them, but Eileen and Stephen, Terry and Joe were, with Anne. The girls sat in the parlour but the young men went through to the backyard to help Mick.

Cathy detained Joe as he went through the kitchen. 'I believe you're going back to sea next week?'

He smiled ruefully. 'Yes. I was hoping to get a job ashore but there's nothing doing.

'You don't like the sea?' Cathy asked.

'Not really, but it's better than being unemployed. I was lucky to get a ship.'

'My dad went to sea when he was young,' Cathy said, 'but he didn't care for it either. He went to see his own father off and saw a pal on a ship and gave him a hand to load. They wanted to catch the tide and were shorthanded so they offered him a job and he went.'

'A Pier Head jump,' Joe said, smiling. He was leaning

363

against the sideboard, watching Cathy rolling out pastry.

'Yes,' she agreed. 'But he was far too young.'

'He only made one voyage then?'

'No,' Cathy laughed. 'He told me he always spent his money then signed on to get the advance note, and that went on for years. He always intended every trip to be his last.'

'Like me,' said Joe.

'Yes, but after he met Mum he got a shore job,' Cathy said. She smiled reminiscently. 'He was very impulsive, you see, and whenever he did anything rash, our old neighbour used to say, "No wonder you did the Pier Head jump, and you're as hare-brained yet."'

'Was that Mrs Malloy?' Joe asked. Cathy looked at him with surprise and he coloured and said hastily, 'Sarah told me about her, that she knew the poet Gerard Manley Hopkins.'

'She didn't exactly know him. He was a priest at St Francis Xavier's and she told me about saying good morning to him in Langsdale Street. She said he must have heard her because he lifted his top hat, but he never took his eyes off something in the gutter.'

'Did she know he was a poet?'

'I don't think so. She said he was reckoned very clever but she didn't think much of his sermons. They were above her head, I think, but of course the Jesuits are clever men, aren't they?'

'Sarah told me that she said he did his best in the service of God.'

'She was a lovely woman, Mrs Mal,' Cathy said softly. 'I think of her so often.'

Suddenly Eileen, Anne and Sarah erupted into the kitchen. 'What on earth are they doing?' Anne said indignantly.

They went into the backyard and there were cries of indignation when they discovered the bike, ready for use, and Stephen and Terry inside the shed with Mick, looking at a model aeroplane that he was building.

'It'll be dark before we start out,' Eileen cried. 'We *thought* you couldn't be all that time mending a puncture.'

With laughter and recriminations they trooped by to say goodbye to Cathy, and Mick carried Sarah's bike through.

Cathy said goodbye to Joe with warm wishes for a safe voyage and a speedy return.

'I can't get over our Joe staying in the kitchen gassing to your mum,' Anne said to Sarah. 'He's usually so shy. But of course she's very easy to talk to, isn't she?'

When they boarded the ferryboat the boys took charge of the girls' cycles, and Terry wheeled Sarah's up the gangway and rode beside her when they disembarked.

They spent a happy day at Thurstaton and when they rode back to the ferry, Sarah rode beside Anne, Joe beside Eileen, and Terry beside Stephen. They sang as they rode along, "Danny Boy", and "Ole Man River", and then another song popularised by Paul Robeson, "Just awearying for you".

Terry rode up beside Sarah, trying to sing in Paul Robeson's deep tones, with his hand on his heart and looking soulfully at her.

'Watch out, you fool,' Anne said. 'You nearly wobbled into us.'

And Stephen told him, 'Keep back. What if a car comes?'

Terry dropped back beside his brother. 'You've got no romance in your souls, you lot,' he complained.

They were near the ferry, and as they free-wheeled down to it, Stephen exclaimed: 'Whew, I'm creased! Wish I could lie in tomorrow like you, Joe.'

'Make the most of it. The last time for a while, brother,' said Terry.

A shadow crossed Joe's face, but he only said quietly, 'Yes, I will.'

When they reached Egremont Street, Sarah wished Joe a good trip and a safe return, before the Fitzgeralds rode off and she turned in at her own door.

'Joe Fitzgerald's a nice lad,' Cathy said. 'Did he tell you we were talking about Mrs Malloy?'

'No, I didn't talk to him,' said Sarah. 'It's just general when we're all out together.'

'They're a nice family,' Cathy said. 'I'm glad you've got a friend like Anne. She reminds me of Norah in Morecambe. We were friends like you and Anne when we were young.'

John soon recovered, thanks to his father's careful

treatment of his injured ankle and the cossetting by his mother and grandmother, although he still walked with a slight limp. He told them that his ankle was healing when he was moved to another hospital and became separated from his companions while travelling there.

He had been cared for by Spanish peasants and had joined with a group of Spanish Militia until he met some Englishmen that he knew. Three of them had made a trench on the hillside but a shell had brought down earth which had buried them, and although they managed to dig themselves out a boulder had fallen on John's foot and reopened his wound.

'A good thing we didn't know all that while you were there,' his mother exclaimed. 'I'd have been out of my mind with worry.'

John put his arm around her and kissed her. 'Sorry, Mum,' he said. 'I didn't mean to worry you.'

Cathy hugged him, happy to feel the old warmth between them. She tried not to feel jealous of the new closeness between Greg and John, and was ashamed of herself when she felt a twinge to see them deep in conversations from which she was excluded.

It was not deliberate on their part, but partly to avoid upsetting Cathy and partly because the discussion went on over many weeks as John tried to sort out his thoughts.

He still collected for Spanish Food Relief but had stopped going to the Club, telling the men there that he needed time to think.

He discussed many things with his father as they worked on the allotment or sat up talking after Cathy had gone to bed. John still felt as strongly about the inequalities in society but was unsure how he could help to change things.

Greg was aware that his son had been disillusioned in some ways and uplifted in others by his experiences in Spain, and hoped that just by listening he could help John to sort out his thoughts and plans.

When John was well enough, he tried hard to find work but it was impossible although he was prepared to do anything. He had already found that there was no hope of his previous job, and sent letters to various offices without success. Now he found that even the most menial jobs were not available to him.

Twice he managed to find a position, once in the kitchens of a big hotel and once labouring on a building site, but both times he was sacked after a few days. The foreman on the building site told him that he was sorry to see him go. 'You've worked well. It's nothing to do with your work,' he said. He refused to say any more and John suspected that he was now on a black list.

Stan Johnson had returned, looking sunburned and well, so Greg was able to spend more time at home. Stan was delighted with the way Greg had looked after his interests and handed him a bonus of fifty pounds.

'You've earned it,' he told Greg. 'You've probably saved me that much and more.'

'But it's too much,' said Greg. 'I'll take something for my overtime but that's too much.'

'Not to me,' said Stan. 'You know the business can stand it, you keep the books, and look at it this way – I couldn't have gone off with an easy mind if I hadn't known I could safely leave everything in your hands. My health is worth more than that to me, so take the money and thanks.'

Cathy was astounded when Greg put the money on the table. 'Fifty pounds!' she exclaimed. 'Greg, it's a fortune. Think of what we can do with it.'

He hesitated for a moment, then said, 'I was wondering, Cath, what do you think of offering it to John for him to get started in something? Stan started selling from a hand-cart and John's not proud.'

Cathy eagerly agreed, but when the money was offered to John he flatly refused to take it. 'No, it's your chance to do something for yourselves. Rig yourselves out in new clothes or buy something for the house. Don't worry about me. If I don't get fixed up, I'll try somewhere else, perhaps London. If there is a black list, it's only a local one.'

He promised not to go until after Christmas, whatever happened, and Cathy could only hope that he could get a job before then.

Some of her neighbours and friends had been shocked to learn that John was fighting in Spain, but they were all pleased at his safe return. Cissie had asked about him every time Cathy had been on a job with her, and she summed up the general feelings when she said, 'I see your lad's home again. Lads get these daft ideas but this'll have cured him. They don't know they're well off until they go away from home and get knocked about a bit.'

'I'm one of the ruins that Cromwell knocked about a bit,' Josie said. Cathy was relieved to see her looking cheerful again. She had been worried and downhearted, chiefly because of some problems her sister was having but also because Edie's off and on love affair had finally ended, and now her wildness was causing trouble between her mother and father.

'As if I haven't got enough on my plate with our Mary,' Josie complained to Cathy after one of these rows.

'Is she no better?'

'Better! She's a hundred times worse,' Josie said. 'You know how she hates men? Well, now she won't even take her change in a shop out of a man's hand. Pip in the Co-op told me he has to put the change down on the counter, and I met the coalman and he said she puts the money on the wall and he has to put the change there too. She won't take it in case she touches his hand.'

'Poor Mary,' Cathy said.

'I'm terrified she'll end up in Rainhill,' Josie said.

'She's not bad enough for a lunatic asylum,' Cathy protested.

Josie said sorrowfully, 'It's not only the change. She's going queer in other ways, too, and I don't know what I can do. I can't bring her here because of Walter and Danny and Frank. It's partly because Mum's gone. She was the only one who could talk sense into our Mary.'

Cathy and Greg, Josie and Walter still made up a foursome for the dance at the Grafton Ballroom every week, and on the surface all seemed well between Josie and Walter, but Cathy knew that their marriage was becoming ever more unhappy.

Sally thought that Josie might be short-tempered because she missed her mother, but Cathy disagreed. 'I thought it would be better because Mrs Mellor was always stirring things up, but it's worse, and I blame Walter.'

'Why? He's a good husband, isn't he?'

'He's not a good father, at least I don't think so. You know Danny wets the bed and Walter beats him for it? Josie tells him the child doesn't do it on purpose. She said you can see that by Danny's frightened little face when he comes downstairs when it's happened, but Walter won't listen to her. It really upsets Josie.'

'I'll have a talk to her. Tell her how to help to stop the bedwetting.'

'And Edie,' Cathy went on. 'Josie knows she's unhappy and that's why she's gone wild, going out with different lads and staying out late. Josie wants to coax her out of it, but Walter's shouting at her and hitting her and he wanted to lock her out one night. Josie said that'd only be putting Edie in more danger. She's nearly distracted. I feel so sorry for her, with one thing and another.'

'Walter's not showing much sense,' Sally said. 'But a lot of men are like that.'

Cathy smiled. 'You sound a bit like Josie. She said the other night that she thinks their Mary might be right after all to dislike men.'

When she thought of Josie's troubles, Cathy felt even more grateful for her own happy life. She still grieved for her father, but she remembered him with love and admiration, and still felt close to him in spirit. In every other way she was perfectly happy.

Even the fear of John's going away to work had been removed. Stan Johnson asked Greg about him and was surprised when Greg told him the type of job that John had been applying for. 'He believes in the dignity of labour,' Greg said with a smile.

'Well, if he wants to practise what he preaches, tell him there's a job going with the chaps who repair my houses, but it's only labouring and paid accordingly.'

John eagerly accepted the job and worked hard at it, and he said no more about going away. He still held long discussions with his father, but not usually about his own affairs so much as the threat of war.

Cathy lay in bed one night, listening to the rise and fall of their voices, and when Greg finally came up to bed she said resentfully, 'You were having a long talk with John tonight. What's he troubled about now?'

'Nothing personal, Cath,' Greg said. 'We were discussing this business about Czechoslovakia.'

'And you stayed up until this hour for that?' she exclaimed. 'You must both be mad.'

Greg and John talked of the possibility of war but most people disregarded the newspaper accounts of foreign affairs.

'Stands to reason,' Mabel said. 'Hitler won't bomb us when he knows we'll do the same to them if he does. We'd just wipe each other out.' And the customers in the shop agreed with her.

Sarah and Anne, flirting with the young men who came in the shop and spending their leisure time in cycling and dancing, had far more interesting things to think about.

'Don't be such an alarmist,' Sarah said scornfully to John, when he said that things looked bad. 'It's all talk.' She truly believed that it was an empty threat until one Sunday in August when she travelled by tramcar to see her friend Maisie in Dovecote.

The tram passed Springfield Park near Alder Hey Hospital and she saw that trenches had been dug in the park.

'Look at them,' a woman said. 'My feller says we'll be at war by Christmas.'

Sarah longed to go home and talk to her father but Maisie was expecting her for tea. Maisie had brothers who would be called up if war came, and she said that two of them had already joined the Territorials. 'I've heard that gas masks have been delivered to different depots,' she said, 'ready to be given out if war starts. Even gas masks for babies.'

Sarah returned home earlier than planned, feeling thoroughly depressed and frightened, but her father reassured her. 'A lot of this is just sabre rattling,' he said. But suddenly, in September, everyone was talking of war.

'It won't be just the soldiers this time,' a customer in the shop said. 'It'll be all of us if they drop bombs. Your brother was in Spain, wasn't he, Sarah? Was he anywhere near Guernica?'

'I don't know,' she said.

And another woman asked, 'Where's Guernica?'

'It's a place in Spain where hundreds of people were killed when German aeroplanes bombed it,' the first woman said importantly. 'That's what we can expect.'

Sarah told John what she had heard but he said, 'People like that should be locked up. Scaremongers! It was different altogether. Guernica was a little town, crowded for market day, and the people there were quite unprepared. Don't worry about tales like that, Sass.'

Although John reassured Sarah, he was privately very worried about the family. 'We're not prepared at all,' he told his father. 'If it comes, the best place for the family would be a cellar, or better still the basement of a big shop because they're reinforced.'

Everybody listened to the news bulletins on the wireless, and people could be seen standing waiting near newspaper vendors, opening the paper as soon as the next edition arrived and searching it for news.

On September the twenty-sixth the Foreign Office warned Hitler of the consequences if he attacked Czechoslovakia, and the following day the Fleet was mobilized.

'And our Joe's still on the high seas,' Anne wept to Sarah. 'My mum says she wouldn't care if he was home and we could all be killed together.'

As Sarah walked home she thought how worried everyone looked, and felt, as she wrote dramatically in her diary, that she was carrying a great weight about with her.

The relief was all the greater when on September the twenty-ninth the Prime Minister flew to Munich and returned waving a piece of paper which he declared meant 'Peace in our time'.

Many people, including Cathy and Greg and their children, went to church to give thanks, and everywhere there was relief and rejoicing. 'I'm really going to enjoy life now,' Anne announced in the shop.

Mabel said sourly, 'I thought you always did.'

'She's mad because she told everyone she was absolutely sure there'd be a war,' Anne whispered to Sarah, but Mabel's ill humour soon vanished and she joined in the general thanksgiving.

Sarah told the family about Anne's words when they were having their evening meal, and added, 'I think Anne's right. I think life feels sweeter now and I'll enjoy everything twice as much.'

Her mother agreed. 'It's the feeling that everything is precious because we nearly lost it, I suppose. Grandma and Peggy went to the pictures this afternoon and when Mr Chamberlain came on the Pathé News holding up the agreement at Downing Street, everybody stood up and cheered.'

Greg and John took the news more quietly. 'It'll give us a breathing space to get ready,' Greg said, and John agreed.

A letter came from Mary which annoyed everyone, although they were all too happy to care about it for long. She wrote:

> Sam says England has come very close to war, but I'm glad to see that one man at least has shown some sense. We saw Mr Chamberlain on the news reels. Fortunately it doesn't affect us, except of course that I worry about all of you.
>
> Sam has bought me the cutest little Pomeranian to keep me company while he's working such long hours. I've called her Peggy, and I've got one set of pink flowered bedding for her basket, and one set of blue. I put a matching blue or pink bow on her collar.
>
> We had a lovely letter from John thanking Sam for the money. So glad he's safely home again. We laughed when we read about Mam's jollop which seems to have acted like a Mickey Finn on him and knocked him out. I could do with some of that for some of the bores here.

'I've a good mind to write to her and tell her to mind her own business!' Cathy exclaimed. 'They've got a cheek, criticizing England, when they don't even live here.'

'Leave it for now,' her mother advised. 'Sleep on it. You might say something you'll regret, and it's only her usual soft talk, anyway.'

'Fancy buying a Pom,' Mick said when he read the letter. 'I'd like an Airedale. Poms are such stupid yappy dogs.'

'It's not only Poms that are stupid,' Cathy said tartly.

Mick wisely made no reply, but took out a book and began to read. He was now sixteen, and had gained five distinctions in his Matriculation examinations. It had been decided that he would stay on at school until he was eighteen when he would take the Higher School Certificate. The headmaster had spoken of his hope that after that Mick would win a scholarship which would take him to university.

With such a future planned for him, Cathy and Greg had been furious when they discovered that he had attempted to join the Royal Air Force. The recruiting officer had taken particulars from him but told him he was too young, in spite of Mick's protests that he was eighteen.

'We'll send for you when you are, son,' the man said firmly. 'Just go and work hard at College until then.'

Chapter Thirty-Two

There was one happy result of the war scare. Edie Meadows' boy friend, the printer, thought he might be called up, so came to see her and patched up the quarrel.

'This time it's for good,' she told her mother. 'Frank's coming to see you and Dad and we want to get engaged on my birthday next week, and married next September.'

Josie was delighted, and with Edie settled there were fewer rows between her parents. Edie was tremendously proud of her ring, a half hoop of diamonds. Anne told Sarah, 'I saw Edie on the tram yesterday. I couldn't ask her about her engagement right away because the girl who was with her knew Helen and she was rattling on, but you should have seen Edie waving her ring about. I had to interrupt and ask her about it before she knocked my eye out.'

'I know,' Sarah said. 'She's made up, and so is her mum. Mrs Meadows was saying to Mum, "Your Sarah'll be next," as though she was consoling her.'

'You can get engaged to Big Feet,' Anne suggested, laughing.

Sarah retorted, 'Not likely.'

Sarah and Anne now went sometimes to modern dances in addition to the ceilidhes and one young man named Donald, nicknamed Big Feet by them, was pressing Sarah to be his regular girl friend.

'No, I don't mind a date now and then but I'm not getting serious with anyone yet,' she said.

'I won't press you to get engaged even, just for people to know we're courting,' he pleaded.

She refused to go out with him on those terms. He persisted in asking her to dance and pleading with her to change her mind, but she was adamant.

At almost the same time, several of the boys from the

ceilidhes who had seemed to accept that Sarah and Anne also had dates with other boys, suddenly began to press them to start serious courtships with a view eventually to marriage.

They were at a ceilidhe one evening, sitting in a large group of the Fitzgeralds and their cousins, the Andersons, when Sarah was asked to dance by a young man she often went with to the cinema or the Ice Rink, Nick Owens. When the dance ended he drew her to a quiet corner near the door.

'I know you have dates with other fellows, Sarah,' he said, 'but I think it's time we started to go out seriously and you gave them the push.'

'You've got a cheek,' she said. 'Maybe I'd like to go out seriously with Jimmy Rafferty or Bob Doyle and give *you* the push.'

His face grew red. 'You've been out with me more often than either of them,' he said. 'I haven't minded you having your fling but now I want to put things on a proper footing, and I don't want you to see anyone else.'

Sarah too was flushed with temper. 'That's very kind of you,' she said angrily. 'It's got nothing to do with you who I go out with. We're not engaged or anything, and you don't own me. I'll go out with whoever I like, and from now on it won't include you.'

'I thought of you as my girl friend,' Nick said, 'but if that's how you feel, maybe I've had a lucky escape. You obviously can't be faithful to one man.'

'I didn't say that,' snapped Sarah. 'But I can tell you, that one man won't be you. It'll be someone who isn't as big-headed or as rude. Goodbye.'

She turned on her heel and stalked back to her friends. Nick dashed out of the door. Sarah was still shaking with temper and Anne said, 'What's up? We could see you were having a row.'

'The cheek of that Nick Owens!' Sarah said. 'Trying to dictate to me who I'll go out with, or rather won't. He's kindly decided that I'm going to go out seriously with him and drop my other friends – without consulting me, of course.'

'It looked as though he got a flea in his ear,' commented Terry, who was sitting nearby.

'I should think so too,' said Anne. Another dance had been announced and a tall willowy young man was making his way towards her, smiling. 'Here's another one who thinks he's the answer to a maiden's prayer.'

Terry leaned towards Sarah. 'Never mind, *alannah*,' he said in a mock brogue, 'I'll be your steady feller.'

'She's not that hard up, are you, Sar?' Anne said over her shoulder as she went on to the dance floor with the young man. Sarah laughed and Terry seized her hand.

'Come on, Sarah. Let's dance in case Nick comes back for the second round.'

'He wouldn't dare,' she said, but Nick did reappear later and came up beside her.

'I'm sorry. I didn't mean that about you being unfaithful,' he said. 'I was just angry. You will be my girl, won't you?'

'No, not on those terms,' Sarah said. 'I'm going to be very sure before I settle down with anyone.'

A few days later Anne had a similar experience with one of the young men she had casually dated for some months, and Sarah said to her mother, 'I don't know what's got into fellows lately. They often went out with other girls as well as with us, but suddenly life's all serious with them.'

'It's probably all the worry about the war in September that's made them think they should get themselves organized,' Cathy said.

Sarah replied flippantly, 'Herr Hitler's got a lot to answer for, then.'

Sally approved of Sarah's determination not to settle down until she was sure that she had met the right man.

'You'll know when you do, love,' she said. 'It might be that you'll know as soon as you see him, or you might come to like someone you already know and suddenly realize he's the one you've been looking for. Don't settle for anything less, pet.'

'I won't, Grandma,' she promised. The feeling of relief after the threat of war was removed still persisted. Sarah thought that it was like being in the condemned cell and then being set free. All her perceptions seemed heightened; flowers were more beautiful, colours were brighter, and the people around her more interesting.

Even the weather seemed better, and as the days

lengthened all the family looked forward to a good summer. Sally's arm had been very painful during the cold weather and the arthritis seemed to be affecting her shoulder and neck too. 'At least my legs are all right,' she said cheerfully to Cathy. 'Not like poor Mrs Mal.'

Cathy had rubbed her mother's home-made liniment into her shoulder and neck and made a red flannel undervest to keep Sally's neck and shoulder and arm warm, but she still suffered in cold, foggy weather.

The bad weather had caused Josh to have a severe bout of pleurisy and Cathy was kept busy helping her mother to nurse him. They put kaolin poultices on his chest, and dosed him with Sally's remedies, and he recovered quite quickly. Cathy was surprised to find that he was a peevish, demanding patient, but her mother was as calm and unruffled as ever in her manner towards the old man.

The short spell of bad weather soon passed and now with Easter approaching and longer days Josh became more cheerful and less concerned about his health.

Greg and John welcomed the longer days for the work on the allotment, although it was easier now because they had divided it between themselves and Michael Burns and his nephew, who had been christened Hector but was always known as Sonny.

'They did most of the work while you were away and I was working long hours,' Greg said to John. 'It's only fair that they should have a share.'

John agreed and they helped Michael and Sonny with seeds and cuttings. The Burns had turned their half of the allotment over exclusively to vegetables, and Greg was amazed at the size and quality and the amount that they managed to grow.

'It's Sonny,' Michael said. 'He's the one who knows what to do.'

'That's a real gift,' Greg said to the boy. 'You should look for that sort of work when you leave school. With a market gardener or the Parks.'

'I'd like market gardening,' Sonny said. 'I like vegetables better than flowers.'

Peggy often came to the allotment with Meg so that she could work on her plot in the next allotment.

'We should have thought of giving her a bit of ground for herself,' Michael said to Willie Smith, the widower who worked the next allotment and had given Meg the plot. 'But it wasn't ours until Mr Redmond made it over to us.'

'She's welcome to the bit of ground I've given her,' Willie said. 'I'm very fond of Meg.'

A few weeks later he nervously approached Michael and asked if he could start courting her.

'You'll have to ask my mam,' Michael said hastily. 'She'll explain to you.' He hurried away to his digging, but Willie followed him and asked for the address.

Michael stayed as long as possible at the allotment, and when he went home found his mother very excited.

'Willie Smith came to see me,' she said as soon as he came in. 'He said he spoke to you and you sent him here.'

'I didn't know what to say to him,' Michael mumbled.

'I was flabbergasted,' Peggy said. 'He came right out with it that he wanted to marry Meg. I had to explain to him the way she was, but he said he knew all about that but he still wanted to marry her and look after her.'

'Was Meg here?' Michael said.

'No, she was over the road. We had a long talk. I told him it was caused by neglect at birth, Meg being a bit backward like. It wasn't handed down in the family, and he said he could tell that because she didn't show any signs of it really, and he thought she only needed a bit of help and watching over, like.'

'So what did you say in the end?' Michael asked.

'I said yes if Meg wanted to, and you know, lad, I had my answer before ever I asked her. The minute she come in she just ran to him and he put his arms round her.' Peggy's eyes filled with tears, and she wiped them on the towel she was holding. 'He'll look after her, Mike, I'm sure he will. It's a weight off me mind for when I'm dead and gone.'

'I'd have looked after her,' Michael said. 'But Willie seems a good fellow.'

'I'm sure I've done right,' Peggy said. 'I never thought I'd see the day, but I'm so thankful.'

Sally knew Willie Smith and had seen him with Meg, and she was delighted at the outcome.

'He's a lad who needs someone to love and look after,' she

said. 'He's very patient with Meg and she's a lovable girl. She'll be made up to have her own house, and you've trained her well, Peg.'

'It'll be like playing house for her, and she won't want to be running round,' Peggy said. The unspoken thought was in both their minds, that Meg would be kept safe from the rough boys who encouraged her to run after them.

'If she's only two streets away, you'll be able to help her with her housekeeping until she gets used to it, and you won't miss her so much. She'll make a lovely bride, with those flaxen curls and her blue eyes.'

Willie took Meg to buy an engagement ring and she chose one with a large blue stone. 'It was only cheap,' he said apologetically, 'but it was what she wanted.' He smiled fondly at Meg as she displayed the ring to her family and Sally, and she flung her arms round his neck and kissed him. Sally thought it all augured well.

John still seemed to be pondering his future, but in the meantime he worked hard for the firm who did Stan's repair work, and in his spare time helped with the Goodfellow Fund. It was run by the *Liverpool Echo* and money was raised in various ways, through the paper, by donations from local businessmen, and also by street collections and various fund-raising activities.

The money was used to provide Christmas hampers for needy families, often the only food they had and John worked indefatigably at the collecting, then parcelling and distributing the food.

He had given up the practice of his religion for some time. But on the morning of Easter Sunday, when the family had gathered in the kitchen in their best clothes before setting out for Mass, John joined them wearing his best suit.

Cathy blushed with surprise and pleasure when Mick asked John if he was coming with them and he nodded. 'I went to Confession last night,' he said, smiling at his mother, but then he glanced over at Greg and grinned and Cathy felt a stab of jealousy. Greg knew about this, she thought.

As they walked down to church, she brooded on the fact that she had been excluded. How often in the past she had waited up for John when his father had gone to bed, and they had sat up talking for hours. John brought all his problems to her then, and they could talk about anything under the sun, she thought. Now she was only told his plans when he had talked them over with his father and decided what to do.

Her anger lasted until she was kneeling in church and she remembered how often she had knelt here before and prayed for an end to the conflict between Greg and John, and that they might be a happy, united family. She looked along the bench at her family kneeling together and felt ashamed of herself. I'm never satisfied, she told herself.

Her thoughts turned to Josie's troubles and she prayed that her sister Mary might be cured. Josie's worries about her seemed to have come to a head, and there seemed no solution to them.

Cathy and Josie had been working at a dinner party when Josie's second daughter, Sophie, had come with a message for her mother. The police at Rose Hill had Mary in the station and wanted Josie to go there immediately.

Mrs Nuttall said she could leave and the other women told her not to worry, but Josie left in tears. Cathy would have liked to go with her but obviously they could not both be spared, and Sophie assured her that she would look after her mother.

When they arrived at the police station Mary was sitting in a small room and a policewoman took them in to her. Mary's dress was torn and there were long scratches down her face. She burst into tears when she saw Josie. The policewoman told Sophie to sit with her aunt and jerked her head at Josie to tell her to follow her out of the room.

'She came in and made a complaint. Said the man next door had tried to rape her. She seemed quite normal but upset, so the charge seemed genuine and was investigated. The man was at home with his wife and the officers saw what was wrong right away, so your sister was cautioned and they left. After they did, your sister was attacked by the women in the street. The officers were called back, and to protect her they arrested her.'

'But the women in the street know her nerves have been bad,' Josie said. 'Why didn't they just send for me?'

The woman shrugged. 'You know what a mob's like,' she said.

'What happens now?' Josie asked. 'She won't have to stay here, will she?'

'No, she hasn't been charged. You can take her home,' the policewoman said. 'But keep her away from that street. She's not fit to live on her own, you know.'

Mary was tidied up and left the police station with Josie and Sophie. 'You'd better run on and tell your dad,' Josie said quietly to Sophie. 'Ask him and the lads to keep out of the way.'

'Do you think it will be all right?' she said doubtfully. 'Will Dad let her stay at our house?'

'He'll have to,' Josie said despairingly. 'What else can I do with her?'

'Should I go and ask Mrs Ward to take her?' Sophie said. 'There's only that old man there and he's in the parlour most of the time, isn't he?'

'That's a good idea. Run on and ask her, love,' Josie said thankfully.

Sally was waiting at the door as they came down the street, and she drew them into the house. Sophie was already in the kitchen setting cups out on the table, and Sally put Mary into a chair by the fire. 'Sit down and rest yourself, girl,' she said. 'And we'll have a cup of tea.'

She talked soothingly while Mary drank the cup of tea and her nervous trembling gradually ceased. A little later Cathy came in. She smiled at Mary and greeted her, then handed Josie four shillings. 'Mrs Nuttall sent your money,' she said. She opened her case and divided half the food within it with Josie, ignoring her protests.

Cathy stayed chatting to Mary while Sally went to the door with Josie and Sophie. 'Don't worry about her,' said Sally. 'She can sleep in my little bedroom for the time being, and Josh will keep out of her way.'

'I don't know what to do,' Josie said. 'I'd take her to our house but you know the way she is, and I couldn't keep Walter and the lads out of the way all the time.'

'Don't worry, and don't try to plan ahead tonight while you're upset,' Sally said. 'It'll all work out.' She gave Josie a small bottle. 'Take two teaspoonsful of that and have a good night's sleep. It'll all look different tomorrow.'

Sally put ointment on the scratches on Mary's face and gave her a sleeping draught before taking her up to bed and lending her a nightdress, and before long Mary was fast asleep.

A few days later Josie and Edie went to see Mary's neighbours. By this time most of the women were ashamed of their attack on her, even the next door neighbour.

'I know you had cause to be angry,' Josie said, 'but you know it's only Mary's nerves that make her do things like that, and she's been a good neighbour to you for years.'

'I know she's helped me out of a hole many a time,' the woman admitted. 'And she's always been good to the kids. It was just – to say such a thing about Fred, and the way the coppers carried on at first till they seen she was, well – a bit doolally. Where is she now?'

'She's with Sally Ward,' Josie said. 'And she's a lot better.'

'She will be,' the woman agreed, 'if Sally Ward's looking after her.'

'Yes, but I can't put on good nature and leave her there,' Josie said. 'And I've got no room. But if she comes back here, I don't want people turning on her instead of sending for me.'

'She'll be all right here,' the woman said, but she added, 'as long as she doesn't start trouble with the coppers for our husbands.'

'One of my daughters is going to stay with her, and I'll keep my eye on her,' Josie said. 'But tell the other women to leave her alone.'

'And tell them if they touch her again I'll come up and belt them, and bring my feller an'all,' Edie said belligerently.

Josie's words or Edie's threats were effective and Mary was left in peace when she returned to her own house, with Sophie staying with her for company. For a while Josie felt that she could stop worrying about her sister.

Josie and Walter still formed a foursome with Cathy and Greg for the dances at the Grafton, and kept up the façade of a happy marriage, but Josie privately told Cathy that she was beginning to hate her husband.

'I don't know what I'd have done if your mam hadn't helped me out with our Mary. When I went in and told

Walter that night that I'd been thinking of bringing her to our house, he hit the roof. I wouldn't have minded so much except for what he said about her. He said: "The place for a loony is in the loony bin, not in my house." He'd had a few drinks, but even so. A drunken mind speaks a sober truth, and he must have thought it.'

Cathy was unable to hide her shock and revulsion at these words and Josie went on, 'I couldn't answer, I was that upset. I just ran upstairs crying and went in the girls' bed. I couldn't lie beside him, I hated him that much.' She was weeping now and took out her handkerchief to wipe her eyes.

'Our Sophie was good. She made me take some of the stuff your mam gave me and I fell asleep. I didn't speak to him for a couple of days but you can't keep it up, can you? Not with the kids watching you.'

'I'm sure he didn't mean it. It was said in the heat of the moment,' said Cathy, but even to herself she sounded unconvincing.

'No, Cathy, I'm finished with him. If it wasn't for the young ones, I'd just clear out – maybe live with our Mary – but I'll have to stay till the three young ones are grown up. I wish I'd had mine closer together so they'd all be grown up now, but I'll make sure I don't have any more.'

Soon after this Josie and Walter stopped going to the dances, though Cathy and Greg still went. In one way it was a relief to Cathy not to have to dance with Walter, but she grieved for Josie's unhappiness and felt almost guilty about her own happiness.

All her family were happy. John had been offered a foreman's job by Stan, but had refused it, saying that he liked the men he worked with and would prefer to stay as he was. 'It's not natural,' Stan said to Greg. 'A young man should want to get on.' But Greg asked him not to press John.

'John's like his grandfather,' he said with a smile. 'He doesn't take the conventional view.'

'Wait until he starts courting,' Stan said. 'I'll bet he'll soon toe the line then.'

John still paid little attention to girls although many of those he met would have been happy to be asked out by him.

He was still avidly reading books and pamphlets, and going for long solitary walks, and his limp had almost disappeared.

Joe Fitzgerald had returned and had found a job ashore as a storeman in Littlewoods Pools, where Eileen also worked. The Fitzgerald family often went out separately, but sometimes they went as a group to the ceilidhes, or cycling on Sundays, always with Sarah as one of the group.

Terry and Stephen had become enthusiastic about ballroom dancing, and were attending Victor's Dancing Academy in Prescot Road. Their accounts of their efforts were so hilarious that Anne and Sarah and Eileen decided to go there too.

'We're not real beginners,' Anne said. 'We can do the foxtrot and the waltz, but I'd like to learn to do the tango and the slow foxtrot properly.'

The system at the Dancing Academy was that beginners were trained on the ground floor, and when proficient attended the dances held in the first-floor ballroom. Anne and Sarah soon graduated to the ballroom, quickly followed by Terry and Stephen, but Eileen lost interest when she met a young man there and began courting.

When Joe returned home they urged him to come to the dances with them. 'The trouble is, he hasn't got any mates with being away so long,' Anne said. 'He'd have to go to the beginners' class on his own now that we're all upstairs, and I think he doesn't like to. It seems daft to say a fellow of his age is shy, but he is. Our Terry would go like a shot, whether he knew anyone or not, but Joe's not like that.'

'I wonder would our John go with him?' said Sarah.

'Do you think he would? That'd be great,' her friend said eagerly. Sarah glanced at her doubtfully. I hope she just wants him to go for Joe's sake, she thought. I hope she hasn't still got a pash on him.

Cathy urged John to go with Joe when Sarah asked him. 'You'll enjoy it, son,' she said. 'They're such a jolly crowd and you could do with some fun.'

He laughed. 'D'you think I'm getting too solemn, Mum?' he asked.

'I do, as a matter of fact,' she said, and John laughed again ruefully and agreed to go to Victor's.

He and Joe became good friends, and enjoyed their

conversations together as much as the dances, but they both learned quickly and moved up to join the dancers in the ballroom upstairs.

John often danced with Anne, and Joe with Sarah, but Terry claimed Sarah for most of the dances. 'She's the only one who can dodge his feet,' Anne said to John. 'He keeps counting, "one two three, one two three," all the time he's waltzing.'

'It's a lie,' Terry called as he danced beside them with Sarah.

'You don't know what I'm saying,' Anne retorted.

Terry said, 'Well, it's a lie anyway.'

John and Joe agreed that war was inevitable, but Anne and Sarah were oblivious to the preparations for it as they enjoyed life to the full. If they thought of war at all they expected that Mr Chamberlain would bring off another last-minute miracle.

In August Sarah was very excited about an invitation to Reece's Grill Room from a young commercial traveller who came in the shop. He was a smart young man with excellent manners. He told her that he had an appointment on Saturday afternoon, but would arrange for a cab to pick her up and bring her to meet him at Reece's.

Sarah was wildly excited. She wore her best dress of midnight blue taffeta, and with it silver sandals and a silver evening bag. Cathy helped her to curl her hair and lent her her marcasite clips to hold back clusters of curls above her brow.

Cathy also lent her the fur cape which Greg had bought her for their twentieth wedding anniversary. 'You'll be the Belle of the Ball,' she said, and Sarah drove off full of anticipation and delight. The young man, Ronald, was waiting for her, and told her that she looked stunning.

The Grill Room was in the basement, and there was a stand at the top of the stairs selling boxes of chocolates for men to buy to impress their partners. Ronald bought her a large box of Black Magic which she carried proudly down to the Grill Room.

The dance floor was small but their table was close to it and Sarah felt very sophisticated as the waiter drew out her chair and handed her a menu. She found Ronald entertaining company as he talked about the various towns he had visited for his firm, and between courses they danced to an excellent band.

The only flaw in her enjoyment was that as they danced Ronald held her very close and ran his hand down her back to press her buttocks, then kissed her and tried to thrust his tongue into her mouth. Sarah kept her lips firmly clamped together and fortunately the dance ended and they could return to their table.

He also pressed his leg against hers beneath the table and tried to press her foot with his, but she quickly tucked her feet beneath her chair, chiefly worried about damage to her new sandals.

These seemed only small drawbacks to an otherwise delightful evening, and Sarah was sorry when the dance was over. Ronald took her elbow as they stepped out of the door, and suggested that they should walk a little before calling a cab. It was a lovely evening, warm but with a fresh breeze, and the street was flooded with moonlight. Sarah readily agreed.

She began to feel uneasy when he slipped his arm around her and squeezed her breast, but she was quite unprepared when he suddenly pushed her into a doorway and leaned heavily against her. His arm was still around her holding her close and the box of chocolates was digging into her chest making it difficult to breathe, but she kept her lips determinedly closed and twisted her head from side to side as he tried again to thrust his tongue into her mouth.

Sarah was so intent on avoiding his tongue that for a moment she failed to realize what else he was doing. He had fumbled with his trousers until his fly was unbuttoned, and was trying to drag her hand down towards it.

She dragged her hand back and kicked at his shin, then gave him a sudden push which caught him off balance and made him stumble backwards for a moment. She used the breathing space to grip the box of chocolates with both hands and bring it down heavily on his head.

It was a casket and quite heavy. The force of her blow made it burst and chocolates flew in all directions. Sarah squirmed away from him and, lifting her skirts, began to run up Parker Street towards Lime Street. She heard a shout of: 'Bloody cheat' behind her, and something about chocolates, but she ran on until she was sure that he was not following her.

Her face felt sticky and one sandal was unfastened. When she reached the Steble fountain she dipped her handkerchief in the water and wiped her face, then fastened her sandal and walked on sedately, although casting many fearful glances behind her.

She had intended to keep the episode from her mother but as soon as Cathy saw her she knew that something had happened. Sarah told her, carefully suppressing any mention of the unbuttoned fly. The experience had upset her and she stayed indoors the following day, but Anne came to see her, and Sarah told her the whole story.

'I've learned my lesson,' she said finally. 'I'll stick to our own crowd in future.'

'And he seemed such a gentleman!' Anne exclaimed.

'Not when he was shouting after me about cheating him,' Sarah said with a faint smile. But then she said seriously, 'I feel cheap, Anne. He evidently thought he could buy me with a night out and a box of chocolates.'

'Well, he thought wrong, didn't he? No need for *you* to feel cheap, Sarah. He probably tries it on with every girl, but you were the one who crowned him with his chocolates.'

Sarah smiled at her affectionately, and Anne said briskly, 'You'll be coming to the ceilidhe tonight, won't you?'

'I don't think I will,' said Sarah. 'I feel really off colour. Nothing to do with last night, but my throat's sore and I'm aching all over. I think I'll go to bed early with some of Grandma's jollop.'

'Stay off tomorrow if you don't feel better,' Anne said. 'I'll tell Mabel.'

'I'm sure I'll be quite well again tomorrow.'

It was fortunate that as she waved Anne goodbye she was unaware that before she was "quite well" again, her life and that of everyone she knew would be changed for ever.

Chapter Thirty-Three

Sarah went to bed early after taking some of her grandmother's cough mixture and fell asleep almost immediately, but she woke a few hours later feeling as though she was on fire. Her throat, arms and legs ached, and the sheets on the bed were soaked with perspiration.

Fortunately the double bed which she and Kate had shared had been replaced a few months earlier by single beds so her sister was undisturbed. Sarah dozed fitfully throughout the night, waking from time to time terror-stricken by strange dreams.

When Cathy came in to call her for work she was horrified to see Sarah so flushed and almost delirious, and to discover the wet sheets.

She gave her a drink of water then changed her bed and pyjamas and made her comfortable, before cooking breakfast for the rest of the family and getting them off to school or work.

Greg came up to see Sarah before he left and was as alarmed as Cathy, although he concealed his dismay from Sarah. He turned her pillows and gave her another drink, smiling cheerfully, but when he went downstairs he told Cathy that he would call at the doctor's surgery on his way to work and ask him to visit.

'What do you think it is?' she asked fearfully.

'It could be rheumatic fever, and if so the sooner the doctor sees her the better. He'll know the best treatment to prevent any trouble in the future.' Cathy told Mick to call to tell her mother and Sally came over a little later.

Sarah was again soaked in perspiration, and Sally helped Cathy to sponge her down, and change her pyjamas and sheets. Sarah refused food but had a raging thirst and drank numerous cups of tea and glasses of water.

389

When the doctor came he told Sarah only that she must stay in bed for a while, but downstairs he told Cathy that she had rheumatic fever. It was important that she should stay in bed for several weeks, lying flat as much as possible, otherwise her heart might be permanently damaged.

As the days passed the fever subsided, but all the skin on Sarah's body gradually peeled, and the pain and stiffness in her arms and legs persisted. At first she was content to lie in bed, sleeping as much as possible and waiting for the medicine to bring relief from pain, but as she began to feel better she became depressed and frustrated at missing the dances and other activities she enjoyed so much.

The family all spent time with her, and Anne was a frequent visitor. Otherwise Sarah spent hours reading. She read the newspaper more thoroughly than she had ever done, and worried about what she read.

When John came to sit with her one night she asked him what he thought about the possibility of war. He said gravely, 'I'm afraid it's inevitable, Sar.'

'You don't think Mr Chamberlain can talk Hitler out of it again?'

'No. I don't know whether these politicians are incredibly naive or whether they just want us to think they are.'

'Mr Chamberlain, you mean?'

'Yes, and Prime Minister Negrin of Spain. Everybody else knows that this Non-Intervention Pact has been a farce, but he seems to believe in it.'

'I don't know what it is,' she said honestly.

'It was an arrangement between other countries that they wouldn't send arms to Spain. France and Britain kept it but Germany and Italy sent arms to Franco from the beginning. Negrin seemed to believe that if he sent the International Brigade home, Italy and Germany would pull out of Spain. Anyone could have told him they had no intention of leaving – it was too good an opportunity for them to try out their tanks and air power.'

'But it was before last Christmas when those men came home, wasn't it? When you went to Lime Street to see them,' said Sarah. 'I didn't think you worried about all that now, John.'

'I just get disgusted sometimes, Sar, at the dirty tricks and the scheming. Mussolini helps Chamberlain by persuading Hitler to hold off last September, and then he gets his reward by Britain recognizing Franco in January.'

Sarah looked puzzled. 'But wasn't it a good thing that Mr Chamberlain signed that pact? At least we've had this year.'

'Yes, and now we're much better prepared,' he said. 'Sorry about the moans. This isn't the time to unload them, is it?' He picked up her book. 'What's this you're reading?'

The next moment his mother plunged into the room, her arms full of ironed clothes. 'You're right, you shouldn't be talking to her about your worries,' she said angrily. 'She's not well enough. If you want to moan, do it to your father, but I thought you'd put all that out of your head.'

John and Sarah were speechless with surprise for a moment, staring at their mother's flushed and angry face, then Sarah said, 'I asked John, Mum,' and he stood up.

'I'm going to the shop, Sar. What would you like?'

'Could I have some dandelion and burdock please?'

Cathy and John left the room and Sarah lay back on her pillows. I must have been very ill, she thought. I've never heard Mum speak to John like that before. Cathy put the clothes away then came back. Her sudden burst of bad temper was over, and she spoke cheerfully about Sarah's progress.

'Only one more day in bed, love,' she said. 'The doctor says you can get up on Friday, if you just sit in the chair at first.'

'Friday! That's the first of September, isn't it? It'll be three weeks on Sunday since this started. I'm dying to go back to the dances.'

'You'll have to wait a while longer. He's only letting you up because you've done as he said so far. You can't take any chances, love.'

Anne came to see Sarah the following evening and Sarah told her that she was to be allowed up, and about her conversation with John.

'I know,' Anne said. 'He's disgusted with politicians. He says they only do what's expedient, not what's right.' Sarah looked at her in surprise and Anne blushed. 'We talk sometimes when we're walking home from the dances. Not just me – our Joe as well,' she added hastily.

She smiled at Sarah. 'We don't half miss you at the dances. Everyone asks about you.'

'I miss going,' Sarah said with a sigh. 'It's only three weeks but it seems like years, especially with all that's going on, the identity cards and gas masks, and the shelters being built. It'll be a different world when I'm back in circulation. What's it like in the shop?'

'Terrible. Nothing but war, war, war from the customers, and Mabel agrees with everyone. I said to her, "Why don't you say what *you* think?" but she just laughed and said it was easier to agree, and anyway the customer was always right.'

'I wonder what they'll do in the bakehouse if Billy and Norman are called up?'

'I don't know about that, but I tell you what I *do* know: they won't go short of jam or mincemeat. You know that big high shelf round the shop, near the ceiling? It's *full* of forty-eight pound jars of jam and mincemeat, and the rooms upstairs are so packed that there are cracks in the ceiling. Hetty says if it falls through, we'll all be killed before the war starts at all.'

'What's she like, the new girl?'

'Hetty? She's all right, but of course she's only temporary until you come back.'

'Whenever that is,' Sarah said with a sigh.

Her friend said cheerfully, 'I'm sure it won't be long. I told Hetty about that fellow you went out with trying to put his tongue in your mouth, and she said it's called a French kiss.'

'Ugh!' Sarah shuddered at the memory. 'The French are welcome to it. Dad doesn't like them, he'd rather have Germans.'

'But he fought them in the last war, didn't he?'

'Yes, but he said the ordinary Germans are all right. French people made them pay for water for dying men, and *they* were supposed to be on our side! Oh, I do hope this is another false alarm, Anne.'

'I'm afraid it isn't,' she said gravely.

Sarah came downstairs mid-morning on September the first, and was surprised to find how shaky she still was. Her mother was machining blackout curtains, and told Sarah that they were already up in the parlour and two of the bedrooms. She was now making them for the kitchen and the girls' bedroom.

Josie came in a little later, looking pale and harassed. 'I just don't know what to do, Cath. Everyone's saying it's not right to keep the children here and they should be evacuated, but I'm worried to death about letting them go. I wouldn't care if I was sure they'd let Eunice stay with the little ones, but she'll be going with the school.'

'Surely they'll let the little ones go with her?'

'But they might get split up when they get there,' Josie said. 'And our Danny – he's fine about the bedwetting usually, but if he's upset about anything he still wets the bed. I don't know what to do.'

'Some mothers are going with their children, aren't they?' said Cathy. 'Mona Ashcroft is going with her baby.'

'Mostly people with young ones,' Josie said. She glanced at Sarah. 'You know, I'd be only too glad to go, the way things are here, but I'll have to be on hand for our Mary. And this wedding next week – Eunice is a bridesmaid for our Edie and she's whingeing because she might have to go away and miss it, and Edie's whingeing because she thinks her wedding might be spoiled and Bert might have to go away.'

'Poor Mrs Meadows, she *has* got troubles,' Sarah said when Josie had drunk a comforting cup of tea and left after some soothing words from Cathy.

'Yes, and no one to share them with,' Cathy said with a sigh. 'Walter's useless, and the sisters-in-law are keeping away in case they have to take any responsibility for Mary. I thank God for your dad and for Mam and my good family, Sarah.'

Later they put the wireless on and heard that Germany had been bombing Poland since five o'clock that morning, and Britain had instructed the British Ambassador in Berlin to request them to stop hostilities immediately or else he would sever diplomatic ties. Sarah and Cathy looked at each other in dismay, but Mick, who had just come in, said cheerfully, 'Hitler still thinks England won't fight, but he's got another think coming.'

On Saturday rain fell heavily, and although Sarah came downstairs she stayed only a few hours then went back to bed. There was nothing on the wireless to distract her from the pain in her limbs or the heavy feeling of foreboding which pressed on her, only gramophone programmes and interminable news bulletins.

There was to be an announcement on Sunday at eleven o'clock. Sarah came down at ten-thirty. At the advertised hour the sombre voice of Mr Chamberlain announced that no reply had been received after the ultimatum and Britain was now at war with Germany.

'He seems upset, doesn't he?' Sarah said. 'I feel so sorry for him, because he's done all he can for peace.'

Greg and Cathy were sitting together on the sofa. Neither of them spoke but Greg put his arm around Cathy and held her close.

She went over to her mother a few minutes later and found her as composed as ever, but Josh's face was grey and he was trembling. 'Never thought I'd see it again in my lifetime,' he mumbled to Cathy.

Sally said briskly, 'We don't know what's going to happen yet. No use crossing our bridges before we come to them.'

Anne came to see Sarah in the afternoon. 'It's almost a relief that something's happened at last. It seems to have been hanging over us for so long.'

'But all men of eighteen to forty-one to be called up,' Sarah said. 'That's practically everyone we know.'

'Our lads are going to join the Irish Guards,' Anne said. 'Terry and Joe and Stephen anyway. Tony hasn't made up his mind yet.'

'We're lucky, I suppose,' Sarah said. 'Mick's too young and Dad's too old, and John —'

She hesitated, and Anne said quickly, 'He's not eligible, is he? He told me the government said a few months ago that men who had fought with the International Brigade would not be accepted in the Forces. I think it's crazy. As though they were traitors! They were mostly just idealists.'

Sarah hid her surprise and said only, 'Mick's enrolled in the messenger service already. All places of amusement are closed, they said on the wireless, dances and cinemas and so on. I wonder will the ceilidhe be on tonight?'

'I've no idea,' said Anne. 'I'd better go, Sar. I saw Tony and Helen on their way to our house as I came here, and she asked me not to be long as there were things to discuss. I think they may be bringing their wedding forward. Helen looked excited.'

'Edie Meadows' wedding is next Saturday,' Sarah said. 'It was going to be a big do but I don't know what will happen now.'

'I should think they'll go ahead,' Anne said. 'Unless something happens before then.' They looked at each other nervously, then Anne picked up her gas mask and said with determined cheerfulness, 'I wonder, will the brides be having to carry these to the altar or wear them for the service? I'll suggest it to Helen and Tony.'

She left and a few minutes later Cathy came into the kitchen. 'Our John is walking back with Anne,' she said. 'He came up just as she was leaving. I'm sorry to leave you on your own but everyone's out in the street.'

'Where's Dad and everyone?'

'He's gone down to the First Aid Post, and Mick's in his element,' Cathy said. 'He's already carried a few messages. He's on duty until eleven o'clock tonight.'

'And Kate?'

'Grandma called her in to cheer Josh up. He's really upset by the news, and we thought Kate would take his mind off it. Albert Ashcroft is the Air Raid Warden for this street, and throwing his weight about already, telling us it's a fine of two hundred pounds or two years' imprisonment for showing a light.'

'We'll be all right now with those blackout curtains, anyway. I'll bet Mr Ashcroft would enjoy reporting someone. He's a horrible man, isn't he?'

'He's bragging about his sons, too. They're in camp with the Terriers so they'll go right into the proper Army, he says.'

'Anne says their boys are going in the Irish Guards. John seems to talk to her a lot,' Sarah said. 'She thinks Helen and Tony might bring the wedding forward from Christmas.'

'Does she? I was just talking to Josie and she's still worrying about Edie's wedding, but I've told her there's no sense in altering the arrangements.' And as though on cue, Josie called and came down the lobby.

'I was just talking about Edie's wedding,' Cathy said. 'Saying you should go ahead as planned.'

'But what if the Germans come?'

'You've got enough food for them, haven't you?' Cathy laughed, but Josie was not in the mood for jokes.

'I feel nearly distracted,' she said, 'what with one thing and another. I was harassed enough about the wedding without this worry as well.'

'I don't think anything will happen this week, Josie,' Cathy said. 'Hitler's too busy bombing Poland, God forgive him, to bother about us yet. Have you made up your mind about the evacuation?'

'Yes, I'm not letting the little ones go. Our Eunice can go with the school because she's old enough to look out for herself, but I'm keeping Danny and Frank here and I don't care what people say about me,' her friend said defiantly.

'It's got nothing to do with anyone else,' Cathy assured her. 'I think you're doing the right thing anyway. Kate leaves school at Easter so I don't have that worry trying to decide what to do.'

Later Sarah walked along the lobby and stood at the door for a moment. Women still stood about in groups, talking. Mr Ashcroft bustled up to them.

'You shouldn't stand about in gangs like this,' he said officiously. 'You make a perfect target.'

'What for? Seagulls?' one woman said derisively, and another folded her arms belligerently.

'Don't talk bloody soft,' she said to him. 'There's no planes going over.'

'There could be,' he said, retreating a little from the angry women.

'Then you should'a sounded your sireen,' she said. 'Listen, if I want to stand on me own parapet no bloody German's going to stop me, and no fussy little bugger like you, neither!'

Sarah went back into the house, smiling. 'I'm glad I went out,' she said to her mother, 'I was just in time for a row between Mrs Gunter and Mr Ashcroft. He couldn't get away quick enough.'

'We can do without fighting among ourselves,' Cathy said with a sigh. 'We'll have enough to do with the Germans.'

'But we're not on our own,' Sarah said. 'It said on the wireless that France and New Zealand and Australia have all declared war on Germany, and in the paper there was an article by a Frenchman. He said France has a big army because their men are conscripted, and an efficient air force and navy as well as the Maginot Line, so they're in no danger.'

'There's nothing wrong with your brain anyway,' Cathy said admiringly. 'You seem well up in all that's going on.'

'Only because I've got time on my hands now, and people talk to me,' Sarah said with a smile.

'Has our John said anything to you about being picked on at work?' Cathy asked.

Sarah shook her head. 'No, he's never mentioned it.'

'He hasn't said anything to me, but Dad said it started when Germany and Russia signed that pact last month. None of the men'll speak to him, but they make cracks among themselves about him being a Russian spy.'

'No wonder he's so fed up,' Sarah exclaimed. 'Why doesn't he tackle them?'

'He said to Dad he didn't go to Spain to fight for Russia, he went to fight for fair shares for all men. He saw real socialism in action there and will never forget it.'

'He told me about that. He said there were no officers and men, just all soldiers as equals and no one grabbing for more for themselves. Everyone just sharing and working for one another.'

'It sounds great,' her mother said, 'but I can't see it working here.'

'I don't think it worked everywhere there, just in that part where John was for a while, but he said it made him realize it *could* happen, and he's glad he went just for that.'

'It's to be hoped these fellows at work don't make him sorry he did! You look tired, Sarah. I'll just nip over to Grandma's and see if Kate's coming back for her tea, then I'll do ours. I'll have to cook for the others as they come in.'

Sarah admitted that she was tired and a little later thankfully went back to bed, but was too unsettled and excited to sleep. Mick rushed in at nine o'clock to gobble some food and collect sandwiches to take with him, but before he went back to the depot he ran upstairs to see her.

'I've just come from Mill Road Hospital,' he said, 'and I saw one of the Fitzgeralds in Everton Road. He said to tell you that the ceilidhe wasn't on tonight so you haven't missed anything. I don't know which one – I think it was Joe.' He rushed away before Sarah could ask any questions.

On Monday morning Josie came in with her eyes reddened by tears. 'I was sorry I'd registered our Eunice when it came to it,' she said. 'She didn't want to go, and all the poor kids looked so bewildered. She's upset about missing the wedding too.'

'She'll be all right,' Cathy consoled her. 'She's with her friends, and the teachers are going to look after them, aren't they?'

Josie began to cry again. 'I took Danny and Frank with me to see her off, and a man came and told me off because I was keeping them at home. I think he was a headmaster. He said the bombing could start at any time, and possibly gas attacks, and I was selfish and irresponsible to keep them at home.'

'Don't take any notice,' Cathy said. 'No one knows what's going to happen.' But she looked uneasily at Sarah.

Most of the children of school age had gone from the street, and it seemed unnaturally quiet. Kate's school was closed as most of the pupils had gone to North Wales and shelters had to be ready before the remaining children could return to school.

The news on the wireless was grim. The *Athenia*, a passenger ship, had been sunk by a U-Boat and about one hundred lives lost. The horror and revulsion at the news was all the greater in Liverpool because so many local men were at sea.

Poland was still fighting bravely, with cavalry officers trying to fight tanks, and the Royal Air Force was dropping thousands of leaflets on Germany, hoping to rouse the German people against Hitler.

The doctor came again and ordered Sarah back to bed, only allowing her to get up for a few hours in the evening, and not to walk about or go out of doors. She felt thoroughly miserable, cooped up, unable to discuss the news except with her own family, and seeing no end to her illness.

Her mother was busy, helping Josie with the preparations for Edie's wedding, but her grandmother often came to sit with her, and told her anecdotes about her early life which made the hours pass more quickly for Sarah, and gave her much to think about when she was alone.

'How is Josh?' she asked one day.

'Not too well. I don't put the news on because it only upsets him, but Kate amuses him and takes his mind off things,' Sally said. 'Everyone's different, Sarah.'

Cathy brought her news of the wedding; some good, some bad. Bert's brother who was to have been best man had gone into the Fleet Air Arm, and his mother said that she couldn't bear to watch the wedding with someone else talking his place. 'Josie flew at her, told her she had two sons and owed it to Bert to be there. I came out quickly. They looked as though they were going to come to blows,' Cathy said, laughing.

'And the good news?'

'Eunice might get home for the wedding. She's staying with two ladies near Pwhelli and they know a man who's driving a lorry to the docks on Friday, staying in Liverpool overnight, and driving back. He says he doesn't mind staying over and going back on Sunday to take Eunice back then.'

'I'm made up,' Sarah said. 'She would never have got over missing being a bridesmaid.'

'Yes, and it sounds as though she's with good people too.'

Saturday was a beautiful morning, sunny and mild, and Sarah stood at the front door to see Edie leaving for church. Eunice and Bert's sister came out first, Eunice almost alight with excitement, both wearing peach-coloured taffeta dresses made by Cathy and carrying bouquets of bronze chrysanthemums.

Edie followed shortly afterwards. She was a buxom girl but Cathy had skilfully cut her white satin dress to give her the appearance of a shapely figure, with a full skirt falling into graceful folds and a short train. Happiness had softened her features and made her eyes bright, and Sarah exclaimed impulsively, 'You look beautiful Edie.'

The bride gave her a brilliant smile, then she was handed into the wedding car by her father and Sarah went back to bed feeling sad.

Anne came to see her after work. 'Less than a week since it started and such a lot seems to have happened! Tony and Joe and Stephen have all applied for the Irish Guards, and I don't know how many of the crowd from the ceilidhe and the dance have gone. Jim Morley off the drums, and Jimmy Osborne, and Big Feet . . . oh, dozens of fellows.'

'Mum says all the young men have gone from the Co-op, nearly,' Sarah said. 'The two young chaps from Peggy's Parlour, they've gone. Er – did you know our John had tried to join up?'

'No. What happened?' Anne asked eagerly.

'He was refused. Supposedly on medical grounds,' Sarah said.

'But he seems quite fit now.'

'I know. They said his foot wouldn't stand up to marching and drilling, but he tried the Navy too and it was no use.'

'So what will he do?'

Sarah shrugged. 'He'll have to carry on with the repair job, I suppose, and hope things will change.'

'The Pools have closed, you know, so our Eileen and Joe are out of work,' Anne said. 'Tony's place had gone on to war work, and Stephen and Terry are all right, but they expect to be called up soon anyway.'

'I feel as though I'm on another planet, stuck up here not seeing people and not knowing what's going on,' Sarah suddenly exclaimed.

'You must be fed up,' Anne said sympathetically. 'Our lads and Eileen would like to come and see you. Could they come tomorrow?'

'I'd love to see them,' Sarah said eagerly. Her mother had come into the bedroom with a tray of supper for them both, and to replenish the fire, and was enthusiastic about the idea.

'I'm sure Sarah would be all right to get up tomorrow for

the day,' she said. 'She's done everything the doctor told her, and a change would do her good.'

Before Anne left it was arranged that she would come on the following afternoon with some of her brothers and sisters. Later Cathy told Sarah that she would light the parlour fire early in the morning so that it would be warm for them to sit there.

Chapter Thirty-Four

Cathy was proud of her parlour and felt it was looking its best on Sunday, with a bright fire burning and roses in a cut glass vase scenting the air.

She had helped Sarah to wash and set her hair, and by two o'clock she was sitting by the fire, wearing her favourite green woollen dress. The stiffness in her limbs made her walk like a marionette so she decided that she would be sitting in the chair when the Fitzgeralds arrived, and stay there until they went.

Anne had said tactfully that they would like to come at two o'clock and leave at five to be home for tea.

'But can't you stay for tea?' Cathy protested.

'No, I'm sorry. We have to go home. There are some cousins coming,' Anne said. Cathy was sure that she was trying to avoid making work for her, but made no further protest.

Terry, Joe and Eileen came with Anne. They said that Stephen had intended to come but had to work a double shift. They had all brought gifts: Eileen a bunch of chrysanthemums and a tin of talcum powder which she said was from her and Stephen, Anne a traycloth to embroider and embroidery silks sent by Maureen, Terry grapes, and Joe a small thick copy of *Pepys' Diary* bound in red.

'It's like Christmas,' Sarah exclaimed, her eyes sparkling. 'Thanks, everyone, and will you thank Maureen and Stephen?' Her father had shown the Fitzgeralds in and taken their coats, and now her mother came to welcome them, and Sarah showed her the gifts.

'I'm not good at sewing but you'll show me the embroidery stitches, won't you, Mum?'

While the others talked to Cathy, Sarah opened her book and saw that Joe had written on the flyleaf: "To Sarah from

403

Joe Fitzgerald. September 1939." She smiled at him and said quietly, 'Thanks, Joe. I'll enjoy this.'

He smiled too and said in a low voice, 'It's one of my favourites. It's good to escape to sixteen-sixty and see they had their problems too, I think.'

Terry had taken the grapes from their bag and unwrapped the tissue paper around them. 'I'm the only proper sick visitor, aren't I, Mrs Redmond?' he said to Cathy. 'I brought grapes.'

'You are indeed,' she said, laughing. 'But if you were a proper sick visitor, you'd eat some yourself. That's what people do.'

'Don't you dare,' cried Anne, and Terry sat close beside Sarah's chair.

'These are all for Sarah,' he said virtuously, 'and I'm going to feed her with them.'

He popped a grape into her mouth and she said indistinctly, 'I can still use my hands, you know.'

'Use them to give him a push, Sarah,' Eileen said, but Terry held her hands in one of his and continued to feed her the grapes.

John popped his head round the door as Cathy carried the flowers out. 'What's all this hilarity?' he said with mock severity. He came in. Terry had released Sarah's hands and gone to put the grapes on top of the piano, and immediately he and Eileen and Anne began to talk to John.

Sarah picked up her book again and glanced at Joe. He leaned forward to speak to her and was about to take Terry's place on the stool beside her when John said, 'Hello there, Joe. I believe your job's kaput.' He walked over and sat down beside Joe and began to talk earnestly to him.

Terry came back to the stool beside Sarah, and the usual wisecracking and mock insults began between him and his sisters, with Terry begging Sarah to take his part and defend him from this monstrous regiment of women.

'I'm a woman too,' she objected.

'You are, *alanah*,' he declared, taking her hand and pressing it to his chest. 'That's your greatest attraction for me.'

He looked up soulfully and Eileen said sweetly, 'What's up? Is there a fly on the ceiling?'

Kate's music lay on the piano and Eileen was persuaded

to play for them. They all sang the ballads she played: 'The Last Rose of Summer' and 'The Mountains of Mourne', and when she played 'Believe Me If All Those Endearing Young Charms', Terry went on one knee before Sarah and sang to her with his hand on his heart.

Later Cathy wheeled in a tea trolley set with cups and saucers and plates of cakes and tiny sandwiches.

'You shouldn't have bothered,' Anne protested. 'We've just had a big dinner and we're going home for tea.'

'You've passed twenty houses since your dinner, as my mother would say,' Cathy said. 'Will you be mother, Anne? And you hand things round, John.'

Anne picked up the big teapot and poured the tea. John came to help and then sat down beside her. Terry insisted on cutting Sarah's cake into small pieces, and offered to hold her cup to her mouth.

'Will you stop it?' she laughed. 'I'll think I've got one foot in the grave before you've finished.'

To Sarah it was all good fun, and she thoroughly enjoyed the laughter and the company, but when the Fitzgeralds had gone, John said to her, 'Is Terry sweet on you, Sar?'

'No, of course not. It was just the part he was playing this afternoon.'

'I don't know. It convinced me,' John said. 'Joe was looking a bit thoughtful, too. Probably thinking it would be another wedding present to buy.'

'Don't be daft!' Sarah said, but in later years she often looked back on that afternoon and wondered. Was that when it all started? If Terry had not brought grapes and sat down beside her with them . . . If John had not come in just when he did . . .

Now, though, she felt invigorated by her happy afternoon, and told her mother that she was going to try to walk over to her grandma's house and make a real effort to make her stiff limbs flexible again.

'Leave it until tomorrow,' Cathy said. 'You've done enough for one day.' The following morning Sarah walked round the house until she was moving easily, then linked her arm in her mother's and walked over to her grandmother's house.

As usual Sally's kitchen was warm and bright, and she

pushed forward a chair beside the fire for Sarah. 'I think Doctor O'Neill's too fussy,' Sarah said. 'Making me stay in bed when I'm getting more and more stiff.'

'As long as you keep warm, girl,' Sally said, 'I think you'll be better up. You'll have to find another doctor, anyway. Peggy says Doctor O'Neill's gone in the Forces.'

'But he didn't say anything, and it's only just over a week since he came,' Sarah exclaimed.

'Well, Peggy says there's a notice in his surgery window telling his patients to find another doctor.'

'I'll have to do that, because he only gave me a sick note for a fortnight,' Sarah said, looking worried.

But Sally said calmly, 'Everything's at sixes and sevens now. I wouldn't worry about that.'

A few days later Sarah went with her mother to another doctor, a harassed, elderly man who gave Sarah a perfunctory examination and told her she could go back to work the following week, but must do no heavy lifting, or work for long hours at first.

Sarah was delighted and it was arranged that she would work from ten o'clock until three for the first few weeks. Hetty was to stay for a while but had already applied for a job in the Ordnance Factory where she could earn more money.

Sarah felt as though she had come back to a different world when she returned to the shop and began to go out and about again. Most of the young male customers had gone and although the dances and ceilidhes were open again, many of the familiar faces were missing.

In October Terry and Joe were called up and sent to Caterham Barracks for training, but Stephen was told that his job was essential war work and he could not be released.

Tony's job as foreman in a small factory was also classed as a reserved occupation when the factory was turned over to light engineering for the Ministry of Defence.

Tony and Helen had brought their wedding forward to the first week in October, and it was a quiet but happy occasion, the last time the family were to be all together for many years. Joe was Tony's best man, and Eileen and Anne were bridesmaids.

While they posed for photographs, Terry looked after

Sarah, introduced her to people and stayed with her until Anne claimed her. Eileen left for the WAAF a week after Terry and Joe went, but Anne and Sarah waited until Sarah was fully fit so that they could volunteer together.

The two brothers who had rented Peggy's parlour were now in the Army, and she had let the rooms to a retired Major and his wife.

'A Major! We're coming up in the world, aren't we?' Cathy exclaimed when Sally told her.

'Peggy says she's not struck on him, but his wife's a nice little woman. The flat they had was requisitioned. Peggy thinks there's some mystery about them.'

'It won't be a mystery for long then,' Cathy said, laughing. 'I'm going in there for Meg to come over for a fitting.'

Willie had asked for the marriage between him and Meg to take place almost immediately so that he could look after her, and Peggy had agreed. He had suggested a quiet affair at the Register Office in Brougham Terrace, but when Meg saw Edie Meadows' wedding, she had pleaded for a dress and bridesmaids like hers.

The wedding was arranged at a local church and Cathy was making a white satin wedding dress for Meg, and bridesmaids' dresses for two of her cousins. She made the wedding dress in a simpler style than Edie's to suit Meg's fragile beauty, and persuaded her to have blue silk taffeta for her bridesmaids.

On the day Meg looked a fairytale bride with a headdress of orange blossom on her flaxen curls and her blue eyes shining with excitement. She was not nervous. 'Willie will tell me what to do,' she said trustfully, and many of the congregation shed tears, touched by his gentle care for his bride.

Josie had been at the church and later that evening came in to see Cathy. 'Are they all out?' she asked.

'Yes, Kate's over at Mam's, Mick's at the depot and Greg's at the First Aid Post. There's nothing doing, but he's training people in First Aid. Sarah and John are at the pictures.'

'It's just I want to talk to you,' Josie said. Her eyes were red and swollen with crying, and she was twisting a handkerchief between her fingers.

'Come in the parlour, then we won't be interrupted,' Cathy said. She slipped her arm through Josie's as they went into the parlour, then switched on the electric fire which now stood in the hearth, and poured a glass of sherry for Josie.

'Drink this and tell me what's happened.'

Josie gave her a ghost of a smile. 'You sound just like your mam,' she said. Then tears welled up in her eyes again. She put the glass down and said bluntly, 'Walter's gone.'

'Gone?' Cathy echoed. 'Gone where?'

'To his lady love,' Josie said bitterly. 'I've been a fool, Cathy. I should have suspected it long ago.' She drank some more sherry while Cathy sat silent, too shocked to speak, while words tumbled out of Josie.

'We had a hell of a row – it's a wonder you didn't hear us. He told me he'd got a job in the BIC in Prescot and was moving to live there. He informed me that now Edie's gone, there's nothing to keep him here. She was always his favourite, and I know that what I always thought was right – he hates the other kids.' She gave a sob and Cathy pressed her hand in silent sympathy.

'I didn't know about this other one at first and said he could go as far as I was concerned, but he couldn't leave it like that. He had to say his piece. He said it was all my fault that things had gone wrong, and now he'd found someone who was worth two of me and was entitled to some happiness after the life he'd had with me.'

'But you were happy,' Cathy said. 'It's only just lately—'

Josie shook her head. 'No, Cath,' she said. 'We had good spells but it's never been really right. I used to blame it on Mam stirring things, but it wasn't that. I gave him all his own way because I felt guilty that he had to put up with Mam, and he was all right while he was the only one considered. When we were very hard up, he always had steak and chops even if me and the kids had jam and bread.'

Cathy stood up and refilled Josie's glass and poured a sherry for herself. She found that her hands were trembling. Josie sipped the sherry and said more calmly, 'I can see it now. When Mam died and the girls were growing up and wanted their own way too, it clashed with what he wanted. Then I was a bit more independent without Mam, and going out to work, and it didn't suit him. All these months, picking fights with me so we didn't speak, then he could stay out and I wouldn't ask where he was! He's been crafty.'

She sat staring at the bar of the fire and twisting her handkerchief nervously. 'I should have guessed. That fellow that brought our Eunice from Wales . . . He told her he slept in the cab so I was urging him to come and sleep here, but he seemed embarrassed and made some excuse. When he went, Walter said to me, "You stupid bitch! Anyone but you would know he had a girlfriend here to stay with."

'I said, "But he's a respectable married man," and he said, "Maybe he's married to a miserable cow like you, and no one would blame him having another woman." Even then the penny didn't drop with me. I must be stupid.'

'You're not stupid, Josie,' Cathy said indignantly. 'You just didn't expect this sort of thing to happen.'

'It was the things he said,' her friend said with a sob. 'He said, "What sort of a life have I had? Lumbered for years with your old mother, then when we get rid of her you want to bring your loony sister here. You're lucky I stayed so long, with that and your nagging."'

'The rat!' Cathy exclaimed. 'He just wants to justify himself. What a thing to say!

'I know. I'd have thought more of him if he'd just told me about the woman and gone, without saying that sort of thing.'

'And he has actually gone?'

'Yes, he had his suitcase packed all ready. It's all been planned. He starts the new job on Monday, and I had a look after he'd left and he must have been sneaking stuff out for weeks. He didn't give me my wages last night, just put a pound down before he went. He said he'd send the same every week, but if he heard I'd been calling him he'd send nothing.'

'You'll manage, Josie,' Cathy comforted her. 'Would you like a cup of tea?'

'I'd rather have more sherry,' she said. 'It's doing wonders for me.'

'Then we'll finish the bottle,' Cathy said, relieved to see her less upset. She filled their glasses to the brim and said cheerfully, 'When the sherry's finished, we'll start on the port.'

Josie talked for a while about Eunice, and about Edie, but she kept coming back to the subject of Walter, remembering signs of his infidelity that she had missed or speculating about the other woman. 'Whoever she is, I wish her joy of him,' she said, but again she wept bitterly.

They heard Kate's footsteps in the lobby, and then her voice calling: 'Mam.'

Josie stood up. 'I'll go before the others come in,' she said. 'I don't want to see anyone.'

'Will you be all right?'

'I'll be fine,' Josie said. 'I should sleep after all that sherry.' She managed a faint grin, and Cathy hugged her impulsively.

'It's a shame it had to end like this, but you'll be all right, Jose. You've got good girls and I'm always here, you know.'

She went with Josie to her own door, and came back just as Sarah and John arrived, closely followed by Greg. Cathy said nothing about Josie's trouble until she and Greg were alone, then she wept as she told him. 'I was never all that struck on Walter but I never imagined he'd do something like this. And saying that about Mrs Mellor's death – that they'd "got rid of" her!'

'I think you hit the nail on the head when you said he was trying to justify himself,' said Greg. 'He's probably ashamed of what he's doing, and looking for someone else to blame for it.'

'I hope he has a terrible life with this woman, whoever she is,' Cathy said vindictively. 'I hope she never gives him a minute's peace, then he'll realize how well off he was with Josie.'

'We'll have to do all we can to help her, but she's no weakling. She'll manage, once she gets over the shock.'

Josie came in to see Cathy again the next morning, and already she was making plans. 'Our Eunice is very happy with those ladies in Wales so I'll leave her for now. Kids are starting to come back home, but she'll be better off there. I'll bring our Mary here and ask the landlord if Edie can have her house, because she doesn't like living with Bert's mother.'

'How is Mary now?'

'She's fine – well, she's not doing any of those things, but she needs watching. Sophie says she doesn't seem able to make her mind up about anything, but she's all right if you tell her what to do,' Josie said. 'She's gone back to work, you know, and the girls in the overall factory are very good with her.'

'I think it's a good idea to bring her here, because that way you'll have Sophie back home as well and she's such a help to you.'

Josie smiled grimly. '*He's* probably thinking I'm sitting here breaking my heart, but I'm already glad he's gone.'

'That's the spirit,' Cathy said. 'And any time you feel downhearted, there's another bottle of sherry in the cupboard.'

'That did me the world of good last night,' Josie said, smiling, but the smile faded fast. 'This'll be a nice titbit for the gossips.'

'It'll only be a nine days' wonder, if that,' Cathy consoled her. 'There's so much else going on these days.'

As Cathy had predicted, Walter's departure was soon replaced as a topic of conversation. Several young men from the street had gone to France with the British Expeditionary Force in September, and letters were starting to arrive from them, and were proudly displayed.

The shipping losses were a constant topic of conversation, especially as three men from the street had already lost their lives at sea.

The children who had been evacuated were beginning to trickle back home as the threat of bombing seemed unfounded. And by Christmas most of them were back.

Cathy's story, that Kate was too near to leaving school to be evacuated, had been accepted, and only Greg knew that it was not the truth. Cathy had not even told her mother what Kate's teacher had said to her.

The teacher had asked Cathy to come to see her and had said forthrightly, 'Kate is eligible for evacuation with the school but I don't think any teacher should be asked to take responsibility for her. She is not advanced academically but she is very – mature. Perhaps you will make your own arrangements for her?'

Anger had flooded through Cathy but she had replied coolly. 'I had no intention of letting Kate go to strangers,

Miss Jones. I have a friend in Morecambe who is anxious to take her if we wish her to go.' But no matter how angry she felt, or how quick her response, Cathy had been upset by the teacher's words. They confirmed what she already feared; that Kate's love of attention was making her encourage the boys who flocked around her, even at her age, and giving her a reputation as a flirt.

Cathy and Greg had taken Kate aside and told her of the teacher's words and the bad reputation she was risking by her behaviour. She stood before them, looking demure and repentant and allowing her eyes to fill with tears which dropped artistically on to her clasped hands.

'I'm just friendly with people,' she said pathetically. 'The teachers are just bad-minded.'

'Well, just be more careful, love,' Greg said. 'Consider how what you do appears to others. We know you don't mean any harm, but don't give the wrong impression.'

'What an actress,' Cathy said, when Kate had gone. 'I'm sure she'd do well on the stage but that's the last sort of life I'd choose for her. By God, Greg, I'm going to keep a close watch on her from now on.'

Meanwhile Kate had run over to see Josh. She had been alarmed by her parents' searching questions, and although she felt she had successfully fooled her father, was not quite sure about her mother. She *was* quite sure, though, that she would always receive uncritical love and admiration from Josh.

Chapter Thirty-Five

Eileen, Joe and Terry each wrote to Sarah. Eileen was suffering badly from homesickness but made a brave attempt to be cheerful in her letter. Sarah decided to write back immediately, and send her some hand cream and cigarettes to cheer her up.

Terry was obviously unused to writing letters. His large untidy scrawl covered two pages, but gave little news about his new life, except that after "square bashing" he had discovered muscles he didn't know he had. He signed off: "Love, Terry."

Joe's handwriting was neater. He asked about Sarah's health, and about her family. He said that Terry had taken to Army life like a duck to water, and was very popular with the other men. "I should be used to being away from home," he wrote, "but I enjoyed those last few months very much and miss my family and friends in Liverpool a great deal."

He was concerned about Eileen, but thought that the first few weeks would be the worst for her and she would soon settle down. He signed his letter, "Yours affectionately, Joe", and she saw a letter he had written to Anne signed in the same way.

Sarah was uncertain what to do about sending parcels to Terry and Joe, but solved the problem by contributing to the parcels sent by the Fitzgerald family.

Maureen was manageress of a wool shop and warned that it would soon be in short supply, so Sarah bought wool of every colour, including khaki, and made balaclavas and gloves to go with the cigarettes and chocolate she contributed. She also wrote cheerful, friendly letters to both Terry and Joe.

She herself was feeling far from cheerful at this time. There was a feeling of anti-climax when the threatened raids failed to occur, and when being at war seemed to mean chiefly difficulties and irritations. Having to remember never to put on a light until the blackout curtains were drawn, and having Air Raid Wardens banging on the door and shouting, "Put out that light," if the slightest chink of light showed. Stumbling home in the blackout, bumping into lamp-posts and falling over obstacles, or finding unexpected shortages of ordinary goods such as batteries for torches.

Sarah's depression, though, was chiefly caused by her poor health which was made worse by overwork. Mabel had gone to train as a nursing auxiliary, and Mrs Dyson's sister was now in charge of the shop. She was a slave driver whose constant cry was "Don't stand about" if Anne or Sarah stopped for a moment.

She did no work herself, but interfered when they were serving customers and complained that they were slow and inefficient. 'If they were any quicker, the place'd go on fire,' a customer said, and Anne and Sarah felt that they had never worked so hard before.

Their day began at eight o'clock, and they rarely left the shop before eight at night. Hetty had departed for a munitions factory and Sarah was now working full-time again. Often when she reached home at night she was too tired to eat or do anything but lie on the sofa.

'Do you have any breaks?' John asked her one night.

'Three-quarters of an hour for dinner,' she said wearily.

'That's ridiculous,' he said. 'You'll have to stand up to her. I'll have a word with Anne.'

Sarah lifted her head in surprise. 'When will you see her?'

He looked self-conscious. 'I pass their house going to work,' he said. 'I sometimes see Anne. You should get together and demand more help in the shop, and have something done about this battleaxe.'

'I think you should too,' Cathy said. 'See Mrs Dyson and tell her.'

The next day Anne and Sarah went together to where Mrs Dyson was filling custard cases in the bakery, and made their complaint. Mrs Dyson rather nervously promised to speak to her sister, and to get more help in the shop.

'I don't think she'll do anything,' Anne said. 'I think she's afraid of Miss Meers. If nothing's done, Sarah, I think we should leave.'

'Our John said that.'

'We'll have to go into the Forces anyway, or be directed into industry before long,' Anne said. 'You'd never pass a medical for the ATS or the WAAFs, and I'm not keen on going after what I've heard from Eileen. If we got a job in a factory doing war work, we'd be doing as much for the war effort, wouldn't we?'

Sarah's parents were both there when she arrived home. She told them what Anne had said.

'I think she's right,' said Greg. 'See what happens about your request, and if nothing is done, give in your notice. It doesn't matter if you have a week or two at home before you find another job.'

Miss Meers was annoyed when her sister timidly told her about the complaint by Anne and Sarah, and after a blazing row with her, they both gave in their notice and left the following week. They both applied to the Meccano factory which was now busy with work for the Ministry of Defence. Anne was accepted, but Sarah failed the medical examination.

She took her employment cards to the Labour Bureau and obtained clerical work with the Ministry of Defence. She was happy there although she missed Anne.

Sarah was puzzled by the situation between Anne and John. She was sure that Anne cared for him, and equally sure that he was interested in Anne, but the affair seemed to make no progress. She spoke about it to her grandmother, and told her that she wondered whether she should try to give matters a push.

'Don't rock the boat, love,' Sally advised. 'Let them work things out for themselves. You might just do more harm than good.'

Sarah took her advice but she was often strongly tempted to ask a few questions of them.

John was having a difficult time at work, having to endure ostracism by the men he worked with who ignored him except to make cutting remarks about Russia.

'I see your pals are doing a good job of carving up poor little Poland, with their German pals,' he was told when

Russia joined Germany in conquering Poland. There were even more savage comments when Russia invaded Finland in November. One man whose brother had died when the *Royal Oak* had been sunk at Scapa Flow was particularly bitter.

At first John tried to correct them and put his point of view, but soon realized it was useless and simply said nothing. Nevertheless he was hurt by the unfounded accusations.

His work had given him some knowledge of building structure and he had enrolled in the Rescue Service where he was learning how to rescue casualties from bombed buildings, although so far there had been no air raids.

To Sarah the war seemed remote at this time. The Pathé Gazette news reels showed the funeral of German and English airmen killed in the raid on the Firth of Forth, and pictures of marching troops in France, but events nearer home seemed more important.

There were often men in uniform at church, at home on weekend leave, and when the twenty to twenty-two-year-old men were called up, three more of her dancing partners disappeared into the Army or Air Force, but so far there had been no casualties among her friends.

She sympathized with the grief and worry of people in the district who had men at sea as the fighting there became more ferocious, but no one she was close to was involved, and her new job and Walter's flight and Peggy's new lodgers seemed more interesting.

Walter had not sent any money to Josie since he left, although she was managing make ends meet with Mary's and Sophie's wages and her own money from the catering jobs. Edie was furious at her father for abandoning his family.

'I'd have thought she'd be on Walter's side,' Cathy said. 'She was always his favourite and very fond of him, wasn't she?'

Josie smiled cynically. 'Twelve months ago she would've been,' she said, 'but she's a married woman herself now.'

When no money had arrived from Walter by the first week in December, Edie took matters into her own hands and later came in to tell Cathy and Sarah the story.

She said that she had taken the tram to Prescot and walked to the BIC factory and waited outside, but so many men came out she decided that it was hopeless to look for her father and was just going back to the tram when she saw him in a shop buying cigarettes.

'I hid round the corner,' she said, 'and followed him. He let himself in with a key to a four-roomed house in Rainhill. I knocked, and when he opened the door I pushed in.'

'He must have got a shock!' Cathy said.

'Shock! He went like a sheet. I didn't half tell him what I thought of him, and he was saying: "I haven't had no spare cash." And I told him, "You had enough for cigarettes and sweets because I seen you buying them, and not an 'apenny for your own children." '

'What an excuse,' Cathy said indignantly. 'His family should be his first consideration.'

'That's what I told him,' Edie said. 'And a bit more besides. And then this little scrag end of a woman with peroxide hair come rushing out. She screeched at me, "I can see why he left you lot." '

'Impudent thing!' Sarah exclaimed. 'What did you say, Edie?'

'I didn't say nothing. I just give her a clout she won't forget in a hurry.' Edie began to laugh. 'I knocked her flying into a plant stand and she fell on the floor with the aspidistra on top of her. You should have seen her little weasely face peeping through the leaves, and soil all over her!'

'What did your father say?'

'Nothing. He just stood there with his mouth open, and I scarpered quick before he come to.'

The next day a card for a catering job came for Cathy and she went to see if Josie had received one. She was scrubbing her front step but stood up and wiped her hands on her sacking apron, and said that a card had come for her also. She was still very thin and pale, but Cathy thought she looked better than she had done for some time.

Josie said she did feel better. 'I know where I stand, and it's much pleasanter in the house. Our poor Mary hardly speaks, but she sits and smiles at everybody and seems happy.'

'Come in for a cup of tea when you've finished the step,'

Cathy said, and when Josie came in later they laughed together about Edie's sortie to Prescot.

'She was upset about what he said about Mary, all the same,' Josie said. 'Did she tell you?'

'No. She just told us what she'd said to him.'

'Shows she was upset,' Josie commented. 'He said he might see me in the street when I go to visit my loony sister in Rainhill Asylum.'

'Rotter!' Cathy exclaimed. 'Pity there wasn't another aspidistra for *him*!' They looked at each other and began to laugh.

Cathy was indignant that John had been refused for the Services but secretly she was relieved. She prayed that the war would end before Mick was old enough to go. She felt that all her family were doing their bit for the war effort. Greg was still busy at the First Aid Post giving first aid training to the many volunteers, and John was training with the Rescue Squad.

Mick had less to do as a messenger as more telephone links were installed, but he still carried some messages and was often on night duty. Sarah was on a fire watching rota, and Cathy herself was now a member of the WVS.

Meanwhile she worried about Sarah's health, Kate's flightiness, and the knowledge that the shipping losses must mean even greater shortages and difficulty in finding food, as well as sorrow for the seamen's families.

Sally had known a period of great hardship at one stage in her married life, when she had to scrape together pennies to buy food and coal. Since then she had always kept a well-stocked store cupboard and a full coal cellar.

As soon as her means permitted, Cathy had followed her mother's example and so far she was not affected by the shortage of sugar, but in early November butter and bacon became rationed to four ounces for each person.

The weather seemed to become worse every day. Coal could not be spared for bedroom fires and every morning the inside of the window panes was covered with frost flowers. The frost on the ground and the roofs was so severe that it looked like snow, and soon that came too, falling so thickly that it was several feet deep in places.

Sarah and Cathy between them had made woollen hats

and scarves, and warm socks and gloves for all the family, but in the bitter cold, with blizzards and icy winds, the plight of more poorly dressed people was pitiful. John gave away his gloves and scarf and later even his overcoat, and Cathy emptied the house of any clothes that could be classed as surplus.

The family joked that they were afraid to go to work in case they came home to find all their clothes gone, but they willingly parted with anything they could possibly spare. Later in the war, when make do and mend was the order of the day, Cathy thought wistfully of the use she could have made of those clothes, but the thought was always followed by the memory of her father's maxim: "Their need is greater than mine", and she had no regrets.

Men coming home on leave told of incredible hardships in unheated camps with no facilities for drying wet clothes, and one of Peggy's grandsons reported sick with frostbite in his toes after a night spent on a Scottish hillside without food or shelter, as the supply lorries were unable to get through to them.

Peggy had soon solved the mystery of her lodgers, or thought she had. 'He's been a Major, all right, out in India,' she said. 'But I think he got thrown out of the Army. He hasn't got no pension anyway, and they don't seem to have two ha'pennies to rub together. She's more of a lady than what he is a gentleman, and she told me her father had plenty of money at one time but made unwise investments.'

'Is her father still alive?' asked Sally.

'No, he died three months after they got married, and I'll tell you what I think – I think His Nibs came home from India on his uppers, and seen what he thought was a cushy number, a single woman living with her well-off father. So he married her, and then the old fellow died and there was no money.'

'He'd lost it?' Sally said. 'On these investments.'

'He'd gambled it,' Peggy said. 'Though there's always money for the Major to get drunk, although they live on the smell of an oil rag. I heard him one night when he was sozzled giving the pay out about her father and the gee gees.'

'Poor woman, it's not her fault,' Sally said.

'No, but he takes it out on her because he was disappointed. She waits on him hand and foot, too, and he gets all the food that's going. She tells me she only has a poor appetite, but she soon finished a plate of scouse one day when she was in with me while he was out.'

'Poor soul,' Sally said. 'Have you been round to Meg's today?'

Peggy's face lit up. 'Yes, I went round this morning. Willie's brought his last in the house because it's too cold to work in the shed, and Meg's helping him with the cobbling. Handing him things and rubbing dubbin on some boots. She's made up.'

Sally smiled. 'I saw them out together on Sunday and they looked very happy,' she said. 'They're very snug in that little house, and it's nice that Willie works at home.'

'Aye, that was one reason I let him marry her,' Peggy said.

Sarah's general health improved but the stiffness in her joints was worse after she had struggled through snow drifts and arrived home wet through. Her grandmother made her a red flannel vest and red flannel knee caps to wear under her stockings. She also wore strips of red flannel round her wrists.

'I won't click with anyone in the office in these,' she said ruefully to Anne.

'Not even Reggie,' Anne laughed. 'I should think he'd like something different, like red flannel.'

'We had a good laugh today,' Sarah said. 'We had air raid drill, and we had to go down to the basement and put our gas masks on, and Reggie said to us that Mr Daulby looked better with his on than without it! When we came upstairs he said he thought Daulby should keep his on and said to him: "Don't you think we should keep these on, Mr Daulby? To know how to work in them."

'Mr Daulby said, quite seriously, "No, Reginald. We won't be expected to work throughout a gas attack." '

'He always rises, doesn't he?'

'Yes, and sometimes Reggie sails close to the wind with him. He was saying today, "I don't want a posthumous VC, thank you," and Daulby said he was proud to fight for his country in the last war. Reggie had told us Daulby was in the stores all through it so he said: "I wouldn't mind a safe job as a cook or in the stores," and Daulby shut up.'

'You like that job, don't you, Sarah? I told the lads when I wrote that you looked a lot better since we moved.'

Sarah still wrote to the three Fitzgeralds who were away from home, and as Joe had predicted, Eileen wrote back to say that she was a lot happier. Terry and Joe had finished their training and were expected home on leave but Joe was suddenly promoted to Lance-Corporal and sent on another course, and Terry came alone.

'Too good to be true that they'd get home together,' Anne said, 'but it might be better for Mum if they come separately. Spread it out a bit.'

Terry looked very smart when he arrived. His uniform was immaculate, his boots shone like mirrors, and he walked with his shoulders thrown back and his head erect.

'You have to walk like this or break your neck,' he told Sarah. 'They give you a cap with a peak like a cheesecutter when you arrive, and the tailor cuts it so that you've got to hold your head back to see where you're going.'

He was disappointed to find so few of his friends still at home. 'They're all over the place,' Sarah said. 'And in all different services. You should see the variety of uniforms in church on Sunday when people come home on leave.'

'I've hardly seen our Anne since I came home,' he complained. 'She seems to be either working or in bed.'

'She's working very long hours,' Sarah said. 'All the factories are mad busy.'

'I haven't seen much of Stephen either. All he thinks of is wangling to be off at the same time as Claire.'

Sarah laughed. 'Yes, he's badly smitten,' she said. 'But she's a nice girl.'

'Another good man gone wrong,' Terry said with a grin. 'My mother seems quite annoyed with Joe for getting made up to Lance-Corporal. She said she wanted us to stick together and look after each other.' He roared with laughter. 'I'd like to see the fellows' faces if they heard that one.'

'How is Joe?'

'Oh, the same old Joe,' Terry said carelessly. 'Not much to say, but I think he's doing a line with a girl in the NAAFI.

He can always get cigarettes. I'll miss them when I go back and he's not there.'

Sarah was surprised at the stab of regret she felt, but Mick came in then, closely followed by John, and the moment passed.

She went to the cinema once with Terry, and once to the ceilidhe with Anne and him, but most of his leave was spent visiting relations. It was a common complaint by men on leave at this time that they were expected to visit their often numerous families, once to say hello and then to say good-bye, and the Fitzgerald family was extensive.

Anne and Sarah were to accompany Terry to the station when he left, and before that he came to see the Redmonds. Sarah had visited a photographer's in London Road for a studio portrait on her eighteenth birthday and a framed copy stood on the sideboard. Terry picked it up. 'This is good, isn't it? Have you got another copy, Sarah?'

'Yes, I got three.'

Her mother said, 'They're in that folder in the sideboard drawer, I think, love.'

She pulled open the drawer and Terry took the folder from her and pulled out a photograph.

'That's great. OK, Sarah? I can have it?' She nodded, and he put it in his wallet. 'I'll pin it up above my bed,' he said, grinning.

'In the gallery?' she inquired dryly.

'Ah, no, *alanah*, the one and only,' he said, with a grin.

At the station he kissed both Anne and Sarah in turn, lifting them up and swinging them round exuberantly while a group of Cheshire Regiment men whistled in admiration and envy. 'Don't be greedy, Mick,' one of them shouted.

Sarah was silent and thoughtful as she and Anne travelled home. She had seen a glance pass between Anne and her mother when Terry asked for the photograph and hoped that they were not jumping to conclusions. She would have been aghast to know that her silence was making Anne think that she was upset about Terry's departure.

Although she liked him, and had been proud to be seen with him, Sarah felt that events were rushing her along faster than she wished, or than Terry realized.

Chapter Thirty-Six

Kate was due to leave school at Easter and Cathy was determined to find her a job where she would not be with young men. One of the shops in town would be best, she decided, Blackler's or C & A Modes, where the staff and customers were predominantly female.

She cunningly stressed how smart Kate would look in a dark dress and white collar when she suggested the idea to her. Kate liked the plan and a position was obtained for her without much difficulty in C & A Modes.

The girl had been disappointed when the plan to send her to Norah in Morecambe for safety's sake was cancelled, but Cathy was thankful that it had not been necessary when Norah told her that many airmen were stationed there.

Cathy's friendship with Norah had been resumed as though there had never been a break in it, and it was a great comfort to her that she could write quite freely to her friend about her worries, knowing that Norah would understand.

Letters from Mary in America came less frequently now. 'Having too much of a good time,' Sally said caustically, and Cathy agreed.

Mary's few letters were filled with details about her little dog and its antics, and about her beach parties and other social events, many of which seemed to take place out of doors.

Cathy had written to reassure her sister that their mother was not suffering any ill effects from the bitterly cold weather, and was not short of food or coal. Mary's comments in reply were perfunctory and Cathy wondered whether she had needed any reassurance or whether indeed she even thought about them.

She mentioned Mary's latest letter when she wrote to Norah, and about the way her sister seemed to dwell on the sunny conditions in California while they were suffering such a winter. Norah wrote back, "Mary was always insensitive, but don't let it get you down, Cath. She would swop all the sunshine etcetera to be over here with Greg, I'll bet."

Cathy smiled at the letter. Only Norah, the friend of her youth, could make such a comment. Her mother had never noticed Mary's attempts to entice Greg, and he had always thought he just happened to be the right sex to interest Mary, Cathy thought in happy innocence.

She burned Norah's letter, feeling more cheerful, and she and Josie worked at a Rotary Dinner that evening.

Cissie turned up with a large dressing on her nose. 'It was the bloody blackout,' she explained. 'The bedroom curtains fell down, so I couldn't put the light on, and it was pitch dark. I held me arms out in front of me so I wouldn't bang into anything but I didn't know the door was open. Me arms went one each side of it and I banged me blasted nose on the edge.'

All the women laughed as they pictured the scene and Cissie was annoyed. 'Youse lot are as bad as Bert,' she said. 'Lying there laughing his leg off he was, and when I yelled at him he said, "First time I knew your bloody nose was longer than your arms." '

Cathy smiled now when she thought of it and Josie said later that she had been the same all day. 'It'd be worth doing the job for the laughs, even if we never got paid, wouldn't it?'

The bitter winter was ending and everyone felt more cheerful as longer days and better weather arrived. Joe Fitzgerald came home on leave and arrived with Anne to see Sarah and her family. Cathy welcomed him warmly and congratulated him on his stripe, while Sarah, suddenly shy, went to make tea.

Her mother was eagerly questioning Joe about the war news when she came back. 'Do you think it's true the Germans are starving?' she asked. 'They did try to bump Hitler off last November, didn't they?'

'That was only a few top men,' he said, 'I think most of the Germans are behind him.'

'I think it'll just fizzle out,' Anne declared, and Cathy smiled at her gratefully.

'Mick's going as soon as he's finished his exams,' she explained to Joe. 'Unless it finishes before then.'

To Sarah it seemed that her mother monopolized the conversation, which was unlike her, and Joe scarcely had a chance to speak directly to her until Cathy went to refill the teapot.

Then he said quietly, 'You look much better, Sarah. Terry said you did, and I agree. I saw him at the Barracks before I came home.'

'He's got your photo up over his bed, y'know,' Anne said, laughing.

Joe glanced at the photograph on the sideboard. 'It's a good likeness. Terry said some of the other men are threatening to ask you for a date. There are a few Liverpool men there.'

'Terry saw it when he was home,' Sarah said, blushing and speaking in a low voice. 'Mum gave him a copy.'

Joe looked up quickly and their eyes met, but before they could speak Cathy came back and began to ask Joe about the food and conditions in the camp he had been sent to. Before long Anne stood up. 'We'll have to get on, Joe. Don't forget the Connollys.'

She turned to Cathy. 'My Aunt Minnie Connolly is my mother's older sister and Terry didn't go to see them. She had a right cob on, and Mum told me to make sure Joe goes there.'

'She's her brother's keeper,' he said, nodding towards Anne and smiling at Sarah, and the next moment they had gone.

'I like that lad,' Cathy said, and Sarah silently agreed.

Joe was only on a week's leave and Sarah saw him again only briefly before he returned to the Battalion. His mother tried to keep him with her as much as possible, and Anne told Sarah that Mrs Fitzgerald had dreamt that Joe had been killed. 'We haven't told him, but that's why she's clinging to him so much.'

'You don't think she's had a premonition?' Sarah said fearfully.

Anne brushed the idea aside. 'No, of course not. It's just that her mind's on such things now.'

'It's a phoney war on land anyway, everyone's saying.

All the news seems to be about shipping losses, ours and theirs. My gran has to come to our house to hear the news bulletins, because Josh gets so upset if she has them on. He's worried about air raids.'

'A woman at work was saying that they'll never be able to bomb us because we've got the Pennines behind us, and if they tried to come round the coast they'd be shot down before they ever got here.'

'I hope she's right,' Sarah said. 'I'll have to tell Josh that or get Kate to tell him. He'll believe her.'

Kate was very much enjoying her new job, she told her mother. She omitted to mention that what she really enjoyed was walking home through the city streets and meeting servicemen of many nationalities who were temporarily in Liverpool.

Kate had inherited not only her mother's brown eyes and dimples, but also her Aunt Mary's straight nose and full-lipped sensual mouth, and a sidelong, provocative glance which Cathy would have remembered seeing Mary using, if Kate had not been careful to hide it from her mother.

She still belonged to the dancing school, and sometimes performed at concerts, although not at the parish rooms.

She had appeared twice in the Christmas concert there once to sing "Bless This House" and once to do a tap dancing number. For that she had worn a brief, full-skirted dress, which she had worn in the chorus line at a dancing school production. She had finished her dance with a high kick which had scandalized the members of the Women's Confraternity sitting in the front rows.

She had not been asked to appear again but had said airily that she didn't want to dance for those old fades anyway.

Cathy worried about her, but Greg was proud of her and insisted that she was only young and skittish and would soon grow more circumspect. Sally disapproved of Kate, Cathy knew, and she could only relieve her worries by writing to Norah.

I'm worried but I can't say why. There's nothing I can put my finger on, just a lot of small things that make me uneasy about her. She seems to be able to do wonders with her pocket money. Mam watches her like a hawk in case she accepts money from Josh, and says that she is sure that she doesn't, but I don't know how she manages to buy so much.

I found a pile of hair brightening sachets in her drawer when I was putting ironing away and they cost threepence each, but she says a girl at work had stopped using them and given them to her. I wouldn't have let her use them, but by the time we'd argued about how she could afford them, I just couldn't face another row and let it pass. I can see now why Mam was so strict with Mary, or tried to be, although she usually managed to get her own way in the end.

Cathy was especially thankful to have Norah's friendship now because she felt that her own family were shutting her out. She was sure that both John and Sarah had fallen in love but neither of them confided in her and she was hurt, especially as John and Greg seemed close and Sarah still spent a great deal of time with her grandmother. Cathy thought that John probably talked things over with his father and Sarah confided in her grandmother but neither Greg nor Sally said anything to Cathy and she was too proud to ask.

The truth was that neither Sarah nor John felt that they had anything to tell their mother. Although Terry wrote fairly often to Sarah and signed the letters "Love, Terry," they were short and flippant and not at all lover-like. Joe's letters were brotherly in tone, and he finished them "Yours affectionately."

John knew that he was falling more and more in love with Anne but felt it was only fair to her to keep silent. He had no regrets about fighting in Spain, but now found himself out of sympathy with the men at the Club yet still an outcast from other people he knew, especially as he had tried several times to join up and been rebuffed.

On April the ninth German troops invaded Norway and Denmark. At first people found it hard to believe the news as these were neutral countries, but suddenly it seemed the "phoney war" was over.

Terry came home on weekend leave later in the month, very excited because Irish Guards had already left, he thought for Norway.

He arrived very late on Friday night and came to see Sarah on Saturday afternoon with an invitation to tea from his mother. She got ready quickly and went back with him to his house, after first taking him over to see her grandmother.

Terry was in high spirits, describing how crates of beer were taken on the train by the other ranks and cases of champagne loaded for the officers as the Irish Guards departed for Norway.

'They'll be legless before they ever get there,' Sally commented, but Terry laughed heartily.

'Not them,' he said. 'It takes a lot to get those fellows drunk.'

Sarah had always been made welcome in the Fitzgerald house, but there was an extra warmth in Mrs Fitzgerald's manner as she put her arms round the girl today and kissed her. She was a gentle, pious woman, deeply loved by her family, but already showing signs of the disease which would soon claim her life.

Sarah saw Anne briefly, but she was working the two o'clock to ten o'clock shift and soon had to leave. Helen and Tony arrived for tea, and Stephen's fiancée Claire, and afterwards Helen and Tony, Claire and Stephen, and Sarah and Terry went in a group to a ceilidhe.

Terry's high spirits set the tone for all of them and they were a noisy merry group, dancing every dance and thoroughly enjoying themselves. Sarah was conscious of the admiring glances when she and Terry were dancing and felt proud, but still had the feeling of being swept along faster than she wished.

A tall, erect old man who took the entrance fee, an ex-Welsh Guardsman now a commissionaire at a cinema, made a great fuss of Terry. 'You can't mistake a Guardsman,' he said when they arrived. 'Smartest body of men in the British Army.'

'I'll bet you say that to all the fellows,' Terry joked, but Mr Powell was not offended.

He came up to their group at the interval and asked Terry about his training, then as the music began again, he shook hands before leaving. 'Look after him,' he said to Sarah. 'You're a lucky girl.'

Terry put his arm round her and laughed down at her as the old man walked away. 'D'you hear that, Sar? You've got to look after me.'

'Silly old fool!' Helen exclaimed. 'Saying she's a lucky girl. *You're* the lucky one, Terry. Sarah would have been married long ago if she'd been able to decide between the fellows who fell for her.'

'And after all that she's finished up with our Terry, poor girl,' Stephen said, laughing and thumping Terry on his back.

Sarah smiled but said nothing. She felt that she would be glad to be home to sort out her thoughts, even though she was enjoying herself so much.

Before the end of the evening Helen whispered to her that the doctor had confirmed that she was pregnant and that the baby was due in November. 'We haven't told anyone yet. We'll tell Tony's mum just after Terry goes back, to cheer her up,' she said. 'But even then I'd like just to keep it in the family for a while.'

They all went their separate ways after the dance. Terry walked home with Sarah, his arm about her waist. There was no moon and when they reached Egremont Street they stood in complete darkness to say goodnight, holding each other close. Terry kissed her, gently at first then more urgently. Briefly she thought of Ronald's rubbery lips, and contrasted them with Terry's firm kisses.

After a moment he raised his head and drew in a long breath. 'That was great,' he whispered. She could only dimly see his face but saw the flash of his teeth as he smiled at her. 'Which Mass are you going to?'

'Nine o'clock,' she said.

'Right. I'll meet you there.' Then, in a quieter tone, 'I think I'd better go, Sar.' He kissed her again, his lips pressing firmly on hers and his hand behind her head, then released her and walked away.

She heard a muffled curse and a laugh as he bumped into something, then his footsteps died away and she went into the house and straight up to bed.

She was glad to be alone, to think things over. Helen's confidences and her remark about keeping the news in the family, as though Sarah already belonged to it, had jolted her. She remembered too Mrs Fitzgerald's warm welcome, and the general assumption that she and Terry were a couple.

Is this what I want? she wondered. She liked Terry as she liked all the Fitzgerald family, but was that enough? I'd like to make my own decision but other people seem to be making it for me, she thought. And yet perhaps others could see that she and Terry were suited to each other.

They came from the same background and their families liked each other, there would be no hassle about religion and Terry was a decent lad who would always treat her with respect, she thought. Yet did she love him? She remembered standing at the gate a little earlier. Terry's firm body when her arms were round him, and how warm and loving she had felt as his lips found hers.

But then she thought that he seemed to care nothing for books and poetry and all the things of the spirit that meant so much to her. The trouble is that I don't really know him properly, she decided. The best thing is to let things take their course. We can be a courting couple but not engaged, and if it doesn't work out when we know each other better, we can break it off and no harm done. With a sigh of relief she turned her pillow over and went to sleep.

He was waiting for her outside the church the following morning. His parents and Anne and Maureen had gone in, he said, but Stephen was working and had been to the seven o'clock Mass.

'Will you sit with our family?' he asked, and Sarah agreed without any misgivings. Anne had changed her work shift for the new week, so after Sarah had been back to the Fitzgeralds' for lunch and Terry had made preparations to leave, the girls went out for a walk while he spent some time alone with his parents.

Later Anne came with Sarah to the station to see Terry off, but tactfully went off to the bookstall for papers for him while they said goodbye. All along the platform couples embraced tearfully. Terry and Sarah held each other closely.

'You're my girl now, aren't you, Sarah?' he said, kissing her gently. 'I'll be going over there soon – I don't think I'll get home again before then, but we'll write often, won't we?'

Sarah kissed him and nodded, her eyes filling with tears. He wiped them away. 'Don't cry, sweetheart,' he said softly. 'I'll see you again soon.'

How often in the years to come did she think of those words and what had gone before them! But now the station was filling with steam from the engine and Anne was back with newspapers and chocolate for Terry. She kissed him goodbye with none of the exuberance of their last leave taking, and walked away, saying, 'I'll wait at the entrance, Sar.'

'All aboard,' the guard shouted. Terry stepped into a carriage but leaned from the window and kissed Sarah again as the train began to move. 'I like it,' he shouted. She carried away a memory of his laughing face and was smiling as she joined Anne.

Her spirits soon sank as the news from Norway began to trickle through. There seemed to be a great deal of confusion. Even the Prime Minister insisted that Narvik had not been taken by the Germans but another less important place, Larvic, but then the fall of Narvik was confirmed.

'If he doesn't know what's happening, there's not much chance for us to find out,' John said.

Sarah defended Mr Chamberlain indignantly. 'He did his best and saved us from war for a year, don't forget, and he's still working hard although he's a sick man. He suffers from gout, they said on the wireless.'

She was even more angry when on May the seventh a member of Parliament, one of Chamberlain's own party, stood up in the House of Commons and pointed at the Prime Minister, saying, 'In the name of God, go.'

Sarah was furious. 'Who does he think he is?' she demanded, 'Leo Amery. Who's ever heard of him? And people all over the world respect Chamberlain.'

Nevertheless, he resigned and a coalition party was formed, with Churchill as Prime Minister, but for a long time Sarah disliked him because he had taken Chamberlain's place. A few days later news came that

Hitler had invaded Belgium and Holland.

Terry had written to Sarah as soon as he returned to Barracks and she had replied, but they had exchanged only a few letters when late in May another was delivered just before she left for work.

It contained only one sheet of paper.

Darling Sarah,
This is it, love. We're off to France. Time to see if all that training was any good. Look after yourself and remember me in your prayers.
See you soon,

Your loving Terry.

She stood with the letter in her hand, her face pale and her fingers pressed to her lips.

'What is it?' Cathy exclaimed in alarm.

'Terry's gone to France.'

'Oh, my God,' Cathy cried, then said quickly, 'he'll be all right, love. Hitler's bitten off more that he can chew there.'

Sarah glanced at the clock. 'I'll have to go, Mum,' she said, but Cathy put her arm round her and kissed her before she left.

A letter card came from France, and Sarah wrote two letters to the address on it. The news from the Continent was confused. An announcement was made that the French were withdrawing to a prepared position to lure the Germans into a trap, but it soon became clear that the German Army was sweeping all before it. The Dutch had flooded large areas but they could do little against the large and well-equipped German Army and Air Force.

Everyone seemed quiet and subdued. 'If only we knew what was happening,' was the general feeling, and those with men in the British Expeditionary Force listened anxiously to every news bulletin though there was nothing to cheer them.

Rotterdam had been blitzed and the Dutch had surrendered, while the roads of Northern France were thronged with refugees, who were being machine gunned by German airmen.

Gradually the news began to seep through of the evacuation of the BEF from Dunkirk, but there was no news of Terry although a few men who had been in France began to arrive home on leave.

'We lost everything,' one of them told Greg, 'I was just glad to get home alive. They just kitted us out and sent us home out of the way, I reckon, while they sorted things out.'

On June the tenth Italy entered the war on the side of Germany, but most people were more concerned with other matters. The news item remained in Sarah's mind only because it was linked with another event. She heard it on someone's wireless set as she turned into Egremont Street. A few minutes later, as she reached Josie's house, she saw a policeman being admitted and heard loud screaming.

She dashed home for her mother and together they hurried over. Josie had stopped screaming and was sobbing. The policeman welcomed them thankfully. 'She's had a shock, missus,' he said to Cathy, who went and put her arms round Josie.

'It's our poor Mary,' she sobbed.

The policeman added, 'She was knocked down by a lorry. He didn't have no chance, with the blackout like, and her in dark clothes.'

'She was killed, Cath, right away.'

'She wouldn't suffer, Jose,' Cathy said. She looked meaningfully at the policeman over Josie's bent head, and said, 'She wouldn't know anything about it, would she?'

'No, big heavy lorry,' he said hastily. 'She was dead the minute it touched her.' He replaced his helmet and moved towards the door. 'I'll leave her with you, then, missus. Send down to the station later for – you know.'

Sarah went to the door with him and thanked him. 'It's a rotten job for you,' she said.

He sighed. 'Aye, and I've got to do it often. This little circle of light they allow from the headlamps doesn't give a driver a chance, especially if people are wearing dark clothes.'

Josie sincerely grieved for her sister. 'She had a rotten life,' she said to Cathy. 'She was only eighteen when she married that swine, and what he put her through twisted her mind. That arrest – it seemed to give her such a shock she just went very quiet like after it. I reckon the time she was here with us was the happiest she'd had since she was a girl at home.'

'Be thankful she had that then, Jose,' said Cathy. 'And a quick and merciful death.' And her friend seemed comforted.

Chapter Thirty-Seven

Men were arriving home on leave who had been evacuated with the BEF and the operation seemed complete, but still there was no word from Terry. Sarah was filled with foreboding. If all the men were home, what could have happened to him?

'We're storming heaven for him. God will keep him in His care,' Terry's mother told her. Mrs Fitzgerald and Maureen spent every possible moment in church, praying for his safety, and Anne told Sarah that she envied them their trust in God.

'I pray for him too, and my faith's a consolation to me, but I can't feel complete trust like Maureen and Mum, especially when I look round at what's happening in the world.'

A few days later Sarah was finishing her day's work and preparing to cover her machine when a note was brought to her desk. She recognized Joe Fitzgerald's handwriting and tore it open eagerly.

Dear Sarah,
We have not had word from Terry but I've been asking around the chaps who were with him at Boulogne, and it seems hopeful to me. Can I walk home with you and tell you? I am waiting outside by the bank.

Love, Joe

Sarah dashed to the window. It was criss-crossed with tape but she peeped between the strips and with a lift of her heart saw Joe outside.

She hurried through her work and soon she was able to go out and meet him. He smiled at her and gave her a brotherly kiss before taking her elbow as they crossed the road.

'Was it all right to send that note in?' he asked. 'I thought you might think it was Terry waiting when you saw the uniform.'

'It was thoughtful of you,' she said shyly.

'I've talked to a lot of chaps who were with him. I don't want to raise false hopes, Sarah,' Joe said, 'but from what I heard, I think he may have been captured. The wounded were taken off, you see, and men who were killed – well, mostly their bodies were seen or fellows saw them get it, but no one I talked to saw Terry.'

'But how could he be captured?' she said. 'I thought the Germans fired from a distance.'

'Some long range,' Joe said, 'but there were tanks and machine guns, and hundreds of Germans with rifles. Our fellows were covering the evacuation but were outnumbered in every way and had to draw back to be taken off by the Navy. There'd be pockets of men cut off and captured, and I think that's what happened to Terry. We'll just hope now we hear from him soon.'

'Would he be able to write if he was a prisoner?'

'Oh, yes,' Joe said. 'He'd be well treated – he'd have to be because of the Geneva Convention.'

'You must think I'm very ignorant,' she said apologetically, 'Dad never talked about the last war, and I haven't read much about it, and this war seems to be such a muddle. You hear different things every day and different versions in the papers or on the wireless.'

'No, I don't think you're ignorant, Sarah,' he said quietly.

They walked along in silence for a few minutes, then Sarah said, 'How's your mum, Joe?'

'Not very well,' he said. 'But she's not as worried as I expected about Terry.'

'She'll be glad to have you home.'

They had reached Egremont Street and she asked him to come in and see her mother. Cathy was pleased to see him and asked how long he was home. 'Only two more days,' he said. 'I had a job to wangle this.'

'It'll be a help to your poor mother to see you,' Cathy said. 'How is she?'

Joe glanced at Sarah, and told Cathy what he had told her and also about his grounds for hoping that Terry was a prisoner.

Sarah saw him again briefly outside church. He was seen off at the station by his brothers and she did not accompany them.

A week later, as Sarah was leaving for work, Anne came running down the street, waving an official-looking paper.

'He's a prisoner of war,' she shouted as soon as she drew near. 'This came. Terry's in a Stalag.' She flung her arms round Sarah. Cathy came out of the house and Sally from across the road, followed by several neighbours, so that the girls were the centre of a jubilant crowd.

'I'll have to go,' Sarah said finally, and Anne said that she must go back to her family.

'Stay off,' she urged Sarah. 'Come back with me.' But Sarah refused.

'No, it's your celebration,' she said. 'And, anyway, I'm in the middle of a document that's wanted urgently.' Anne looked surprised but hurried back to her family and Sarah set off for work.

She was not only confused about the war, but also about her own feelings. She was happy and relieved that Terry was safe but thought that she would have felt the same if it had been Stephen or Tony in the same situation. If it had been Joe – but she turned her mind quickly from the thought. Joe had always thought of her only as Terry's girl, she told herself, and felt ashamed that she could feel like this at such a time.

Resolutely she turned her thoughts from Joe and towards Terry, a prisoner-of-war, far from home, but she felt a hypocrite when people rejoiced for her, and unable to show the jubilation friends expected.

'You take it quietly,' one of the girls in the office said. 'If it was Peter found alive when I thought he was dead, I'd be turning handsprings.'

'This is Sarah's way,' another girl said. 'We're all different.'

France had surrendered and signed an Armistice with Germany, but the mood of dismay and bewilderment in Britain after Dunkirk had speedily altered to belligerence after a speech by Churchill in which he said, 'We shall fight them on the landing grounds, we shall fight in the fields and in the streets, we shall fight in the hills, we shall never surrender.'

On the day that France surrendered Cathy and Josie were working on a Rotary Lunch with Cissie. She announced that she was glad to hear the news. 'Foreigners!' she said with contempt. 'They're all the same. I'm sorry for them, like, but we're better off on our own. We've got our lads back and we know where we are now.'

There was a large photograph of Churchill on the wall with his cigar at a jaunty angle, and his feet planted wide apart. Cissie went over to it. 'Look at him, God love him,' she said. 'Like a bloody little bulldog. He's a match for any Jerry.'

Even Sarah had to admit that she felt safer with Churchill in charge. The two letters she had sent to France were returned to her by the Post Office, and a week later a letter card came from Terry from the Stalag. He had tried to make his writing smaller and neater, but all he could say on the card was that he was well and in good spirits, and looking forward to letters. He sent his regards to Sarah's family and signed it "Your loving Terry". Sarah and John and Cathy wrote to him immediately.

John was growing more and more frustrated and angry that he was not allowed to fight for his country, and he found a receptive listener in Anne. 'Why won't they have me?' he said. 'I'm an Englishman. I love my country, yet they won't let me fight for it. Everywhere I try I'm refused, just because I fought in Spain.'

'It's stupid,' she agreed.

'And what really makes me mad,' he said bitterly, 'is that some of the Varsity men who were in Spain are in the Foreign Office or the Intelligence Service. Of course they could pull strings through their families or old schoolfriends, yet I'm still treated like a traitor.'

'I should think people in Intelligence or the Foreign Office could do more harm if they were traitors than an ordinary soldier,' Anne said.

'Exactly,' he agreed. 'I know some fellows who don't want to fight. They say it's a Capitalist war, fought for money. I don't believe in war myself, I think there are better ways of solving problems, especially when you think of what happened last time, but now we *are* at war I'm keen to do my bit for England and they could use my experience.'

'Pity you can't pull strings. It's the class system again, isn't it? A man at work says the class system here is as bad as the caste system in India.'

'And at the moment I'm an Untouchable,' John said ruefully.

He envied Mick who had his future so clearly mapped out. The examinations for the Higher School Certificate were taking place, and when Mick had finished them he intended to go right into the Royal Air Force. He was eighteen years old in June and intended to register without waiting for the results of the examination. Early in July he was called for a medical examination.

'I suppose that's because I've been pestering them,' he said cheerfully. He was sent to Padgate near Warrington for the medical examination and inoculations, and issued with uniform and kit. Within a week he was sent to Morecambe and billeted in a guest house with five other men, not very far from Norah's place.

Cathy was delighted to hear that he was near enough to visit her friend, and received a letter from Norah inviting her to come for a few days and see Mick.

"I've got airmen billeted here," Norah wrote, "but Minnie and I have our own bedrooms, both with double beds, and if you and Greg would like to come, I could go in with Minnie and you could have my room."

Cathy accepted gratefully, and Greg came with her but had to return the same night, after seeing Mick drilling beside the road and talking to him at Norah's house. But Cathy stayed overnight and saw her son again before leaving. He seemed happy, had already made many friends and enjoyed drilling, even though they had only very old rifles with the firing pin filed down because they were too worn to be fired safely.

Now that Mick had gone away, Cathy found that she was not nearly as worried as when she was anticipating the departure. This was partly because she had so many other things to occupy her mind. The war news was bad. German planes were attacking shipping in the Channel and U-boats were taking a toll of shipping on the high seas.

Later, when queuing was a way of life, Cathy looked back on these days as almost a time of plenty, but when shortages were a new factor, life seemed very complicated.

She was worried about John's frustration and Sarah's situation with Terry away until the end of the war, and also about Greg whom she felt was overworking. Stan had never resumed all his responsibilities in the firm and Cathy was annoyed about the amount of work that was left to Greg.

'It's all very well, Stan looking after his health, but what about yours?' she demanded. 'I'll bet he's not doing any Civil Defence either.'

'I don't mind,' Greg said. 'I enjoy it.' But Cathy was still vexed.

'You look tired out,' she said. 'And then sitting up talking to John till all hours . . . I wish you'd learn sense.'

The news that Hitler was planning to invade England brought a mixed reaction. July the eighteenth was considered a likely date. On that morning Mrs Gunter was scrubbing her step when Sally came out to do her shopping.

'Did'ya hear the quare fella thinks he's invading us tonight?' Mrs Gunter called across to her.

'I hope it keeps fine for him,' Sally said.

'Let any dirty German put his foot on my step!' Mrs Gunter shouted. 'I'd give him a clout he'd never be the better of, and then I'd put me bucket over his head.'

Her next-door neighbour, a mouse-like little woman named Chandler, came out on her step. 'I've put a carving knife ready on the hatstand,' she said. 'My feller says anywhere I could reach up to to stab a German'd ruin him for life.'

Sally went off down the street, wishing that her lodger could take the same attitude as the women. Josh seemed to have completely lost his nerve. Street shelters had been provided but most people believed that they would be safer sheltering under the stairs, and Sally had cleared out the cupboard which ran back under hers.

She had put cushions in there, and blankets, and a tin of biscuits and a jerrycan of water. The first air raid warning sounded soon after midnight on June the twenty-fifth and as Sally came downstairs she was amazed to see Josh rush from the parlour and through to the kitchen. By the time she reached it he had dived under the stairs and was cowering at the extreme end of the cupboard with his arms cradling his head.

Sarah was on a fire-watching rota, but she was off that night and came over to see Sally.

'Are you all right, Grandma?' she called. Sally stepped quickly out of the cupboard and came to meet her. 'Don't come out,' said Sarah. 'Where's Josh?'

'He's in there,' Sally said, ushering her towards the door. 'Go back home, love.'

Sarah looked puzzled but obeyed. The drone of planes could be heard and searchlights criss-crossed the sky, but nothing happened and the All Clear was soon sounded.

Sally said goodnight curtly to Josh and went to bed. And she presumed that he had soon returned to his room. Sally said nothing about the incident, but every time the warning sounded Josh bolted like a rabbit to take refuge under the stairs.

The same thing happened each air raid warning, but Sally never discussed it with Josh or told anyone else.

On the night of August the seventeenth, when the air aid warning sounded just after midnight, Cathy brought Kate over to Sally. 'Can she stay with you, Mam?' she asked. 'We're all on duty.'

Josh was already cowering under the stairs but it was impossible for Sally to refuse so she talked loudly to Kate so that he would be warned. He was sitting on one of the stools Sally had provided when Kate crept in, and managed to talk normally to her for a while. Sally pulled closed the door which shut them off from the kitchen, to try to minimize the heavy drone of the bombers and the rattle of the anti-aircraft guns, and prayed that the raid would be over before Josh betrayed his cowardice to Kate.

Suddenly there were loud crumps as high-explosive bombs fell on the docks. Inside the house, crockery fell from shelves and pictures from the walls.

Kate flung herself into Sally's arms, and her grandmother held her close. 'All right, love,' she said. 'It'll soon be over.'

An unpleasant and unmistakable smell filled the air and Kate raised her head and wrinkled her nose in disgust.

'Josh has been to the lavatory,' she whispered, but Sally hushed her.

'It's with the house being disturbed,' she said firmly. 'Something to do with sewage.'

She spoke in a low voice and Kate gave her a sardonic glance but soon the All Clear sounded and Sally told her she could go as her mother would soon be home.

Josh remained under the stairs. Sally put a jug of warm water on the washstand which was behind a curtain in the parlour, then she went to the understairs cupboard.

'I've put some water in your room, Josh,' she said. 'Leave your clothes outside the door and I'll attend to them. I'm going to bed. Goodnight.'

He made no reply but later Sally heard him moving about for some time before she fell asleep. There were no clothes outside his door, but later when Sally went to the midden she discovered newspaper-wrapped parcels which must have contained the soiled clothes. She reflected that it was the best solution as Josh had plenty of clothes, and far less embarrassing for both of them. Now nothing need be said. And if Kate opens her mouth, she thought grimly, I'll soon close it for her.

She swept up the broken crockery and made breakfast, then called Josh. 'Only a pudding basin and two cups went,' she said cheerfully as he shuffled into the kitchen. 'I'll leave the pictures down, I think.'

Cathy arrived as they sat down to breakfast. 'Are you all right, Mam?' she asked. 'Kate said some crockery was broken. I told her she should have swept it up for you.'

'I sent her to bed,' Sally said. 'She needed the rest for work this morning, and it didn't take me five minutes.'

Cathy had simply said good morning to Josh, and he had barely raised his head, but now she told them about trying to catch a budgie which was flying around. Sally laughed but Josh made no response. When her mother went to the door with her, Cathy whispered, 'Doesn't Josh look ill?' She had been shocked at the change in him. His once ruddy face was grey, his cheeks were sunken and his shoulders bowed.

'He's not well,' Sally agreed.

'I haven't seen him for a week,' Cathy said, 'I can't get over such a change. And you're a bit upset too, Mam.

It's Sunday today, you know. No work for Kate.'

'Of course. I don't know whether I'm coming or going,' Sally said, and Cathy kissed her impulsively.

'Sarah's not fire-watching tonight and I'm not on duty either so we'll be here if anything starts,' she said. 'We'll all go in together, either under your stairs or ours. Greg thinks we should go in the street shelter, you know.' But Sally shook her head decisively.

'No, me and Josh'll go under our stairs and you go under yours.'

Later that day Mick arrived home on leave. 'Mick!' Cathy exclaimed when she opened the door. 'Why didn't you let us know?'

'But I did. I sent a card,' he said. 'Aren't you going to let me in?'

Cathy laughed and flung her arms around him. 'Oh, it's great to see you, son.'

Greg, Sarah and Kate were all at home and all delighted to see Mick. He looked very smart in his uniform with a strip of white in the glengarry he wore at a jaunty angle and a two-bladed propeller badge on his sleeve.

'I thought it was a dog's bone,' Kate said when he told them why he wore it, and that it meant that he was now a Leading Aircraftman.

He had been briefly in London, at St John's Wood, and told them that his squad drilled at Regent's Park Zoo and had their meals there. 'What about the animals?' Kate asked.

'We let them watch,' he said. 'The baboons and the monkeys imitate us. They're going to be issued with rifles to defend the Zoo.'

Kate looked at him suspiciously. 'I never know when to believe you,' she said.

Cathy was relieved to hear that Mick was being moved from London, but not so pleased when she heard that he was going to Scarborough. 'They've been having it bad on the East Coast, haven't they, as well as in London?'

'Don't worry about me,' Mick said easily. 'Only the good die young, you know.'

Mick told them that he would be billeted in a girls' public school in Scarborough. 'Unfortunately, the girls have been evacuated, like the animals from the Zoo,' he said, winking at Kate.

Later, when Mick had gone to see friends, Cathy said to Greg, 'He's made up, isn't he? I hope it doesn't make John feel worse, seeing him so settled.'

'No. John'll be glad to see Mick happy,' Greg said. 'Has he mentioned changing his job, by the way?'

'He only told *me* he was applying to the Ordnance Factory,' she said.

'That's all he told me,' Greg said hastily. 'He's a stubborn blighter, you know, Cath. While he was having a bad time at work about his politics, he wouldn't leave. Yet now that gang has gone and he likes the fellows he works with, he applies for another job.'

'I suppose he wouldn't give in to that crowd,' she said. 'But he wants to do war work, if he can't get into the Army.'

'I think he talks a lot to Anne,' Greg said. 'She's a good listener, and his own generation, of course.'

'She's a nice girl,' Cathy declared. 'I hope—' She looked at Greg and smiled. 'I'm match-making.'

'Why not?' he said as he stood up and kissed her. 'She'd get a nice mother-in-law, anyway.'

After their evening meal Sarah went to wash the dishes and Mick came out to dry them. 'How's the boyfriend?' he asked.

'All right, I think,' Sarah said. 'He can't say much on those cards, but Joe says he'll be well treated.'

'I thought Joe would be more your sort than Terry,' Mick said casually. Sarah stood with her hands in the bowl, rigid with shock. Was it so clear? Could other people tell how she felt? But he went on calmly, 'I only saw them a few times, but I was surprised when it was Terry you settled for.'

'You're the only one then,' she said bitterly. 'Everyone else seemed to have me paired off with Terry before I knew what was happening.' She looked at Mick and forced a smile. 'I'm not grumbling,' she added hastily.

'Both nice fellows,' said Mick. 'What about John and Anne? What's happening there?'

'Search me,' Sarah said inelegantly. 'Neither of them say anything to me, and Grandma told me not to ask.'

She had recovered from the shock of Mick's words and

said curiously, 'Why did you say that about being surprised, Mick?'

'Just that I thought you and Joe were well suited, and Terry seems a bit flip for you,' he said. He grinned. 'Must be the well-known attraction of opposites.'

'Must be,' she agreed, but respect grew in her for Mick's quick perception. No one else, she was sure, saw her and Terry as anything but a perfectly matched couple, or suspected all that lay unspoken between herself and Joe.

He had been home again on leave, and they had been unable to resist seeing each other frequently on one pretext or another, but Joe's manner to her was scrupulously brotherly and Sarah was as careful to treat him in the same way. Only when they looked at each other did they betray the longing that they felt for each other, but no one else noticed.

Sarah had received several cards from Terry and one had greatly annoyed her. He had written as usual that he was well and in good spirits, and then had added: "Don't worry, Sarah. There are no frauleins available here."

She was furious. Big head, she thought. Little does he know that I'd be *glad* if he met a fraulein, but he must know there are plenty of men available to me. She was never tempted, though, because her heart was filled with love for Joe.

Later she felt ashamed of her thoughts and wrote an affectionate letter to Terry. She and Joe wrote to each other sometimes, stilted letters saying nothing of their feelings though each could read between the formal phrases.

Sarah had been careful not to let her grandmother see her with Joe, knowing that her eyes were as sharp as Mick's.

All the family were worried about Sally at this time. She looked tired and worn, and they thought that the strain of the air raids was telling on her. Sally never betrayed the real reason. She had no fear of death, and the air raids would not have worried her, but every time there was a raid her strength was sapped by Josh's clinging to her, whimpering with fear, and even more by concealing his behaviour from everyone.

Peggy still came in for a cup of tea every morning, but Josh kept to his room except for meals now. 'Did you see that funny light in the sky last night?' Peggy said one morning. 'It was these incendiary bombs, the Major said.'

'Is he still giving his views?' Sally said dryly.

'He'd get on your nerves,' Peggy declared. 'You're lucky with a quiet old man like Josh. The Major's always giving the pay out. He listens to every news bulletin, and he told me Lord Haw Haw said Liverpool was finished. Nearly everyone dead, and the few that were left starving.'

'I never listen to that fool.'

'Neither do I,' Peggy said, 'but I can't stop the Major telling me. I went to Meg's shelter last night, but I believe the Major wouldn't go under the stairs or in the street shelter, and wouldn't let his wife go either.'

'Have you heard from Michael?' Sally said, anxious to turn the conversation away from shelters and air raids.

Peggy readily talked about Michael and Meg. 'I'm made up Willie failed the medical when he was called up,' she said. 'He's as good as gold with Meg. All through the raids he sat there with his arms round her, telling her stories, and she never bothered about the crash bang wallop going on outside.'

I could do with Willie here, thought Sally ruefully.

Chapter Thirty-Eight

John was notified that his application for a job in the Royal Ordnance Factory was successful, but on the same day was told that one of his frequent attempts to join the Army had been successful also.

'Which will you take, son?' Cathy asked.

'The Army,' he said without hesitation. She sighed, and he said gently, 'Sorry, Mam, but you know how long I've been trying for it.'

'Yes, I know. What shift is Anne on?'

'Afternoons,' he said. 'I think I'll slip round there now and tell them.'

He dashed away and Cathy was not surprised when they returned at lunch time with Anne proudly wearing a three-stone diamond engagement ring.

'Anne's dad was on nights so he was home and I could ask,' John explained. 'We went right away for the ring.'

'No sooner the word than the deed with you,' Cathy said, smiling.'You'll have to cure him of being so headstrong, Anne.'

'Headstrong!' John exclaimed. 'You can't say that, Mum. The way I've felt about Anne for ages, but I couldn't ask her while I had this stigma on me.'

'I didn't see it as a stigma, John,' she said quietly. He kissed her and Cathy flung her arms round both of them.

'I'm made up, and everyone else will be too. It's what we've all been hoping for.'

There was a light knock at the open front door and Sally came down the lobby. 'Mam, quick,' Cathy cried. 'Tell her, John.'

'We're engaged,' he said with a beaming smile, while Anne shyly held out her hand to show the ring.

'What kept you?' Sally said sardonically to John, but she

took Anne's hand and looked at the ring, then kissed her warmly. 'Welcome, love,' she said. 'He's a lucky lad, and we're lucky too. Look after him, girl, and I know he'll look after you.'

Anne's eyes filled with tears. She flung her arms around Sally and kissed her with fervour. 'I will,' she promised.

'Hey, it's me you've got to say that to,' John said, laughing.

Anne had gone to work when Sarah and Greg arrived home, but they were delighted with the news, and so was Kate.

'Can I be a bridesmaid?' she asked.

'That's up to Anne,' her mother said, and Kate declared that she would ask her.

Sarah was thrilled with the news and delighted when Anne came the following morning to walk to work with her and show her the ring. 'I can't possibly tell you how pleased I am,' Sarah declared. 'Mam says our John's walking on air and I feel as though I am too. Although not the same, of course,' she added hastily. 'I know it's different for him, but I'm so pleased, Anne.'

'I feel a bit mean flashing my ring around while Terry's away,' said Anne. 'But I'm sure he'll soon be home to give you yours.'

'Don't worry about that,' Sarah said. 'And don't let it spoil your pleasure, Anne.'

She had wondered sometimes if Anne had encouraged the idea that she and Terry were a courting couple because she wanted to strengthen links between the Fitzgeralds and the Redmonds, but she knew that if so, her friend's actions were simply from unconscious longing, not a deliberate ploy.

All Anne's family were pleased about the engagement, particularly her mother. Mrs Fitzgerald looked more frail every day, Sarah thought. She often went to see her because she was fond of her, as well as to hear any news of Joe, and was always warmly welcomed.

'It does her good to see you,' Mr Fitzgerald said. 'I worry about us all being out so much, but what can you do?' He was working long hours and fire-watching, and Maureen was now driving an ambulance. Stephen had been sent to Newcastle to organize another factory for his firm.

The air raids continued and Sally hoped that Josh might become accustomed to them, but his terror was still as great. On the night of August the thirtieth he was not sheltering under the stairs when Sally came downstairs in answer to a warning siren. She knocked at his door. He couldn't sleep through this, surely? she thought, as the heavy throbbing drone of hundreds of bombers filled the air, adding to the noise of anti-aircraft guns and loud explosions.

Cathy came running in in her WVS uniform. 'You and Josh'll have to go to the street shelter. It's too bad to stay under the stairs. Kate's gone with Josie's family.'

Sally turned to her, looking bewildered. 'I can't wake Josh,' she said. Their eyes met. Cathy came and took the handle of the door.

'Wait here, Mam,' she said, but Sally followed her into the room. Josh lay in bed, curled up in a foetal position, with his face buried in the clothes. Cathy bent over him then stood up and shook her head.

'He's gone, Mam,' she said. The next moment there was a tremendous crash. The house shook and glass fell from some of the windows. Cathy flung her arms protectively round her mother and pulled her to the floor.

'Whew, that was a near one,' she said, helping Sally to her feet. 'Look, Mam, we can do nothing for Josh now, not even bring a doctor because the living need them more. You'll have to come to the shelter.'

For the first time, she thought, her mother seemed like an old woman, bewildered and docile. Cathy brought her a coat, her handbag and a warm shawl, but before they left Sally suddenly reasserted herself.

'Help me to straighten him out,' she said, turning back the bedclothes from Josh. Then, when his limbs were straight, she took two pennies from her purse and laid them on his eyelids, and drew the sheet over his face.

All this time bombs were falling and the house seemed to vibrate as some fell nearby. 'We'll have to go, Mam,' Cathy urged. 'I'm on duty.'

'It must have been his heart,' Sally said as they left the house. The sky was filled with the glow from incendiary bombs, and the noise was deafening. 'It's like Bedlam,' Sally gasped, as they hurried along. 'Thank God he's spared this.'

Peggy was in the shelter, as well as Kate and Josie and her family, and Cathy was able to leave her mother there and hurry back on duty.

'I hadn't got time to get to Meg's,' Peggy said. 'That first one come so fast, I just run in here.'

'Where's Josh?' Kate said pertly. 'Was he too frightened to come?'

Sally frowned at her. '*Mr* Adamson is dead,' she said severely, 'and I'll thank you to show more respect.'

Kate fell silent as Peggy and Josie exclaimed. Peggy said in alarm, 'Was it a bomb?'

'No, he had a heart attack,' Sally said. 'You know his heart's been bad for years.' There was another tremendous explosion and they could hear distant shouts and screams.

'Good God, I wonder where that was?' Josie said. 'Maybe I *should* let these two go away. Our Eunice is safe there in Wales.'

'Ah eh Mam, don't make us go away,' nine-year-old Danny protested, and five-year-old Frank smiled at his mother.

'I like it,' he announced. 'It's exciting.' His two front teeth were missing, and all the women smiled at his eager expression. Sally took two bars of chocolate from her handbag and gave one each to the boys.

'That your iron rations, Sal?' Peggy laughed.

'Yes, I'm like the Boy Scouts. Always prepared,' she said. She was already recovering from the first shock of Josh's death and reflecting that it had been merciful, coming before he had experienced what was happening now and before anyone else knew of his fear.

'I wonder if that sailor got through?' Peggy said. 'There was a seaman here but he made a run for it to reach his ship.'

'He was in a shelter in Longview last night, and he said they had a fine time. Someone had a melodeon and they were all singing,' Kate said.

'It's a wonder you didn't offer to give him a performance,' Sally said sharply, but the next moment there was an explosion which threw them all to the floor.

'Merciful God!' Josie screamed, clutching her boys, and instinctively Sally threw her arms round Kate as they fell.

She had given Josie the shawl to wrap about the little boys

a few minutes earlier, and they were muffled in it as they all fell. Everyone was too shocked to speak for a moment, then Frank peeped up from the folds into his mother's face. 'Are we the only ones left, Mam?' he asked. 'Are all the others dead?'

'No, lad, we're all here,' Peggy said. Sally found that she was shaking, less with the shock of the explosion than with fear for the rest of the family.

'I wonder what's happened to my lodgers?' Peggy said to her.

'I'm worried about Cathy and Greg and Sarah,' Sally said quietly. 'They're all in different parts too.'

A woman at the end of the shelter screamed, 'Jesus God!' after every crash, and another one moaned quietly, 'Oh, God, will it never end?' But the little group round Kate and the boys felt that they had to keep up a brave front for the sake of the children, although Kate would have been annoyed to hear herself classed as one of them.

At long last the All Clear sounded and they stumbled wearily from the shelter, stiff and exhausted. The sky was lit with the flames of burning buildings, and the street was littered with broken glass and fallen chimney pots and slates, but as they picked their way along, a woman clutched at Sally's arm.

'Oh, Mrs Ward, I've been looking for you. Me neighbours's lad's been killed. Will you come?'

Sally left Kate with Josie and without hesitation took up her familiar role of comforter to the afflicted. Anxiety about her own family still gnawed at her, but some time later Sarah came to the door of the house. 'Will you tell my grandma we're all safe?' she said. 'My mum and dad are still on duty and I'm going to get a few hours' sleep before I go to work.'

She was dirty and dishevelled, and the woman asked where she had been. 'Fire-watching,' she said. 'We had a lot of incendiaries. We put them out with sandbags so we got a bit dirty.'

'They got Mill Road Hospital,' the woman said. 'My sister lives just by there and she said it was terrible. Women were having babies coming down in the lifts, and all the ambulances and everything were messed up.'

'Were the ambulance drivers all right?' Sarah said in alarm. Joe would be heartbroken if anything happened to Maureen, she thought, but the woman looked doleful.

'I don't think so,' she said. 'Some of them were killed, and I seen some being put into ambulances from other hospitals.'

Sarah found the next day that Maureen had been injured, but fortunately not seriously. Cathy went with her mother to visit Mrs Fitzgerald and was shocked by the change in her.

'I'm glad Maureen's only slightly injured,' she said to Mrs Fitzgerald.

The sick woman smiled weakly. 'It's a hard time for mothers, isn't it?' she said. 'We used to worry about the men in the last war, but now we've got to worry about the girls as well. How is your lad in the Air Force?'

'Still enjoying life,' Cathy said. 'Mick was born under a lucky star.'

'Like our Terry,' said Mrs Fitzgerald. 'I'm glad he's a prisoner and out of the fighting, but his luckiest day was when he met Sarah.' She put her hand on the girl's and smiled at her.

'Like our John when he met Anne,' Cathy said. 'I can't tell you how pleased we all are to have her in the family. She's a lovely girl and our John's lucky – and he knows it.'

While they talked Sarah sat with her hands tightly clasped and her head bent, feeling a hypocrite and wondering how they would all react if they knew how she felt about Joe.

Suddenly she heard his name. 'Our Joe's at Dover now. Tony told me they think Hitler's going to invade down there, but he says the Air Force is beating them to a frazzle. I don't know how he knows it all. Your lad isn't down there, is he?'

'Mick. No, he's still training,' Cathy said. She smiled. 'He wrote to John who showed me the letter. He said they're in this school, used to be a girls' boarding school, and there's a bell on the wall with a notice: "Ring for a mistress". '

Sarah looked rather nervously at Mrs Fitzgerald, knowing how pious she was, but she was smiling, 'They'd have a good laugh out of that.'

'He got more than a laugh,' Cathy said. 'They were

ringing it and fooling round generally, and the end of it was they got put on "Jankers", shovelling coke. It seems Jankers means fatigues, but that wouldn't worry Mick. He'd only get a laugh out of it.'

Mrs Fitzgerald looked slightly better when they left, but Cathy said sadly as they walked home, 'Poor woman, she's not long for this world, Sarah. I could break my heart for that poor lad, a prisoner, not able to get home and see her.'

'Depends if the war's over in time,' said Sarah.

'But it won't be, will it? I don't think she'll live more than a few months, if that, and Churchill reckons we've still a long way to go.'

She looked at Sarah's downcast face and said more cheerfully, 'Still, who knows, love? It could finish next week for all we know. Hitler seems to have bitten off more than he can chew anyway.' Sarah nodded, aware that her chief concern was the grief facing Joe if his mother died.

Greg had attended to all the details for Josh's funeral, according to instructions he had left with Sally together with the money. He also gave the name of the solicitor who had drawn up his will, and Greg contacted him.

Cathy and Greg were angry when the will was proved to find that Josh had left all he possessed to Kate, and not even mentioned Sally or her kindness to him. 'There's no fool like an old fool,' said Cathy. 'All Mam's done for him all these years, and to leave everything to Kate!'

'Nearly a thousand pounds,' Greg said. 'I know what Railway wages are, even for a senior clerk, and he couldn't have saved so much if Mam hadn't taken next to nothing from him for his rent and keep.'

'I'm disgusted, after all you've done for him,' Cathy said indignantly to her mother.

Sally smiled. More than you know, she thought, remembering the past few months, but she said calmly, 'I don't want his money, love, I've got all I need, but I hope it won't be the ruin of Kate.'

'I'll see that it isn't,' Cathy said grimly.

Kate was delighted with the news, and asked for some of the money to buy the clothes she craved for. Cathy went with her to town, determined that the spending would be kept within bounds as she and Greg had explained to Kate that most of the money would be invested for her.

In spite of her determination, Cathy had to admit when she came home that Kate had bought all that she wanted. 'I should have asked Mam to take her,' she said. 'I'm too soft.' But as Kate often reminded them after clothes rationing was introduced the following June, her spending spree had been a wise investment.

Cathy was pleased that Kate also asked that Sarah should have some new clothes, and that all the family should have some treat from her money. She went to show her new clothes to her grandmother. Sally's only comment was, 'Very nice,' but later she said to Cathy, 'Kate pays for dressing. She's growing a lovely-looking girl.'

'She looks a lot older than her age,' Cathy said. 'You'd never think she won't be fifteen until March.'

'Our Mary was the same,' Sally said. 'Some girls mature quicker than others. That reminds me – there's another letter from her. She's really worried about London.'

Cathy was puzzled by her mother's tone until she read the letter. Mary had written that everyone in her community had been shocked and desperately upset when they heard that the *City of Benares* and the *Empress of Britain* had been sunk while carrying children to Canada. "What sort of monsters will kill little children?" she wrote. "And poor London. We hear all about the dreadful devastation there and the lives lost, and my heart bleeds for them."

The rest of the letter was filled with the usual details about her dog and her social life. Cathy handed it back with a wry expression on her face.

The air raids on Liverpool had been increasing in intensity and length. Now they usually lasted most of the night, sometimes in one long raid and sometimes with warnings at intervals throughout the night. 'We're up and down to the shelter like bloody yo-yo's,' one woman complained to Cathy. 'You just get to sleep and the warning goes. When you get back upstairs and get your head down, it goes again.'

The previous night, November the twenty-eighth, had been a particularly bad one. The raid started soon after seven o'clock and lasted for nearly eight hours. Incendiaries, high explosive and parachute mines had fallen in various parts of the city. A parachute mine had made a direct hit on a large shelter beneath a school and it was impossible to estimate the number killed as it had been packed with the passengers from two tramcars, and people from a shelter that had already been bombed as well as the regulars.

A tram conductor told Cathy that Garston Gas Works had been hit, and although the area round Egremont Street had escaped damage everyone had been awake all night as bombs crashed down and enemy planes droned overhead, and the sky was lit with the glare of incendiaries and burning buildings.

'I wonder what she thinks we're doing, just reading the papers?' Cathy said.

'Mind you, it's our own fault,' her mother told her. 'We've hidden all this from her in case it worried her.'

'Sam should know,' Cathy said. 'He's got business contacts here. But I suppose he's kept quiet for the same reason, in case she's worried.'

Cathy had much to worry her at this time, with her sons away from home and Greg on duty with a First Aid team most nights and Sarah fire-watching, but she felt surprisingly cheerful. I suppose it's because everyone's in it together, she thought, and everyone wants to put the best side out.

Life was surprisingly normal, too, in many ways. She still went out on catering jobs and usually managed to enjoy them. She and Greg had stopped going to the Grafton dances, as they were thronged now with soldiers, sailors and airmen in every conceivable uniform, and the girls who came to dance with them. Cathy and Greg felt that they were the wrong generation for the dance, but they always had at least one night out at the cinema and supper afterwards.

Kate was an avid filmgoer, and she and her friend Daisy spent nearly every night at one of the cinemas. Her parents were unaware that they were usually accompanied by foreign servicemen.

Sarah and Anne went more often to the cinema than to dances now. Anne summed up their position one night when they had been to a dance in Eberle Street, organized by the department Sarah worked for. They had danced together for most of the evening, only occasionally with the few men who were present, and Anne said as they walked to the tramstop: 'Dances don't seem the same now, do they? We always enjoyed the dancing but I suppose without realizing it we were enjoying the flirting too, and looking out for possible boyfriends. We're a pair of grass widows now, aren't we?'

'Neither fish, fowl nor good red herring, as my gran would say,' Sarah agreed.

'I don't mind though, do you?' Anne said. 'After all, we've found the men we want, and the war can't last forever.'

Sarah was silent. It was true she had found the man she loved, but it was Joe not Terry who made her uninterested in other men. Sometimes her secret seemed too hard to bear and for a moment she was tempted to confide in Anne. What would she think? But a tram clanged to a halt beside them and the moment passed.

Maureen Fitzgerald had recovered and been discharged from hospital, and Eileen came home on Christmas leave. Mrs Fitzgerald seemed to rally, and for several weeks after Christmas the progress of the disease seemed to be halted. Stephen also came home from Newcastle for Christmas, and the family held a conference, with Sarah included, to decide how much to tell Terry about his mother's health.

Tony Fitzgerald turned to Sarah. 'What do *you* think? Should Terry have some warning? We don't want him to be worrying while he can't get to see her, but would it be too much of a shock if we only told him if something happened to Mum?'

Everyone looked at her and she said hastily, 'I don't know. You know him better than I do.'

A blush swept over her face as they all looked surprised, but Helen said firmly, 'Yes, it's not fair to put this decision on Sarah. I think we should vote on it, and ask Joe for his opinion too before we decide.'

'That's a good idea, Helen,' Anne said.

And Maureen added in her quiet voice, 'I would vote not to tell Terry yet. Mum doesn't seem much worse to me than when I went into hospital, and some of the nurses I talked to there told me that often there's what they called remission in Mum's disease. People have spells of months, even years, when they're not cured but they don't get any worse.'

'In that case I vote with Maureen,' Helen said, and all the others agreed, including Sarah.

'I was going to vote that way anyway,' Anne said, 'because our Terry would close his eyes to it if we warned him, and it would still come as a shock to him.'

Sarah told her father about the discussion when she was at home but her mother was out. Greg worked in a team of four First Aid men who were called to incidents to give medical aid and decide whether the casualties should go to hospital or to a rest centre, and he had come in covered in dust, with his hands and face scratched and cut.

He went into the yard to take off his clothes and shake the dust from them, while Sarah made supper for him. When he had washed and come back into the kitchen, she asked where he had been.

'Sawney Street, a pretty bad one,' he said. 'I got into a cellar to put a tourniquet on a chap who was half buried there, and a priest came in after me to give him absolution. The stuff above us was a bit rocky and the rescue man was going mad. He was saying, "Come ed, Father," and then to me, "Hurry up, lad. One of yiz come out, for God's sake."

'He thought we'd bring it down, shuffling round each other, and sure enough we got the lad out, then the priest, then he just pulled me out like a baby as it all came down.'

Greg laughed. 'He was so indignant! John trained for that work. We could do with him here now.'

'He's happy where he is though,' Sarah said. She told her father about the discussion at the Fitzgeralds' while he ate his supper, then he gave her a cigarette, lit one for himself and sat down beside her by the fire.

'I see you had a letter from Terry this morning.'

'Yes,' she said listlessly. 'No news though, of course.'

'Does it depress you to get them, Sass?'

'Oh, no, it means he's all right,' she said quickly.

'Of course, but Joe's letters are more interesting,' he said. Sarah glanced at him, her face flaming, but he was smoking and gazing into the fire. She said nothing. They sat for a while in silence while thoughts tumbled about in her mind.

Then Greg threw his cigarette into the fire and put his hand on hers.

'You're not happy, love, are you?' he said gently. Sudden tears filled Sarah's eyes and a sob escaped her. Her father's arms went round her and she buried her head in his shoulder.

'Oh, Dada, what can I do?' she wept. 'I've made such a terrible mistake.'

'You're not the first to do that, love,' he said. 'Do you want to tell me?'

She nodded and wiped her eyes, then said, 'I was stupid. It was all a joke at first, Terry pretending to be my boyfriend and singing daft songs, and then with the war everybody seemed to pair us off. When he was on leave everyone was working shifts except me so we went about together, then he came to say goodbye to Mum and saw my photo and asked for it.'

'It all seems to have been very haphazard,' Greg said.

'It was,' Sarah said. 'At the station Anne went off and left us together, and everyone was sort of emotional, and we just sort of got carried away, I suppose. Terry wanted to have a girl to write to and have a photo like the other fellows, and I suppose I liked the idea of a boyfriend,' she said honestly. 'It wouldn't have lasted though, Dad. I knew really that I didn't love him and he didn't love me, and then I realized how I felt about Joe.'

'And what about him?' Greg asked.

'He feels the same way, I know he does,' she said, her voice soft. 'Although we can't say anything. We couldn't do a dirty trick on Terry while he's stuck there, and I *am* fond of him, like a brother.'

'So you and Joe have said nothing to each other?' Greg said, and when Sarah shook her head, continued, 'You've both behaved very honourably then.'

'Yes, but sometimes I feel I'll *burst* if I don't talk about it!' she exclaimed. 'I saw Joe when he came on leave but only so he could tell me about Terry, and then when he came again we knew when we looked at each other but we didn't say anything and no one noticed. Except Mick. He didn't see us then, but when he was home he just said casually he thought Joe was more my sort than Terry.'

'Not much escapes Mick,' Greg said. 'I think he's right, love, but you're right too. You can't tell Terry while he's away, so you'll just have to mark time until the war's over. It won't be easy, love, but you'd never forgive yourself if you did anything else.'

'I can't bear it,' she blurted. She gave a sob which she tried to turn into a cough. 'Joe comes on leave in a fortnight, and I don't know how I'll bear to see him and say nothing. I nearly told Anne one night.'

'Don't do that,' Greg said quickly. 'Talk to Joe. There's only one decision you can make, but make it together. You'll feel better when you've got things straight between you, but say nothing to anyone else. I won't even tell Mum.' He smiled ruefully. 'She'll never forgive me if she ever finds out, but this is one secret it's best for everyone to keep between the three of us. If you feel you have to talk about it when Joe's gone, talk to me, love. I'll always be ready to listen.'

Sarah sat up and smiled faintly. 'I feel much happier now, Dad, just to have talked about it. I know it won't be easy, but if we *know* . . .'

'You can sort it all out when Terry comes home,' Greg said. 'He may have thought on the same lines himself, that you were both a bit impulsive.'

'He'll have had plenty of time to think,' she said.

'There'll be a lot of adjustments to make when this is all over,' Greg said thoughtfully. 'Youngsters who've gone away as boys and come back men. People who marry in haste before men go abroad, then grow up and grow away from each other. You won't have that problem, anyway, love.'

'No thank goodness,' she said. 'We'll just have to take things as they come, and if Joe and I know about each other I can stand it.'

'And be discreet,' he said.

'Like Grandma says, keep a still tongue.' She kissed her father gratefully. 'Thanks, Dad.'

Chapter Thirty-Nine

Cathy was relieved to see that her mother looked better in spite of the disturbed nights. She worried about her living alone but Sally insisted that she was quite happy and would prefer not to let her parlour again. She and Peggy spent a lot of time together, and she also visited Cathy and the family frequently.

Her remedies were still in demand and she was often called on to comfort or counsel her neighbours. 'You're a one woman ARP service, Grandma,' Sarah said to her, laughing.

'I like to keep busy,' Sally said placidly.

Cathy was also pleased to see Sarah looking less strained. She's accepted the fact of Terry's being a prisoner, Cathy decided. All her children were happy now: Kate because of her legacy, and Mick and John because they were leading the life they wanted, with the added bonus for John that he was engaged to the girl he loved.

Mick's examination results were impressive, and a master from the school came to see his parents and told them that he would have been able to go to Cambridge if the war had not broken out. 'Still, education is never wasted,' he said. 'He will have these results to open doors for him after the war, and I'm sure he will be very successful in life.'

'I'm sure he will,' Cathy said, suppressing a smile. She had suddenly thought of her mother's comment that if Mick fell down the lavatory he would come up with a gold chain round his neck.

Joe came home on leave in January, and Sarah wondered how she was going to see him alone. She was hurrying out of the building at six o'clock when the messenger called her. 'Miss Redmond, a soldier gave me this note for you.'

Sarah felt as though her legs had turned to jelly but

managed to say coolly, 'Thanks, Norman. It'll be from my brother.' She walked away, opening the note.

Joe had written: "I must see you, Sarah. I'm waiting to the right of the door, holding a torch."

Sarah turned right. A little way along the front of the building she could see the slightly darker bulk of Joe with a dimmed torch shining down on his glossy boots.

'Sarah,' he said, 'I didn't know how I'd see you in the blackout.'

She began to laugh, in spite of her agitation. 'You know that's what the girls on Lime Street do,' she said. 'The street walkers. They shine a torch on their legs.'

'Now how does a respectable girl like you know a thing like that?' he said, taking her arm. She laughed again but said nothing and they walked slowly up the hill. In an angle of the wall by the Picton Library, Joe drew her into his arms. 'Sarah, I've got to say it – I love you.'

She turned her face up to his. 'And I love you, Joe,' she whispered. His lips came down on hers and they clung together, Sarah's arms tight around his neck.

'I had to tell you,' he said finally. 'I couldn't go on any longer and I had to know if you felt like this too.'

'I do, Joe,' she said. 'I always did, I think.'

'I did from the first time I saw you,' he said. 'I was going to say something, then I realized you were Terry's girl.'

'But I wasn't,' she interrupted. 'Not when I first knew you, but you went away and Terry and I – we just sort of got thrown together.'

'I feel every kind of heel and rat,' he said. 'My own brother! But I can't help it. I just had to say it, Sarah.'

'I'm glad you did,' she said. 'But we can't hurt Terry, Joe. Now we know, we'll just have to go on like before.'

'I know,' he agreed. He seemed suddenly to realize what Sarah had said about herself and Terry. 'What did you mean about being thrown together?'

'I mean I was never really in love with Terry, and he wasn't with me. It was just fooling around as a joke, and then people seemed to pair us off.'

'But he thought you were his girl. He had your picture above his bed.'

'But even that – he just asked for the photo because he

462

saw it, and then on the station there were couples saying goodbye and Anne had left us on our own. Even then I thought we could see how it went and break it off if we wanted to, and no harm done. I didn't foresee this.'

Joe kissed her again hungrily and she responded as fiercely, then when he released her said self-consciously, 'I sound as though I'm making excuses, as though I'm trying to justify feeling like this when Terry—'

'I don't think so for a minute,' he said. 'I'm glad to know what really happened, but I know it doesn't alter anything.'

'I didn't love Terry, Joe, and he didn't love me. If we'd had time, we'd have realized it and gone our own ways. But the way things have worked out, we can do nothing until after the war, can we?'

'You know, Sar, I feel a lot better about Terry, about being disloyal to him in my thoughts, but I wouldn't do anything that would hurt him,' he said. 'It's not going to be easy, but we'll have to keep it dark about how we feel till then.'

'I talked to Dad,' Sarah said. 'Well, he practically asked me. He noticed I was depressed when I heard from Terry, and happy when I got a letter from you, and I was dying to tell someone. He won't tell anyone else, not even Mum. He said we've behaved honourably, and that it might be all right when Terry comes home because he'll have changed too. I don't mean have met someone else, but grown up and realized this was a mistake.'

'I hope he's right. You're sure he won't say anything?'

'Absolutely,' Sarah said. 'Not if he says he won't, not Dad.'

They kissed again then she said, 'We'll have to go, Joe. Where do they think you are?'

'Church,' he said with a grin. 'God forgive me.' They kissed again and clung together then walked slowly home. At the corner of Egremont Street they kissed again in the friendly dark.

'This will have to last me for a while now. Oh, Sar, I love, love, love you. I loved you from the minute I saw you.'

'And I love you, and I always have.'

' "They never loved who loved not at first sight," ' Joe said. 'Time to put the mask on now, love.' He gave her a swift kiss, and Sarah whispered goodnight and walked away.

She was relieved to find the house empty when she went in, and a note on the table that her dinner was in the oven and her mother would be home at eight o'clock. She looked at herself in the mirror, seeing with dismay her bright eyes and the happiness in her face. Good thing no one was in, she thought. I'll have to be more careful.

Fortunately Claire and Stephen announced their engagement while Joe was home, and said that they planned to marry in June, and in the excitement at their plans attention was diverted from him.

Joe and Sarah had intended to resume their relationship as it had been before they declared their love, but they found it was impossible and managed several surreptitious meetings before the end of his leave.

'Just for this leave,' they told each other, and after that they would be as brother and sister again. Stephen was home on a week's holiday so he saw Joe off from the station, but Sarah pleaded illness and came out from the office in time to wait in a doorway near the side entrance to the station to see him pass. She thought she was unobserved, but she saw him speak to Stephen who dashed ahead into the station. Joe turned back and kissed her passionately.

They had only a moment before he had to dash after Stephen but when he wrote to her from camp he said that he had seen her and asked Stephen to get him cigarettes. "It meant so much to me, that kiss, Sar," he wrote, "and to know that you would contrive to be there."

John came on leave in April, and he and Anne announced that they planned to marry in September, unless John was ordered abroad before then, in which case they would marry on his embarkation leave.

Only a few weeks earlier Claire and Stephen had cancelled their marriage, and Anne said to Sarah that she hoped no one would think that might happen to her and John. 'Never,' Sarah said emphatically. 'I was always a bit doubtful about Claire and Stephen anyway. Good thing they found out in time.'

John went back on May the first. There was a

comparatively light air raid that night, followed by eight nights when it seemed that every bomber Hitler possessed was sent over the Liverpool area. Air raids had continued throughout the early months of the year but never, it seemed, with such ferocity.

Cathy, Sarah and Greg were all on duty, and Sally and Kate spent the first night in the street shelter trying to comfort Josie's children as one explosion followed another and fires made everywhere as bright as day.

'There's thousands of them,' a woman in the shelter said.

Sally said quickly, 'Some of them are ours.'

When the night ended, Josie said that she was taking the family out of Liverpool. 'They're not going through another night like that,' she said, and Peggy urged Sally and Kate to come with her and Meg to Chrissie's in Huyton.

Sally refused to go to Chrissie's. 'She's got enough with all your family,' she said. 'Didn't you tell me that thirty-two people slept there during the Christmas raids?'

'She'll fit us in,' Peggy said. 'I'd take the Major and his wife but he won't leave the house or let her either.'

When Cathy and Greg came home they added their pleas to Peggy's. 'You don't have to go to Chrissie's,' Cathy said. 'There are rest centres, and we'd feel easier if you were out of this. You and Kate can look after each other. She couldn't go to work today anyway.'

'I don't need to,' Kate said. 'I don't want another night like last night, Grandma.'

It was Greg who clinched the argument by saying wearily, 'Look, Mam, anyone here who doesn't need to be is another potential casualty, and we've got enough to deal with already.'

Sally agreed to go, but stopped to make a pan of scouse ready for the workers coming home to Cathy's house, and was taken by surprise when an ARP man came to the door.

'Mrs Ward? Place for you and your granddaughter in the lorry for Huyton.'

'But what about my neighbours?'

'Mrs Meadows is in the lorry with her family,' he said, and Peggy came out of her house carrying a blanket.

'I'm going with Meg and Willie,' she called. She jerked

her thumb at the house behind her. 'They're staying. Ta ra, Sal.'

There were mattresses on the floor of the rest centre and helpers who made Sally and Kate and the Meadows family as comfortable as possible, but only the children slept.

The air raid began at six-thirty and went on until after five o'clock the following morning. The noise was continuous. An ammunition ship had been bombed the previous night and the cargo was still exploding, to add to the noise of high-explosive bombs and land mines and the crash of falling buildings.

'I wish to God Cathy and Sarah and Greg were here,' Sally said to Josie. 'God knows what's happening there.'

Sarah had been fire-fighting in the office block, but the incendiaries were too numerous for them to deal with, and they were ordered out of the building by the Fire Brigade. Moments later a bomb fell on the burning building, and Sarah and two other girls were brusquely told to "scarper" by a warden.

Buildings were burning all around. Sarah picked her way over the criss-crossed hoses and the masses of debris. She sometimes helped in a canteen and as she walked down a street of small houses which had been demolished, she was seized by a woman who worked there.

'Sarah Redmond, thank God! Take these people to the school shelters. Someone will look after them there.'

She pushed a woman and some children towards Sarah who realized that they were from a house which lay in ruins beside them. A man's arm was sticking out of the rubble, fingers outstretched. The woman kept repeating, 'It's him. It's him. The cat done that to his nail. The cat done that to his nail.'

She pulled away from Sarah, looked down again at the hand with its blackened nail and began again her sad refrain, but a priest came up beside her.

'He's dead, Ada,' he said. 'I gave him absolution but he's dead. They can't get him out yet in case the whole thing goes, and there are others further back. Be a good girl now, and go along. Take your children.' To Sarah he said, 'Take them to the playground shelter and say Father Hewlett said they have to be looked after.'

Sarah gathered the family together, three children between about four and ten years old and the woman, and took them to the shelter where they were wrapped in blankets and given hot tea. She stayed to help the relief workers who were trying to brew tea and make sandwiches in a corner. 'Our rest centre was hit so we brought what we could save here,' one of them explained.

When the raid was over she began to make her way home. In almost every street she passed there seemed to be houses missing, sometimes almost the whole street, and she began to hurry, fearful of what she would find. In such wholesale devastation, surely Egremont Street could not have escaped unscathed? When she came to the corner, she stood still, rooted in horror.

Her grandmother's house, and Peggy's, and others on that side of the road, were just piles of rubble. Her own house, although still standing, was without windows or door or chimney pot. Thank God Grandma wasn't there, was her first thought. She felt a touch on her arm and her mother stood beside her. Neither of them could speak, but only stare at the ruin of Sally's house and the state of their own. Finally they roused themselves and went to their house, stumbling over bricks and a brass coal scuttle, and the remains of a dog kennel.

They got inside and looked around. Window frames had slipped to strange angles, and the floor was littered with crockery and ornaments and fallen plaster, but it seemed there was no structural damage. 'Good solid houses these,' Cathy said. It was some time before Greg joined them, and he agreed that the house could be repaired.

He told them that the Major had been buried when Peggy's house was hit, and killed, but his wife had been blown through the window and survived. Later Sarah saw her picking over the rubble, then standing looking dazed with a pan in her hand which she had dug up.

She told them without emotion that her husband's jugular vein had been severed and he had bled to death before he could be reached.

Peggy and Sally were told about what had happened before they saw the remains of their houses. Peggy's only comment on the Major was 'Serve him right,' but she took his wife with her to stay with Meg.

The house opposite to Meg and Willie's had been hit, and a brass bedstead hung half out into the street with coats still hanging on the wall behind it, but Meg's house was unharmed. She and Willie had been in a basement shelter all night.

In later years when Sarah looked back at those days and nights of horror, she marvelled that what would have been unimaginable even a year earlier so soon became almost a normal way of life.

She marvelled too at the resilience of people who could still shout jokes to each other after a night of continual bombardment, with death and destruction all around them.

Most of all she looked back with wonder at the fortitude shown by her grandmother and Peggy Burns who could accept the loss of their houses and all that they had collected during a long lifetime, with the comments, 'No use crying over spilt milk,' from Peggy, and, 'What can't be cured must be endured,' from Sally, and even a joke, 'I never liked that ornament anyway.'

Sally could have told her that she and Peggy had lived long enough to realize that people were more important than possessions, and none of their immediate family had been killed although several were injured.

Cathy's left arm was scalded when a tea urn exploded when the rest centre was hit, and Peggy's son Ritchie, who was a fireman, was injured and her eldest son Rob and three of his family trapped for two days in a cellar before being rescued uninjured.

Seeing the Major's widow with the pan had given Sarah the idea that she might salvage something from Sally's house. It was just a pile of rubble but there were gaps here and there. Poking about, Sarah saw a hollow where the table had been blown against the grate. She moved some bricks and in the gap saw her grandmother's handleless teapot and a pipe of Lawrie's which had stood on the mantelpiece.

Cathy was almost as delighted as her mother to see the teapot. 'I remember that from when I was a tiny child,' she said. 'We always felt safe because there was the handleless teapot to fall back on. It saved my bacon many a time, even after I was married.'

Sally tipped out a pile of silver and a few coppers. 'I haven't bothered so much these last years,' she said, 'but I remember this when your dad lost his job. I'm thankful to have it back, love.'

In June Hitler invaded Russia. Clothes rationing was introduced also, and Anne told Sarah that she was more concerned about the clothes rationing than the invasion.

'I should have got everything for the wedding before it happened,' she said. 'It's going to make things very difficult.'

'I've ruined some of my clothes fire-watching' Sarah told her. 'Lewis's rigged their fire-watchers out with wellingtons and clothes and tin hats. We got nothing, needless to say.'

'I've got more money than I ever had,' said Anne, 'but I've been working such long hours I haven't had time to spend it. I wish I'd made time.'

A few weeks later she told Sarah that she had changed her mind about the importance of the invasion of Russia by Germany. Instead of being regarded as an enemy, Russia was now welcomed as an ally, and Anne said this made a difference to John.

'He says suddenly the fellows are all agreeing with him instead of arguing,' she said, laughing.

'He's not arguing there, too, is he?' Sarah exclaimed. 'I thought he'd left all that behind when he went in the Army.'

'You know John,' Anne said lightly. 'He'd cause a row in an empty house. Actually he says it's quite different to civvy street. These are more discussions than arguments, but he was making the point that in Spain he was fighting Fascism, just as he is now.'

'He used to be always arguing with Dad,' Sarah said, 'but they seem quite pally now.'

Anne laughed. 'Must be something about eldest sons,' she said. 'Tony was always like that with our Dad too.'

'What about the other lads?' Sarah said, longing to speak of Joe in whatever context.

'No, they were all right. In fact, Joe and Maureen always used to act as peacemakers because Mum used to get upset about the rows. Joe used to say that some American, Mark

Twain I think, said when he was sixteen he thought his father knew nothing, but by the time he was twenty it was surprising what the old man had learnt.'

Sarah smiled happily, knowing that her face was hidden as they walked through the dark streets, but she only said, 'Mick never fell out with Dad.'

'Mick never fell out with anyone, did he?' said Anne. 'I hope he can get home for the wedding to be best man.'

'He will,' Sarah said. 'He's waiting to go to Grading School in Yorkshire, but he'll only be there three weeks, and should be in Manchester in September.'

Help had poured into Liverpool after the "May Blitz", as it was being called, and the Redmonds' house had been quickly patched up. Sally had moved in with them, and the arrangement worked well. All the family loved and respected her, and Mary wrote from America that she was "ecstatically happy" that her mother was with the family.

She also sent numerous parcels of food and clothes which she claimed were "part worn" on the customs declaration so no coupons were claimed for them. Both clothes and food were very welcome, and Sally and Cathy laughed about the parcels which used to come from Fortnum and Mason as they unpacked the chocolate and sugar and dried fruit. 'You're not going to turn your nose up at this, are you, Mam?' Cathy asked.

'This is different,' Sally said. 'Those parcels seemed like charity – as though she thought we were starving – but I suppose she meant well.'

Sally used some of the food to make a magnificent cake for Anne and John's wedding, and more of the food was put aside for the wedding breakfast.

The small back parlour in her house had been made into a bedroom for Mrs Fitzgerald, who had become weaker and more frail although she was as gentle and uncomplaining as ever. It was a bright, sunny room. Tony papered and painted it, and all the family made it as comfortable as possible for their mother. It soon became the heart of the house.

Cathy had been to see Mrs Fitzgerald and suggested that the wedding breakfast should be held at her house. She had agreed.

'It would help my mother to get over losing her house if she could organize it,' Cathy said tactfully.

Mrs Fitzgerald pressed her hand and smiled. 'I can see why Sarah has such a lovely nature,' she said.

John had two weeks' leave, Mick had finished at Grading School and had a week's leave before moving to Heaton Park in Manchester, Joe and Eileen both obtained leave and Stephen a week's holiday, so all the family except Terry were home for the wedding in September.

Sarah and Eileen and Kate were bridesmaids, and all looked very pretty in long pale pink dresses with wreaths of flowers in their hair. Kate had acquired the material for the dresses, a bolt of taffeta which, she told her mother glibly, came from a fire damage sale.

Anne looked beautiful in a dress of white organdie, with a headdress of orange blossom and a bouquet of white roses and carnations. Maureen had borrowed a wheelchair for her mother, and Mrs Fitzgerald was able to watch Anne and John being married. Maureen quietly wheeled her away before the Nuptial Mass which followed, and drove her home.

Later Maureen drove her mother to the Redmond house. She spent a short time there, greeting the guests and hearing John's speech in which he thanked her for the gift of her daughter. Anne and John came to her and kissed her.

In her weak voice she said, 'I'm so glad to have John as a son. I know you'll be very happy. God bless you.'

The effort exhausted her. Her husband tenderly wrapped her in a blanket and carried her out to the car.

'Go back, Patrick,' she said when she was settled in the car. Sarah had come out with them, and Mrs Fitzgerald held out her hand to her. 'Sarah will come with us, won't you, love?'

Sarah readily agreed, and when they arrived at the Fitzgeralds' she helped Maureen to put her mother back to bed. Maureen went for medicine for her as the sick woman lay back with her eyes closed. 'Now lettest thou thy servant depart in peace,' she murmured, then took Sarah's hand.

'I won't be here for your wedding, love,' she said faintly. 'Whichever one you marry.'

Sarah's hand tightened on hers with surprise and Mrs Fitzgerald opened her eyes.

Her lips were almost bloodless but she smiled weakly at Sarah who bent closer to hear her as she whispered, 'I saw the way you looked at each other. Don't hurt Terry, love.'

'We won't, I promise,' Sarah said as quietly. 'When Terry comes home, we'll try to sort it out.'

'That's good children,' the sick woman whispered. She lay for a moment in silence, still holding Sarah's hand, then she opened her eyes again. 'Don't make a mistake, love, and ruin your life. Marriage is forever, don't forget.'

Maureen had come back and stood quietly beside them as Sarah bent her head, too choked with tears to speak.

'Don't cry, pet,' said Mrs Fitzgerald. 'Terry'll be all right, but Joe – look after him.' Sarah nodded. Tears were now running down her face, and Mrs Fitzgerald raised her other hand and touched her cheek, then her hand fell back weakly. 'Don't cry, love. Be happy. You and Maureen can help each other.'

She looked up at Maureen who bent and kissed her. 'Don't talk any more, Mum,' she said. 'You must rest now.'

Sarah gently pressed Mrs Fitzgerald's hand, then withdrew her own and moved away from the bed, while Maureen gave her mother medicine. Within minutes she had fallen asleep and Maureen took Sarah's arm and drew her out of the room.

'Go up to the bathroom and wash your face, Sar,' she said. 'Destroy the evidence.' She smiled. 'I'll make us a cup of tea.'

When Sarah joined Maureen in the kitchen, she felt self-conscious but the other girl said quite naturally, 'I guessed about you and Joe too, but only because we're so close. No one else knows.'

'My dad does,' Sarah said. 'He guessed too, and we talked about it, but he hasn't even told Mum. I feel a bit awful about that.'

'Don't,' Maureen said. 'It would only worry your mother, so you're both keeping quiet for her sake really.'

'Our Mick didn't exactly guess,' Sarah said, 'but he said

he was surprised about Terry. He thought Joe and I were a better match.'

Maureen nodded. 'You think you're being so careful,' she said, almost to herself, then looked at Sarah's puzzled face. 'I know what you're going through,' she said. 'Did you wonder why Mum said we could help each other?'

'No, not really.'

Maureen said quietly, 'I've been in love with a married man for nine years and two months. Does that shock you?'

'Oh, Maureen, no. You weren't shocked about me and Joe, were you? I know how it happens now.'

'We did knitted baby clothes in the shop and he came in to order some. He seemed so lost. When they were ready I took them to his house, and that's how it started. His wife caught poliomyelitis – you know, infantile paralysis – after the baby was born, and she blamed him.'

'But why? That's unreasonable,' Sarah exclaimed.

Maureen shrugged. 'She's not a reasonable woman,' she said. 'Never was. My poor Chris has a terrible life. I think she hates him, but she wants him there to make him suffer.'

'Does she know about you?' Sarah asked. Maureen shook her head.

'It would be another stick to beat him with,' she said bitterly. 'Anyway, there's nothing *to* know.'

There was a sound at the door and Maureen went into the hall. 'Joe,' Sarah heard her say, then they went into Mrs Fitzgerald's bedroom. A few minutes later Maureen came to the kitchen and called Sarah out.

Joe was standing by his mother's bed. Sarah tried not to look at him, but was unable to resist a glance and their eyes met. 'Is everything all right?' she asked.

'Yes, going with a swing,' he said. 'I came to see —'

'We know why you came, don't we, Mum?' said Maureen, and Joe looked up in alarm. Both Maureen and her mother were smiling. Maureen lifted Mrs Fitzgerald higher on the pillows. 'Now you can go back together,' Maureen said, and Mrs Fitzgerald held her thin hands out to them.

'God bless you,' she said.

They walked slowly back to the wedding reception while Sarah told Joe what his mother had said. 'Nobody who knows has condemned us, Joe,' she said. 'But to have your mum's blessing – it makes me feel better, and yet stronger to resist temptation.'

Joe nodded. 'Mum and Maureen,' he said, 'they're both alike. Gentle, but as strong as iron about principles. If they agree —'

'Your mum said Maureen and I could help each other,' Sarah said, 'and Maureen told me about Chris, just a little. We were talking when you came.'

'Did she? Poor Maureen, and poor Chris. That's what I mean about her being strong. He has a hell of a life but he's married, and you know – "In sickness and in health", whatever sort of a sham the marriage is and always has been. I think her faith helps her.'

They had reached Egremont Street. Joe turned and looked deeply into her eyes. It was dusk but people were passing. He said quietly, 'I can't kiss you.' He squeezed her hand tightly. 'I love you, Sar. We'd better not go in together. I'll smoke a cigarette here.'

She went into the house, trying to hide her happiness, but in the general festivity it went unremarked. Her parents and Anne and John asked about Mrs Fitzgerald, and Sarah said that she was in bed and comfortable and very happy about the wedding. Joe followed her a few minutes later and mingled with the guests.

Sarah felt guilty because everyone was concerned about Terry being away and that she was alone. She lost count of the number of people who said consolingly to her, 'Never mind. Your turn next when Terry comes home.'

Mick was near her on one occasion and she said in exasperation, 'I wish they wouldn't! I'm not jealous of Anne, and I'm in no hurry for marriage anyway. I feel a hypocrite.'

'You and me both,' he said cheerfully. '*I've* got people coming to shake my hand and tell me I saved Britain. They think I'm a fighter pilot.'

'It's the uniform,' Sarah laughed. 'And that speech by Churchill.'

'I know,' said Mick. 'At first I told them I'd only had twelve hours' flying instruction and made one solo, but now I just smile and say nuffin.'

Anne's going away clothes had been brought to the house

and Sarah and Eileen helped her to change, then the bride and bridegroom left. They went first to see Anne's mother, then to a hotel in Chester overnight, then on to a honeymoon in North Wales.

Anne hugged Sarah before she left. 'I always wanted you for a sister,' she said. 'And soon we'll be doubly related, won't we?'

Joe was standing near. Sarah blushed deeply. Joe moved closer. 'Well said, Anne.' He kissed her and shook hands with John, and under cover of the outbreak of kissing and farewells was able to kiss Sarah too. 'Our turn soon,' he murmured, and she felt as though she was lit up with happiness for everyone to see.

Chapter Forty

Anne and John returned from their honeymoon to spend the last few days of his leave with the others in Liverpool, but at a family gathering John almost immediately became involved in an argument with Tony and other Fitzgerald relations.

Germany was being bombed by the Royal Air Force, and John said that it was indefensible to bomb cities where civilians, including women and children, could be killed.

'How can you say that?' Tony exclaimed. 'When you look around Liverpool? The Maguire family, six of them, wiped out, and Mrs M'Gee's daughter and three small children killed.'

'And Grandma's house bombed,' said Kate.

'Two wrongs don't make a right,' John said stubbornly.

His father said mildly, 'You won't find many people to agree with you, John. I remember a chap in our First Aid team standing beside a bombed house at the height of a raid and shaking his fist at the bombers overhead. He shouted, "You wait, mate. You'll get yours. We'll flatten Berlin." We'd got to a woman and child and managed to save the woman but the child died while we were there. I suppose the thought of vengeance made it easier to bear.'

'Most people would agree with that chap,' Tony said.

Kate added, 'Our John's always out of step with everyone else.'

'So was his grandfather,' Sally said calmly, 'and he was usually proved right in the end.'

'There's nothing we can do to prevent it, anyway,' Anne said. 'And there'll be a lot of things that we can't decide the rights and wrongs of until the war's over.' She smiled at John, and he smiled back at her and said no more.

'Anne is just the girl for John,' Sally said later to Cathy.

'As your dad would have said, she'll give him the ballast he needs.' And Cathy agreed.

It had been a small family gathering as Eileen and Stephen, Mick and Joe, had already left. Before he went, Mick told his mother and father that he would soon be going to South Africa or Canada for flying training, but for security reasons they would not be told where or when until his departure.

For Sarah and Joe there was a bittersweet feeling about his leave. They contrived to spend many hours together, with some help from Maureen and from Cathy's father, yet all the time there was the worry that they would be seen together, and the guilty feeling that they were betraying Terry.

At every meeting, too, it became harder to keep their feelings under control. Shortly before Joe left they went to see the film *Dangerous Moonlight*, to which the accompanying music was hauntingly sad. Suddenly Sarah's tears began to flow and she leaned her head against Joe's arm, trying to stifle her sobs and stem her tears, but it was impossible.

They had been sitting with clasped hands but carefully apart in case they were recognized as eyes grew accustomed to the dark, but as Sarah's weeping continued Joe forgot caution and held her in his arms. 'Don't cry, darling,' he whispered, 'don't, Sar,' trying to mop her tears. But although she sat up again, tears still poured down her face.

They were near the end of a row and he whispered, 'Do you want to go out?' She nodded and they went into the foyer, where Sarah went into the Ladies'. When she came out she had managed to compose herself and had splashed cold water on her face, but tears threatened again as she took Joe's arm and they went into the dark street.

They stepped into a shop doorway and Joe held her tightly trying to comfort her, but his kisses became more and more passionate. Sarah responded eagerly but as his body pressed against hers and his hands found her breast, she drew in her breath and pulled away.

'No, Joe,' she said urgently. 'Terry —'

Joe took his hand from her breast and put his arms more loosely about her but she could still feel his heart beating as he groaned, 'Damn Terry, damn him! Why did he have to be such a bloody comedian?'

'It was my fault too,' Sarah wept. 'I must have been mad.'
But Joe had recovered himself.

'No, love,' he said gently. 'It wasn't anyone's fault. How
could we know this would happen? We all thought we might
be killed or wounded, no one thought of being taken
prisoner and being away till the end of the war.'

'I'm sorry, Joe, carrying on like this,' she said in a choked
voice. 'It was just – the music – and the years we'll have to
wait, and suddenly it was all too much to bear.'

'I know, love, I know,' he said, kissing her gently and
stroking her face. 'But, Sar, I can't be sorry we love each
other, in spite of all that.'

'Neither can I,' she said softly. They walked about for a
while before returning to Egremont Street, and kissing
goodnight.

Sarah had said that she was going to the pictures with a
friend, letting her mother believe that it was a girl she
worked with. When she returned home her mother and
grandmother were sitting knitting beside the fire.

'Good picture was it?' Sally said, looking quizzically at
Sarah's face blotched with tears.

'Yes, very good.'

'A lovely picture – I cried all night,' her mother laughed,
and Sarah managed a faint smile in return.

A few days later Joe went back to his unit. He was very
sad to leave his mother, fearing that he would never see her
again. He was right.

Mrs Fitzgerald died peacefully less than a month later.
The family knew that her end was near as she had been given
massive doses of morphia which the doctor had withheld
until this time, and had lain in a drugged sleep for days, but
she was greatly loved, and they all grieved deeply at the loss
of her.

Mr Fitzgerald was devastated. Maureen undertook
the task of sending the sad news to Terry. She received a
letter from him, grief-stricken at his mother's death and
concerned for his father, but to Sarah he wrote that
he found it hard to believe that his mother was really
dead.

"My life before coming here seems so unreal now,"
he wrote. "It's as though it was someone else living through

the events I remember. I suppose it will only seem real when I come home."

'Not a very tactful letter,' Cathy said to her mother when Sarah had gone out after showing them it.

'She doesn't seem to mind anyone else reading her letters,' Sally said.

Cathy shrugged. 'I suppose she feels that plenty of other people have seen them before she gets them, with censorship and all that, and he never writes anything very loving, maybe for the same reason.'

Joe and Eileen were given a short compassionate leave for the funeral, and Sarah was glad to have the opportunity, however brief, to comfort Joe.

She also tried to comfort Anne, but she was less close to her now although they were still good friends. Anne worked with girls who, like herself, had husbands away in the Forces, and inevitably she had more in common with them. She was reluctant, too, to parade her happiness in her marriage before Sarah, because of her situation with Terry away and marriage impossible before the end of the war, and Sarah was always afraid she might betray her love for Joe to Anne, so gradually she became closer to Maureen.

With Maureen she could speak freely about Joe for as long as she wished, and could hear details about his childhood and other things which she longed to know about him. Maureen could talk to Sarah about the man she loved, and they spent many hours sitting together in the quiet house or out walking, becoming very close friends.

'You're the only one I can talk to about Chris, now that Joe's away and Mum's gone,' said Maureen. 'Poor Mum. I miss her in so many ways, yet I shouldn't wish her back when she was suffering so much.'

Mrs Fitzgerald was already a sick woman when Sarah first met her, looking older than her years with grey hair and a face lined with suffering. Sarah was amazed when Maureen showed her a photograph of her mother as a young woman, with large dark brown eyes and jet black hair, and a clear pale complexion.

'But, Maureen, she's so like you and Joe,' Sarah exclaimed. 'Almost Spanish in appearance.'

'Yes, the rest of the family are like Dad, with dark hair

and brown eyes, yet quite different from us,' Maureen said with a smile. 'Mum came from the West of Ireland, you know, and they reckon sailors from the Spanish Armada were washed up on that coast and some of them married Irish girls. That's where the Spanish look comes from.'

'Isn't that strange?' Sarah said. 'Mick said he could picture Joe dressed like a toreador.'

'Joe is like my brother Patrick who died. I think that's why Mum was so fond of Joe, although she never showed favouritism.'

'You were always very close to your mother too, weren't you?'

'Yes, partly because I was the only one who remembered Patrick,' Maureen said. 'I was three and he was six when he died, and Tony was seven months old. People thought Tony would console Mum, but he was a big boisterous baby and Patrick had been such a quiet little boy.'

'I don't know how people can bear to lose a child,' Sarah said.

'What can you do? You've just got to carry on, especially when you have other children depending on you. I think it was only when Joe was born and was so like Patrick that Mum began to get over it, as much as she ever did. Well, they're together now,' Maureen said with a sigh.

She was able to talk to Sarah about her own unhappy love affair. 'Chris and his wife should never have been married,' she said. 'But she was like Claire. They're predators, those sort of women. They track men down and know just the sort to choose – easygoing fellows who don't like to hurt a girl's feelings, and who'll take the line of least resistance by letting themselves be married out of hand. Our Stephen was lucky that he was moved to Newcastle and had time to see what was happening to him.'

Maureen told Sarah that Chris's wife had behaved like an invalid during her pregnancy, then later she caught polio. The child was brought up by her sister and died of diphtheria at five years old. 'She blamed Chris for everything that happened, and she's determined to make him suffer,' said Maureen. 'She hates him, but he has to be there to look after her.'

Joe came on leave again in July but it was more difficult

for Sarah to spend time with him. They had to be more circumspect because of the light nights, and Joe's father wanted to have him with him as much as possible. Even though she felt frustrated, Sarah could not begrudge the grief-stricken and bewildered man the comfort of spending time with his son.

Mick had been sent to Canada for training and his letters showed that he was blissfully happy.

> Quite a comfortable journey. No names, no pack drill but we were in a luxury liner, zigzagging to dodge the U-boats. Great to have white bread, not to mention the other food. We went from New York to New Brunswick by all night train. There for a few weeks, then Elementary Flying School. I can't wait!

'He's happy anyway,' Cathy remarked. 'It was always his dream to fly but I never thought it would be this way.'

Letter cards came infrequently from Terry. Sarah wrote regularly to him, although it was becoming increasingly difficult for her to think of something to say. She told him about Mick being in Canada, although unsure if it would pass the censor, but evidently it did.

Terry wrote in reply:

> I envy Mick in Canada. The chap I have been with right through comes from Liverpool but worked in Canada for years before the war. After hearing his description of the open spaces, climate and opportunities there, I've decided it's the place for me. I'm not going to spend the rest of my life at a factory bench.

He must have read the letter through and decided that he had not mentioned consulting Sarah about his plans. He added a postscript: "PS I'm sure you'd like Canada, Sarah."

She was cheered by the letter and copied it to send to Joe. He agreed with her that Terry's dreams for the future were obviously not of marriage and settling down.

Joe was still stationed near London, and John, now a

Corporal, was in Norfolk training recruits. Mick returned from Canada in the spring, bearing gifts of nylon stockings and dress lengths of material for his sisters and mother and grandmother, all carefully chosen to suit each one, and cigarettes and a lighter for his father.

He had been commissioned in Canada and returned to England with the rank of Pilot Officer. He went for four weeks' acclimatization training as flying in England – hilly, crowded and with blackout – was very different to flying in Canada, then on to Operational Training for flying bombers. Mick enjoyed it all.

While he was home on leave he talked to Mrs Gunter who was renowned for her lack of tact. When he went back, she said to Cathy, 'I see that lad of yours is *still* training. Seems a waste, doesn't it, when most of them get killed so soon?'

All the fears that Cathy had tried to push to the back of her mind rushed back and she dashed into the house, unable to reply. From then on she listened in terror to the news bulletins, waiting for the words which told of the numbers of aircraft which "failed to return".

'But Mick's not operational yet,' Greg tried to comfort her. She could only think of the mothers who had lost their sons and think that Mick too would soon be in danger.

Sally was a great comfort to her. She had never been more glad of her mother's calm good sense, and was so grateful that she was living with them.

Kate was not quite so enthusiastic about having her grandmother in the house, to watch her closely and to listen to what Kate described to herself as her "white lies". She blamed her grandmother when her parents suddenly became strict about the men of many nationalities whom Kate had been dating.

She was told that she must bring them home to meet the family, and when she protested Cathy told her that people had been asked to show hospitality to these boys who were far from home.

When she realized that her parents were adamant, Kate began to bring the young men home, and a procession of Dutch sailors, Australian and Polish airmen, and Canadian soldiers came to collect her and then returned later for supper with the family.

Gradually, though, as her other escorts moved on, Kate brought mainly Americans to supper or to tea on Sundays, and as time passed it became one American in particular. He introduced himself as: 'Eugene J. Romero, Ma'am, always known as Gene,' when Cathy came forward to welcome him.

He was a quiet and likeable young man, but he soon made it clear that he would stand no nonsense from Kate. He was missing from the house for a few weeks, and when he reappeared told Cathy that Kate had stood him up on a date to go out with someone else.

'I guess every dog is entitled to one bite,' he said, 'but it doesn't get to have a second one, not in my book, and Kate knows that now.'

He checked her too when she announced that he knew Uncle Sam. 'No, honey, I don't know him. I know of his business, but that's not the same thing.'

'I like that young man. He's just what Kate needs,' Sally said. 'What a pity he's not English.'

'Why, Mum? You don't think they'll marry surely? He'll have gone home before Kate's old enough.'

'She's seventeen, and an old seventeen,' was all Sally would say. 'She writes plenty of letters to America to our Mary. Let's hope she'll write as many the other way if she goes.'

Just before Christmas 1942 a baby girl was born to Helen and Tony, and did much to console Mr Fitzgerald. Joe came home on embarkation leave shortly afterwards, and he and Sarah were able to spend more time together because his father was now preoccupied with the new arrival. But Sarah had begun to worry that people were beginning to suspect their relationship, and was too nervous fully to enjoy the leave.

Several friends wrote to Terry and she was afraid that someone might tell him about her and Joe. Her common-sense told her that it was unlikely, but much to her later regret, she allowed the fear to cloud their time together. Joe remained in England for a couple of weeks, then in March she received a letter from him from North Africa.

Because Sarah and Joe wrote so frequently to each other, he had been sending his letters to her enclosed in ones to

Maureen. When women registered for compulsory war work in May 1942, Maureen had been directed into clerical work in an office near to Sarah's because of her injuries in the "May blitz", so they were able to meet every day for Sarah to receive her letters.

Joe wrote cheerfully and lovingly, telling Sarah how much she meant to him and saying that all was going well, but the news bulletins were not so cheerful. Sarah dreaded to see Maureen bearing a telegram with bad news, but by May General Alexander could tell Churchill that the Tunisian campaign was over.

Sarah thought that this meant that he would soon be home, but instead his Battalion was ordered to Italy. The tone of his letters was still cheerful: 'This isn't Italy as I pictured it. We've had rain, hail, and snow, and bitter cold, but we'll come here together some day, Sar, when the sun is shining. It won't be long now, sweetheart.'

Sarah wished that she could be so optimistic, but like most people was thoroughly fed up with the war. How much longer was it going to drag on? people wondered. The earlier defiant mood, when Britain stood alone and everyone was united against the common enemy, had gradually drained away. Life seemed full of petty problems, with shortages and queues and fussy self-important officials to contend with. Everyone was suffering from boredom and weariness as the war dragged on, and most people had grief or worry about someone to add to their troubles. Mrs Gunter's son had been lost on a convoy to Russia, and one of the Ashcroft boys had gone down with the *Prince of Wales*. Michael Burns had been taken prisoner in Burma, and Peggy had received only one printed card from him in over a year.

'I wouldn't let the wind blow on him when he was little,' she mourned, 'and God only knows what's happening to him now.'

Mick was now flying with Bomber Command, and the nightly toll of aircraft reported on the news bulletins struck fear in all their hearts. In addition Sarah was often sick with apprehension about Joe, made all the worse because she had to hide it. Sometimes she felt that the deceit needed to hide her love for Joe was more than she could bear, and sometimes she felt that she almost hated Terry, although she knew it was not his fault.

Anne came often to the Redmond house now, to see John's family and to talk about him, and Sarah felt sure that someday she would slip up when they talked about the brothers and Anne would realize that it was Joe not Terry that Sarah hoped to marry when the war was over.

This brought her back to the weary treadmill of wondering how Terry really felt about marriage; how she could possibly tell him about Joe if he had spent these years of captivity planning for marriage and a home and family. Yet how could she bear to part from Joe, or for that matter bear to marry Terry while she loved Joe so much?

The news bulletins and newspapers gave details of the Anzio landing in which Sarah knew the Irish Guards were taking part, and in February came the news which she had dreaded. She was called out of the office to a waiting room to find Maureen, ashen-faced, with the news that Joe had been wounded. 'They don't give any details,' she said. 'Only that he's wounded and is in hospital in Naples.'

They stared at each other, afraid to speak, then Maureen said fearfully, 'As long as it's not his eyes.'

Sarah replied, 'Or a very bad wound. That he'll live.' They clung together then Maureen wiped her eyes and told Sarah that she had rung Tony at work.

'He's going to tell Dad,' she said, 'but he thinks we shouldn't tell Eileen or Stephen or Terry until we get more news. Anne knows – she was at home when it came.'

Only two days later Sarah and Maureen each had a letter from Joe, written from the field dressing station before he was taken off by boat for Naples.

"I have been slightly wounded, love," he wrote to Sarah, "in my arm and leg but they are not bad wounds. Scribbling this in case you are notified. All my love, Joe."

Sarah went immediately to see Maureen, but whatever her feelings either of sorrow or joy about Joe, she had to conceal them at home, although she could talk freely to her father when they were alone.

Cathy's concern was mainly for Anne as Joe's sister, although she said to Sarah, 'I'm sorry for you too, love. How could you have sent more bad news to Terry? Poor lad, locked away from everyone and his young life going past.'

So is mine, thought Sarah. My youth is going, marking time, waiting for this damn' war to end to sort out my life. If only we could see some hope of its ending.

Suddenly it seemed that her hopes were realized. Joe managed to improve enough to rejoin his battalion, or the remnants of it, and they sailed for home on 7th March. They berthed in Liverpool, and Joe managed to pass a note for Sarah to a docker, but troop trains were waiting at Riverside Station and before the note reached her Joe was on his way to London.

He was given leave almost immediately and she waited for him with a light heart. Mick had completed a tour of operations and was now grounded for a while, John was still in England, and her father said that the tide of war had turned.

'Everything's in our favour now. The Russians have beaten Hitler, and soon we'll have the Second Front and finish things off.'

Joe agreed when he arrived home. 'I think we're on the last leg now,' he told Sarah. He showed her the wounds in his arm and leg when they were alone in the Fitzgerald house. The scars were deep and blue in colour, and he said they were made by an anti-personnel fragmentation bomb. 'It burst on the ground as I ran past with a machine gun under my arm,' he said, grinning. 'A lot of blood but not much damage.'

They had a very happy leave, helped by Maureen and by Sarah's father, but she had one uneasy moment. Vesuvius had erupted while Joe was in hospital in Naples. He was describing to Cathy and Greg and Sally how the patients had watched the molten lava from the hospital windows.

Sarah was listening with shining eyes fixed on Joe when she felt that she was being watched, and looked up to find her grandmother's eyes on her.

'Isn't that exciting, Grandma?' she said quickly. 'Gosh, the places people are seeing now, just because of the war.'

Before Sally could reply there was a knock at the door, and the next moment Mick was among them. Immediately all the attention switched to him. 'I sent word I was coming, honestly,' he laughed. 'You'll probably get it tomorrow.'

His face was grey with dark shadows beneath the eyes, but he was as cheerful as ever, and wore his battered cap at a jaunty angle.

'You could do with a new one, lad,' Sally observed.

'No, Gran, that's how we like them,' he said. 'I jumped on that when it was new so that it would look well worn.'

'Whatever next?' Cathy exclaimed, looking at him fondly. It was pure happiness to her to have her son back under her roof and to know that he was safe, at least for a while.

Later Gene arrived and was introduced to Mick and there seemed to be an immediate rapport between them.

Kate was eighteen years old in March, and she and Gene announced their engagement on her birthday. Cathy and Greg could find no fault with the young man, except that marriage to him would take Kate so far from home.

American officers had visited the family and seemed to approve of the marriage, although Greg wondered if the family's relationship with Sam and Mary in the States had something to do with that.

Kate had exchanged letters and photographs with Gene's family, and Mary and Sam had also been in touch with them, so Kate seemed assured of a warm welcome when she went to America after her marriage.

Chapter Forty-One

John came on leave a day before Mick went back so for the first time in years they were able to spend a short while together. Before Mick went he said to Cathy, 'Don't worry about me, Mum, will you? The fellows say I bear a charmed life, and it's true, you know. You always said I was born under a lucky star.' And she was comforted.

She told Greg about Mick's words as they were preparing for bed, and said that she would try to think of them when she heard of the bombing raids. She was brushing her hair and leaned forward to look in the mirror.

'Oh, look, Greg, I'm going grey,' she said in dismay. He came to sit beside her on the side of the bed and put his arms round her.

'So am I, love. But when your hair has turned to silver, I will love you just the same.'

'It's all right for you. Grey just makes a man looks distinguished – like an office manager and partner,' Cathy said, her dimples showing as she laughed.

Greg had worked very hard to restore the woodyard after the air raids, and to deal with the problems of repairing damaged housing. Stan Johnson had showed his appreciation by making him a partner. Six office staff were now employed, and Greg was also office manager.

'The way I used to worry about money,' Cathy went on. 'With the worries we've got now, it seems stupid ever to have worried just about making ends meet.'

'That's because we've got as much as we need now,' Greg said. 'Listen, Cath, we could afford a better house. What do you think about moving?'

'I've never thought of it. There's nothing wrong with this house,' she said in surprise.

'But wouldn't you like hot water and a bathroom and a

garden?' Greg said. 'And it can't be very pleasant for Mam to see that empty space where her house was every time she steps out of the front door.'

'You mean Mam would come with us?'

'Of course. We'd have to see how she felt about moving before we looked round.'

Cathy pondered for a moment. 'I wouldn't want to move far,' she said. 'What about a house like the Fitzgeralds'? They've got hot water and a bathroom.'

'Yes, but that's such a big house, with attics and cellars, Cath. Don't forget, we'll soon be only a small family. John married, and Kate and Sarah before long, and who knows what Mick will do after the war. We'll just think about it anyway.'

Cathy had given up the catering job after the "May blitz", partly because she had less need of the money but chiefly because few of the old staff remained. Josie was now working full-time, Freda had remarried and moved to Scotland, and Cissie was now working in a café on the Dock Road. Her house had been destroyed in the air raid in which her husband Bert had been killed, and Cissie now lived with her sister, Queenie.

'We fight rings round all the time,' she told Cathy when they met one day. 'Me and our Queenie never got on, even when we was kids.'

'Can't you find anywhere else to live then?'

'I couldn't live nowhere else while she's got room for me,' Cissie said in a scandalized voice. 'We're flesh and blood, remember.'

Many people who were "bombed out" had to make arrangements to live with relations, but not many were as successful as Sally's move to Cathy's house. Although she had not admitted it, she had been finding it more and more difficult to manage her own home, but in Cathy's house she could do as much or as little as she pleased, and know that she was always loved and needed.

Cathy would have been lonely at this time without her mother's company, with so many of her friends dispersed. She worked several hours a day at the hospital on a constantly changing rota so she made no new friends, but spent happy hours with her mother, talking over old times and planning for the future.

Maureen had suggested that Anne and John should turn two rooms in the Fitzgerald house into a flat for themselves and her father had agreed, so Anne and John spent a blissful leave making the rooms into a home for themselves.

Joe had gone back to London but when the Battalion, few of whom had returned from Italy, was made up to strength they moved to Hawick in Scotland. It was obvious by now that the Second Front was about to begin, and Gene was one of those who were moved down the coast to where troops and equipment were being organized for the invasion of France.

John had been promoted to sergeant and shortly afterwards was also moved down to Eastbourne ready for the invasion. By this time it had been confirmed that Anne was pregnant and that the baby was due in January. She told Sarah that she was terrified that John would be killed before the baby was born.

'Don't worry,' Sarah said. 'Joe says this time it's going to be different altogether from Dunkirk because Hitler's had such losses on the Russian Front and in other places, and we're so much stronger with our own troops and the Americans and the others on our side.'

'I hope he's right,' Anne said. 'I know we've been lucky having John in England for so long, but just now I'd love to have him home.'

She seemed suddenly to think of Sarah's long wait and said hastily. 'You and Joe are good friends, aren't you? I haven't seen him much on his leaves, with the shift work. We'll all be strangers by the time this is over. I wonder if Terry will have changed?'

'He probably will,' Sarah said, blushing. 'We'll just have to wait and see.'

In June the invasion of Europe began and John was among the first wave of troops. Gene landed a few days later but it was July before Joe went out with reinforcements.

'It's like a switchback,' Anne complained as she listened to the news with Cathy and the rest of the family. 'One day everything's going well and you think it'll soon be over, and the next day they're held up again.'

'Don't worry, love. I'm sure John will be home before the baby's born,' Cathy comforted her, and for a while it seemed she would be right.

In late September Joe wrote of the wonderful welcome they had received when they liberated Brussels, of the lights being turned on and the flowers and fruit and wine heaped upon them, and the kisses from everyone from nine weeks to ninety. Once again hopes were raised at home, but there was bitter fighting still to come.

The end was near as Germany was overrun, and on May the fourth the unconditional surrender of all German Forces was announced, to take place on the following day.

By that time Anne's baby, Gerald John Redmond, was four months old. 'It's history repeating itself,' Sally said when he was born. 'John was born when his father was away in the Army.'

'Yes, but John will learn by my mistakes,' said Greg.

'And by mine,' Cathy said quickly. They smiled at each other, all the bitterness of those years forgotten.

Sarah took part in the celebrations on VE Day but with a sinking heart as she thought of the months ahead. Already, as Germany was defeated and prisoner-of-war camps liberated, the prisoners had begun to come home. Lorry-loads of men drove past the office where Sarah worked and the girls had made huge "Welcome Home" banners, and hung them from the windows when the convoys were expected, ringing a handbell so that the men would look up and see them.

'Wouldn't it be exciting if you saw your boy friend on one of the lorries?' a colleague said to Sarah, but she had warning of Terry's arrival in a letter from France. It was formal in tone with a few "darlings" scattered in it. Like currants in a cake, she thought.

She was surprised to learn from Maureen that Terry had written to his father asking if he could bring his friend Frank to stay as his father, his only relative, had been killed when his house was destroyed by a landmine.

The Fitzgeralds all gathered for Terry's homecoming. Eileen had been demobilized, but she was a quiet, sad girl now. She had been married to an Air Force pilot who had been killed three weeks after their wedding, and to Sarah seemed greatly changed.

Stephen had arrived home on holiday, Helen and Tony

were there with their small daughter, and Anne and Maureen were already at home with their father. Only Joe was still away in Germany, and for once Sarah was glad that he was absent.

Sarah decided to go to the Fitzgeralds' house on the evening of Terry's arrival, and felt a hypocrite when Mr Fitzgerald praised her for her thoughtfulness.

'We'll want to have a good look at him,' he said apologetically, 'but there's plenty of room in the house for you two to go off on your own later.'

Now that the time had come, she felt terrified. So much depended on what happened in the first few hours after she and Terry met.

She worried about what she should wear. After the years of clothes rationing she had only a few dresses and had worn each of them when she was with Joe. Her best dress was the one made from the deep blue material that Mick had brought her, but that was Joe's favourite.

Fortunately her grandmother handed her some clothes coupons. 'Get yourself a nice dress, love,' she said.

Sarah hugged her, feeling her pleasure in the gift mixed with guilt and worry about what people would think when they knew the situation. Why am I so thin-skinned and such a worrier? she thought with exasperation. I wish I could stop it and just let things happen. Kate would.

She said this to her father when all the rest of the family were in bed. 'We're all a bit on edge these days,' he said. 'And it's worse for you with this problem, and being a natural worrier anyway, and sensitive to other people's feelings.'

'But why am I like this?' she said. 'I'm sure I don't want to be. I'd like to be the same as Kate.'

'Oh, well, we are what we are, I suppose. You've just inherited different characteristics. Grandma told me once that when she was young she would worry over a pin. She was talking about you at the time.'

'I hope I've inherited other things from her but I could do without that trait,' Sarah said ruefully.

Greg smiled at her. 'It makes you what you are, love,' he said. 'And we don't want you to be any different.'

Sarah had planned to leave Terry alone with his family when he arrived and go later to the Fitzgeralds', but Tony came to escort her there shortly after his brother's arrival.

'This chap Frank is with Terry and so far hasn't left his side for a minute, so I think your tact was wasted, Sarah,' he said. 'You'll find Terry changed in some ways. I suppose he's grown up.' He squeezed her arm affectionately. 'Of course, you're not the quiet little girl you used to be.'

How nice all the Fitzgeralds were, Sarah thought, and how much she liked them. The thought was followed by another: I hope they don't turn against me.

As they drew near the house, Tony released her arm. When they saw Terry's tall figure waiting, Tony moved on quickly, clapping his brother's shoulder as he passed him, and Sarah and Terry moved towards each other.

But he looks just the same, she thought as Terry took off his cap and bent to kiss her. There was no passion in the kiss and Sarah only laid her hand on his arm. They smiled self-consciously at each other, and Terry crooked his arm for her to slip her hand through.

'Does it all feel very strange?' Sarah asked as they strolled along.

'Yes, it does. I suppose I expected things to stand still – well, I knew there'd be changes, I suppose. Mum —'

'Yes, it's sad for you,' she said gently. 'But she would have had a lot of pain if she'd lived.'

'So Maureen told me. *She* hasn't changed much, but the others – all these marriages, and a new nephew and niece.'

'Was it bad for you over there?'

'In some ways. We got fed up with time dragging past, but the Germans were all right. We got pally with some of the guards and were sorry when they were sent to the Russian front, poor blighters.'

'It said on the news that prisoners were treated badly.'

'Some were, I suppose, but we were lucky. The main thing was Frank and I managed to stick together, even for working parties. That reminds me – we'd better get back. He's a bit shy with the family.'

Maureen opened the door to them. She detained Sarah to whisper, 'Well?'

'All right,' Sarah whispered as Terry went ahead. 'I don't feel strange, I feel quite easy with him, but it's like being with Tony.'

'You haven't talked?' Maureen asked.

'No. He wanted to get back to Frank,' said Sarah. Maureen grimaced and led the way into the room. Terry introduced Frank to Sarah. He was a thick-set young man who to Sarah seemed far from shy as he joined in the conversation in which the family told Terry of events over the years.

'Yes, I think you wrote to Terry about that, didn't you, Sarah?' he said several times, and she began to feel glad that she had written nothing very personal in her letters.

A little later Frank suddenly leaned forward and said to Sarah, 'What do you think about Canada, then?'

Sarah realized that Terry, sitting beside her, was making frantic signals to Frank. A blush spread over her face but she could think of nothing to say.

Tony stepped in quickly. 'What do *you* think of Liverpool? Do you see many changes?'

'I do. Even from the bit we saw coming here. It all looks shabby and dirty, and the people! What a miserable-looking bunch. The Jerrys look more cheerful, and they've lost the war,' Frank said.

There was a stunned silence then Helen said sharply, 'Liverpool's been knocked about, and people are shabby maybe but I wouldn't say they were miserable. They'll be able to buy new clothes soon, and rebuilding's started.'

'It's just that I remember Liverpool as such a lively place, and I've talked about it like that to Frank,' Terry said tactfully. They all felt that he must often have to smooth feathers ruffled by Frank.

Maureen brought in tea and sandwiches and said to Terry, 'I've put yours and Sarah's in Dad's den.' They went into the little room and Terry took Sarah's hand.

'Sorry Frank blurted that out about Canada,' he said. 'I want to do what you want, Sarah. It's been a long time for you to wait, with everyone else getting married. Do you want us to get married right away?'

Sarah shook her head, then with a rush of courage she said, 'Do you think we should? I mean, when you went away, Terry, it was only a last minute thing about being your girl, and even then I thought if it didn't work out we could part with no hard feelings. It was just circumstances that made the difference.'

'That's true,' he said. 'But, Sarah, five years is a long time to wait. You don't think we should get married right away?'

'Do you want to?' she said. 'Tell me honestly, Terry.' He hesitated and she said, 'I think we're both fumbling about. You think we should marry because it's been so long, or rather you're *prepared* to marry for that reason. And I feel that if you've been planning marriage I should marry you, but if you'd rather go to Canada with Frank, I think you should.'

Terry listened to her in amazement. 'By God, Sarah, you've changed! You're so confident, so – so grown up. I could never have imagined you talking like this.'

She blushed. 'I took Maureen's advice,' she admitted, 'I said a little prayer before I started.'

Terry's hearty laugh rang out and he leaned forward and kissed her. 'I'm very fond of you, Sar,' he said. 'I appreciate all your letters. They've been an anchor.'

'And I'm very fond of you, Terry,' she said. 'I like all your family, but now we've got it settled that we're good friends but don't want to marry, I can tell you.' She took a deep breath then said in a muffled voice, 'Your Joe, Terry. I love him and he loves me. We didn't say anything for a while, and when we did we didn't do anything underhand. We decided that we couldn't do anything until we knew how you felt.' She gave a wavering smile. 'I was relieved when you spoke about Canada.'

'Well, bloody hell!' he said. 'I'm just surprised,' he added hastily. 'Our Joe. Still waters run deep.'

'We didn't deceive you. We didn't make any plans or tell anyone. We thought we'd wait until the war was over and you were home and we could see how things worked out. Maureen and my dad are the only ones who know. They guessed just by seeing us together. It's such a relief to know we agree, Terry, that what we feel for each other isn't enough for marriage.'

'It's a relief to me too, Sarah. After a while I began to realize I'd pushed you into this situation, but there was nothing I could do. I know you didn't want to send me a "Dear John" letter while I was there, and I didn't want to send one to you. Thank God we're all sorted out now.'

The next moment the door opened and Frank walked in, but Terry firmly ushered him out again.

Sarah stood and Terry put his arms round her. 'So that's settled then, Sarah? No wedding for us. I'll go to Canada with Frank, and you'll marry Joe and live happily ever after.'

'And you don't mind that it's him?' she said.

'No, it'll keep you in the family,' Terry said with a grin. 'The more I think of it, the more I see how well suited you are.' He gave her a quick kiss. 'Come on, let's go and disappoint the family.'

'Don't mention Joe yet,' she said quickly. 'I want to tell Mum and Grandma first.'

They went in and Helen looked up inquiringly. 'Wedding bells?'

'No,' Terry said. 'Sarah and I had each decided it wasn't a good idea, but neither of us wanted to send a "Dear John" letter. We've sorted it out now.'

'Good,' Maureen said briskly. 'How about a drink, Dad? You're not usually so slow in that direction.'

There were exclamations from some of the family, but no one looking at Sarah's and Terry's happy faces could doubt that it was a joint decision and the right one.

Later, when Terry walked home with Sarah, he said he was surprised that the family took it so calmly. 'They're all more concerned with the changes in their own lives,' she said. 'The children and houses and all that.'

Sarah's family welcomed Terry warmly and he was introduced to Gene who was sitting in the kitchen with them. Kate flourished her engagement ring with its large diamond under Terry's nose. 'I suppose you'll be buying one of these for Sarah?'

Terry ignored the question. 'Now I know I feel old,' he said. 'You engaged, Kate! You were only a sprat when I went away.'

Greg asked questions about Terry's journey home and conditions in Germany, and conversation was general until Terry stood up to go. Kate and Gene had already left. 'I'd better be off,' he said.

Sarah said laughingly, 'Yes. Frank will be like a hen on a griddle.' She went to the door with him and returned almost immediately.

'Who's Frank?' Cathy asked.

'Terry's friend. He's staying there but they'll go together to

Canada soon.' She looked at the amazed expression on her mother's face. 'Terry and I aren't getting married, Mum.'

'But you both looked so happy,' Cathy murmured.

'Yes, but for different reasons,' Sarah said. 'The way Terry explained it at his house, we both knew it wouldn't work but neither of us could say it in letters in case the other one was still planning to marry. We've sorted it out now. Terry's going to Canada with Frank, and I'm going to marry Joe.'

'Joe Fitzgerald, you mean?' Cathy exclaimed.

'Yes, Mum. We've known for a long time, since Dunkirk, but we couldn't do anything until Terry came home.'

Cathy looked from Greg to her mother. 'Did you know?' she asked.

Greg said nothing but Sally said calmly, 'I didn't know but I guessed, just seeing them together. But Sarah said nothing, so neither did I. I could have been wrong.'

'Oh, Grandma, you don't think we were sly, do you?' Sarah said.

Sally shook her head. 'No. I could see you were in a cleft stick the way things were, but I think you and Joe are better suited.'

'So do I,' said Greg. 'I like Joe.'

'Yes. I like Terry too,' Cathy said, 'he's a nice lad. But Joe – I'll be made up to have him as a son-in-law. All the same, Sarah, I don't think you're sly, but you're more crafty than I gave you credit for to keep it dark all this time.'

She flung her arms round her mother. 'I'm so glad you don't mind, Mum,' she said. 'It was hard to hide it from you but we had to do it.'

'As long as the Fitzgeralds don't mind and Terry isn't hurt,' said Cathy.

'Hurt! He's relieved,' she laughed. 'It was all a sort of joke at first. If he hadn't seen that photo and asked for it, he'd never have thought of me as his girl.'

'So it was all my fault for framing the photo,' Greg said. 'You see, Gran, it's always my fault.'

'Remind me to cry for you when I've got time,' Sally said dryly, but she was smiling and Sarah knew that she was pleased at her news.

Sarah slipped away to send a note to Joe immediately,

and Cathy looked at Greg. 'What next?' she said. 'And you don't seem surprised either. I must go round with my eyes shut.'

'No, You were just sure that Terry was the one,' he said. 'I think they behaved honourably in keeping it quiet.'

Sarah received an ecstatic letter from Joe. He told her that he had asked for special leave to see his brother before he went to Canada. It had been granted and he would be home in a week's time. Terry planned to sail to Canada within a month. Maureen told Sarah that she would be sorry to lose him so quickly, but not at all sorry to see Frank go.

'He's so tactless and clings to Terry like a leech,' she said. 'Anyone but Terry would be driven mad but he doesn't seem to notice. Just says there's plenty of room in Canada, if we say anything.'

Joe saw Terry alone when he came home, and he told Sarah that they had had a good talk and now his brother knew exactly how things had happened. 'I thought he might want to punch me,' Joe said, 'but it all went great. We're still good pals.'

Sarah took a week's leave and they spent every possible moment together. Joe was still in uniform and everyone smiled on them as they walked along in a golden dream with their arms around each other or sat entwined on a park seat.

Other people seemed remote to Sarah. Only Joe was real, and the love which they had tried to hide now seemed almost tangible as they moved through the days in a blissful dream.

To Sally they were like herself and Lawrie in their courting days. He was often in her thoughts as she smiled tenderly to see Sarah and Joe, lost to the world as they gazed into each other's eyes.

All too soon the week sped by, but before Joe went back they chose a neat three-stone engagement ring. Everyone admired it, then Kate announced: 'I've got news too. Gene and I have fixed the wedding for the first week in October.'

Cathy was vexed that she had chosen to announce the wedding at what should have been Sarah's moment, but Sally told her not to worry.

'I'd like to see anything that'd worry those two this minute.'

Terry went to Canada in September and Mick was demobilized and came home, but not for long. He told them that he had considered going to Cambridge but had decided to go into industry instead, with a friend from his squadron.

'We're going to make plastics,' he said.

'Plastics? What are they?' Cathy asked.

'It's a new idea,' he said. 'We'll be able to make things like buckets and bowls, even something that looks like leather or glass but isn't.'

'Ersatz, you mean, like the Germans?' Cathy said doubtfully.

'No, they were substitutes and not good ones. These will be just like the real thing, but much cheaper. We could make a glass slipper that wouldn't break.'

'And what will you use for money?' Sally asked.

'We've both got good gratuities and we've been saving,' said Mick.

'I suppose you know what you're doing, Mick, but it seems chancy,' his mother said doubtfully.

'If it fails we'll do something else,' he said cheerfully. 'I'm afraid I'll be moving away though. We've taken a small factory in the Midlands.'

'So Greg was right,' Cathy said to her mother. 'The house is emptying out. What do you think about moving, Mam?'

'Are you sure you want me to come?' Sally said. 'You and Greg could be like Darby and Joan.'

She smiled but Cathy knew that she was serious and said quickly, 'I'll tell you what, Mam. I'd rather go to live in Norris Street again with you, than have a dream house without you. I'd be lost.'

'In that case, I think it's a good idea. It breaks my heart to look round Everton now, with all the empty spaces where people I knew used to live. There's nothing to keep me here.' She glanced up at the mantelpiece where the handleless teapot and Lawrie's pipe stood in the place of honour. 'I'll take those and I'll be settled anywhere.'

'Anne and John have been promised a prefab,' Cathy said, 'so Sarah and Joe can have their rooms until they get a house. Of course Joe won't be back in England until after Christmas, and he'll still have a few months in London before he's demobbed, Sarah says.'

'Do you ever hear about Miss Andrews that took your house in Norris Street?' Sally said. 'I remember Peggy telling me that her brother was an Air Raid Warden and nearly drove everyone mad, but I've never heard any more.'

'Neither have I,' said Cathy. 'Freda used to tell me about the street but now she's gone to Scotland I don't hear anything. I know Mrs Parker is in Belmont Hospital. She went senile and none of them would look after her, and poor Grace Woods died before her husband so she didn't get her wish.'

The atomic bomb was dropped on Hiroshima on August the sixth and on Nagasaki three days later, but the full horror of it was not realized by people at home. Five days later Japan surrendered and Peggy came running round to see Sally.

'At last,' she said. 'It's all finished, and our Michael will be home. I've got his room all ready.'

Peggy had lived with Meg and Willie for a while after her own house was bombed but had been unable to resist interfering and spoiling Willie's careful efforts to make Meg self-sufficient. Fortunately a house became empty nearby and Peggy moved there, ostensibly to make a home for Michael's return.

When she was finally notified that he had been traced and brought to hospital in London, she travelled to see him with her eldest son Robbie. Sally went to see Peggy when she returned and found many of her family with her, all very distressed.

'Sally, he's just a skeleton,' Peggy wept. 'What he must have gone through!'

Even burly Robbie was in tears as he walked up and down the room, clenching his fists. 'If I could just get my hands on those yellow devils,' he kept repeating, 'I'd kill them, so help me God! I'd kill them.'

'Never mind, Peg,' Sally tried to comfort her. 'At least he's alive and they'll give him every care.'

'The doctor said they'd build him up but it'll take months,' Peggy said. 'But he'll never be the same again, Sally. My poor lad.'

It was a relief to Sally to come back to her own family and their happy house. 'There's not many as lucky as us, love,' she told Cathy.

'I know, Mam. We've all got safely through the war, and now three of them have got good partners. I wouldn't wish for a nicer girl than Anne, and Joe's perfect for Sarah, and a lad I'm very fond of. Gene's a nice boy, too, although I don't suppose we'll see much of him or Kate either when they go to America.'

'I wonder who Mick will bring home?'

'I don't know. I'm prepared for anyone from a hottentot to a dowager,' Cathy said. 'If he does as well as the others in marriage, I'll be happy.'

She had intended to hold Kate's wedding reception at home, but Kate had other plans. She told her parents that Gene would like to be married in the little chapel at the camp as he often acted as altar server in the Mass there, and the priest would like to marry them and say their Nuptial Mass.

The family were invited to the Officers' Mess a few days before the wedding and were overwhelmed by the hospitality they received. 'And that wasn't even the wedding reception,' Cathy said as they drove home.

'Kate will take to that life like a duck to water,' Sally said. She had been reluctant to go but Greg had pointed out that she would have to go there for the wedding so she might as well get to know the place beforehand. In the end she had enjoyed the evening.

Joe was not able to come home for the wedding but Sarah wrote him such a detailed description he said he felt as though he had.

With a baby in the family again, Christmas 1945 was a quiet but happy one for the Redmond family, but early in the New Year Cathy was saddened by the death of Eleanor Rathbone, MP. Cathy had admired Miss Rathbone all her life and campaigned for her in her youth, but a few days after the death was announced she was cheered by the news that Joe was coming home on disembarkation leave.

He had suggested getting married on this leave but Sarah said she would rather wait until he was demobbed in May. "I don't want to be parted again after we're married," she wrote, but several times during Joe's leave regretted that they had not married when he suggested.

The months soon passed, with frequent weekend leaves, the excitement of Kate's departure to America, and viewing the new house which Cathy, Sally and Greg were to move into after the wedding. It had been built pre-war and was a modern, well-planned house with a bathroom and hot water and a garden front and rear. It was not far from the allotments which the Burns family now worked so Peggy could often come to see Sally, and Sally could take the tram to see her.

Joe came home in May and with Sarah made the arrangements for their simple wedding. The wedding reception would be the last festivity in the Egremont Street house.

Only the immediate family were at the wedding of Sarah and Joe, with Peggy as Sally's guest, and it was a simple but moving ceremony. Even the priest who married them was visibly affected by their shining happiness and obvious love for each other. He said that he would not preach a sermon, only say that he wished every couple he married were as sure of happiness as Sarah and Joe. He walked to where they knelt at the altar and placed his hands on their heads. 'Go with God, my children,' he said and they felt truly blessed.

They spent their honeymoon in Anglesey, and came to see Sarah's parents and grandmother when they returned. Anne and John came too with the baby, and they all sat round discussing the war and what it had meant.

'Was it worth while?' Anne said.

Joe replied immediately, 'I think so. If you'd seen those people when we liberated Brussels – it was an evil regime. And the concentration camps! I don't believe in war and I hope we never see another but Hitler had to be stopped.'

'Yes, but –' John was beginning.

Sarah interrupted, 'Don't let's talk about war. Can't we talk of happier things?'

John picked up the baby from the rug where he was playing and sat him on his knee.

Cathy leaned forward and stroked his head. 'What about Gerry?' she said. 'What sort of a world will he grow up in?'

'A much better one, Mum,' said John. 'All the things that Grandad worked for will come true soon with the Welfare State. "Security from the cradle to the grave." It took a war to do it but it's come at last. I wish he had lived to see it.'

'He didn't think it would come in his time, lad, but he hoped it would come in yours, and thank God it has,' said Sally. 'I've been thinking about him a lot lately, I suppose because Sarah and Joe put me in mind of us when we were wed.' She laid her hand on Sarah's. 'I hope you won't have the hardships we had to face when Lawrie fell out of work.'

'They won't, Grandma,' John said eagerly. 'There'll be unemployment pay, proper pensions for widows and old people, and medical care for everybody, milk for babies and schoolchildren.' He glanced at his mother. 'And even family allowances at last.'

'I helped Miss Rathbone to campaign for them when I was young,' Cathy explained to Anne. 'Miss Rathbone – there's someone else who died before she got what she'd always fought for.'

'But she knew it was coming,' John said.

'And you campaigned?' Anne said admiringly to Cathy. 'We didn't do anything but enjoy ourselves, did we, Sar?'

'No. My only ambition was to be happy,' Sarah said. She smiled up at Joe. 'I've realized *that* anyway.'

'And what about this little fellow?' Greg said, taking the baby from John. 'I suppose you've got all sorts of ambitions for him?'

'No. Only for him to be happy. I think that's the best we can wish for our children. I hope he has more sense than I had, but he'll make his own mistakes,' said John.

'If he's happy and healthy, I'll be satisfied,' Anne said. 'I think Sarah's ambition is the right one.'

'I wonder if he'll realize how hard the fight was for what he'll probably take for granted,' said John.

'I don't doubt you'll tell him,' Sally said dryly.

'No, I won't, Grandma. I'll let him find things out for himself.'

'He'll grow up in a different world anyway,' said Joe. 'And so will all our children. People hoped for a better world after the Great War but it didn't come off. This time I think it will.'

'I hope you're right, lad,' said Sally. 'Forty years ago Lawrie thought good times were just around the corner, but maybe this time it really will be a better world.'

'It will, Grandma,' John said eagerly. 'A better world for everyone.'

'And especially for Gerald John Redmond and his generation,' Cathy said, laughing and cuddling the baby.

He looked round their smiling faces and clapped his hands, crowing with delight.